W9-AWF-885

BLIND LUCK

BLIND LUCK

A Novel by
Ben Cooper

HP *Heritage Productions, Ltd.*

Houston, Texas
1998

The following songs are quoted and used by permission.
All rights reserved.

"Woman Goin' Crazy on Caroline Street" by Jimmy Buffett
copyright © 1976 MCA Records, Inc.

"Do You Believe in Magic?" by John Sebastian
copyright © 1965 Trio Music

This is a work of fiction. All names, characters, places and
incidents are either invented by the author or are used fictitiously.
Any resemblance to any actual person, living or dead,
is unintended.

Library of Congress Catalog Card Number: 98-92759

ISBN 0-9663548-7-7

Manufactured in the United States of America

First Edition

Published by Heritage Productions, Ltd.

Houston, Texas

To Jody
My wife and best friend.
Thanks for your support.

Special thanks to Bill, Mary, Shirley,
Debbie, Trish and Jody D.

When they call the roll in the Senate, the Senators do not know whether to answer "Present" or "Not guilty."
—Theodore Roosevelt

The trade of governing has always been monopolized by the most ignorant and the most rascally individuals of mankind.
—Thomas Paine

Suppose you were an idiot. And suppose you were a member of Congress. But I repeat myself.
—Mark Twain

Power tends to corrupt, and absolute power corrupts absolutely.
—Lord Acton

Sure there are dishonest men in local government. But there are dishonest men in national government too.
—Richard M. Nixon

Our country is now taking so steady a course as to show by what road it will pass to destruction, to wit: by consolidation [of power] first, and then corruption, its necessary consequence.
—Thomas Jefferson

The budget should be balanced. Public debt should be reduced. The arrogance of officialdom should be tempered, and assistance to foreign lands should be curtailed, lest Rome become bankrupt.
—Marcus Tullius Cicero, 63 B.C.

A billion here and a billion there, and soon you're talking about real money.
—Sen. Everett McKinley Dirksen

This country has come to feel the same when congress is in session as when a baby gets hold of a hammer.
—Will Rogers

1

Gary Stephens looked at the piece of paper. *What kind of sick joke is this?* he thought to himself. "Maybe it's not a bad idea," he whispered out loud. Nobody heard. He shook his head and sighed, *I can't believe I even thought that.*

He was about to toss the letter in the trash, just as he had with all the other "Letters to the Editor" that he had received over the years from crackpots. He looked at the letter again. Plain, eight and a half by eleven, stock copy paper. Centered, all caps, bold, courier 10 point type face. No salutation and no name or signature. Most letters from crackpots were signed, even if it was signed "Bat Guano."

Stephens reread the note.

```
I WILL KILL ONE SENATOR OR REPRESENTATIVE
EVERY WEEK UNTIL TAXES ARE LOWERED AND
WASTEFUL SPENDING IS STOPPED!
```

He took it more seriously this time. He grabbed at the envelope the letter had come in as though it was about to fly away. Again, all caps, courier, 10 point:

```
MR. GARY STEPHENS
EDITOR, PHOENIX TRIBUNE
16532 E. 22ND ST.
PHOENIX, AZ 85001
```

The envelope was postmarked Scottsdale, Arizona. It was marked PERSONAL AND CONFIDENTIAL.

Gary Stephens graduated from The University of Pennsylvania with a degree in journalism more years ago than he really cared to remember. He went to New York and worked many years with several newspapers. The awards on the walls reminded him of the early days when he would do anything for a story. He didn't just want the story, he had to be first with it. Then all the stories started to sound the same. Crime was rampant. Corrupt politicians. Watergate was the last straw. HE should've broken that story, but he had slowed down. It was time to move on.

Stephens landed a job as staff reporter with the Phoenix Tribune. The pay was decent enough. Considerably less than New York, but it was much cheaper to live in Phoenix. He was happy. He had his own column and he could write about anything he wanted. His editorials became extremely popular. When the editor died unexpectedly, Gary Stephens was offered the position. He gladly accepted.

Gary reread the letter. Nothing had changed. He moved the arrow on the computer screen to the "Message Center" icon and pressed it. A list of names instantly popped up on the screen. He used his mouse to move the arrow over the name Tim Brooks - his assistant editor - and clicked the left button. The screen quickly went blank and just as quickly the message center popped up.

You are sending a message to: Tim Brooks. The computer filled in the name and message address. Enter your message now: COME IN HERE NOW! Gary typed the message and pressed "Enter." He moved the arrow over the "Send" icon and clicked the right button. The message was sent. *Easier than dialing the phone.*

Tim Brooks was at his desk when his computer terminal beeped. He looked at the screen:

> Message to: Tim Brooks
> Message from: Gary Stephens
> Message: COME IN HERE NOW!

Tim read the message and bolted out of his chair toward his boss's office. He had never seen a message like that from Gary. *What the hell did I do?* He thought.

"You wanted to see me?"

"Come in and close the door."

"Read this," Gary said as he handed the letter across his desk. Gary noticed Tim's hand was shaking as he reached for the letter. Not much, but noticeably. He now studied Tim's face for a change in expression. There was a very noticeable change. Tim read the letter and looked up, reread the letter and look up again.

"What do you think?" Gary said as Tim looked up the second

time.

"Is this for real? Where did you get it?" Tim wasn't sure if this was a joke, a test, or for real, but he knew he had better take it seriously. "This is winter, and this is Phoenix. I'm sure there are several Congressmen in town."

If he believed the letter or not, Gary decided he was going to call the police. There was no way he would sit on a letter like this. He could just imagine the repercussions if he said nothing, and a Congressman was killed.

"Tim, I'm going to call Pete and I want you to make a couple of copies of that letter for us. I've touched it and you've touched it, but I'm not too concerned about that. I seriously doubt that they would find any fingerprints on it anyway. After you make the copies, come back here. Don't tell anybody about this. I want to keep it quiet for now. I would think that it's probably just a crank letter, but damn it, it's too plain. If it was bogus, I think it would be longer, more details."

"You're not going to print this?" Tim interrupted.

"I'm not sure. I want you back in here. You, Pete and I will discuss it. I don't want to give copycats any ideas."

Tim thought about it for a second and decided his boss was absolutely correct. Sometimes it is better to keep the news from the public. This was one of those times. The one thing he had learned from Gary Stephens is that reporters should respect people's privacy, especially victims' privacy. Gary got his point across by firing a young reporter who stuck a tape recorder in the face of a mother whose daughter had just been found. The little girl had been raped and murdered. The Tribune reporter was just one of a crowd of reporters that surrounded the hysterical mother, asking stupid questions and taking pictures. It didn't matter, the kid was fired. Gary had made his point. It was a good point. All the other reporters still do it, and that kid is probably still doing it. But not at the Tribune.

Pete Mitchell had been a detective with the Phoenix Police Department for ten years. He met Gary Stephens five years before he became a detective. There had been a huge apartment fire. The largest disaster in Phoenix history. The residents were going crazy. Most had just lost everything they owned. A few had lost loved ones. Every TV and newspaper reporter in the state seemed to be there sticking a camera and microphone in some poor soul's face.

Every reporter except Gary Stephens. He was there, but he stayed out of the way and watched. Pete was working crowd control. He noticed Gary and kept an eye on him. He knew that he was up to something, reporters just don't act like that. Gary did. When the fire was out and all was under control, Pete introduced himself to Gary and expressed his appreciation for staying out of the way. Even though there was 15 years difference in their ages, they became instant friends.

"Pete, this is Gary, can you come to the office?"

"Is it important?"

"Yes!"

"Give me ten minutes."

"Thanks, bye."

"Bye."

The Phoenix Police Department was only two blocks from The Phoenix Tribune Building. Nobody really remembers which came first or why they were so close, but it sure came in handy. Pete decided he could get there just as quickly by walking. By the time he got out of one parking garage and into another, he could be there. As he walked, he tried to remember another call from Gary Stephens like the one he had just received. He couldn't remember one.

"Go right in, Pete, they're waiting on you."

"Thanks." He probably would have anyway. Gary had given him no clue as to what was going on. In the five minutes it took to walk the two blocks, Pete must have thought of about 50 different reasons for this visit. He had not thought of the right reason.

"Hi Pete, thanks for coming." The two shook hands. "You know Tim Brooks."

"Yes, of course." They shook hands as well. "I have a feeling you didn't invite me over for coffee." Pete could sense the seriousness in the room. He had hoped to lighten it up a little with his coffee comment. He did. Both Gary and Tim let out deep breaths and smiled for the first time since reading the letter.

"When I got in this morning, this letter was on my desk," Gary said handing the piece of paper to Pete. He paused and watched Pete's face, waiting for a change of expression. There wasn't one. When Pete looked up, Gary continued, "the Post Office delivers our mail directly to our back door, usually by six A.M. Our mail room sorts it and distributes it by nine. I was here right at nine and it was on my desk. Unopened. The envelope is marked 'personal and confidential'." He handed the envelope to the detective. "As soon as I read the note, I called Tim in. We both read it. We both have touched it. I had Tim make some copies and I called you. It's now," he glanced at his watch, "about quarter of ten and you know every thing we do."

Pete read the note several more times while he was listening to Gary. Each time it still read the same:

```
I WILL KILL ONE SENATOR OR REPRESENTATIVE
EVERY  WEEK  UNTIL  TAXES  ARE  LOWERED  AND
WASTEFUL SPENDING IS STOPPED!
```

Pete looked at the envelope then at his watch. Still only about a quarter of ten. "Do you know if there are any Senators or Representatives in Phoenix now?" Pete asked. He knew the answer, but he hoped they had all left. No such luck.

"We've been checking on that," Tim answered. "We know our Senator Fisher and Senator Robbins of New Mexico are in town. There is a story in the morning paper about them. They were attending some sort of gala last night. We don't know where Robbins is staying, but Fisher has a home in Mesa. I am pretty sure Senator Carson of Texas and Senator Dailey of New Jersey are in town. No word on any Representatives, I'm sure some of our local guys are in town."

"You know I need to take this letter."

"Of course."

"What are you going to print?"

"Right now, nothing. If nothing happens, nothing gets printed."

"And if something happens?"

Gary paused for a few seconds before answering this one.

"I really don't know. If this gets out, everybody may be trying to kill a Congressman. But if it gets out that I had this letter and didn't use it, ethics or no ethics, I'll be looking for a job. Let's see what happens. I'll let you know before I do anything."

"Fair enough, I appreciate it. You know, I'll have to call the FBI on this one."

Gary nodded. He hadn't thought about it, but of course the FBI would have to be notified. He wondered when they would get there.

Pete was out of breath when he arrived back at his office. He hadn't timed it, but he was sure he had just set a record. He checked his Rolodex and dialed the local FBI number. He spoke to Special Agent Alexander Christian. After listening closely to the details,

Agent Christian was genuinely interested. He said he was about to leave for the Indian reservation and would come over as soon as he could. The entire conversation took less than five minutes, but Detective Mitchell liked Agent Christian. He hoped the feeling was mutual.

The phone on his desk rang. He answered it before the first ring had stopped. "Detective Mitchell, can I help you?"

* * * * * *

The Honorable Jeffrey G. Carson, senior Senator from Texas sat under the umbrella at the Desert Green Country Club in Paradise Valley, Arizona. Senator Carson just turned 55 years old. He had been in Texas politics since graduating from the University of Texas Law School in 1963. He often bragged about the time he was introduced to the undertaker that LBJ used to "dispose" of certain parties.

Carson was in very good shape. He prided himself on the fact that he looked younger than many of his constituents who were still in high school when he was first elected to the Texas House of Representatives.

Senator Carson sat at the round wrought iron table with the three other members of the foursome waiting for their scheduled tee time. As usual, Carson dominated the conversation.

"I thought she wanted me because of my great body," Senator Carson chuckled, "or, at least because she knew I was a Senator, but she was a hooker! Maybe 25 years old, blond hair and a body that wouldn't quit. Well worth the two hundred and fifty dollars." The Senator let out the rapid-fire belly laugh that he was well known for. Senator Dailey of New Jersey, Congressman Knox of Virginia and Congressman Daniels of New York laughed along with Senator Carson.

"Two hundred fifty dollars for sex is kind of high, no matter what she looked like," Congressman Knox protested after the laughter had subsided.

"Congressman Knox, as one of the younger members of the House, you have much to learn. First of all, it was one of the best fucks and greatest blow-jobs I have ever had - so you know it had to be great - and I bet the young woman was working her way through college. So the two hundred and fifty dollars will go on the expense account as a contribution to further education among the disadvantaged. The TAXPAYERS will pay for it. We all got fucked last night." A roar of belly laughs came from the table.

"Shush now," Senator Dailey said as the waiter approached the table, "we don't want to pull a Leona Helmsley." They all chuckled quietly as the waiter got closer.

"Where's Arturo?" Senator Carson asked before the waiter could say anything.

"He took a day of vacation," the waiter replied without much enthusiasm. "What can I get you all today?" Still not much enthusiasm.

"Bloody Marys all around?" Carson asked as he looked around the table. Everyone agreed that Bloody Marys sounded good and the waiter walked off to get their orders, never showing any enthusiasm whatsoever.

"Can you believe that, damn wet-back taking a day of vacation." Again, belly laughs all around for Senator Carson's comment.

The waiter promptly returned placing a Bloody Mary, with a stalk of celery in each, in front of each of the gentlemen.

"Will there be anything else?" the waiter asked, again, with absolutely no interest in the answer.

"No, tee-time is in 15 minutes," the senior Senator said, directed more at his party than to the waiter. The waiter laid the check on the table and left. Never giving the four men at the table more than a second glance.

After a few more tales about his conquests over the opposite sex, Senator Carson suggested they finish their drinks and head to the first tee. They all tipped their glasses and finished what was left. Congressman Knox picked up his celery stalk and took a bite. The other three men just looked at him. Another belly laugh.

Their golf clubs were in the carts and the carts were waiting for them as they approached the first tee box. At Desert Green Country Club you have a choice of caddies or carts. Although Senator Carson often jogged two or three miles a day, the championship course at Desert Green was 6,799 yards long from the blue tees. Add zig-zags needed to chase errant shots and the distances from one green to the next tee box, the gentlemen agreed they did not want to walk over five miles, even if it was very early spring in Arizona.

Senator Carson was the first to tee off. He pulled his Great Big Bertha driver out of the bag and walked onto the tee box. He bent over to tee-up his Titlest DT90 golf ball. He thought about telling the story of how he got one gross, 12 dozen balls, with *The Honorable Jeffrey G. Carson* specially engraved - at taxpayers expense, but he remembered that he had told this group that story on more than one occasion.

Perfectly teed up, with *The Honorable Jeffrey G. Carson* pointing the exact direction he wanted the ball to fly, he took one practice swing, addressed the ball, waggled, then with a swing even some pros had praised at recent Pro-Am's, drove the ball 265 yards straight down the middle of the fairway. He always held his back-swing as he watched the ball fly its designated course.

"AHHHHHH!" Senator Carson yelled as he uncoiled from his back swing, dropping his driver, clutching his abdomen as he bent over.

"Are you O.K.?" the other three men asked almost simultaneously as they came running to the Senator's side.

"Oh, I, I don't know," the Senator responded as he was finally able to straighten up. "I just had a sharp pain, kind of like a cramp in my stomach." He took a couple of deep breaths as he arched his back to stretch his stomach muscles. "I'll be all right." The remaining members of the foursome teed-off and they all climbed into their carts. The two Senators always rode in the same cart.

"Are you sure you're O.K. Jeff?" Senator Dailey asked as he drove to where his ball had landed. Senator Carson was about to say, "I'm fine," but before he could get the words out he again grabbed his abdomen as he doubled over in obvious pain. Instead of, "I'm fine," he was barely able to say, "I'm not sure."

"Stop the cart," Carson said as he inhaled deeply.

"Jeff, what the hell is wrong?"

"I don't know, just stop the fucking cart!"

Before the cart had completely stopped Senator Carson was climbing, or falling, out. Senator Dailey applied the foot brake, jumped out of the cart and got to the other side to see his friend on all fours, wrenching in pain.

"Come on Jeff, get back in the cart, I've got to get you back to the clubhouse."

"No way," were all the words that Senator Carson could utter before the coughing attack started. Violent dry heaves soon followed.

"What's wrong?" Congressman Knox was yelling as their cart approached the scene. They had not seen Senator Carson leave the cart but they could tell something was wrong. Dreadfully wrong.

"I don't know, but something is very wrong with Jeff. Go back to the club house and call an ambulance." The cart was turned around and the two Congressmen were headed toward the club-house before Senator Dailey could finish his sentence.

The dry-heaves had turned into projectile vomiting.

"Lay down, Jeff, help is on the way," even as he spoke, he knew his friend was not hearing him.

"Oh, Jesus," Senator Dailey said as he watched what was happening to his friend.

The vomiting had become violent. The undigested Bloody Mary came up. The Senators body was now convulsing uncontrollably as his eyes rolled up into head. He was losing control of his bodily functions. He began to urinate.

"Oh, God! Come on Jeff, hang in there, helps on its way," Senator Dailey pleaded. *What can I do?* He thought. He leaned over to try and help. To do anything that might help. A loud "Arrg," came from the body as it tightened up into the fetal position. The tightening forced gas and defecation out of the Senator's body. The red in the vomit was no longer from the Bloody Mary.

Senator Dailey turned from the now lifeless body and vomited. He was relieved that the red in his vomit was from the Bloody Mary. He still felt sick.

Congressmen Knox and Daniels had called 911 and were waiting outside the clubhouse when the ambulance arrived. They had planned to escort the ambulance to their friend but it wasn't necessary, Congressman Daniels simply pointed to the crowd that had gathered in the middle of the first fairway. The two men followed in their golf cart.

One female golfer had taken too long of a look and she was now shaking uncontrollably as tears flowed down her cheeks.

The ambulance pulled around the Senator's golf cart and backed into position. The paramedics opened the doors and began pulling a stretcher out all in one motion. The two E.M.T.'s had barely moved a step toward Senator Carson when they froze in their tracks. They each saw the Senator's body at the same time. Phoenix is not the most violent of towns, but the two had seen their share of knife wounds, gun shots and automobile accidents.

Automobile accidents were always the worst. The body was not always in one piece. But when you arrive on an accident scene and see the mangled steel of what had at one time been an automobile, you are prepared for a mangled body. The victim of an automobile accident usually goes quick too. There's lots of blood, but you tell yourself that the victim didn't feel a thing.

Both paramedics stared at the body of Senator Jeffrey Carson for a moment. His face had a look of horror on it. He was laying in a puddle made up of a mixture of his own vomit and blood. His once white shorts were now stained with his urine and defecation. His hands dug into the soft Bermuda grass. There was no telling yourself this man didn't feel a thing.

Mark Donnels, the older of the two E.M.T.'s left the stretcher and moved closer to the body. The stench was horrid. Mark lightly pressed his hand on the side of the Senator's throat. There was nothing. He didn't really expect to find a pulse.

The first police unit arrived as just as Donnels was checking for a pulse. The ghastly sight also stopped the veteran officer in his tracks.

"Any pulse?" Officer Cline knew there wouldn't be.

"No." Donnels moved toward Officer Cline. "We just got here a few minutes ago, haven't touched a thing."

"Good." Officer Cline said as he looked to see how his partner was doing disbursing the crowd that had gathered. There were no problems. Most wanted to leave.

"Better call a detective on this one," Cline advised his partner. "Go ahead and cover him, Mark, we're going to be here awhile."

Mark Donnels and Officer Cline had worked together on numerous occasions. This was one of the worst either could remember.

2

"Detective Mitchell, this is Officer Cline in Paradise Valley."

"Good morning Officer Cline."

Paradise Valley is the smallest of several towns that border Phoenix. They have a police department, mostly for traffic patrol, burglaries and various misdemeanor crimes. Anything major, they call Phoenix. This was major.

"I was wondering if you wouldn't mind coming out to Desert Green Country Club? We've had a death out here."

Somebody's always dying out there. The average member has to be 70 years old, Pete thought to himself. "Another heart attack?" he asked.

"I don't think so." Officer Cline didn't really mind the sarcasm as there had been a number of heart attacks at Desert Green. "According to witnesses, he had stomach pains, went into some sort of convulsions, began vomiting blood and died within a few minutes."

"And he IS dead?"

"Very, SIR," Officer Cline didn't appreciate the question. The emphasis on "SIR" let Detective Mitchell know it.

"I'm sorry, Officer Cline. That's not really what I meant. Why do you need us on this one? Sounds like it could be some kind of poisoning, send him to the coroner's for an autopsy."

"That's what we planned to do, but we really would like some help on this one. The victim was a Senator from Texas."

"Carson?"

"Yes sir, how did. . . " Detective Mitchell didn't let him finish.

"I'll be right there. Don't move him." Pete hung up the phone and looked at his watch. 10:15 A.M.

"Shit!" Most of the office heard him.

"Fran, call Agent Alexander Christian at the FBI. He's supposed to be on his way over here. See if they can get a hold of him and have him meet me at the Desert Green Country Club in

Paradise Valley." Detective Mitchell was through the double plate glass doors that led to the winding stairs to the first floor before he finished his sentence. His extremely efficient yet underpaid secretary had comprehended enough to make the telephone call.

* * * * * *

Agent Christian was waiting when Detective Mitchell arrived at Desert Green. Mitchell was surprised.

"I was on my way to Salt River when the call came in. Evidently the local cops decided to call us right after they called you. It's your jurisdiction, but it's definitely an FBI case."

Detective Mitchell was a little surprised by Agent Christian's appearance. He was six feet tall but a little on the thin side. Maybe 180 pounds. Brownish blond hair. He wore glasses, but Mitchell was still amazed at the deep blue of his eyes. Early 30's, mid 30's Pete would find out later, Agent Christian looked young for his age. In the dark suit, he looked more like an accountant than an FBI agent. The men began walking toward the area on the first fairway that was roped off by yellow POLICE LINE - DO NOT CROSS tape.

"Of course we are going to conduct an investigation, but I don't think we'll come up with too much. I'll give you everything we find. I'm afraid this is the first layer of a big pile of shit."

The agent's head snapped to look at the detective.

"The letter," Mitchell said, not believing that Agent Christian had forgotten about the letter.

"Yes?" Christian replied, now stopped.

"It said they would kill one a week." The detective was beginning to wonder about the FBI agent who was now in charge of the investigation into the murder of one of the most powerful men in Washington.

"Oh, yes, 'I will kill one Senator or Representative every week until taxes are lowered and wasteful spending is stopped,' I had forgotten the 'one every week' part. This IS going to be a pile of shit." Both men managed smiles. Detective Mitchell was again impressed. He had read the letter to the agent exactly one time, over an hour before, and now the agent recited it back to him verbatim. They continued toward the yellow tape.

Senator Carson lay on the ground where he had gasped his last breath. He had been covered with a white sheet. The crowd of curious onlookers had been replaced by reporters. One of the police officers had mentioned the Senator's name over the radio. Most newspapers, television and radio stations monitor the police bands. And a race was on for the "scoop."

Detective Mitchell looked about at the throng. Video cameras, microphones, note pads, still cameras. "Eyewitness" and "Big 5 News" helicopters were circling above. *Everybody looking for an angle,* he thought, *if they only knew about the letter.*

Agent Christian walked over to the Senators body and lifted up the sheet. He was expecting the worst, but there was no hiding his emotions as he viewed the body. Detective Mitchell was right behind the agent.

"There is really no need for us to look," Mitchell said softly, "I guess it's just that lust for the macabre that human beings have. The same reason everybody slows down to look at a wreck on the freeway." Alexander Christian agreed. Both men knew that looking at the dead man would add nothing to the investigation. But they had to look.

Detective Mitchell looked at the emergency medical technicians and said, "a mobile crime lab should be here in a few minutes. They will go over the body and vacuum the surrounding area. When they're finished, they'll release the Senator's body and you all can take it to the morgue."

Both E.M.T.'s nodded. They quietly thought about the task ahead for the members of the crime lab as they vacuumed the fluids Senator Carson had expelled. They also thought about what the lab would do with the substance once it was back at the lab. At the moment, the two emergency medical technicians were very glad they were not members of the FBI crime lab.

Detective Mitchell looked for Officer Cline. He saw about half a dozen officers attempting to keep the reporters away from the scene and went that direction. Agent Christian was right beside him.

"Officer Cline?" Mitchell said just loud enough to be heard over the clicking cameras and the journalists broadcasting their live remotes.

"Yes." Cline responded, as he moved toward the two men.

"I am Detective Mitchell and this is Agent Christian of the FBI," Mitchell said. They all shook hands.

"FBI? Christ, bad news really travels fast."

"Actually, there's more to this than we can disclose at this time," Agent Christian said. "I understand you were first on the scene?"

"Yes."

"What can you tell us?"

"Why don't we head up to the clubhouse, my sergeant has set up a command post."

The three men began walking toward the clubhouse. As they walked, Officer Cline briefed them on what he knew.

"It seems the four Congressmen had one drink each on the patio before teeing off. Finished the drinks maybe two or three minutes before they got to number one tee. Senator Carson was first to tee-off. He seemed to have a cramp or something when he swung. The others teed-off and they headed toward their balls. Didn't go 150 yards before Carson started yelling for Senator Dailey to stop the cart. He fell out of the cart, went into convulsions, and. . . " Officer Cline paused and looked around the golf course ". . . and, well I guess you know the rest." They did.

Officer Cline continued, "the other three Congressmen are in the Green room. I've got a guard on the door. I've had the press notified that someone will make a statement. I guess that will be you Pete," he looked at Agent Christian and said, with what looked like a smile of relief "and I have officially turned the investigation over to you. If you need me, call the station." Officer Cline shook hands and headed toward the exit sign.

"Well, Agent Christian, I am going to make a brief statement and see how many reporters I can piss off." Both men laughed for the first time. While Detective Mitchell was making his statement to the press, Agent Christian decided to start his investigation by interviewing the remaining three Congressmen.

* * * * * *

White settlers arrived in 1867 to find an extremely hot and arid climate. Impressed by the area and the remains of a primitive irrigation system built by prehistoric Indians, settlers named their settlement Phoenix, after the sun-bird that arose from its own ashes.

The regional office of the Federal Bureau of Investigation was established in Phoenix in May, 1919. Its main purpose was to keep an eye on the federally protected Indian reservations. In the early days it was the one of the worst assignments an agent could get. Winters weren't bad, but in summer, the temperature often soared to above 120 degrees. An agent would have to survive the summer, without air conditioning, to enjoy the winter. Luckily, nothing much happened in Arizona in those days. Indians would occasionally get drunk and wander off the reservation and find their way into town. Usually the sheriff would round them up and take them back. The FBI might hear about it, usually they wouldn't. No one in the Sheriff's office wanted to write a report. Most days at the FBI office were spent trying to stay cool, waiting for the sun to sink behind the mountains. The desert nights were cool, and quite pleasant.

After World War II the population of Phoenix exploded. By 1990 the population had increased 15 fold. With the influx of people came the same problems which plague all major cities. Hurt by pollution from automobiles and increased crime, but helped by air conditioning and the Great Central Arizona Project which, when finished in 1985, delivered over three and a half billion cubic meters of fresh water per year to the city, Phoenix thrived.

Movie stars were vacationing and buying winter homes in the area. Resorts and country clubs with beautifully manicured golf courses were being built at an enormous rate. Phoenix had become one of the most sought after assignments for FBI agents.

Alexander Christian went to the University of Houston on a golf scholarship. Of the eight golfers on the team, he was the worst. But being the worst golfer on a team that produced two NCAA National Championships in four years and had four players become professionals on the PGA tour, with two of those players among the top 20 all-time money winners, was not bad. He still wore one of his national title rings. He graduated Cum-Laude with a degree in Criminal Justice. One of his grandfathers had been the sheriff of a small town in southwest Ohio and his other grandfather had been a cop in New York City. Alexander Christian had always wanted to be a cop.

Christian joined the FBI the Monday after graduation. He quickly became known in Washington. If it was critical, call Alex! It was pretty much expected around the Bureau that Alexander Christian would someday head the FBI. Many thought that Special Agent In Charge (SAIC) - Phoenix, would be his last title before Assistant Director.

Detective Mitchell looked around the small conference room. The room was full. He wasn't sure who everyone was, but he could guess. FBI, Secret Service, Sheriff's Department, Alcohol, Tobacco and Firearms, himself and a few others from the Phoenix Police Department, and he would guess that the CIA was represented as well. Quite a collection of law enforcement, he thought.

At precisely 2:30 PM SAIC Alexander Christian cleared his throat as he stood in front of the podium. It got everyone's attention.

"As most of you are aware, this morning at approximately ten-fifteen, Senator Jeffrey Carson of Texas died while playing golf. Most of you have most of the details, but I am going to give you everything we have at this moment. I don't want anyone to be in the dark about anything. First of all, we do not have an official cause of death. An autopsy is being performed as we speak. Unofficially, we believe he was deliberately poisoned. At nine o'clock this morning Gary Stephens, the editor of the Phoenix Tribune, received a letter. The letter stated that a Senator or a Representative would be killed. It also stated that one would be killed every week until, and I quote, 'wasteful spending is stopped'. The packet we handed you as you came in has a copy of the letter in it. Right now, I am taking that threat very seriously." He paused to take a drink of water while everyone scrambled to read their copy of the letter.

Christian continued, "Mr. Stephens immediately called Detective Mitchell with PPD who picked up the letter and immediately called me. This was just before ten o'clock. At ten-fifteen, I heard of the Senator's death at the Desert Green Country Club in Pleasant Valley. I went straight there and met Detective Mitchell. This is what we have: Somehow someone, most likely our killer, posed as a waiter and served the four gentlemen Bloody Marys, one of which was laced with poison. The waiter then disappeared. We believe he was tall with either light brown or blond hair. It seems that other than Senator Carson, four people saw him: The bartender, who assumed he was a new waiter, Congressman Knox, Congressman Daniels and Senator Dailey. We got a composite from each witness, and each composite could be a totally different person. Evidently no one paid any attention to the guy. By the time Senator Carson dropped dead, the waiter and the Bloody Mary glasses were gone. I suspect that our killer is out of Arizona by now. I know it's not much, but it's all we have at the moment. I will be in contact with each of your departments to let you know what we need from you. Any questions?"

"Do you think it was a professional hit?"

"My first thought was 'no way', too many people could have seen our suspect. But now I'm not sure. Quite frankly, we have less to go on than we have had on some professional jobs. They're working up a possible profile right now. We'll fax it out as soon as it's ready."

"You mentioned the Tribune has a copy of the letter, are they going to print it?"

"My understanding is that they weren't going to unless there actually was a killing. I'm guessing that they will now. It's quite a scoop."

"Any idea why the Tribune got the letter?"

"No. It could be because the killing was going to be here in Phoenix. I'm guessing there's more to it, but that's just a gut feeling. I have nothing to back it up."

Agent Christian continued, "as soon as we get an autopsy report, I'll get a copy out to all of you. We've got 15 agents on their way here. For now, we are setting up our command here at this office. Depending on what happens next week, it may be moved to Washington. We will keep all of you informed. Contact us here if any of you come up with anything."

The various law enforcement officers began filing out of the room. The mood was somber. They all knew what lay ahead for them.

Detective Mitchell waited for most of the people in the room to leave before he approached Agent Christian.

"When I reached you on the phone this morning, I didn't realize I had the top guy," the detective said as he extended his hand to the agent. As Christian shook his hand he said, "when the phone rings around here, whoever has a free hand picks it up. I'm glad it was me. It's not official, but I'm pretty sure I will take charge of this case. By the way, I wanted to thank you for calling us as soon as you did. Unfortunately, it didn't help the Senator."

Detective Mitchell nodded in agreement. "Be sure to call PPD if there is anything we can do to help." Christian said he would as Mitchell said goodbye.

3

"After many months of planning, we have now moved to the operation phase. I would like to propose a toast to execution - no pun intended." The six men and three women seated around the rectangular table all uttered a subdued laugh as they raised their glasses to toast. This is what they had planned for months and each was happy that the plan was now underway.

To themselves, each also wondered if they could continue with the plan. They would only be taking the lives of the corrupt of the corrupt. They were planning to kill as many politicians as it took. But they were only going to kill the ones who deserved it. Many people think no one "deserves" to be killed, but these are people that the American public put their trust in. The people voted for the politicians because they believed what they said. Then, once elected, they proceeded to lie and cheat and totally desecrate the office to which they had been elected. And then, cover it up with more lies and dishonesty so they would be re-elected. So they were going to be eliminated.

Eliminated in such a way that other elected officials who may be considering the bribe, be it a plane ticket, a woman or a suitcase full of money, would think twice before accepting. They were going to kill the worst of the bunch. It was all justified in their minds. But this was not a group of homicidal maniacs. And although happy their plan was started and confident it would work, they all realized they had taken the life of a human being, so there was no grand celebration. There was no grand celebration, but no one in the room was mourning the death of Senator Jeffrey G. Carson either.

"And I would also like to toast Todd Evans on a job well done." Russell Lewis said. Again the glasses were raised. Everyone looked at Todd and nodded. The mood around the table could not be described. It was the ultimate paradox. One man was dead, more were to die. They had all planned it, and now it was done. They could all go to prison for life. Nobody mentioned that option. Todd smiled as he was toasted.

Russell Lewis was considered the ring leader. He was over six feet tall and well built, although the large quantities of beer and pizza were beginning to affect his waistline. His brownish-green eyes and long eye lashes transformed his average looks to well above average. There was no official title and there was never a vote. Technically, there was no ring to lead, just a group of friends. But somehow Russell was looked to as the leader.

Nobody really remembered who actually started the group. All anyone could remember was that every Thursday night, between 9:30 and 10:00 o'clock, people would start meeting at the Pizza Palace on Sixth Street. Sixth Street was "the drag" in Austin, Texas. If you went to school at the University of Texas, or any other school in Texas for that matter, you spent a lot of time on Sixth Street. Russell could remember being invited one Thursday night his sophomore year.

He couldn't remember who was there, or how much beer was consumed. But he could remember leaving when told that the place was closed and that no more beer would be sold. He also remembered that the bill, for several large pizzas and many pitchers of beer, was about twenty five dollars. He thought for sure the bill should be at least seventy five, but it was not his place to argue. Every one pitched in and the pot totaled almost fifty. The bill was paid and the rest was given to the waitress as a tip. Russell quickly figured out why the bill was only twenty five bucks.

The Pizza Palace immediately became Russell's Thursday night hang out. Every week there would be old and new faces around the table. Some would become regulars and return week after week, and some were never to be seen again. Russell became a regular. Some nights there may have only been the five or six regulars, and some nights each would bring someone and there might be 15 or 20 people crowded around the table.

As the years went on, the "regulars" became a close-knit group of friends. They all had things in common - other than beer and pizza - and they all associated with each other on a daily basis. This was the early beginnings of a group of educated, fun-loving, law-abiding citizens, who had just masterminded the murder of a United States Senator.

Todd Evans was what most people would describe as typical. Tall, six feet two inches, but not overly tall by today's standards, 185 pounds but not well built. Not considered overly attractive but by no means unattractive, Todd was average. No one would take a second look at him, and no one would remember him. He was counting on this when he posed as a waiter and slipped poison into the drink of Senator Carson.

Todd graduated from the University of Texas with a degree in accounting, but would be much happier doing something else, anything else, as he put it. Having worked for seven years for a small pipe distribution company on the east side of Houston, he made a good salary and was up to four weeks of vacation per year. His job was routine and he could take off just about when he wanted. He volunteered to make the first "hit." In fact, had he not volunteered to do it, it may not have been done. Everybody loved talking about it and planning it, but no one was really wanted to be the trigger person.

"We all worked very hard at planning this." Todd Evans was addressing the group, "and I imagine we are all feeling a little strange right about now. We, er I, er we, whoever, just killed one person and the ingredients are set for a second within a matter of days." Everyone stared at Todd. At the same instant goose bumps ran over everyone's bodies.

Todd had told them he had an idea for the second on "the list" but never mentioned it again. To be honest, most members of the group never thought they would go through with one murder, let alone two. Todd Evans noticed the look he was getting from his friends and decided to explain.

"I know that we had agreed that Senator Williams of Illinois would be number two. When we were planning to kill Carson, I came up with an idea for Williams, so I did it on my way back from Arizona."

Kathy Beck, the youngest of the group at age 20, excused herself and ran from the room.

Kathy was introduced to the group when she started dating one of the members of the group. She was liked by everyone and soon became very close friends with one of the other girls. Kathy and her boyfriend split up right before he decided to accept a teaching job in South Carolina, and since everyone in the group liked her better anyway, she stayed in the group.

Now Kathy Beck was locked in the bathroom curled up in the fetal position on the floor. She was shaking uncontrollably. She felt nauseous. She'd been a part of the planning, even added some ideas. She had no idea why her stomach was in knots, but could only assume the thought of actually killing someone had made her sick.

It was just talk. Talk over drinks. Nothing serious. She sat on the floor with her head leaning on the toilet. Almost without warning, Kathy's stomach heaved and expelled the undigested remains of the asparagus casserole she had eaten for dinner. As she rested on the shiny white porcelain, she looked into the bowl. The sight of the asparagus caused her to vomit again, more violently than before.

In the dining room, Todd Evans continued, "I knew that we wanted Williams next, and I figure they are going to tighten security around all the Senators, so I thought it would be a good idea to set a trap."

The group sat silent. They were just beginning to accept the idea that they were all party to murder, and now they were learning that they were involved in two murders.

"Are you going to give us the details?" Russell Lewis asked.

"I think we should wait a bit. One murder a night is enough, agreed?" At this everyone agreed.

"Kathy's been gone a while, do you think someone should check on her?" Eric Moore asked. For the first time everyone noticed that Kathy had been missing a while. Julie Hanson, Kathy's best friend, said she would check on her.

The atmosphere seemed to lighten some and Julie left to look for Kathy. Several separate conversations started around the table and Eric Moore moved closer to Todd.

Eric Moore was also a University of Texas graduate. He landed a decent job with the Phoenix Tribune right out of college but was fired for, what he thought, was doing his job. He migrated to Houston and worked for the *Houston Post* until it was bought out and he was let go. For nearly a year he had been living off unemployment and free-lance money.

"If you've got it set up so Williams dies, I need to get a message to the paper." He said to Todd. He paused, searching for the right way to put it. After a few seconds, when he determined that there was no better way, he said, "we don't want somebody else to get . . .credit." Both men thought about this for a second and the pure absurdity of it, wanting to be sure that they get the credit, hit them like a tone of bricks.

"What in the hell are we doing?" Todd asked, and the two began laughing. At first it was a disgusted laugh, then it became an uncontrollable hysterical laugh. An enormous amount of tension was being released. It was amazing how much better both felt when they finally calmed down. They drank their beers and Todd explained his plan to Eric. Eric said he would mail his next "press release" tomorrow.

Julie came into the room and said she was taking Kathy home. She assured everyone that she was all right, but it all was a little much for her. The same thought raced though everyone's mind at the exact same time: *Can Kathy handle this? Will she tell anyone about this?* Nobody really thought about it while they were making the plans, but all it takes is one weak link and everybody is in prison.

Russell Lewis was thinking about it and he had a feeling everyone else was too.

"Julie, before you leave can you bring Kathy in here for a minute?" he asked. Julie nodded and left the room. It was only a matter of seconds before she returned with Kathy. The room had gotten quiet. Russell was sure everyone was thinking the same thing he was. Julie entered the room with Kathy in tow. Kathy, her face as white as the porcelain throne, was walking under her own power but it was obvious she was leaning heavily on Julie.

"Kathy. . . " Russell began.

"Please," Kathy interrupted. "I know this doesn't look good, and I don't know why I feel like this." She was using every bit of energy she could to control herself. "Killing this guy really doesn't bother me. I'm with you. Please, you all can trust me." Everyone gave her a sympathetic smile and a nod of assurance as Julie helped her to her car.

Later that evening Kathy experienced more vomiting. Her temperature spiked to 103. She was diagnosed with the flu. Three days later she was seven pounds lighter but feeling fine. Kathy Beck would never eat asparagus again.

4

Russell Lewis turned his 1986 Dodge 600 convertible around as soon as he heard the report on the radio. Saturday morning traffic in Houston is usually light, so Russell decided to take the Southwest Freeway to Fondren, and Fondren to Richmond Avenue. He drove to the tenants' entrance and punched the security code on the keypad. If he had used the visitors entrance, he would have had to call the apartment and had someone open the gate for him. Most everyone who visits these apartments know the tenant's code - *1234. The wrought iron gate slowly swung open and Russell sped past as soon as it opened far enough to squeeze through.

It was a beautiful morning and the top was down on the Dodge. Russell pulled into the closest parking space, killed the engine and jumped out of the car without opening the door. He didn't run, but walked very briskly to apartment 213. He took the steps two at a time and was at the top in seconds. Russell knocked on the door hard enough to be heard inside, but not so hard as to startle anyone inside. In a few seconds Todd Evans opened the door. He was wearing walking shorts and a T-shirt. No shoes or socks. The T-shirt said "Music people are crazy. . . Kerrville Folk Festival."

Todd Evans hardly had a chance to say "good morning," before Russell pushed his way past him to get inside the apartment. Russell moved Todd out of the way so he could close the door and lock it.

"Geez Russell, what the hell is wrong?" Todd asked.

Russell walked to the couch, sat on the edge, put his head in his hands for a few seconds, then looked up and said, "I guess you haven't had the radio on."

"No," Todd answered, beginning to get an idea of what was up.

"I heard it just a few minutes ago, Senator Williams was found dead at his home this morning."

"Did they say how he died?"

"No, how DID he die?" Russell was staring at his friend. The emphasis was on DID.

"You want a beer?"

"It's 8:30 in the morning, are you kidding?"

"It's a bit of a long story, I could go for a cold beer."

Russell thought about it and said, "me too, that's not a bad idea." They both smiled and Todd went to the refrigerator and pulled out a Michelob and a Budweiser. He twisted the tops off the bottles and put each in a koozie. He handed the bottle of Bud to his friend and sat in a chair next to the couch. Both men took a long pull on their bottles of beer.

"I knew that we wanted Williams," Todd Evans began, "and I knew that once we got started and did one, security would be beefed up and getting to another Senator would be tough. There are too many Representatives to watch, we'll be able find one that's vulnerable. But the Senators are going to be under tight security, which they have been. We've been hearing about it the last couple of days. I think every Senator has at least one FBI or Secret Service agent with them at all times. They check their houses and cars and food and drink."

Todd paused to take a drink of beer.

"I know you had it in place for a while, but how'd you do it?" Russell was getting anxious to get to the meat of the story.

"As you know, I researched Williams movements the same time I was researching Carson. They were number one and number two on our list and I really wanted to get them first. I found out Williams had a summer house outside of Springfield, Illinois. It's very secluded. Sits on a lake with a panoramic view of the lake. He owns all the acreage around the house and there's only one road in. If anybody tries to approach the house, either by land or water, they would be seen, as long as somebody is looking. They probably were the last few days, but they weren't before Carson was killed. In fact, I found a key above the back door. I thought I might have to make it look like a burglary, but I just unlocked the door and walked right in." Again he paused to take a drink of beer.

Obviously the story was not moving along fast enough, Russell began asking questions. "You said the FBI was checking houses, do you think they checked his? What did you do? HOW did you do it?" Todd, much more relaxed now that most of the bottle of beer had landed on his empty stomach, patiently waited for the questions to be rattled off. He was really beginning to enjoy this. He almost wished he could call a press conference and tell his story to the world. Finally, he continued, "have you ever heard of Anszoid?"

Russell shook his head, "no, I can't say that I have, what is it?"

"It's some really nasty shit made by Randy's company. They sell it to companies who dilute it and make pesticides. At full strength, you only have to breathe one part per thousand and you're dead in two minutes."

"That Anszoid really does sound nasty. I'm surprised Randy gave you a bottle. If you broke the bottle in a crowded area, you could really cause some problems."

"Last year Randy told me about this stuff and how bad it was. I didn't think much about it at the time, but for some reason I remembered the name. I guess I thought I might look for it on the label if I ever needed to buy some pesticide. Anyway, last fall I was on the east side and I thought I would stop by Randy's house. Nobody was home but the garage door was open. I needed to pee, so I walked through the garage into the back yard and did my thing. On the way back, I saw all the little brown bottles on the shelf. Several of them were labeled 'Anszoid'. They had screw on tops and then tape wrapped around the cap. I knew the stuff was bad but I figured I'd be O.K. So I took one bottle, put it in a brown paper bag I had in the car, and brought it home. I've had it in the refrigerator ever since. I don't think it's full strength, but I don't know how much it's been cut. I don't think even Randy, and you know he's a little scatter-brained, would keep full strength Anszoid in his garage. It was obviously strong enough to do the trick. I was pretty sure it would be." Todd paused to take a drink of beer.

"In the refrigerator? Are you crazy? As deadly as that is, what if a little bit leaks out? You open the door and wham, you're history."

"Randy said the hotter it got, the more deadly it was. It's usually used at room temperature or above, and it's very potent, even diluted. But when it's cold, it doesn't produce as much gas, or toxic fumes or something. Anyway, I got the impression it was much safer to keep it cold.

"I have also managed to get a hold of some respirators and cartridges. So I found an old hypodermic needle that I had around for some reason, packed everything up very well in a very solid suitcase, along with the cyanide I used on Carson, and flew to St. Louis from Phoenix. I rented a car and drove to Springfield. His place was pretty easy to find. First thing I did was check all the doors. They were all locked. I started thinking about the best way to break in. Just for the heck of it, I looked under all the flower pots and welcome mats, then I ran my hand along the ledge above the door. Bingo, there was a key."

Quite pleased with himself, Todd paused for dramatic effect and took another drink of beer. One more drink drained the bottle and he went for another. Russell wasn't ready yet. Todd returned with the beer and continued his story.

"I had an idea of what I wanted to do before I got there, but I checked the fridge to see what was in it. I didn't find anything I wanted to use in there, and besides, I bet that was the first place the FBI looked, and I didn't know how this stuff would work cold. The FBI probably threw out everything that could have been tampered with. So I went into the bathroom that connects to the master bedroom. There it was. The tube of toothpaste. I took the tube of toothpaste outside, put on my respirator, filled the hypodermic with about two CC's of Anszoid and slowly injected it into the tube. I stuck the needle about half an inch into the toothpaste and slowly worked the needle around as I injected the stuff. I was hoping to make a little cavity just below the surface. When it was all injected, I withdrew the needle, rubbed the paste around a little to be sure there was a seal and put the cap back on. I took the needle off and threw it as far as I could into the lake. I rinsed the hypo in the water and washed off the rubber gloves I was wearing. I then put the gloves, the hypodermic and the vile of Anszoid in a Ziplock bag. I put that bag in another Ziplock bag then took the toothpaste back into the house and put it back exactly where I found it. I made sure I hadn't left any foot prints or anything, and left. I locked the door and put the key back where I found it. I gathered up my Ziplock bag of goodies, took off the respirator, loaded it all in the car and got the hell out of Dodge. I stopped in some small town somewhere between Springfield and St. Louis and dropped the Ziplock bag in a dumpster."

Todd sat back, took a few sips of beer and looked at his friend. Russell sat quietly drinking his beer. He was replaying the whole scene over again in his head. He couldn't help but wonder what would have happened if a member of the local law enforcement would have stumbled across his friend running in and out of Senator Williams house wearing a respirator.

Russell Lewis smiled and said, "well, I guess it worked."

* * * * * *

Gary Stephens handed the letter to Alexander Christian. Special Agent Christian had a good idea what was in the letter. He had heard the news of Senator Williams death at 6:00 A.M. Phoenix time. When Gary Stephens phoned him at 9:05 A.M., he knew immediately that Senator Williams had not died of natural causes, as the preliminary reports had stated.

Wearing rubber gloves and holding the letter by the corners, Christian began reading the letter:

```
I WILL KILL ONE SENATOR OR REPRESENTATIVE
EVERY WEEK UNTIL TAXES ARE LOWERED AND
WASTEFUL SPENDING IS STOPPED!
```

So far, identical to the first letter, Christian thought. But there was more.

```
SENATOR WILLIAMS WAS NUMBER TWO.
```

Special Agent Christian could only stare at the letter. A thousand different thoughts raced through his mind. He was barely conscious of the fact that his stomach was beginning to tie itself up in knots. He kept staring at the letter hoping it would go away. His worst fears had just been realized. The first letter was not a decoy to lead the FBI on a wild goose chase when Senator Carson was in actuality the only target. This was a true conspiracy. Someone, or someones, had carefully planned and executed the murder of two United States Senators. They had sent letters to a newspaper office telling that they were going to do it, and they have done it. There is no reason to believe that they are not serious about killing a third and a fourth and a fifth. . .

Alexander Christian looked up and realized everyone was staring at him. He tried to think about how long he might have been staring at the letter. He said, "it's obvious we have a major problem here. Gary, I appreciate you keeping a lid on this the past four days. It's going to come out now. There is no way we will be able to keep this quiet. We are going to have to beef up security for all Congressmen and it will be noticeable. You can run your story in the morning paper. I am going to call a press conference for 8:00 A.M. tomorrow. At that time I will give everyone else the news."

Gary Stephens simply nodded and said "thanks." Twenty years ago he would have killed for this opportunity. It was every reporter's dream. But it wasn't twenty years ago, and even though he could see the Pulitzer being handed to him, he really wished someone else had received the letters.

Special Agent Christian, and the two agents with him, said goodbye to Gary Stephens and his assistant, Tim Brooks, and left.

"Tim, I want you to handle the column."

"What?" Tim Brooks was stunned. He had been sitting there totally envious of his boss. He would love to have a story like this. "Are you kidding? This may be the biggest story of the decade, it's fallen into your lap, you get to publish it, actually have the paper in your readers hands, before the FBI announces it to the world. Why don't you do it?"

"You are going to break the story. We've been talking about this story for almost a week. Anybody in this office could write a decent column. But it's not going to end there. It might if I write it, but I'm not going to write it, you are. When you break a story like this, you have to keep being first. Everybody is going to be buying the Phoenix Tribune looking for another scoop. I don't have the desire, or the drive, to be first with every development of this story. You do. You're young and you're ambitious, and I think you can handle it. This story will make you," Gary Stephens paused so that the next line would sink in, "or break you. Do it well, and you will be able to write your own ticket. Do a half-assed job and everyone is going to know it. You will be unofficially black-listed."

"Thanks Gary, I won't let you down. You'll have a draft by three o'clock."

Gary nodded and said, "by the way, I expect that this will keep you busy full time. I will have someone else fill in as assistant editor for a while."

Tim hadn't thought about this twist and he wasn't sure how he felt about it. He wanted the story, but thought he would do his old job too. He was sure he wasn't being demoted, but something didn't sound right. He realized he probably had a puzzled look on his face and decided that he would think about it awhile before he said anything he might regret. Besides, he thought, Gary is giving him the story of the decade. He said goodbye and went straight to his desk.

Gary Stephens leaned back in his chair. A thought had struck him earlier, and although he had given it some thought, it hadn't bothered him until it popped into is head a second time. It was when he was wishing that someone else had received the two letters stating that a Senator would be killed and he thought, *why did I get these letters?* After the first letter he assumed it was because he was the editor of the Phoenix Tribune and Senator Jeffrey Carson was killed in Phoenix. But now he gets a second letter, very similar to the first, except it mentions Senator Williams by name, and he gets it just about the same time Williams is found dead. As he thought about this, his adrenaline began to kick in and the old investigative reporter's blood began to boil. He almost called Brooks to tell him he wanted the story back. "Nope," he said to himself, "I don't want the story. Besides, Brooks would kick my butt, boss or no boss. But I am going to find out why I got the letters. I am going to find out why."

5

Special Agent Alexander Christian entered the small conference room at exactly 5:00 P.M. There was one rectangular table with ten chairs around it. Nine of the chairs were occupied. Christian stood behind the tenth chair at the head of the table. "Last week," he began, "Senator Jeffrey G. Carson was murdered here in Phoenix. This morning Senator Williams of Illinois was found dead at his summer home outside Springfield. The preliminary reports led us to believe that he died from natural causes. However, around nine this morning Gary Stephens, editor of the Phoenix Tribune, received another letter. This letter is very similar to the one he received last week, except it mentioned Senator Williams by name as number two. The lab has the letter now. We will get copies to you as soon as we can. Because of the nature of the first letter, we beefed up security on several members of Congress whom we considered high risk targets. Williams was on our list. I should be getting a detailed report of the security measures taken and how he died later this evening. I will brief you all on that as soon as I can." Christian paused to look at the group assembled around him. Three FBI agents, three Secret Service agents and three from the United States Marshall's office.

He continued, "I have called a press conference for eight o'clock tomorrow morning. The Phoenix Tribune will run a story about the threat letters and the two deaths in their morning edition. Quite frankly, the shit is going to hit the fan."

The room was full of muffled sounds. Some of the sounds were sardonic laughter and some of the sounds were moans about what was about to happen. Alexander Christian sat down and looked around the table. "Does anybody have any questions, comments, suggestions, opinions?" The room was remarkably quiet.

* * * * *

Word of the two Senators' deaths quickly spread among members of the group. It was decided that everyone should get together. To some, it was a celebration. To others, it was to satisfy the need to hear that what had happened was necessary. They were not murderers, but revolutionaries, of sorts. Whatever the reasons, they all wanted to be together this evening.

They decided to meet at Kathy's house. In private conversations among one another over the past few days, most had agreed that Kathy was the weak link. Everyone, including Kathy, seemed committed to the quest - cleaning out Congress - but if only one person told someone outside the group, or acted in a way that was out of the norm, the whole world would come crashing down upon them and they all would all spend a very long time in prison.

Kathy lived in a small frame house in West University Village. West U, as it is known to the locals, sits almost in the heart of Houston. A small community with a mixture of small older homes, and newer, larger brick homes. The smaller, older homes were being torn down to make room for the new, bigger homes.

Kathy's father worked for an oil company in Houston for many years. When the opportunity to manage an office in London came up, he jumped on it. The agreement was that Kathy would go to school and live in the house while her parents were in the U.K. She was given enough money to pay all the bills and live comfortably. She loved the arrangement but did miss her family on occasion.

Russell Lewis arrived a few minutes before six and rang the bell. Kathy opened the door. She was wearing a backless sun dress that came about half way up her thighs. Russell was shocked. He knew Kathy was a beautiful woman, but tonight she was stunning. She put her arm around him and pulled him close to her. He could fell her breasts pushing through the thin material of her dress and his shirt. She kissed him on the cheek and told him to come in. For the first time since he had met her, Russell didn't want to let her go. It took all his willpower to turn her loose. He couldn't put his finger on it, but something was different about Kathy tonight.

From the first time Russell saw Kathy over a year earlier, he had a crush on her. At the time, she was dating one of his friends. Russell accepted the fact that he and Kathy would never be more than friends. They became good friends. They usually sat together when the group met for pizza and had a great deal in common. When Russell's friend, Kathy's boyfriend, moved, Russell wanted to ask Kathy out. Feeling the best way to ruin a wonderful friendship was to start dating, he made a point of hiding any romantic feelings he was having toward her.

"You're the first here, can I get you something?" Kathy said as she turned and led him toward the den. Russell's brain froze. His heart was racing in his chest. All he could do was walk behind her and stare. The flowered sun dress hung from Kathy's shoulders, clung perfectly around her waist then swung from side to side across her hips as she walked. Russell watched her hips swing and studied her legs. Absolutely perfect. He had always felt that he was in love with her, but he had never experienced this type of feeling.

She stopped, turned and said, "Earth to Rus." Russell shook his head as he snapped out of the trance.

"I'm sorry, I was thinking about something else," he said.

"Cold beer?" Kathy said as she smiled.

Russell uttered a yes as he felt himself slipping back into the trance. He watched her as she went to the refrigerator for his beer. The beer was on the bottom shelf. Kathy bent from the waist to get one. As she bent, her sun dress moved up slowly exposing more of her legs. As she reached the beer, her sun-dress reached her panties, exposing every inch of her legs. Kathy turned around and handed Russell the beer. He wanted so badly to pull her close to him tell her how much he loved her.

Russell took the beer and twisted the top off. He was wishing that no one else would show up. He never wanted to risk losing Kathy as a friend by asking her out, but tonight he wanted to be with her. He thought back over the year or so that they had known each other and tried to determine why, all of a sudden, he felt he had to take a chance and tell her how he felt about her.

The doorbell rang and Kathy went to answer it. Russell knew everyone else would show up, but he had to hope. He couldn't move as he watched Kathy walk to the door. *God, she is great,* he thought to himself. Russell studied her perfect legs as she answered the door. It was Eric Moore. Kathy stretched to put her arms around Eric to hug him. As she stretched, her sun dress rose exposing more of her legs. Russell just stared. It reminded him of a poster for a James Bond movie.

Kathy offered Eric a beer and poured herself a White Zinfandel. Russell wanted to stay and watch her retrieve the beer from the bottom shelf of the refrigerator, but Eric pulled him into the den.

"It looks like we are two for two," Eric said as he extended his right hand to shake Russell's.

"We got a little lucky, I think. Did you get a letter to the Tribune?"

"Personally delivered it this morning."

"You're kidding, how?"

"First of all, I didn't want the newspaper, and the FBI, to get the letter before Williams died. If they knew we planned to kill Williams, they probably would have hidden him away somewhere. He never would have found Todd's surprise. I've been watching the wire service on the Internet very closely the past few days. Last night, just after midnight, a one line report came across that an ambulance had been dispatched to Senator Wendall Williams summer home in Illinois. I figured it was Todd's work, so I took a chance. I printed out my letter to Mr. Stephens and grabbed the first available flight to Phoenix. It was expensive just to fly there and turn around, but I thought it was important that they know that we were responsible for William's death. Anyway, I took a cab from the airport to the FBI offices. I was wearing a dark suit and sunglasses. I didn't smile or make small talk with the driver. I'm sure he thought I was an agent. I walked from the FBI office to the Tribune, it's about two blocks. There's a mail slot in the front door. I slid the envelope through the slot. One thing about newspapers, no matter what time of day or night, even if the front door is locked, there are people milling around. I'd be willing to bet the letter was on Gary Stephens' desk when he got to his office."

"Then you took a cab back to the airport and came home?"

"Yep, since I mentioned Williams by name in the letter, I wanted to be sure it got there after he was dead, but before they knew it."

Eric could tell Russell was a little worried. Kathy had heard most of the story and was looking very worried. Both Eric and Russell remembered how she had reacted to the death of Senator Carson less than a week earlier, even though she said it was just a bug.

Eric continued, "I can't imagine the FBI searching every passenger list of every flight that went in and out of Phoenix the past few days. Or, checking with the cabs to see if anybody was taken to or picked up from the Tribune. Remember, I had the cab take me to the FBI building. That should confuse the hell out of em. Anyway, I'm a reporter, if by the far-out chance I'm ever asked about that trip, I'll say I wanted to interview a FBI agent about a story I was working on. Not a big deal."

Russell had time to think about it and he was comfortable with it. The chances of anyone connecting Eric's flight to Phoenix with the murder of Senator Wendall Williams in Illinois was extremely remote.

"Couldn't you have E-mailed him a note via the Internet?" Eric Asked.

"I could have, but I'm pretty sure they could trace that right back to my apartment."

"Oh, I thought all that just got lost in cyberspace."

"No, it's all connected. I have an Internet address and anything I send out will have that address on it. I could sign up for access and give a fake name and address, but some computer systems have built in caller ID systems on them that log the number I call from every time I call. That's how they've been busting all the perverts that are trying to trade child pornography."

The doorbell rang and Russell suggested to Eric that he answer it. Russell took the opportunity to move next to Kathy.

"Are you O.K." he asked, taking her hand.

She was a little surprised by this. She liked Russell, very much, but there had never been a hint of romantic involvement between them. She wasn't sure if this was, or if he was just being concerned. Whatever the reason, it helped. She felt much better.

"I'm fine, thanks."

They looked into each others eyes and for an instant they both felt that everything really was fine.

Eric returned with Todd Evans, Mark Flanagen, Annie Simmons, Gene Thompson and Robert Green.

"I picked up Annie, and Gene, Mark and Bob pulled up the same time we did." said Todd who was carrying a red and white Igloo Playmate ice chest. "Who wants a beer," he asked. Russell hugged Annie and shook hands all around before pulling a cold Budweiser from Todd's ice chest and easing his way back to Kathy. Her smile relieved him. Maybe something was clicking, he thought. He returned her smile then realized that all eyes were on him.

Todd Evans was the first to speak. "Well, that's two."

There was a simultaneous "here, here," as everyone clinked there beer bottles and wine glasses together. Again, everyone looked at Russell.

"This should really crank some people up," Russell said. "Since we didn't hear anything about the first letter after Carson's death, obviously they decided to try and keep it hush hush. I don't know how they kept it out of the papers." He looked at Eric who gave an I-don't-know-either type of shrug. "But I can't imagine the Phoenix Tribune sitting on this now. They have to realize that there will be a leak and they will lose the greatest scoop of their lives."

Everyone nodded in agreement.

Julie Hanson had entered the room while Russell was talking. She was Kathy's best friend and always let herself in without knocking. The usual greetings were exchanged. Julie poured herself a glass of wine and joined the group.

"A long time ago, when we all first started talking about this, we had an idea of what we wanted to see happen. I'm not sure any of us thought we would actually get this far, but we have. Now comes the hard part. We have to let our intentions be known. That's where Eric comes in handy. I now nominate you as, not only the writer of our demands, but as our historian. It will be your responsibility to be sure that what we have done, and what we are about to do, is documented for future generations." Russell said.

Although everyone was in basic agreement with what Russell had just said, the way he said it generated a round of boos and hisses from his friends. A well needed round of laughter followed the boos and hisses.

"We must also define a clear set of objectives," Russell was on a roll, "we have to send a letter which states the minimum actions Congress can take to reduce waste before we strike again."

These comments ignited debates the level of which the group had not seen in years. The newest member of the group, Kathy, had never seen such heated discussions. She was amazed that two people could go after each other in such a way that they might come to blows any second, then one would get up and get the other a beer, and they would move on to something else.

Before anyone realized it, it was three in the morning. The Domino's pizza boxes were as empty as the Igloo ice-chest. Mark said that he really needed to leave and he got no resistance from the people who had ridden with him. Robert, Eric and Todd also agreed it was a good time to leave. Even though absolutely nothing was formally agreed upon, the consensus was that the evening was the most fun they had all had in a very long time. They would each try to piece the evening together over the next few days, then get together again and actually try to make some plans.

Russell purposely delayed his departure. He wanted Kathy to tell him that she wanted him to stay. Stay and they would spend the rest of the night and early morning making mad passionate love.

"Julie, would you like to go ahead and sleep here tonight?" Kathy asked.

"Sure, I really shouldn't be driving."

It seemed like it was everything Russell could do to keep from crying. He felt as though his heart had just been ripped out. He quickly said goodbye, giving both women a hug. His hug lasted a little longer, and was much tighter, with Kathy.

By the time he got in his car, a tear had begun rolling down his cheek. He began talking to himself. "What in the hell just happened? I can hardly breathe. I feel like there's a refrigerator on my chest. When I saw her tonight I felt as though I couldn't live without her."

His head snapped up as a light came on in the corner of Kathy's house. *Must be her bedroom* he thought to himself. For a moment he thought about getting out of the car and sneaking up to the window to see if he could see in. He quickly abandoned the idea and started the car. He looked again at the light coming through the window. He put the car in drive and slowly drove down the street. He thought about Kathy. He thought about Julie with Kathy. He should be in there, not Julie.

6

Special Agent In Charge Alexander Christian was exhausted. If he wasn't talking to people in person, he was on the telephone. He hadn't slept in over 24 hours. He wished he had slept. He was no closer to the killer, or killers, of the two U.S. Senators than he was the day before. He had just finished reading the front page article of the Phoenix Tribune. In less than an hour he would be holding the biggest press conference of his life. He looked out his office window at the street below. He couldn't remember the last time he saw such a congregation of news vehicles. The Branch Davidian stand-off outside Waco, Texas came to mind. He hoped his press conference would turn out better than the Branch Davidian stand-off.

Alexander checked his watch and decided he had just enough time to hit the head, splash some water on his face and grab a cup of coffee before he had to face the music.

He used a paper towel to dry his face. He studied himself in the mirror. *I LOOK O.K.,* he thought to himself. The butterflies in his stomach were unmistakable, but he didn't really feel nervous. Anxious was a better word. He was totally prepared. Soon it would be over and he would be able to get back to the task of finding the killers. A task that had very few roads, all of which were dead ends.

For a brief moment he thought about golf. If he could have only cut out an average of three or four strokes per round, he would be in some other part of the country right now preparing to tee-off on the first hole of a round of golf where he would have a chance at winning over a quarter of a million dollars. *When this is over, I'm going to start playing more golf,* he thought to himself.

The briefing room at the FBI office in Phoenix was rather small. It could have been twice it's size and it still would have been too small for the crowd of reporters who had gathered. Luckily, the lobby was fairly wide and quite long. It was the only logical place to hold the press conference. A makeshift stage was assembled at one end, with a podium set in the front of it. The sound engineers all worked together to make sure that all the microphones were mounted on the podium and the miles of cable all ran to the correct trucks. An unidentified intern stood behind the bank of microphones and counted "1. . . 2. . . 3. . . 4. . . testing 1. . . 2. . . 3. . . 4." He repeated this process several times until everyone seemed satisfied that his or her microphone was working properly.

At precisely eight A.M. Special Agent Alexander Christian stepped up to the microphone and introduced himself. Shutters began clacking, strobes firing and motor-drives winding. The Agent hoped they would all run out of film very quickly. He took a deep breath as he looked around the room. The strobe lights fired again as the motor-drives sped film though the cameras at 18 frames per second. The banks of spot lights which had been set up turned the crowd of people into one large mass of silhouettes.

His posture perfectly erect, he stared straight ahead into the lights and began. "Good Morning. Thank you for coming. Last week, Senator Jeffery Carson of Texas was killed as he played golf at the Desert Green Country Club. It's been determined that the cause of death was cyanide poisoning.

"Late Friday night Senator Wendall Williams of Illinois was rushed to the hospital with what was thought to be a massive heart attack. It turned out that Senator Williams was also poisoned. Our lab is attempting to determine what kind of poison was used. There are in fact, a number of poisons that affect the respiratory system. What these poisons do is cut off the flow of oxygen from the lungs to the brain. The brain tells the lungs it needs air and the lungs work harder. The heart pumps harder trying to send oxygen enriched blood to the brain until it basically explodes. The symptoms are almost identical to those of a stroke.

"Before, minutes before to be exact, the death of Senator Carson, we received a letter stating one Senator or Representative would be killed each week until Congress stops wasting money."

The outburst from the crowd of reporters was deafening. They shouted exclamations to each other and generally made a commotion that is expected after hearing a comment such as the one they had just heard. Before Christian could continue, the reporters began yelling questions at him. He took the opportunity to take a drink of water, then held his hands out signaling the crowd to calm down.

As the noise level subsided, Agent Christian continued.

"Yesterday morning we received another letter stating the

exact same fact, as well as naming Senator Williams as the next victim."

Agent Christian stood patiently waiting for the second outburst to subside. "We, the FBI and Secret Service, quietly informed every member of the House and the Senate and beefed up our security on them. An exact copy of both letters will be released to the press in due time. We did not release this information after the death of Senator Carson because, one, we did not know, and we still do not know, if the purpose of the killings are for the reasons stated, or if the letter is an attempt to sway our investigation in a different direction. Two, we are in the middle of an investigation and the less known by the public, the better. And three, a crime of this nature often spawns copy-cat crimes. We were hoping to avoid this. Unfortunately, after the death of Senator Williams, it had become very difficult to keep the situation a secret.

"Our investigation is moving along, we have several leads, and I will keep you all informed. I am sorry, but that is all I can tell you at this time. Thank you very much for coming."

Ignoring the questions being shouted at him, Agent Christian turned and walked off the make-shift stage.

7

"All I saw were the highlights on the CNN this afternoon. I was sound asleep when it was on this morning. I didn't even think about setting the timer to tape it." Russell said to Todd Evans and Eric Moore. The entire group was coming to Russell's apartment to discuss the events and what they wanted to do next. Todd and Eric had arrived early. Although everyone was involved, it was Todd Evans and Eric Moore whose heads were the furthest in the noose. Russell Lewis was not far behind. Tonight would be serious. No beer. Actually, the mere thought of beer made their stomachs turn and roll.

The three men worked on an agenda for the evening while they waited for the others. The first thing they discussed was whether or not they wanted to continue. They had killed two human beings, worthless human beings, but human beings nevertheless. Now that two were dead, would the remaining members of Congress change? Did these deaths put any kind of scare in them at all? If not, how many would they have to kill? When they originally derived the plan, a number never came up. Maybe they thought that they would kill one or two U.S. Senators and the rest of Congress would immediately pass a balanced budget, eliminate all of the pork barrel spending and overhaul social security so that only those who paid into it would get something out of it. No longer would a person be able to say alcoholism was a disease, get on social security and be able to sit around all day and drink beer.

Eric Moore said, "when the Social Security system was enacted in the thirties, the world was in a depression. Government decided it should try to put some of the out of work men to work. They built roads, national parks, bridges and dams. If you wanted to work, and you were lucky enough to get on, you worked hard and you made money. Not much money, but it was a hell of lot better than no money. Just about everybody WANTED to work. Today there is unemployment insurance, social security, welfare, food stamps and homeless shelters. Nobody wants to work. Why work? Bust your ass all day for five bucks an hour. Then Uncle Sam takes over seven and a half percent of that for social security. No thank you, just don't work. Stay home and have kids. Uncle Sugar will pay you to have kids. You can't support a child on what the government pays you for one, so have four or five. At five hundred bucks a month per child, that's 2,500 dollars a month, and they pay most of your rent to boot. Why send the kids to school? They know the system. The little girls will have babies. The boys can fend for themselves. Become an alcoholic or addicted to drugs. Remember, those are diseases now, you'll get Social Security. Somebody in the neighborhood knows a doctor that will commit you. Get on the Uncle Sugar payroll and you're set for life. Nobody ever checks. Don't worry about the money, all of those middle class yuppies are paying big bucks into the system as well as putting big bucks into IRA's and 401k plans. They will never see a penny of the social security money. There will be plenty of others to spend it on, as long as they keep making cheap beer."

"That was mighty preachy Eric. What's wrong, is your unemployment about to run out?" Todd could not resist the zinger. Eric didn't like it, but did not say anything. His unemployment benefits were about to expire.

The rest of group arrived at Russell's and it wasn't long before they remembered why they had hatched this plan in the first place: One hundred and seven thousand dollars to fund research into the sex life of the Japanese quail. One point two million dollars to study the breeding habits of the woodchuck. One million dollars to study why people don't ride bicycles to work. Nineteen million dollars to examine gas emissions from cow flatulence. Two hundred and fifty thousand dollars to study television lighting in Senate meeting rooms. One hundred sixty thousand dollars to study if you can hex an opponent by drawing a X on his chest. Fifty-seven thousand dollars for gold-embossed playing cards on Air Force 2. The list is endless.

It was all business tonight. Not nearly as much fun as last night, but everyone knew that they needed to get something accomplished this evening. And at a decent hour. Most of them would have to get up and go to work in the morning.

Eric Moore took notes. By the end of the evening it was generally decided that, One: They would not send a of list demands, but wait and see if anything changed over the next few weeks. Two:

A list of "victims," was made. This was Gene Thompson's area of expertise. He had a Ph.D. in History from the University of Missouri and was the most politically active of the group. He was also the oldest. At one time he may have had political aspirations himself, but having been overweight to one degree or another his entire life, he decided he would never be elected in this the television age. Three: They would concentrate on a member of the House of Representatives. There were a lot more of them than there were Senators (the "even less Senators now" comment helped ease the mood considerably) and it would be much harder to protect all of them than it would all of the Senators. It was also reasoned that since they had killed two Senators, the FBI might think they may go after a third. Four: Each person would very discreetly research a couple of the potential victims. Try to find out which ones would be the easiest and safest to get to. Five: While researching these potential victims, think about how to do it. Remember. The element of surprise was over. They are going to be on guard. And, six: The FBI doesn't have a clue. They had all by now seen most of the press conference. The FBI agent said they had several leads. Bull Shit. They have nothing. And it had to stay that way.

A few glances at watches reminded everybody that it was getting late. Russell took the cue. "This has been good. Why don't we meet Thursday night," he paused and looked at Kathy, she nodded her head up and down, "at Kathy's. We'll go over what we've got then and have some beer and pizza." Eight hours ago this comment would have gotten some serious groans, but the effects of the night before had pretty much worn off. Beer and pizza was beginning to sound good again.

Everyone said their good-byes and left. Kathy was last. She slowed down so the others could get out the door and down the steps. She stopped at the door and turned around to face Russell. She put her arm around his neck and pulled him down to her. She kissed him on the lips. It lasted much too long for a friendly good-bye kiss.

"I really missed you last night," she said, then turned and went through the door, closing it behind her. Russell stood looking at the closed door for what seemed like an eternity. He finally recovered enough to make it to the couch where he collapsed. He rubbed his lips with his index finger and removed the trace of lipstick left behind by Kathy. He held it under his nose and smelled the lovely aroma. He then put his finger to his lips and fell asleep dreaming of Kathy.

8

"Son-of-a-Bitch. The FBI ain't got shit. What the hell are they doin'? Why haven't they arrested these killers? 'Cause they ain't got shit! I oughta slash the FBI budget. Maybe that would stop these crazy son-of-a-bitches. They want us to cut spending, I'll cut the God damn FBI budget. I can't eat, can't sleep, I don't even feel safe going out and finding some whore to give me a blow-job." Senator Chuck Abernathy was yelling at his two aides. The two aides knew why he was so upset. If all the Senators were ranked in order by most corrupt, Jeffrey Carson would have been number one, Wendall Williams number two and Chuck Abernathy number three. There was not much separating one from three, and two were dead.

Seven years ago Lisa Thompson was a Freshman at Harvard when she met Senator Abernathy. She loved politics. She was president of every class in high school and was freshman student body president at Harvard. She was brilliant and attractive, had it not been for a somewhat pale complexion, caused by chronic anemia, she would have been considered beautiful.

She had blond hair, blue eyes, high cheek bones and a beautiful smile. Her legs were long and thin. Too thin, she felt, and too white. She normally wore white pantyhose to hide her legs, which, although she didn't realize it, were magnificent. Her breasts were well developed and perfectly shaped, without the help of medical science. She looked amazingly like a Barbie Doll.

She planned to get her political science degree and go straight to law school, probably at Harvard. Her aspirations were to become the first woman President of the United States, and there was a very good possibility she would. She definitely had the ambition. It was a dream come true when she was selected as an aide to Senator Abernathy of Florida, her home state.

Her dream was shattered within minutes of meeting Mr. Abernathy. He was charming, articulate, sincere, even flattering as the aides were introduced in his office. Pictures were taken for the Florida papers. Lisa Thompson was on cloud nine. He excused the journalists by saying there was much work to be done. He asked Lisa to stay as he wanted to give her a special project. Chuck Abernathy smiled and shook hands with each reporter and the other aides as they left. He closed and locked the door.

He motioned for Lisa to sit as he took his seat in his oversized leather chair behind his desk. He didn't say a word. He stared at Lisa. He stared at her legs and at her breasts. It was obvious what he was looking at. A few seconds were fine. She could handle it. But he was burning a hole right through her. She became noticeably uncomfortable.

Finally, he stood, walked around his desk and sat beside her. She was wearing a yellow blouse, gray skirt of medium length and white pantyhose. She sat with her legs crossed allowing more thigh to show than was covered by her skirt. He put his hand on her leg at the knee and slowly slid it up her leg. Lisa said "please don't," and politely removed his hand from her leg.

Chuck Abernathy put his hand back on her knee, this time pulling her knee abruptly toward him, causing Lisa's legs to uncross and spread for a brief moment, until she regained her balance and could bring her legs back together.

"Nice, very nice," he said as Lisa stood and backed away. She was silent as she stared at the Senator. In a few short seconds her dream had turned into a nightmare. "Come on, sit back down, I was just testing the water. Me and you will go swimming in that water one of these days. I had to see if the water was hot now, if it was I'd jump right in. No need for me to put it off if you were ready, but I guess you're not. That's O.K., I can wait. Your water will get hot one of these days." Abernathy smiled and laughed as he went back to the oversized executive chair behind his desk.

Lisa was in shock. She couldn't move. She wanted to run and grab the reporters and bring them back in and tell them what had happened.

"Oh lighten up, babe, I'm just having a little fun with you. I bet you want to run from here and tell the world what I just did. Well, go ahead. I'll deny it. I'll tell everybody the first thing you said to me was that you would sleep with whoever it took to get to the top and then I threw your happy ass out of my office, so you ran to the reporters with this cock and bull story. Who do you think they're going to believe?"

Lisa had a few minutes to regain her composure. This had been a tremendous shock to her, but she hadn't gotten where she was by being a pushover. She sat back down.

"What if I just walk out?" She asked.

"You will miss out on the learning experience of a lifetime. I am one of the big dogs on this hill, and Capital Hill is the biggest hill in the world. I would like to say, 'I don't really give a hairy rat's ass what you do, but that's not true. The system up here runs on favors. You scratch my back, I'll scratch yours. Shit rolls downhill. Remember. . . "

"And this is the biggest hill," Lisa interrupted.

"You are good. I knew you would be. I do favors for the President of the United States and my aides do favors for me. The President helps me out and I help my aides out. It all flows downhill. You are an attractive woman. If there's one thing I've learned over the years is that good-looking women hang around with good-looking women. I want you get to know the other girls around here. You keep me in a fresh supply of young good-looking women, as well as doing a good job for me as an aide, and you will go far, very far. But I'm holding out for the day when you say 'Chuck, I want that assignment and I'll give you the best fuck of your life for it'."

"Don't hold your breath, Chuck." Lisa said, already immune to his style.

Abernathy leaned forward in his chair and said, "by the way, you can call me Senator, Senator Abernathy, or Mister Abernathy. The only time you can call me Chuck is when you're about to do something that rhymes with it."

It had been seven years since that first meeting and she still hated the man. She had learned more about politics in the those seven years than most people would learn in a lifetime. She also learned a lot about people. At the ripe old age of 26, she knew the kind of person she didn't want to be. She was in law school now, Harvard, but she still had time to work for Senator Abernathy. More time this year than last. Her first year of law school left very little time for the Senator. He had missed her too. She did her job well, she would make a very good Senator. Lisa had also found women for him that he used to only dream about. He had really missed that.

She stared at the Senator. He had always been crude, but seldom was he this blunt, especially with witnesses. But two of the Senators closest comrades were now dead. He was scared. Lisa

Thompson had hated this man from the first day she met him. He had what she wanted and she knew that all these years of tolerating the bullshit would pay off ten-fold someday. She just didn't think it would be this soon.

Lisa looked at the other aide in the office and said, "Bill, would you excuse us for a minute please."

Bill glanced at the Senator for approval. He got the nod and left the office. Lisa was basically in command in the office. She was over the entire staff. When the Senator was not around, her directions were followed to the letter. If the Senator was in the room, every member of the staff would wait for approval before doing anything Lisa asked.

Senator Abernathy sat in his oversized leather chair and stared at Lisa. He couldn't remember her ever dismissing a member of his staff in front of him.

She walked to the front of his desk, put her hands on the desk and leaned over, bracing herself on the Senator's cherry desk. She was wearing a loose white cotton blouse tucked in to a navy skirt. The top two buttons of the blouse were undone. Anyone sitting on the other side of the desk would have a lovely view of a good portion of two very beautiful breasts. The Senator didn't try to make eye contact. His eyes were glued to her chest.

"I have a proposition for you, *Chuck*."

The Senator's eyes immediately looked up at hers. She didn't smile. He stared deep into her blue eyes for several seconds. Without saying a word he reached up and unbuttoned a button of her blouse. Then another. With both hands he reached inside her blouse, under her bra and slid his hands down around her breasts. She stood motionless allowing him to squeeze her breasts until she knew he would do just about anything she asked.

When she felt he was hooked, Lisa straightened up and buttoned her blouse. The Senator almost fell out of his chair leaning forward to stay with her breasts as long as possible.

"I said I have a proposition for you." Lisa sat in same chair she sat in the first day they met. "They're going to get you, you know." She paused to let this sink in. He was scared and she knew it. "Look at who they killed. I'm surprised you weren't number one on the list." He heard what she said, but his mind was still on her breasts. "You should resign." This got his attention. Part of him had been at attention for a while, and she knew it.

"Are you out of your fucking mind?"

"They're going to kill you if you don't quit. Come up with a good reason. Resign. Appoint me interim Senator until a special election can be held. You will support me as your hand picked successor. I'll become the elected Senator from the great state of Florida and I will make sure you have all the female companionship you can handle, and you won't have to worry about public opinion."
She spread her legs slightly so the Senator could look up her skirt. She let him look for several moments. It didn't matter, she knew all he would be able to see was the reinforced area of her panty hose. But it did the trick. If there was an ounce of blood left in his brain, it all just shot straight to his penis. The little head was doing the thinking for the big head.

"So we hop over to the couch for a quickie, then I go out and tell the world that I'm resigning for personal reasons and you should take over?"

"That's not how I had it figured, but if that's all you want, sure."

The blood was beginning to return to his brain. "What did you have in mind?"

"First of all, no quickie on the couch, as you so eloquently put it. Can you get away without the S.S. following you?"

"Sure, I just have to tell them I don't want them. Why in hell would I want to do that?"

"So you could meet me somewhere, maybe like Florida, tomorrow night, where I will do the ultimate favor for you. Then I will come back and you will go to your home where the following day you will announce your retirement. I will come up with your speech. You will go out with a bang. Then you will appoint me to finish out your term."

Senator Abernathy sat quietly. He was not going to resign. But what could she do if he reneged after an evening of great sex? He would have really liked to ponder the ramifications a bit longer before he agreed.

Lisa leaned back in her chair and said, "and there's nothing I won't do, if you know what I mean, Chuck."

The Honorable Chuck Abernathy opened his top left desk drawer and pulled out a key. He took a pad of paper a began writing as he spoke. "This key is to bungalow 3C at the Palm Court Resort, 25 Caroline Street, Key West. It's got a private drive in the rear and sits quite a ways from the other bungalows. Very private and very soundproof." He smiled and she smiled back.

"Can you make it there by tomorrow afternoon?" He asked.

"We had better make it two days. I will get there either tomorrow evening or Friday morning. You get there no sooner than Friday afternoon. You have to be damn sure no one knows we are together. It would be the end for both of us."

Lisa would have preferred somewhere a little easier to get to than Key West. Key West is a four hour drive from Miami. The only other option is to fly into the Key West airport. It was too small, there was too much risk of being recognized. She would have to make the drive.

"I have to agree with you on that. If word of this arrangement got out, it could ruin you," the Senator said.

Lisa ignored the implication that it would ruin her and not him as she took the key and the address and left the Senator's office. As she closed the door behind her, she had the urge to vomit.

Senator Abernathy adjusted himself behind his desk. His erection had made him very uncomfortable but he was not going to do anything about it while Lisa was in the room. He would never give her the satisfaction of knowing that she had aroused him.

He leaned back in his chair and thought about the upcoming affair. *I am going to enjoy her in every way imaginable. Very possibly for an entire weekend. Then she will fly back to Washington and I will announce how sorry I am, but I am forced to dismiss the aide that has served me so well over the past six years because she has made, what I consider, lewd and lascivious advances toward me.* He smiled.

9

Lisa Thompson proofed Senator Abernathy's letter of resignation. She had written it as soon as she left his office, but decided to wait and reread it after she calmed down. She made a few subtle changes before she printed the final draft. She did not expect him to sign it, she was sure he had a plan of his own to discredit her after their weekend fling.

It actually surprised Lisa that the Senator, after all the years she worked for him, might think she was so naive to believe he was going to resign and appoint her his successor. Then it dawned on her that the Senator was probably thinking with the wrong head again and she understood why he was not thinking clearly. Of course, the deaths of Carson and Williams were two very good reasons to resign.

There was no need to take a chance that he might get suspicious, so she prepared a letter of resignation, just as she had said she would. Lisa looked over the letter one last time before she placed it in a nine by twelve manila envelope and laid it on his desk. By the time he found it, she would be on her way to Florida.

The Boeing 737 landed on time at Tampa's International Airport. Lisa stayed in her seat as the passengers filled the aisle wrestling with their carry-on luggage. The main door opened and the line began moving slowly toward the front of the airplane. As the crowd in the aisle thinned, an older gentleman with a nice tan stopped, allowing Lisa out of her row. She smiled and said "thank you," as she stepped in front of him.

Lisa's brother Larry was waiting for her at the end of the corridor. She scooted around a couple of the slower moving senior citizens as soon as she saw him. Larry was two years older than Lisa and had always been very protective of his little sister. Lisa waited patiently as the crowd squeezed through the last bottleneck before leaving the airline's gated area. She grabbed her brother by the neck and hugged him.

"It's so good to see you. Mom and dad are so exited they can't hardly stand it. I am to. It really is good to see you," he said.

"It's good to see you too." Lisa said, wishing she was visiting under different circumstances.

"I was going to bring your car to the airport because it hadn't been run in a while and you said on the phone that you had to drive somewhere. I had the oil changed and it's running great, so I decided to drive my Jeep. Your car is a little too small for me."

"Thanks. You always have taken care of your little sister."

Lisa explained that she had no checked luggage and she was more than ready to get out of the airport. On the drive from Tampa to Winter Haven, Larry caught Lisa up on the activities of the family as well as the gossip about her old friends. The hour drive only seemed to take a few minutes. She was sorry the drive was over until she saw her parents come out of the house.

When Lisa went off to college, she fully expected to come home for the holidays and summers. Once she began working for Senator Abernathy, all of her free time was spent in Washington. She always made it home for Christmas, but some years that was the only time she saw her family. She missed them dearly.

Lisa was opening the door of the 1997 Jeep before it stopped. She jumped out and ran to her mother. She hugged her and kissed her, then hugged and kissed her father before hugging her mother again.

The Thompson family went inside where Mrs. Thompson had a late lunch prepared. They sat around the kitchen table drinking iced tea and talking about what was happening in their lives. Lisa did most of the talking. After all, she was about to graduate from law school, Harvard Law School, and she worked for one of the most powerful men in the country.

Lisa's family was extremely proud of her. Larry, a civil engineer who had graduated from Florida State was the most proud. There was no sibling rivalry, he was very happy that his little sister was doing so well.

"You said you weren't going to be able to stay long. What do you have to do?" Lisa's mother asked.

Lisa had been anticipating the question. She didn't like lying to her parents, but she certainly couldn't tell them the truth this time. "The Senator has asked me to come and talk to a couple of large contributors who are complaining that he is not doing enough for them. He said these people like me and that I could convince them that he is doing everything he can for them at the moment. I don't really mind doing it, and it gave me a chance to see you all for a while. I have to leave tonight in order to meet with them tomorrow, but I should be home either late tomorrow or Saturday. I hope I can get back tomorrow, I booked the latest flight out Sunday night, I have a class I have to attend Monday morning. Senator Abernathy said he has business in Miami all next week, that's why he couldn't meet these people. But since he's out of the office, I have to get back to Washington as soon as I can."

"Honey, are you sure you're not working yourself too hard? Florida, Boston, Washington. You know you look a little pale."

"Mom, I'm fine. Really. And I always look pale, you know that. Please, don't worry about me. As soon as school is over, I'll come home and stay a week."

"We would all really like that."

Each member of her family agreed it would be nice to have her home for a week. Lisa excused herself and went to her bedroom. It was exactly as she had left it almost seven years ago. Having been one of the most attractive and most popular girls in high school, Lisa was invited to every formal dance that came up, beginning her freshman year. At every dance she had a picture taken of her and her date. The pictures covered most of one wall of her bedroom.

Lisa went into her closet and pushed the row of prom dresses aside. Beneath the dresses were shoe boxes which contained a pair of matching shoes for each prom dress. She pulled out the middle box on the bottom row and carried it to her bed.

She looked at the plain white shoe box several seconds before opening it. The Beretta .22 pistol was wrapped in white tissue paper inside the box. She unwrapped the gun and held it in her hand. The clip and a small box of 50, .22 caliber long-rifle rounds were in the bottom of the box.

Holding the pistol, Lisa looked at the pictures on her wall until she found the one of her and Bobby Humphries. It was the Junior Prom. She was a freshman, Bobby was a junior and friend of her brother. Lisa had a crush on Bobby and told her brother who promptly hinted to his friend that he should ask her to the prom. Although Lisa was only a freshman, most of the boys at the dance were envious of Bobby.

The summer following the Junior Prom, Lisa spent a lot of time with Bobby. Lisa couldn't remember how it came up, but she mentioned that she had never shot a gun before. Her father and brother went hunting quite often, but would not take her or even teach her how to shoot.

Bobby volunteered to teach her and picked her up one morning and took her to the woods. He brought along a Beretta .22 caliber long-rifle semiautomatic pistol. In the woods, Bobby taught Lisa how to load the bullets into the clip, how to put the clip into the pistol and load a bullet into the chamber by pulling back on the breach. He explained the safety and the importance of keeping it on. They fired several rounds until they ran out of cans to shoot. He gave her a box of 50 bullets and told her to keep the gun and practice whenever she wanted.

Lisa hid the gun in the shoe box her prom shoes had come in and forgot about it. She and Bobby dated another month or so until he became more sexually active than she wanted to be. They remained friends and would talk when he came over to visit her brother. He never asked her for the gun back.

It had been at least eight years, at her brother's and Bobby's high school graduation, since she had last seen him. As she wrapped the semiautomatic pistol in the white tissue paper, she wondered what happened to Bobby. She would ask Larry about him, if she thought about it, when she got back from Key West. She would never ask.

Lisa loaded six bullets into the clip and placed the gun and the clip in her overnight bag. It had been ten years since she had fired the gun. She wondered if ten year old bullets would still work. She didn't have time to test them and she knew it would not be a good idea to buy new.

Lisa put her overnight bag over her shoulder and looked at the wall of pictures one last time. It brought back a flood of wonderful, and not so wonderful memories. She looked at Bobby and wondered if her life would be different had she given in and had sex with him. She looked at the pictures of her and Gary Douglas. They had dated over a year, beginning when she was a junior, and had gone to several formal dances together. She thought she loved him and when he became more sexually active, Lisa did too. He was her first. As she looked at his picture, she wondered what ever happened to him.

After putting her overnight bag in her 1989 Toyota Celica, Lisa kissed and hugged her brother, father and mother. She got in the car and as she was buckling her seat belt, Larry bent down and put his head in the window.

"What's going on sis?" He asked.

"Nothing, what do you mean?"

"I'm not going to say anything to mom or dad, but something's up, I can tell. You're acting differently. Where are you going?"

"Don't worry about me, I'll be home by Saturday at the latest," Lisa said kissing her brother on the cheek before pulling out of the driveway.

* * * * * *

The group was a buzz with excitement. It was in every newspaper. On every television station. All the radio talk shows were talking about it. The entire country was talking about how some group or "faction," as most news reports referred to it, was demanding that government stop being so wasteful, or they would kill members of Congress.

They had already killed two senior members of the Senate. This was a faction to be taken extremely serious. The President had made this case the top priority of all federal law enforcement agencies.

Analysis of polls by CNN, CNBC, The Washington Post and others, as well as comments from listeners of call-in radio and television shows, showed the country was evenly divided between those who supported this faction and their methods, and those who thought they were just like any other terrorist group and should be stopped immediately.

Everyone was early for the Thursday night gathering. They were all giddy. Acting almost like children. Each had stories to tell of conversations they had heard, and that they had had about the faction. They especially enjoyed telling about the different theories people have about who is involved.

It was very hard not to tell them that they are so wrong it wasn't even funny. Everyone was happy to be together again so they could finally talk about it.

Russell Lewis unofficially called the meeting to order. Eric Moore kept unofficial notes. Everyone was anxious this evening. Even those who hadn't been that involved were psyched because of all the hype.

Russell started, "who has come up with a suggestion for our next. . ."

Before he could finish names were coming at him from every

direction.

"Ted Thomas."

"Jack James."

"Carl DeFoure."

"Janet Logan."

"Ted Kennedy."

"Wait, slow down," Russell stopped the flow of names. "I think we need a little more organization here."

There was some light hearted jeering along with a few more names being tossed out until Gene Thompson interrupted.

"Wait. Calm down. I probably know more about politics and politicians than anyone here, so this is what we will do. Y'all throw out a name, one-at-a-time, and I will tell you if there are any particular reasons he or she should not be considered."

"Seems like a good idea," said Eric.

"How about Ted Kennedy? Everybody knows about him. We could do it for Mary Jo." Said Annie Simmons.

"No," said Gene. "Next."

"Wait, what do you mean 'no', aren't we going to discuss it?"

"O.K., he had one brother killed in World War II. He had a brother get his head blown off in Dallas. He had a third brother killed in L.A. He meets a woman at a party, gets a little on the side of the road, and sends her on her way. She drives off a bridge and drowns. Instead of telling the truth, he says he was driving, and, well, you know the rest of the story. His brain is basically fried from all the booze and I'm sure his liver is just about history. He lives on a compound surrounded by guards. We couldn't get within a mile of him. Why bother?"

Annie was somewhat shocked. She had never received a tongue lashing like that from Gene. He was always the quiet one. He would smoke his cigars, drink wine and pretty much just listen to what everybody had to say, occasionally straightening people out who were straying a little far from reality.

"How 'bout Jack James, Representative from Beaumont?" Annie asked. A little sheepishly this time.

"Excellent choice!" Boomed Gene. "Next."

Annie glared at Gene. She thought he was being facetious. Gene stared back at Annie. This was the most fun he had in a long time. "Annie," he said, "I'm serious. James is a perfect candidate. He has screwed the people of Orange County for over 20 years. He thinks he is invincible. I talk with lots of politicians every day. They say he thinks there is no way anybody could get to him. He says security cramps his style. Jack E. James is a drunkard, a womanizer and one of the most crooked public servants I know."

"I agree," said Russell. "In fact, I thought about him too. I did a little checking and I have an idea that should make Mr. James the Late Representative from Beaumont. If nobody has any objections, we will make Representative James our next target."

There were no objections. In fact several were relieved. Julie Hanson, Robert Green and Mark Flanagen enjoyed the company, they were all close friends. When the "plan" was first being talked about, it was fun. It gave them all something to talk about other than work. Now that everybody everywhere was talking about it, they really enjoyed knowing what 200 million other people didn't. But to plan and execute a murder, they weren't quite ready. Privately, they each hoped that this wasn't going to turn into a quota type thing where each one would have to kill at least one to be accepted.

"My plan, and it's just a basic plan, not totally thought out yet, needs a female accomplice. Any volunteers?" Russell asked.

"I will," Kathy said. Russell was hoping she would.

"It could be dangerous."

Kathy looked at him silently for a second before she said, "I can handle it."

"I need a pickup truck. Who can hot-wire a truck?"

Serial killers yes, petty auto thieves no. Everybody looked at each other. There were a few chuckles which turned in to laughing which gave way to hysterics. The same thought had struck everyone at the same time. They were involved in the death of two United States Senators, but nobody knew how to steal a pickup truck.

As the laughter subsided, Eric said, "I can probably find you a truck, is it all right if it has a key?" There was more laughter. The mood was high anyway and the beer was beginning to kick in.

More names were tossed around for future reference. James would be the second from Texas, so it was agreed that they should concentrate on Representatives from other states. There was no shortage of corrupt politicians, and they all had one thing in common. They thought they were invincible. Most were refusing tight security.

"Eric," Russell asked, "what about a letter to the newspaper? Can you send one? Do you want to hand deliver one to the Chronicle? You can't fly to Phoenix every time. . . ."

Eric Moore interrupted, "I've already thought about it Russell,

I'm working on a 'this is why we are doing it, and we've decided that one-a-week is not necessarily the rule' letter. We may kill two in one day or we may skip a few weeks, let the heat cool. If we see changes in Congress, we may not do any unless they start going back to their old ways."

Everyone thought Eric's idea was great. 'One-a-week' would be hard to accomplish. It's not easy to knock off a person a week and not get caught. Not getting caught was the key.

It was agreed that Representative Harvey Babineaux of Louisiana should be the next target after James. He made Heuy P. Long look like Mother Theresa. Todd Evans suggested that everyone discreetly gather information on him. His likes, habits, what he eats, where he eats, etc. They should try to make his death either very creative or extremely grotesque. He would be number four, and if Congress wasn't changing by then, they should kill him in such a way that they would have to take notice. "We can't kill all of them," he said.

Mark Flanagen added, "that's Louisiana. I bet we could hire some Coon-Ass from the swamps to kill him and then leave body parts all around L.A." "L.A." was the state abbreviation for Louisiana. It also stood for "Lower Alligator" country.

"Why not mail body parts to other Congressmen? That would shake them up," said Robert Green. Robert was the least serious member of the group. No one replied to his comments. He let it pass.

Individual conversations began again and the talk was mostly about who had said what about the events of the past week. No one could imagine the rush they got when every conversation they heard was about something they, in some part, were responsible for. Each person in the room knew that is was Todd Evans who actually killed Senators Carson and Williams, and each one felt that, even thought they were not directly involved in the deaths, they certainly could have stopped it by saying "dumb idea, let's not do it," and it probably would have stopped. Each person also thought that if caught, they would go to prison for a very long time.

Eric excused himself. He wanted to start working on his letter to the Tribune. If Russell managed to kill Representative James on Saturday, then he wanted the letter to be in Phoenix. If for some reason Russell missed, the letter would also explain why there were no deaths this week. Eric told Russell he would call him on Friday with the details of the truck. He said "goodnight," and showed himself out.

It was only ten-fifteen, not very late compared to some evenings which went on to three or four in the morning, but the week had taken its toll. It was easy to watch Letterman or Leno and realize it was past midnight and you had to get up for work at six. One night was easy, five in a row and you started getting tired.

Russell asked Kathy if she would mind if he stayed so he could tell her about his plan. She said sure. Those of the group who heard this knew it was for their benefit. They looked at each other and winked. When two people move from being friends to falling in love, it's extremely obvious to all other mutual friends. Russell and Kathy were extremely obvious.

Russell watched Kathy as she said goodbye to the last of their friends and closed and locked the door. She was wearing a white spaghetti-strapped romper. By clinging in just the right places, it showed her figure off without seeming pretentious.

Kathy could be the average girl-next-door, when she wore blue jeans, a too large T-shirt, little make-up and her hair down. She could also look like a super model. When she made herself up, styled her hair, or when she wore an outfit that would show her off, she was beautiful. The weight the flu had knocked off of her came from her hips and thighs and she had become drop-dead beautiful. She had the straightest teeth money could buy and a smile that made her irresistible. Watching her close the door, Russell wondered how Kathy thought of him. He knew they were good friends and he was pretty sure she was ready to move to the next level. He had always been afraid to try anything, the thought of losing her as a friend was not worth it.

As Russell thought about how he would make his move, he tried to think if she had given him any signs recently that she wanted to be more than friends. He could not think of any. Maybe the kiss from the other night, it seemed like more than a good night kiss. Russell was ready. Tonight he would make a move. If she was not receptive, he would back off quick and hope he hadn't ruined their friendship.

His train of thought was broken as Kathy put her arms around his neck and kissed him. Russell put his arms around Kathy's waist and held her close. They had moved to the next level and she was the one who had initiated it. It could not have worked out better.

Russell maneuvered Kathy to the couch and they laid down, side by side. They continued to kiss. Russell caressed her shoulders and back. Her skin was soft and smooth. He loved touching her. He rubbed the back of her legs from the base of her bottom to as far as his hand would reach down her leg. He eased his hand under the romper and on to her cheek area. He touched her panties and began to slide his hand under when she stopped him.

"No, Rus, please don't."

Realizing only minutes ago he was wondering if she was interested in him, and now he was trying to put his hand in her panties, he knew he was moving too fast. Even though they had never even gone out on a real date, they had known each other for over a year. The fact that he had fallen deeply in love had confused him. He moved his hand back to her shoulder.

"I'm really sorry. I. . . "

"Don't be. I'm just. . . " It was Russell's turn to interrupt.

"Please, you don't need to explain." He kissed her again.

The two laid on the couch kissing and talking for hours. Mostly kissing. Russell didn't attempt to touch her again.

"Kathy, can you kill another human being?"

Kathy laid her head on Russell's chest and took his hand and held it in hers. She was so quiet Russell thought she might have fallen asleep.

"For a long time I have listened to you all explain why we are doing this. I think it started out as a joke. Some joke, huh. We are already involved. I don't know what would happen if we were to get caught. I'm 20 years old and I have fallen in love. I don't want to spend the rest of my life in prison. I don't want to see the man I love go to prison."

Russell was flabbergasted. He wanted to jump off the couch and do a thank you dance to the love gods. He kept listening instead.

"Part of me says let's quit and move somewhere until this has blown over. Then I remember what everybody has said about why we're doing this and I think that maybe, just maybe, something good will come out of it. My, maybe, our," she emphasized the word 'our', "children will have a better life because of it." Kathy laid her head on Russell's chest where he could not see her face. "I love you very much. I have for a long time. You seemed to have just noticed me and I don't know why, and I don't care, I'm just glad you did. I trust you. If you think we should kill James, I am behind you. If you want me to kill him, tell me how." She raised her head and looked into Russell's eyes. "If you tell me you love me, I will make love with you."

Russell brushed the hair off her forehead and said, "Kathy, I cannot think about anything for more than a few minutes without thinking of you. I love you very much." Kathy smiled and kissed him gently on the lips. Russell ran his hand across her upper back pulled the spaghetti straps off her shoulders and down her arms bringing the top portion of the romper with it. Kathy bit her lower lip as the descending material exposed her breast. Russell released the strap and put his hand on her breast.

Kathy, resting her head on Russell's shoulders, closed her eyes. She was just about to cry when she felt Russell pull the strap to her romper back over her shoulder. She looked up at him. He was grinning from ear to ear.

"If you don't make me wait too long, I can wait 'til the honeymoon," he said.

Kathy tried to give him a go-to-hell look for what he had done, but she couldn't keep from smiling. They fell asleep on the couch.

10

Nobody knew it, or at least nobody remembered it, but it was Eric Moore who first brought up the fact that something needed to be done to make Congress stop all the waste. He knew he could always crank Gene Thompson up. Gene, the political activist, thought like all politicians. Sure, there may be some waste in Government, but it is all necessary. If it ever got really bad, the people could make change with the power of the vote.

Even as the words would leave Gene's mouth, he was in fact believing it less and less. A Senator is convicted of having sex with an underage campaign worker and he wins his next election by a landslide. "Sure, he got caught with his pants down. She told him she was 18. His wife forgave him. We should too. And besides, he got that new army base put in our state. Look how it's helped the local economy down there." Of course the federal government had to buy 50,000 worthless acres from the Senator at an extremely over-inflated price to put the base there. Even Gene Thompson was becoming cynical of the political system he loved.

One evening, quite late, after several pitchers of beer, Eric Moore suggested somebody should just start shooting the most corrupt politicians out there until the rest of them wised up and started doing what they were elected to do. One person at the table agreed, then another. Soon everyone was saying how great the county would be if our government was actually "of the people and for the people."

Someone said it would be great if the elected officials just lived up to their campaign promises. Gene Thompson said that most of them did. The public demanded it. Gene was drunk. Someone else asked Gene, since 1900 how many men who were elected President of the United States said in their campaigns that they were actually going to institute new taxes or raise old taxes. Gene thought for a moment and said he didn't think any actually said they were going to increase taxes, in fact most said they would reduce taxes. Gene was getting it from all sides. Someone asked if there were income taxes in 1900. Gene said no. Someone asked if there were social security taxes. Gene said no. Someone else started to ask Gene a question, probably about the deficit in 1900, when Gene stood up, said, "O.K., why don't we shoot a couple of the bastards and get the ball rolling," and walked away from the table.

No one had ever seen Gene react like this. His best friend Mark was stunned. They had yanked Gene's chain once too often and the fuse burnt quickly. The table returned to normal and when Gene returned from the bathroom, he had also calmed down. He later confided to Mark that he was doing a little chain yanking of his own.

But the fuse was lit. Some nights politics and killing Congressmen never came up. Sometimes it would come up, and they would all say that they really should do it, but there would be nothing more said. The idea never went away. It began to crop up more and more during the election year. It seemed every time a politician opened his or her mouth, the bull would fly. Everybody, including Gene Thompson was getting tired of it.

Eric Moore sipped the cold Miller Lite he had poured into the long-neck frosted glass. As he contemplated the letter he was about to write, he wondered how much he would miss a cold glass of beer in prison. A voice inside him said, "don't worry about it. It's hard to drink beer when you're on your knees and elbows and some guy named Bruno is. . . " Eric shook the thought from his head. It was all too real.

Eric started typing:

> We have killed two United States Senators. We will kill more unless wasteful spending is stopped and taxes are lowered.
>
> We will no longer attempt to kill one per week. We may kill one, we may kill more. We may skip a week. If we see changes in Washington, we may not kill for a month. We may stop altogether. Our actions are dictated by those in Washington.
>
> As voters, we tried other options. They all failed. We voted for people who said they would make changes. After elected, they changed. They went from being honest concerned citizens to being just as corrupt as the incumbent they replaced.

This will be our final correspondence. Our goals
are known. We are doing this for our childrens' sake.

Eric reread the letter and spell checked it. He thought about
things he wanted to add to the letter, but decided it was fine as is. He
positioned the arrow over the little picture of a printer on the top of
the computer screen and clicked the left button on the mouse. The
hard drive rattled as it spun. A message appeared on the screen. He
clicked the 'print' box and in seconds his last letter to Mr. Gary
Stephens at the Phoenix Tribune rolled out of the printer.

Eric reread the letter and, satisfied that it was what he wanted,
clicked the little picture of an envelope on the top of the screen. A
box appeared, Eric typed in the address information and pressed
print. The printer flashed the message *Load #10 Env.* which Eric
did. The envelope disappeared into the bowels of the printer only
to reappear seconds later with the address neatly printed in the lower
right hand corner.

Eric clicked on "File" then "Exit" to exit the word processing
program. A box appeared with the message *Document unsaved.
Would you like to save?* There was a "yes" box and a "no" box. Eric
clicked the "yes" box. The hard drive spun and a message appeared
with a space to name the file. Eric typed "Kill3.DOC" and pressed
enter. The hard drive spun and the screen cleared. The Windows
main menu appeared.

Eric sipped his beer as he looked at the blank screen. He
thought about Bruno. Double clicking on the "W" icon, he restarted
the word processing program and began typing:

Senators Carson and Williams were poisoned by
Todd Evans. Several of us knew he was going to do it,
but we didn't know when or how. As of this date, two
more names have been given serious consideration.
One, most likely, will be this weekend. Russell Lewis
is planning one with the help of Kathy Beck. I am not
aware of the exact plan.

Eric went though the save routine, named the file "killers.doc",
and exited the program. He stared at the screen while he finished his
beer. After several long moments, he pressed the UTILITIES icon,
changed to the "DOCS" directory, highlighted "killers.doc" and
pressed "delete." A message popped on to the screen asking Eric if

he would like a "secure" delete, meaning the file could not be undeleted. He pressed "Yes."

* * * * * *

Lisa Thompson pointed her Toyota southeast. Her idea was perfect. Shoot the S-O-B and let everyone think is was this strange sect that was going around killing Congressmen. Unfortunately, she didn't have a well thought-out plan. The idea was spur-of-the-moment and now she was trying to plan as she went.

She should have taken time to formulate a plan and stick to it. The first kink was Senator Abernathy suggesting Key West for their rendezvous. There was simply no easy way to get to Key West, if you didn't want to be recognized. Many tourists fly in and out of Key West daily. Most flights are shuttles, on small airplanes. Maybe nobody would recognize a photograph, but chances are, someone would. It would only take one person to make a positive identification that Lisa Thompson was at the Key West airport on or about the day the Senator was murdered.

Lisa's only option was to drive. She had not slept much the night before and now she faced a seven hour drive from Winter Haven to the Keys. Seven hours would give her plenty of time to think, but she knew sleep was going to be a problem. She had already decided that she should spend as little time as possible in bungalow 3C. Criminal law had taught her that the police are usually very good investigators. Since they will be investigating the death of a U.S. Senator, the top investigators from the top law enforcement agencies will go over every inch of bungalow 3C. The less time spent in the room, the less evidence they would find.

Somehow, out of the corner of her eye, the sign caught Lisa's attention. The sign badly needed paint but she could make out *BUBBA'S RENT-A-HEAP-CHEAP*. Lisa slowed down and turned onto the shell driveway. A 14x80 trailer sat surrounded by an eight foot decaying cedar fence. She stopped in front of the door where a sign read "OFFICE."

Lisa turned off the ignition and sat for a moment looking at the trailer. When she thought her story sounded believable, she got out of the Toyota and walked to the trailer door. She wasn't sure if she should knock on the door or walk right in, or, turn around get the hell out of there. She decided to walk in without knocking.

The man behind the counter was watching *All My Children* on the small portable TV. *Must be Bubba,* she thought. He was tall, muscular, not handsome, but attractive. He wore a T-shirt that made some sort of reference to "a big Johnson," khaki shorts and well worn boat shoes. Bubba made a moaning sound when he heard the bell that was mounted above the door ring as Lisa opened it. His attitude was, how dare anyone come in here and interrupt me during my show.

Bubba almost swallowed his Skoal when he saw Lisa. She was wearing loose fitted shorts, white tank top and no bra. Trying not to be obvious, Bubba couldn't take his eyes off of the area where Lisa's nipples were making a slight but noticeable outline in the tank top.

She gave Bubba her sweetest smile, which he tried to return. Unfortunately, the sight of Lisa had made him forget about the pinch between his cheek and gum, and when he tried to smile, the brownish combination of tobacco and saliva drooled down his chin. He uttered a few expletives and spit into his coffee cup.

Lisa couldn't help but smile as she watched Bubba blush. She stared at Bubba's large green eyes. They were hypnotic. She felt a shortness of breath come over her as her heart began to race in her chest.

"Can I help you?" He asked trying overcome his initial blunder.

"I need to rent a truck."

Bubba didn't say a word. In his opinion, she was the most beautiful woman he had ever seen. His heart was in his throat.

"Do you rent trucks?" Lisa was beginning to wonder about Bubba.

"Uh, yea, sure, I mean, yes, I have a truck." Bubba had said exactly what he meant, too. He didn't have a truck for rent, he owned a truck. But there was no way he was going to let her walk out of his trailer/office.

"It's the best vehicle on the lot. A 96 Ford Ranger Extended Cab, automatic, AM-FM cassette, cruise control. . . " Bubba would have kept going, he was proud of his truck, but Lisa cut him off.

"That sounds perfect, how much?"

Bubba had to think fast. It was after all his personal truck, but he would have given it to her for free. Maybe his friends in town would see her driving it. "Same rate for all the cars, $20.00 a day, unlimited miles." Bubba was proud of himself, he had thought on his feet. There was no way she would turn down 20 bucks a day. He had second thoughts about the unlimited mileage portion though, what if she was planning to drive to Alaska?

"I'll take it," Lisa said giving Bubba her sexy smile this time. Bubba didn't try to return it. "Can I leave my car here?"

"No problem. Here, fill these out." Bubba handed her a basic one-page rental agreement. Bubba stared at Lisa's breasts as she filled out the agreement.

NAME: Lisa wrote the name Katie in the space and thought about what last name to put down. Obviously Bubba watched too much television to use Couric. Smith was too obvious, Thomas was too close to her own. Jackson. Sure, sounds a little like "Kate Jackson," but he won't notice.

> NAME: Katie Jackson
> ADDRESS: 1101 Main St.
> CITY: Winter Haven STATE: Florida

Lisa left the zip blank and wrote in a phone number without an area code. Hopefully Bubba wouldn't notice. She thought about using a different town, but she knew she would pick the town Bubba grew up in. Then she would have to play do you know so and so? Lisa and Bubba were roughly the same age and in small towns, they would have to have known some of the same people. The next line asked for the drivers license number. Lisa opened her purse and took out her license. She copied the number onto the form, transposing two digits near the end. If there was a great computer somewhere that the listed every auto rental in every state and the FBI could access it, Lisa Thompson would not be in it. Lisa signed the agreement *Katie Jackson* and gave it to Bubba.

As she was putting her drivers license back in her purse, Bubba asked to see it. *Jesus! No problem, I didn't expect it to be that easy.* Lisa handed the license to Bubba.

Bubba looked at the picture and looked at Lisa and attempted his sexy smile. Lisa had to swallow hard not to laugh and the result was an extremely wide smile. Bubba was in heaven. He was about to hand the license back when he did a double take.

"Uh," Bubba was confused. He was looking at the license and the rental agreement. The names didn't match. They weren't even close.

Lisa didn't give him time ask. "That's why I need the truck. I'm getting a divorce and I haven't changed the name on my license yet. Lisa K. Thompson is my legal married name. I hate the name

Lisa so I always go by Katie, my middle name."

To make the point, Lisa pointed at the K on her license. To point out the initial, Lisa leaned as far over the counter as she could. Her breast was almost touching Bubba's hand as he held the agreement. The agreement was suddenly the last thing on Bubba's mind.

Lisa continued, "I have always gone by Katie, and I can't wait to get rid of anything that connects me to my husband." As Lisa stretched, the outline of her nipple became very clear. Bubba seemed to be in a trance. "I need the truck to pick up the last of things and then I'm free." Bubba still hadn't said anything. Lisa grabbed the agreement along with Bubba's hand and pulled it toward her. "I'll change my damn name." She said with an extremely stern look that said, *Bubba, you are about to blow any chance you had with me.* Bubba's hand pressed hard against Lisa's breast as she pulled the agreement toward her. He jerked his hand away.

"No, it's O.K. I'm sorry. I just. . ." Bubba took the agreement from Lisa. What he wanted to say was that he wanted to protect his truck but he would give up every truck he would ever own if she would move her stuff into his trailer and grow old with him.

"I'm really sorry," Lisa said with her sad look, "I'm just so tired. I can't wait for this to be over. I'm so close. You've been really sweet." She leaned over the counter making sure her bra-less breasts rested directly on top of Bubba's hands. She felt Bubba try to pull his hands away. *What a sweet guy,* she thought to herself. She pulled him close so he could not move his hands from under her breasts and kissed him on the cheek. She held him, counted to five slowly, kissed him on the cheek again and straightened up. At that moment, had she asked Bubba to go to Key West and shoot Senator Abernathy between the eyes, he would have done it.

Bubba reluctantly gave Lisa the keys to his truck. That meant she was about to leave.

"How long are you going to be gone?" he asked.

No more than two days, I may be back tomorrow evening."

"Maybe we could have dinner or something."

"I would like that," Lisa said. As she turned to leave, she thought about having dinner with Bubba. There was a certain sincereness about him she hadn't seen in a long time in Washington or Boston. Maybe she would have dinner with him.

Bubba followed Lisa to her car where she got a few cassette tapes and her overnight bag. As they walked to the Ranger, Lisa asked, "what's a Big Johnson?"

Bubba's face turned red as the Florida sunset. His brain froze. No thinking on his feet this time. She handed the Toyota key to Bubba, paused for a second, then gave him a hug. As she pulled the truck out of the shell drive, she waved goodbye. Bubba was still trying to think of a way to tell her what a "Big Johnson," was.

11

Friday morning Senator Chuck Abernathy explained in no uncertain terms that he was going out and he did not want to be followed. He would be back, he needed some air. If he even thought he was being followed, jobs would be lost!

The blue Buick Park Avenue Abernathy owned was not hard to follow. The Secret Service agents were staying several cars back. They knew Abernathy could not actually have them fired, but he could make their lives miserable. They also knew if they lost him, their lives would be made miserable by other members of the SS.

Going with the flow of traffic in the left lane of the freeway, Abernathy suddenly accelerated, cut across two lanes of traffic and took the exit, just missing the barrels sitting in front of the concrete divider. The Secret Service agents could only watch the Senator as they drove past the exit, still in the left lane.

"He must have known we were behind him and that there was no way we could get over to that exit. You better radio in that we lost him," the driver said as he watched Abernathy disappear under the overpass.

Reluctantly, his partner made the call and explained the situation. Within twenty minutes Senator Abernathy was relocated at Dulles International Airport. He was preparing to board a flight to Fort Lauderdale. The Secret Service was relieved, he was no longer their responsibility. The FBI would be waiting for him in Florida and they would follow him from there.

The Secret Service briefed the Florida FBI Duty Officer of Senator Abernathy's successful attempt to lose the agents assigned to him. They also explained the Senator's morals and what they thought he might be up to. The FBI decided, in light of the recent murders, they should attempt to follow, and protect Abernathy. It was also decided if Abernathy rendezvoused with an underage girl, the agents were to intervene and let him know they were watching.

As long as no laws were being broken, the agents were only to make their presence known. The Senator should have enough sense to bail out of any planned sexual encounters with a minor if he knew the FBI was watching him. If the agents witnessed a crime, kidnapping, prostitution, drugs or sexual assault on a minor, Abernathy would be detained.

Senator Abernathy walked off the airplane carrying a briefcase and a small flight bag. He wore gray slacks, white shirt with a blue and red tie, and navy sport coat. His walk was slightly impaired from the endless supply of Scotch and waters supplied by first class air travel.

As he walked past the two plain-clothes FBI agents on his way toward baggage claim, the agents noticed his eyes looked glassy. They allowed him a reasonable head start before following. As he got near the end of the long aisle that led to baggage claim and passenger pickup, Abernathy turned to the left, instead of the right, as the agents expected him to.

"What's to the right?" One of the agents asked as they picked up their pace some.

"Restrooms and telephones, that I know of," the other said. They walked as fast as they could without drawing attention to themselves.

As the agents got to the end of the corridor, they saw the bank of telephones, the Men's and Women's restrooms and a single door marked "Private." The door marked "Private" was locked.

"He's got to be in the head."

"Go in and check, I'll wait here."

One agent went in and immediately came back out.

"There's nobody in there."

"I know, look." The agent pointed toward the tarmac. The two agents watched as Senator Abernathy boarded the Bell helicopter and took off.

"Could you read the numbers?"

"Barely. It looked like N83MI, but I'm really not sure. I do know it was a Bell 206BIII Jet Ranger, early 90's model, probably a 1991. That bird costs over six hundred grand. Do you think it was the Senator's?"

"It wouldn't surprise me. N83MI is what I thought the number was too. Let's call it in and see if the DEA has anyone in the area. They headed north, didn't they?"

"Took off to the north, below radar too. I expect they will make a swing back to the south or west, staying just under radar. That's the same way the druggies fly. If the DEA has a radar plane in the air, they'll already be watching them. If not, we're not going to find them."

The agents called the information in from the pay telephone. By the time they returned to their car and checked in, the DEA had informed the FBI that they had not seen the Senator's helicopter.

* * * * * *

Eric Moore dropped the letter in the box at the post office substation. He thought, but wasn't positive that all mail was put directly on a truck and taken to the main Houston post office downtown where it was sorted and canceled with a date stamp.

Even if it was postmarked at the substation, Eric couldn't imagine how it could be traced back to him. He put a quarter in the pay phone and dialed Tony Murphy. Tony was an extremely large, not tall, but round, Irishman with very blond hair. His mother was Sicilian and demanded half his name be Italian. He delivered beer to the convenience stores and strip clubs along Telephone Road.

Tony's beer route was one of the worst in Houston. But he could always convince owners to buy more beer than they needed. Especially when the person who moved the most beer in a contest week would win tickets to Hawaii or Florida. Tony had a certain charm about him people liked. Telephone Road was known as "Hooker Haven." When you deliver beer to sleazy bars, you get to know sleazy people.

Eric Moore met Tony when he was doing a story on prostitution in Houston, and why it should be legalized. There were basically four types of prostitutes. Street walkers, girls who worked at the strip joints then went home or to a hotel with a customer, girls who worked in the "private modeling studios" and call girls. The price went up with each group, Eric discovered. The girls, for the most part, got better looking as the price went up. But, unfortunately it was just as dangerous for a street walker as it was for a call girl. Obviously the street walker had the best chance at being busted. Surprisingly, the girl at the topless bar was least likely to be busted. She could pick and choose her customers, Eric reasoned.

In his article Eric wrote that legalized prostitution would protect both parties. One of the main reasons police departments use to justify the resources they spend to round up hookers is that the girl often gets beat up or murdered, and quite often the John would be robbed. The street walkers laughed about how they could suck a man off and clean out his wallet at the same time. They would always pick up a few extra bucks and the Johns would never go to the police. So, according to the police, they were protecting both parties. The police never mentioned that hookers very seldom carried guns or shot at cops.

Eric's idea was that they should open houses of prostitution and license the prostitutes. To get a license, the girl, (or guy, there would be no sex discrimination) would be subject to an AIDS test and a drug test. If she was HIV positive, she wouldn't be licensed. If she was drug positive, she would have to attend drug classes which would be funded by a special tax levied on the licensed prostitution houses. Any one receiving a license would also be required to receive counseling so that the state could be assured that she was a prostitute because she wanted to be, not because someone was forcing her to. All fees for licenses, as well a "trick tax," would go to providing shelters for homeless or abused women and children. Sales tax generated on the tricks would go to the city and state the same as all other sales tax.

Eric's story got state wide attention. It also almost got him fired. Most men liked the idea. But between the Baptist ministers (Catholic priests seem to favor the idea) and the women's groups, especially a few women on the Houston city council, legalized prostitution was never a consideration in Houston.

Eric had bumped into Tony at several of the bars where he was meeting with hookers. Each time they talked they became better friends and ended up having drinks on several occasions. Tony was the type every successful newspaper person needed. He either knew what was going on or knew how to find out. Eric learned a lot about the street from Tony.

Tony was home and answered the phone on the second ring. He was happy to hear from Eric. Eric explained what he needed and Tony said no problem. When did he need it? They agreed to meet later that evening. Eric asked how much and Tony said no charge, he was happy to hear from him again. On second thought, Tony said it would cost him a steak dinner. Eric agreed and hung up. It was good to talk to Tony again.

* * * * *

The FBI decided that the Phoenix office should be designated HQ. One Senator had been killed in Arizona and one had been killed in Illinois. It was anybody's guess where, or even if, the next would take place. It was logical to establish Phoenix as headquarters for several reasons. One, The Phoenix Tribune was only a few blocks away and for some reason seemed to be involved. They had received two letters warning of the impending murders. Too late to save the Senators, but they were in fact warned. There must be a reason the Tribune received the letters. It was very possible, the FBI reasoned, that whoever was behind the murders was right there in Phoenix.

The other reason for establishing HQ in Phoenix was Alexander Christian. He was undoubtedly one of the top agents in the county and most likely would have been chosen to head up the investigation anyway. Keeping him close to home would make him more comfortable. HQ could be in Phoenix, Washington or the North Pole. With current electronics, it really didn't matter.

Agent Christian had designated the largest conference room "command central." No less than a dozen extra phone lines were wired into the room. Television sets, computers, printers, fax machines and multi-line telephones were all connected. Nothing would happen in the world with out being known in this room.

Cots were set up in some of the offices and special arrangements were made to have food catered in. The gym on the top floor had showers. Work around the clock. Sleep, eat and shower, especially shower, as needed were the standing orders. If you were totally burned out, go home, try to relax, spend some time with your spouse. It had been five days since Senator Williams was murdered. No agent had gone home.

The agents were busy. Hundreds of leads needed to be followed up. All had led nowhere. FBI specialists developed a profile of the type of individual or individuals they may be dealing with. The lives of the two dead Senators were thoroughly researched.

Agent Lori Anderson entered the operation center. She carried the FBI files on Senators Carson and Williams.

"Which one would you like to hear about first?" She asked Agent Christian.

"Carson, then Williams. Just the highlights, please," he said, having a good idea what the files would contain.

"You know, in the sixties and seventies, Hoover encouraged agents to dig up dirt on members of Congress. He liked to use it against them. You wouldn't believe the amount they collected on

Carson. Most of it is old, I don't think anyone would give this stuff a second thought today."

Lori paused as she turned the yellowed pages. She paused and looked at a page. "He was named by Korean Businessman Tongsun Park as one of the payoff recipients, but was never charged." She thumbed through a few more pages then closed the file. "A few other suspected bribes, but that's about it. According to the newspapers, he, like most politicians, goes for the legal graft."

"Legal graft?"

"As you know, legally, lobbyists cannot give members of Congress gifts worth more than one hundred dollars. A loophole allows legislators to accept airfare, hotel accommodations and meals if they are attending a legislative conference or taking part in a celebrity golf or tennis tournament. Carson was staying at a five hundred dollar-a-night resort, meals and green fees included, and being paid two thousand dollars for participating in a 90 minute panel discussion. He's taken fifteen of the vacations in the past year. Why should he take a bribe?"

Christian breathed a sigh of disgust and said, "what about Williams?"

"For all his seniority, he was considered shy and occasionally self-effacing. His shyness did not prevent him from getting his share of the pie. He had been criticized for accepting money, for his campaign, from the Banking and Securities Industries just before a Senate vote on securities legislation. In 1989 he was videotaped by a Chicago, Illinois television station talking to the mother of a 17 year old girl he had been having sex with. In a follow-up interview, the girl told the television reporter Williams had paid her to have sex with him. The first time when she was 13. In the videotape, Williams suggested that he might get the woman a government job. The FBI said there was no evidence that he was offering the woman a bribe for her silence. The girl refused to testify."

Christian shook his head and said, "what was Williams background?"

Agent Anderson looked at the file a few moments to refresh her memory. "He was an attorney, evidently not a very good one, before he entered politics. He spent ten years in the House of Representatives before winning a seat in the Senate. One reason he ran for office was because he could not hold a job. He had worked for four law firms in five years after he graduated from law school. He was trying to make a go of his own practice, the quintessential ambulance chaser, when representatives of the Teamsters approached him about running for Congress. He was broke and accepted their offer. Several years ago he was instrumental in shaping a bill deregulating the trucking industry into a form more acceptable to the teamsters. He now owns a five hundred thousand dollar home in Georgetown."

"That's about what I expected from these two. I don't need to hear anymore."

"I've got the list of people who we think might have a motive." She handed the lists to Christian and the other agents in the room.

The agents couldn't believe two men could have so many enemies. The list of possible suspects was quite long. By comparing two lists, one of Senator Carson's suspected enemies and one for Senator Williams suspected enemies, a single list became much smaller. The names on the new list were given top priority. Had Senator Carson been alive, he would have been at the top of Senator Williams list, and vise versa. Todd Evans name was not on either list.

12

Lisa spent the night in a cheap but nice motel along U.S. 1 not far from Florida City. Money wasn't a problem. Senator Abernathy had given her plenty from his "campaign fund", a stash of hundred dollar bills kept in his office safe. The plaid shirt and baseball cap she found in the truck made a good disguise. She bet Bubba missed his Bubba Gump's Shrimp Company hat.

The drive across the Keys was one Lisa always enjoyed. Some people hated it. Almost four hours of basically one long bridge with a few small towns in between. Bubba's truck ran great. She pushed a Jimmy Buffett tape into the deck and turned the volume up. With her Bubba Gump hat, Buffett tape and the fresh air blowing in the open window from the gulf, she felt fantastic.

U.S. one dead ends in Key West. It had been a while since she had been to Key West but it seemed like yesterday. She found Duval Street and followed it to Caroline Street. The song *There's a woman going crazy on Caroline Street* came on. Lisa smiled and sang along.

> *There's a woman goin' crazy on Caroline Street,*
> *stoppin' every man she does meet, sayin' "if you'll be*
> *gentle, if you'll be sweet, I'll show ya my place on*
> *Caroline Street."*

Bungalow 3C was exactly where the Senator said it would be. There was a private drive and the whole area was extremely secluded. She opened the door and looked around the room. Nicely decorated but not overdone. It had a sitting area and a kitchenette with a bar separating the two. She walked through the only open door to the bedroom. A king-sized bed in the middle of the room. That figured. A closed door to the right and an open door to the left. The open door led to the bathroom. She assumed the closed door was a closet.

It was noon and she had no idea what time Senator Abernathy was going to show. She sat on the edge of the bed and ran different scenarios through her mind. She felt as though everything was finally planned pretty well.

From her overnight bag Lisa retrieved the gun. A Beretta 22 caliber semi-automatic with an seven shot clip. She pulled the breach back to be sure there was not a round in the chamber. Had there been a clip in the handle, this would have forced a round into the chamber and cocked the hammer into the firing position. She pointed the small pistol at a pillow on the bed and squeezed the trigger. It wasn't a "hair" trigger, meaning the slightest touch would release the hammer, but it was soft. She recocked the gun and checked the safety. Push on with the thumb and off with the index finger. Surely it was designed that way she thought. *You can't accidentally pull the trigger if your finger is pushing the safety button.*

Lisa slid the clip into the handle until she felt it catch. She slowly pulled back the breach and watched as one .22 long rifle bullet popped out of the clip and followed the grooves into the barrel. The gun was now loaded and cocked. She double checked the safety to be sure it was on and put the gun under the mattress at the head of the bed.

Looking around the room, making a mental note of everything she had touched, Lisa Thompson sat down on the end of the bed and waited.

* * * * * *

Eric met Tony at Bo Bo's. Bo Bo's is a small, somewhat seedy diner east of Houston in the small town of Channelview. Bo Bo's received it's 15 minutes of fame, the fame that Andy Warhol said everybody would enjoy during their lifetime, when a woman met a man there, allegedly, to hire him to kill the mother of a teen-age girl, just so her daughter could become a cheerleader at the local junior high. The plan fell through, but Bo Bo's was mentioned in the subsequent movie.

Tony briefly explained the easiest way to steal a truck. First, you had to hunt a baited field - the east side of Houston. That reminded Tony of a story.

"There was this old coon-ass living in the swamps of LA. He got down on his luck and he had heard that if you needed money, you should go to a bank and borrow it. So the old coon-ass drove into town to see the banker and asked him for a $500 loan. The banker asked what kind of collateral he could put up. The coon-ass asked what collateral was. The banker said collateral was something he would let the banker hold and it would become his if he didn't pay back the loan. The coon-ass thought for a minute and said 'I've got Phydeaux'. The banker ask what a Phydeaux was. The coon-ass said Phydeaux, the world's greatest huntin' dog. The banker said he didn't think a dog was worth $500. The coon-ass said sure he was, he would show him. So they drove out to the woods and the coon-ass let the dog loose. Phydeaux ran into the woods for a while and when he came back, he pawed the ground three times. The coon-ass said that means there were three birds in the woods. The banker didn't believe it, so they walked into the woods. They flushed out three birds. The banker said it was just luck. They drove a little further and stopped and Phydeaux ran around the woods and come back and pawed the ground twice. The banker said 'two birds?' and the coon-ass said 'yup'. They walked into the woods and sure enough, they found two birds. The banker agreed to do the deal. Six months later the old coon-ass had made some money and he took it back to the banker. He asked the banker where his dog was. The banker said he went crazy and he had to shoot him. The old coon-ass said 'You shot Phydeaux! What happened?' The banker said, 'It was the first day of hunting season so I took Phydeaux out to my favorite spot. He jumped out of the truck and took off in to the woods. He was gone a really long time. I thought he was lost. Then he finally returned and he was wet with sweat and was foaming at the mouth. He picked up a stick in his mouth and started shaking his head back and forth. Then he jumped on my leg and started humping me. I kicked him off but he picked up the stick again, started shaking it and humping on my leg. So I kicked him off again and shot him'. The old coon-ass said, 'Oh no, he was trying to tell you that there were more fuckin' birds out there than you could shake a stick at'."

Eric and Tony laughed at the joke. Tony would always laugh at his own jokes. Luckily, Eric thought, this one wasn't that bad.

"You need a pickup truck, you come to the east side of town. There are more fuckin' trucks out here than you can shake a stick at." Tony said. He laughed again.

It was Friday afternoon, pay day, and thousands of construction workers would be getting off work and heading to the nearest check cashing outlet - in their pickups.

Tony explained the procedure to Eric. "I'll drop you off at one end of the parking lot. You casually stroll through and look in the windows. If you see keys, see if anybody is watching. If not, jump in and take off. I'll hang around to see if anyone gives chase. If they do I'll block 'em in or cut 'em off, but you should be long gone before they find out you're gone. If nobody tries to follow, I'll meet you at my place. We'll put the truck in the garage and I'll bring you back for your car. If you don't see a truck with keys, or if anybody is looking, ANYBODY, keep walking and I'll pick you up on the other side of the parking lot." Eric understood why he had to do the leg work. Tony was much too large to be agile and he was not exactly inconspicuous. Tony gave Eric the route he should follow when he finds a truck.

The first two parking lots had several trucks with keys in them but too many people were around to take the risk. They decided to try an ice house. Ice houses were all over east Houston. Almost as common as pickup trucks. An ice house was a small building, usually with garage doors which were open during business hours. The building housed a bar, a dart board and a couple of pool tables. Beer and wine were typically the only beverages served. And wine only on a rare occasion. Seldom did an ice house have a liquor license, which meant you could bring in your own bottle and buy set-ups.

The first ice-house they drove past was no good. The open garage doors looked onto the parking lot. The parking lot of the next ice house was behind the building and out of view. Tony dropped Eric off at the far end and waited as Eric walked across the parking lot looking in the windows of the trucks.

The keys were hanging in the ignition, pulled out just far enough to turn off the electronic device designed to remind the driver that the keys were in the ignition. Eric stopped beside the Dodge Ram pickup, looked around, saw nobody, and tried the door. It opened. He stepped in and started the truck. Slowly, Eric backed out and eased through the parking lot. He got to the main street and turned right, the opposite direction of the open garage doors, and was out of sight. Tony waited and watched. After 30 seconds, he eased out of the parking lot and followed Eric. Nobody had seen them.

* * * * * *

At five minutes after five on Friday evening, Senator Chuck Abernathy walked into Bungalow 3C. Lisa Thompson jumped off the bed from where she had hardly moved in hours. The Senator met her at the door to the bedroom.

"In the bedroom. You can't hardly wait." He said with a smirkish grin.

Before Lisa could answer, the Senator had grabbed her, pulled her to him, put his mouth over hers and stuck his tongue deep into her mouth. Lisa felt her skin beginning to crawl as he slobbered into her mouth. This was the part she had been dreading the most. He thought they were there for a week-end of pure unadulterated sex. She had to let him kiss her, even though it made her sick to her stomach.

The Senator slid his hand up her leg and under her shorts. He was rubbing and squeezing her bottom when she felt his attempt to stick his middle finger in her anus.

It was a natural reflex that pushed the Senator away. The look she received scared her. She quickly recovered and said, "please, not there." She looked at him with sad puppy dogs eyes.

"We'll save that for later. I guarantee you'll like it," He said, his harsh look softening.

Lisa nodded and fended off his next advance by reaching up to remove his sport coat. They were standing face to face. She unbuttoned the top button of his shirt as he grabbed her breasts and began squeezing. With all of her might, she grabbed the Senator's shirt and pulled. Buttons popped and flew. Lisa dropped to her knees and pulled on Senator Abernathy's belt. She looked up at him and smiled. He put his hands on his hips and stared down at her. This was what Chuck Abernathy, United States Senator lived for. A beautiful young woman was in front of him on her knees. He was God.

Lisa pulled the Senator's pants and boxer shorts down with a single tug. He stepped out of his pants as Lisa pushed him onto the bed. It was as though he was following a rehearsed script. The Senator scooted backward and laid down with his head resting on the pillows. Lisa stood at the foot of the bed. She unbuttoned her shorts and very slowly unzipped the zipper. As her shorts fell to the floor, she pulled her T-shirt over her head. She stood and let the good Senator admire her while she contemplated her next move.

Lisa could not contain herself. Joe Stud. The woman killer. After all of the boasting and bragging, this man had not only the littlest, but the ugliest penis she had ever seen. Not that she had seen that many, but the Senator's was particularly ugly. She had always felt sorry for the women she had fixed up with Abernathy, but now she really felt for them. Pay back time was close. To keep from laughing Lisa was oohing and aahing. The sounds reminded her of the X-rated movies she had had to watch in her The Law and Pornography course.

On all fours, she straddled the Senator. Letting her breasts barely touch the his body, Lisa worked her way up from the foot of the bed. The Senator tried to force Lisa's mouth onto his manhood, but she kept inching forward. She lowered herself so that the ugliest penis she had ever seen disappeared between her breasts. The honorable Mr. Abernathy relaxed as he moved his hands from Lisa's head to the sides of her breast. He pushed her breasts together to increase the friction as he rocked his hips back and forth.

Whatever the Senator did from this point on, Lisa could not have cared less. Her main concern was that he remain preoccupied. She moved quickly to a point where her bottom was over his stomach and her breasts hung just over his mouth. She lowered herself until the Senator's mouth found a nipple. He began sucking like a baby that hadn't eaten in a week. His hands were all over her. Rubbing, squeezing.

Lisa rested most her body weight on her left arm as her right arm reached over the mattress. She could barely touch the .22 caliber semi-automatic pistol with the tip of her finger. She did her best X-rated movie imitation moan and shifted to the right. The moan wasn't wasted. The Senator took the cue and promptly began licking and sucking her other breast. He was oblivious to anything other than his mouth, his hands and Lisa's perfect breasts.

Senator Abernathy slid his thumbs underneath her panties and pulled down. Because she had straddled the man's obese belly, her panties barely came down past her hips. Though not far, it was enough for the Senator's right hand to slide between her legs. Lisa grabbed the gun the exact same moment the Senator grabbed Lisa. Sliding the gun along the bed, Lisa slowly raised from the waist. As she rose the Senator put his middle finger against her anus and pushed it in. Lisa put her index finger against the safety of the gun and pushed it in.

Lisa raised into a sitting position, forcing the Senator's finger inside her. As she got to a point where she no longer needed her hands for balance, she pointed the pistol at the Senator's left eye.

Senator Abernathy smiled and said, "I knew you would like it." He opened his eyes just in time to see a flash. He would never see the bullet that would rip though his eyeball, travel though the eye socket, shred the gray matter most people call brains, and lodge into the back of his skull.

Lisa stared at the smiling Senator. One eye was open and the other was gone. The good eye was staring at her. The bang made by the gun was louder that she had expected. As her adrenaline level lowered she realized her ears were ringing. She would know in a matter of minutes if anyone else had heard the shot.

Senator Abernathy continued to stare and smile at Lisa. She slowly waived her hand in front of his eye. He didn't blink. She pushed the safety on the gun in and looked at her ex-boss. She had never seen a dead person before. She didn't know what she was expecting, but this wasn't it. Other than a small trickle oozing from the Senator's bad eye, there was no blood.

Over the past 48 hours, Lisa had thought of dozens, maybe hundreds of clever little antidotes she would say as she looked over The Honorable Chuck Abernathy. Ex-United States Senator. At the moment she couldn't remember one.

Suddenly Lisa bolted from the bed. It had taken nearly a minute for her to realize that the late Senator's finger was still inside her. She landed on the floor, her panties across her thighs. She looked at the Senator. His hand was between his legs, middle finger pointing skyward.

Lisa pulled her panties up and put her shirt and shorts back on. She put the gun back in her bag. Using a wash cloth from the bathroom, she began to wipe anything she may have touched. She had been very careful not to touch much. She could only imagine how many different women's fingerprints were in bungalow 3C. She wanted to leave most of them as they were.

Taking the hair brush was genius, Lisa thought to herself. She had noticed the brush full of hair in the restroom of the place where she had eaten breakfast. Though repulsive, she wrapped it in a paper towel and put it in her purse. She retrieved the brush, and holding it by the paper towel, pulled a piece of hair off and laid it on the pillow next to the Senators head. As she laid strands of hair around the body, where she thought they might fall naturally, she checked very carefully for any of her own hair. She found none.

Satisfied that there was absolutely no trace that Lisa Thompson had ever been in bungalow 3C, she even washed the dreaded middle finger that was still pointing skyward, she closed and locked the door, placed the "Do Not Disturb" sign on the knob and left Key West.

The inland road from the Keys bypasses Miami, and a lot of congestion. It also bypasses random drug checkpoints that may be set up around the main South Florida airports.

Lisa still needed to dispose of a few items. A Beretta .22 caliber semi-automatic pistol in particular. It doesn't take long on the inland route to reach the swamps and levees which are quickly being turned into resorts and golf courses.

It was dark and traffic was light. When she could see no cars in front or behind, she pulled over at the next swamp. She ran to the edge of the swamp, being very careful in the dark not to go too far, threw the gun, the clip, the bullets, the hair brush and the wash cloth into the murky water.

Lisa drove all night, stopping only for gas and to use the restroom. It was still dark when she arrived at Bubba's Rent-a-heap-cheap. Exhausted, she parked in front of the trailer, wrapped Bubba's plaid shirt around her and fell asleep.

The rapping on the window frightened Lisa. She was dreaming that she was Senator Abernathy, and someone was holding a gun six inches from her eye. The gun had fired, but the bullet had barely left the barrel. She could see the bullet coming at her, but she couldn't move. The movement of the bullet was barely noticeable. It just kept coming straight at her. As she awoke, she hoped that Senator Abernathy would spend eternity looking at the bullet coming at his eye.

"Are you O.K.?" Bubba said as he peered through the truck window. He was looking at his shirt. He may never wash the shirt again.

"I'm fine, thanks," she said. In fact, she had a headache, she was hungry and her right ear was still ringing from the gunshot.

"Come on in, I'll get you a cup of coffee."

"That really sounds nice, thank you."

Lisa followed Bubba into the trailer. He was wearing shorts and a T-shirt that said "Margaritaville."

"I like your shirt."

"Thanks." After the "Big Johnson" incident, Bubba didn't want to talk about T-shirts. "Sit down, how do you like your coffee?" He nodded at the sofa.

Lisa barely got the word "black" out when every emotion that had been building within her since she first thought of killing Senator Abernathy came bursting out. She began crying and shaking uncontrollably.

Bubba hurried to the sofa and put his arms around Lisa. She literally climbed on top of him, pushing him backward on the sofa. Lisa buried her head into his chest and cried until she fell asleep.

When her breathing became rhythmic and he felt he could move her with out waking her, Bubba carried her to the bedroom and put her in his bed. Lisa woke but pretended to be asleep as Bubba carried her to his bed. She was tired, but the emotional freight train that hit her had moved on down the track. She felt as long as Bubba held her, it wouldn't come back. Bubba gently pulled off her shoes and pulled a sheet over her. He leaned over, kissed her on the cheek and said something she couldn't understand.

As Bubba was getting up, Lisa felt the freight train coming back. She put her arm around Bubba's neck and pulled him down on top of her, kissing him harder than she thought possible. She squeezed Bubba until he could hardly breath. She plunged her tongue deep into his mouth. But the train wouldn't stop coming. She raised up in the bed, her body shaking, pulled her tank-top over her head and said through quivering lips, "make love to me." Bubba laid still, looking at Lisa. Her crying became uncontrollable. She began pounding on Bubba's chest and screaming "fuck me. God damn it, fuck me."

Lisa attempted to unbutton her shorts, but her hands were shaking too violently to work the button. Bubba pulled her close to him and held her as she cried. As he caressed her hair he told her everything would be O.K. Divorce must be a horrible thing, he thought.

13

Friday morning, after sleeping with Kathy on the couch, Russell was stiff and tired. He wanted to stay with Kathy but he needed rest. He also needed a plan. He told her he needed to work on some details and would call her later.

Russell's grandfather had purchased a sizable tract of land just outside Friendswood, a small community south of Houston. At the time, Russell's Grandfather was heavily criticized for spending most of his savings on what was considered worthless land. In the summer, the land was dry and hard, nothing could be grown on it. When it rained the land became gumbo, causing cattle to get hoof rot. For many years the land was indeed worthless.

As Houston grew and people moved to the suburbs, the area southeast of Houston boomed. Clear Lake City, home of NASA, and Friendswood became two of the fastest growing areas in the country. Developers bought large parcels of land to build "master planned communities." Russell's family sold the land in the early 80's, just before the downturn in the Houston economy, for a rather substantial amount of money.

A trust was set up so Russell could live well without working. Not great, but well. If he wanted a new car or to take exotic vacations, he would have to work. Russell received his degree in computer science. He was an excellent programmer. Since programmers were in extremely high demand, Russell could work when he needed a little extra money and he could play as much as he wanted.

Russell had worked for two months straight when the group started getting serious about it's plan. He wanted to be sure he would be able to stay at home and follow the proceedings closely. He was very glad now that he did. He was planning to take Kathy to Vegas on Monday. He needed the money.

Russell napped and showered and made a few phone calls. Gene Thompson had told him that every Saturday, when he was in town, Representative James would go to a small rodeo arena outside of Port Arthur. He claimed he liked to get out and meet the people, but everybody knew he usually took some young cowgirl home.

James was in town. He would probably be at the rodeo arena. He and Kathy would be there. If he hit on Kathy, Russell would kill him, literally. That was the plan. The "how" was worrying Russell. He had several "if - thens" in mind but, frankly, no idea what was actually going to happen. He was very worried about Kathy's safety.

The phone rang and Russell picked it up on the first ring. It was Kathy. She apologized for calling. Said she was worried. She hadn't heard from him all day. She wouldn't do it again. Russell assured her he was glad she called and she should call whenever she wanted. He wanted her to. He said if she didn't mind, he would come over. She didn't mind.

As he was leaving, the phone rang again. Russell smiled and thought to himself, *she can't get her mind off me.* He picked up the phone and said "hi."

"Hi," said the voice on the other end of the line. A man's voice. It surprised Russell.

"Oh, hi Eric what's up?" Russell said, disappointed it wasn't Kathy.

"I've got your truck. Full of gas too. I just parked it in a safe place for the night. When do you need it?"

"In the morning. Are you busy tomorrow?"

Suddenly, Eric thought of Bruno. He had mailed the last letter to the Tribune first thing. He had just stolen a truck. He was involved.

"Not really, do you need help?"

"I really could use another driver. All you need to do is meet us somewhere and we'll take the truck. Then you follow us in my car. My basic plan has James picking up Kathy and then I will follow him and kill him. It would be nice to have a second car just in case I lose him. I would hate to think of what would happen to Kathy if I didn't stop the son-of-a-bitch."

"I bet you would. I'll help. But if I'm driving your car, why did you need the truck?" Eric assumed he didn't want his own car around in case anyone saw them.

"I hope to have Kathy get him in the street and I'm going to run his ass over. Don't want to fuck up my front bumper."

The two picked a time and a place to meet. The rodeo usually went from three till six or seven. Russell planned to get there around five. He didn't want to be too early and he didn't want to get there too late and risk that James had already left with some other poor unsuspecting cowgirl.

On the way to Kathy's, Russell stopped at the supermarket and bought flowers. It had been a long time since he felt like this. In fact, he couldn't honestly remember ever feeling like this. He was truly in love. He hoped to be married in less than a week. Later in the evening he would ask her to go to Vegas with him and get married. Her family was in England, his was either in Florida at their winter home or in Vermont at their summer home. He hadn't talked to them in several weeks because they were in the moving stage. They would have a formal reception later in the summer if Kathy wanted, or they would wait and get married later, but he was going to ask her tonight and hope she would agree to Vegas. After last night, Russell was sure she would say yes. He thought he would wait until after she agreed to marry him to tell her about his plan to kill Representative Jack James. There was a slight possibility she would have to sleep with James if the plan was a total bust. Russell decided he would kick the door in and personally cut the Representative's throat before he would let that happen.

Kathy loved the flowers. She thought getting married in Vegas would be great, but Monday was really soon. She would think about it. Next week-end would be better. Surely he could wait a week. After all, he never asked her out in the year and a half they had known each other. Russell felt like shit. She was right. He told her so. Then he told her about his plan. She thought it was a good plan. She also had some good ideas of her own to add to it. She thought it would work and assured Russell that if things got bad, a hard knee to Mr. James's groin would give her plenty of time to get away. Just don't be too far away.

* * * * * *

Lisa woke to find herself sleeping on Bubba's bare chest. She laid perfectly still waiting for the freight train to come roaring back. So far so good. She was pretty sure she remembered everything from the past few days. She hoped she remembered everything.

She remembered the latest episode with Bubba and she remembered he was wearing a shirt. She wondered what else he had taken off. She slowly raised the sheet and looked. She was still wearing her shorts and Bubba was still in his. She looked at his sleeping face. *What a wonderful, kind and gentle man he is,* she thought. She eased out of the bed and picked up her shirt and shoes. "Good-bye, Bubba," she said softly.

In the "office" portion of the trailer Lisa found a pen and a piece of paper. She wrote:

> My dearest Bubba,
> You are the most kind, gentle and thoughtful man I have ever met. I am sure I have fallen in love with you. Unfortunately, I cannot stay with you, nor can I ever see you again. You must believe me that I will never forget you or what you have done for me. There will always be a special place in my heart for you. I will love you always.
> Lisa K. Thompson.

Lisa found the keys to the Toyota in the first drawer she opened. She left the note to Bubba on the counter, quietly slipped out the door and in to her car and drove home. She was thinking about Bubba. Senator Abernathy was nothing more than a faint memory.

When Bubba awoke and realized Lisa wasn't in the bed, he knew she was gone. He didn't want to get up. As long as he was in bed, there was a chance she would come bouncing through the door. He decided he couldn't stay in bed forever. Bubba found Lisa's note and wished he had stayed in bed forever. "I love you too, Lisa."

* * * * * *

"I'm at a dead end," said Tim Brooks, assistant editor of the Phoenix Tribune, and now one of the most famous newsmen since Woodward and Bernstein. His copyrighted article had hit the news wire hours before the FBI held their press conference. His article had been fabulous. It would most definitely win him a Pulitzer. Almost a week had passed since his original article had come out and fresh news was hard to find.

He had interviewed the FBI agent in charge of the case, Alexander Christian. The good news was that he was able to get several exclusives with Agent Christian. The bad news was that even the exclusives didn't give him much more than every other reporter in town had. Having an office two blocks away from FBI headquarters for what was becoming the biggest case in history was a definite advantage.

"I know exactly what you mean," Gary Stephens said. "I did a little digging myself. Just to see if I could come up with anything. I talked to Pete Mitchell, my friend who's a detective here and he said everybody is up against a stone wall. Every lead the FBI has is coming up empty. He said they have a few straws to clutch, but nothing solid. Of course they know the same group is responsible for two reasons. The most obvious is the two letters, but they used poison in both murders. They are really checking every place in the U.S. where you could possibly get cyanide and Anszoid. Mitch thinks they are keying on the Anszoid. That's not that easy to get. It's really dangerous shit and only manufactured by one company, in Houston, and the company is very careful about who gets it, how much they get and what they plan to do with it. Cyanide, on the other hand is pretty common. I wouldn't imagine you could just walk into the corner drug store and ask for it, but it's used in a lot of applications and there is not that much control over it. It's the poison of choice in most of the tampering cases. My advice is to hang loose. Keep digging but don't write if you don't have anything. Every paper in the states, hell, maybe even the world, is waiting for your name to come over the wire so they can print it. If you send them garbage, you will lose credibility fast. Make them wait."

"You're right. I guess that's why you're the boss. I was thinking I had to get something out every day. That I needed to keep my name on the front page. But if they kept printing bullshit from me, pretty soon they will stop printing me."

"I'll make a reporter out of you yet," Gary said jokingly. "It's going to be a beautiful Saturday afternoon. How about some Mexican food and a margarita."

"That really sounds good to me."

"Great, you're buying, Mr. Pulitzer."

Gary Stephens and Tim Brooks decided on taking separate cars to La Hacienda. Gary was going to go home afterward and try to relax. Tim wanted to go back to the office. He had a few more ideas he wanted to check out. Leaving the building, they held the door open and waited for Hal, the mailroom boy. He was just returning from the post office with the Saturday morning mail.

"It's a little late for mail isn't it?" Gary asked.

"Not really sir, we always wait till after eleven on Saturday.

For some reason the post office doesn't get all the mail in the box 'till after 10:30 or so. They're short handed on Saturdays is what I've heard," Hal replied.

Gary nodded at Hal and motioned Tim through the door he was holding open.

"Nice kid," he said as the door closed behind him.

"Yea," Tim agreed.

Hal continued to the mailroom with the mail, including a one page letter addressed to Mr. Gary Stephens. Postmarked Houston, TX.

14

The phone rang in Russell Lewis' apartment. After the third ring, the machine answered the call. "Hello, this is 771-7744. I am not able to answer your call right now, but please leave a message after you hear the time and date. Thanks for calling." A computer generated voice said, "Saturday, April 13, 10:05 a.m., please record your message now."

"Russell, this is Gene. Listen. I should have told you but I just forgot. A lot of people who know Jack James calls him 'Jessie James'. Not because he has robbed the people of Orange County blind, but because he always carries a gun on him. I'm really sorry, I should have remembered that before now. Be careful." Gene hung up the phone. He thought for a minute and pressed re-dial on the phone. After the message, date and time, he said, "be sure you erase the previous message." He wished he could warn his friend. He tried Kathy's house. The machine picked up and he listened to Kathy's message. After the beep, he hung up the phone. One incriminating message was good for a lifetime.

"I guess it wasn't important or they would have left a message." Kathy said as she sat up in the bed. She leaned over to kiss Russell on the lips and said, "what time are we meeting Eric?"

"We're meeting at a truck stop just before the San Jacinto River around three."

Kathy looked at the digital clock next to her bed. "Then we have plenty of time." She slid back down next to Russell and kissed him.

Russell was thinking about the previous evening. It had gotten late and they both knew that Russell would not be going home. They decided that they would sleep together. Sleep together, but not make love. Kathy led Russell to her bedroom and excused herself. Russell stripped to his shorts and got in bed. He thought about baseball. He thought about Jack James. He even thought about his mother. He tried singing the theme song to *The Beverly Hillbillies*.

Anything so he wouldn't think about the bulge growing in his shorts. *I want to wait,* he kept telling himself.

Kathy returned after what Russell thought was an eternity. She was wearing a Mickey Mouse T-shirt that hung to mid-thigh. She turned out the light and crawled in bed next to him. Kathy put her head on his chest and said, "I love you." Russell stroked her hair, "I love you, too." She fell right to sleep.

Russell had spent the night thinking about Kathy and Representative James. What if something went wrong? He would never forgive himself. Kathy stirred and moaned and opened her eyes. Her eyes opened, but the lights never came on. She looked at Russell as though she was saying "who are you and why are you in my bed." He said nothing and she rolled to the other side of the bed and went back to sleep. She wouldn't remember waking up.

Russell looked at Kathy. She was beautiful. Even with the small amount of light that filtered in from the street lamp outside, he could see her clearly. She was making a slightly noticeable wheezing sound as she exhaled. He fell asleep watching her.

Russell's thoughts came back to the moment as he kissed Kathy. As they came up for air Russell said, "Kathy, I love you very much. I do want us to spend the rest of our lives together." Kathy started to speak but he cut her off. "If we go though with what we have planned for today, the rest of our life may only be today." This scared Kathy. He had wanted it to. "I think it's a good plan, and if we do this, I don't think I could kill anybody again. Maybe the country will be better because of what we are doing, and most likely, it won't change shit. I will do what ever you want."

Kathy thought for a long time. She looked around her bedroom, she looked out the window, she looked at her stuffed animals. She did not look at Russell Lewis. Russell didn't say anything, he just waited. The silence was lasting too long. He was about to say forget it, it was a stupid idea, that they had nothing to gain and everything to loose. It doesn't matter what the group thinks, they would have to understand, when Kathy sat up in bed and pulled her T-shirt over her head. She wore nothing underneath.

"Let's make love for a couple of hours then go kill the son-of-a-bitch."

* * * * * *

Agent Alexander Christian had lost all track of time. The conference room which had become the command center for operation *BLIND LUCK* was located in the center of the FBI building. Even if there had been windows, they would have been covered by the maps, charts, newspaper clippings and time lines that hung from the walls.

The reason for naming the operation "blind luck" was twofold. First, it was determined that who ever killed Senator Carson was a novice. No professional killer would take the risk of being identified later. It was blind luck that every composite drawing the police artist drew, based on witnesses from the Desert Green Country Club descriptions, were totally different. Secondly, it was the opinion of the FBI agents assigned to the case, that to find these killers would require some blind luck.

One of the series of telephones rang and Alexander Christian picked it up on the first ring. "Christian here."

"Good afternoon Alex, this is Chill." Christian knew Agent Childress very well. They both entered the academy at the same time and were roommates during "basic."

"Hi, Chill, tell me this is a social call."

"It may be. I just thought you should know that Senator Abernathy of Florida has disappeared."

"God damn, he's on the top of our list of possible targets, weren't your guys watching him?"

"Secret Service was assigned to him. But he dismissed them late Thursday night. They argued and he got real nasty. Threatened all kinds of shit if he spotted any of them watching him."

"They left him alone?"

"Not entirely. When he left his apartment in Washington they had a loose tail on him. We didn't have time to hook up any electronic surveillance. He got in his car and drove like a maniac. Cut people off to make right turns from left lanes, circled blocks several times before going down a one-way alley the wrong way. You get the idea. Needless to say, we lost him on the freeway. An agent spotted him at Dulles, he took a flight to Fort Lauderdale. We had our Florida people waiting, but he had someone waiting for him at a private door. He got in a helicopter, registered to the Great South Florida Land Development Company, and we never saw him again. Florida is his turf. If he wants to get lost, he can very easily in Florida. By the time we got a bird up he was gone. My bet is he wasn't in the air two minutes before they sat him down at a car and he drove away. Nobody's heard from him since. That's the real reason I called, he is usually pretty good about checking in, even when he's banging a 16 year old girl in a cheap motel somewhere in the Everglades."

"That's a pretty disgusting thought."

"He's a pretty disgusting S-O-B."

"Chill, I hate to say it, but I hope to hell he's banging some poor 16 year old right now."

"Me, I'm not so sure. I'll keep you informed. Bye." The line went dead before Agent Christian could say "goodbye." He hung up the phone. He hadn't realized it, but every agent in the room was hanging on his conversation. He filled in the parts they couldn't hear.

One of the agents in the room said, "if our guys couldn't follow him and now they can't find him, maybe the bad guys can't find him."

"Unless the bad guys set him up," another agent said.

"I'd bet on it," said Agent Christian. "I'll bet somehow they dangled a very cute little sixteen year old girl in front of him and told him it had to be private, don't be followed, and she's yours for the weekend. Probably said she was a runaway. Found her at the bus stop. They've given her some money and some coke. She'll do anything you want."

"But if it was our group, how would they set it up?" Asked the first agent.

"Easy," answered Agent Christian, "call him on the phone. Tell him you're the big cheese of the Florida Cheese Company. Tell 'm you need a favor. A bill passed or an amendment blocked, some B.S. Abernathy says he would love to help, but he just doesn't know if he can. They ask him if his line is secure, like they know what they're doing. He says 'sure it is'. They say they are big supporters. Know what he likes. They have something for him but he has to come to their place, wouldn't want anybody to find out. They bandy back and forth, letting a little more come out each time, and soon they have told him they have a sixteen year old who is just pretty as a picture and he can literally have his way with her. Do anything he wants, they don't care. If he wants her to fall in a swamp afterward, they can arrange it. If he wants to keep her around a couple of months, maybe send a friend over to visit, that's O.K. too. The honorable Charles D. Abernathy is on his way to Florida before his dick gets soft."

The room was absolutely silent. Everybody knew what went on with some of these guys but to hear Agent Christian say it turned their collective stomachs.

"I hope it is our gang setting him up," said the youngest agent.

"Agent Bates, I will pretend I did not hear that, considering the circumstances. It will not leave this room. No matter what our personal feelings, we have a sworn duty to uphold the law. You will never insinuate that you would like to see a member of the United States Congress dead. Is that clear?"

"Yes, Sir."

"Good, now, find out everything you can about The Great South Florida Land Development Company. Call Agent Childress in Washington. He probably already has a file."

"Yes, Sir."

Agent Christian winked at the young agent as if to say 'think it, don't say it'.

* * * * * *

Russell couldn't keep his eyes or his hands off Kathy. She had the most beautiful face and perfect body he had ever seen, let alone been with. They kissed deeply as Russell touched every part of her body. There were no objections from Kathy. She had fully given herself to him.

"I think it's time to get up and get dressed, we have to meet Eric soon," said Russell. Kathy couldn't hide her surprise, or shock, at what she had just heard. They had been on the bed kissing and gentle caressing each other's bodies in a typical prelude to love making. Kathy assumed they would make love before they went in search of James. She positioned herself on top of him resting herself on her elbows.

"What?" was the only thing she could think of to say. She had heard him very clearly, but as he repeated the question, she had a few moments to think. She loved the fact that he could go as far as they had and then suggest they stop. She was thinking that Russell had to be the most wonderful guy she had ever met. But she was also thinking that she was about as *ready* as she had ever been in her post-virginal life. Never had she experienced such prolonged foreplay. It was usually kiss, kiss, touch here, feel there, then wham bam thank you Ma'am.

Kathy was more than *ready*. She looked at Russell, who was

still wearing his shorts. He was ready too. If she said she didn't want to wait, she wanted it, needed it, now, would he think she was a slut? With one sentence she was totally confused.

"We really ought to get up. We need to eat and meet Eric," Russell repeated.

Kathy sat upright on the bed. She pulled her knees up to her chest.

"Russell," she said with the saddest puppy dog eyes she could fake, "do I not excite you? I don't know what is going to happen today, I wanted to be with you now. Did I do something wrong?" It's never too early to start training the man you plan to live the rest of your life with.

Russell took Kathy in his arms and said, "I'm sorry, that's not . . . I mean. . . of course. . . "

Kathy figured he had suffered enough and stopped him by putting her mouth on top of his. They made love.

Russell Lewis and Kathy Beck were like two different people. They were in love and they had made love. A wall that had been between them had been torn down. Each truly believed the other loved them. No longer were they worried that a stupid or misinterpreted comment would cause the other to storm out of their life forever. It wasn't just because they made love. There was more to it. Though intangible, it felt like a ton of bricks had been lifted from their shoulders. No longer did they have to feel they were walking on eggshells around each other.

The smiles were permanent fixtures on both their faces as they showered together and got dressed. Russell told Kathy to wear the white romper she had worn the other night. He ask if it was expensive as it might be ruined. Kathy didn't like the thought of the clothes she was wearing being ruined. She pictured the good Representative ripping them off her and raping her while Russell was driving around Beaumont looking for her. As bad as it made her feel, she never stopped smiling.

"It was around twenty five dollars, not much, but I really like it. What do you mean by 'ruined'?"

"It's a rodeo arena, you might sit in cow shit or something." It was the "or something" that worried both of them.

"Bring a change of clothes anyway. You will probably be the only one anybody will see. If they start looking for us, I don't want you wearing the white outfit."

"I'm just curious," she asked, "why do you want me to wear it anyway? Why not blue jeans?"

"When the cops start asking the cowboys who saw you for a description, they are going to say 'she was wearing a white dress type thing with real thin straps on the shoulders. It came down just below her ass. Man, did she have a great ass and legs.' They'll spit and be so proud of themselves that they could identify you. The cop will say 'how tall was she? What color was her hair? Was her hair short or long?' The cowboy will think a minute and say, 'she really had a great ass and legs."

"You shouldn't flatter me like that you silver tongued devil," Kathy said with a laugh.

"We don't have time for you to enjoy my silver tongue."

"Tonight?"

"I promise."

It was a great to be alive and in love.

15

Gary Stephens pager vibrated just as he was reaching the top of his back swing. He kept his eye on the ball as his hips rotated to clear the way for his arms. His shoulders turned and his arms came through the ball. His hands uncocked at the precise time to deliver the clubhead through the hitting zone. Unfortunately, the clubhead hit the ground a full six inches before it reached the ball. The metal clubhead skipped into the ball sending it less than a hundred yards down the driving range.

Gary looked around but no one seemed to notice, or to care if they did notice. It was a driving range, not Augusta. Gary looked at his beeper. 11111111 was displayed. It was the paper. He pressed the little button on the side and the date and time flashed on the screen. 1:48 p.m. *I should have gone back to the office with Tim, or at least home. I wouldn't have wasted a bucket of balls,* Gary thought to himself. He picked up his clubs and walked to the parking lot. *Somebody will use them.* He was right. No sooner had he put his clubs in the trunk and someone was busy hitting the golf balls he left behind.

If it was important and he was needed at the office, the code was seven number "ones" sent to the pager. If they just wanted him to return the call, a single "one" was sent. Gary didn't count them, but there was a bunch of one's. On the way, he used the car phone to check in. He was needed in the office. It was important.

Gary Stephens was full of mixed emotions. It was an absolutely gorgeous day. It had damn well better be important to bring him back to the office early. He had planned to come in later to go over the Sunday edition. On the other hand, Gary was thinking, this might have something to do with the Congressman murders. He hoped not. He didn't want another Congressman to die. Although, after reading one of Tim's articles about the two Senators, he wasn't sorry either one was dead.

Phoenix was very enjoyable this time of year. The orange trees were full of oranges. The weather was fantastic. The crazy heat that plagues Phoenix in the summer was still a few weeks away, if they were lucky. Many of the snow birds had already flown north. Gary was enjoying the drive. He was in no hurry. Whatever it was could wait another five minutes. The investigative reporter juices that had rushed his body the week before had quickly evaporated into Phoenix sunshine.

Gary pulled into his spot near the employees' entrance. As he walked through the double glass doors, Tim Brooks was waiting.

"You got another letter."

"What's it say?" Gary's pace increased dramatically.

"I don't know."

Gary stopped in his tracks, faced Tim and said, "what do you mean, 'you don't know?'"

"It was addressed to you. It didn't say personal or anything on the envelope, it so they opened it. I think it was Hal that opened it. They always flatten the letters out and put them in a stack. Then they put them into the folder of whoever it is addressed to," Tim said as they started walking again.

Gary could have done without the lecture on mailroom procedure at the Tribune.

"When Hal looked at the letter, he didn't see a name on it. In order to look for a name on it, he had to read it. When he realized what it was, he found the envelope, put the letter back in it and called me."

The two men got on the elevator and waited for the door to close.

"He knew as soon as he read the first few lines what it was. He said he put it back in the envelope and brought it straight to me. It's sitting on my desk as we speak. I didn't want to touch it. We can explain Hal's fingerprints simply enough, but if mine and yours are on it, then the FBI may get a little pissed that we passed the thing around the office before calling them."

Gary thought about it and Tim had done the exact right thing. "Did you call the FBI?" He asked.

"No, I thought I would wait for you. Several reasons. If Hal was over zealous and just read an irate letter to the editor, we would look pretty stupid. I figured the FBI will be here in about two minutes after we tell them we have another letter, assuming it is another letter. I thought you would at least like to look at it before we turn it over."

"You thought right, Tim."

"I had lots of time to think about it while I was in the lobby waiting for you."

Both men were smiling as they reached Tim's office.

The mood changed quickly as they looked at the envelope resting on Tim's desk. They both stared at it like it was a rattlesnake, coiled and ready to strike. A small crowd was gathering around them. News travels fast in a newsroom.

Gary picked up the envelope. The mail room had run an opener along the top fold and cut a perfect slice along the top. Gary pulled the letter out and unfolded it. He looked around at the faces that had gathered and began reading to himself.

> We have killed two United States Senators. We will kill more unless wasteful spending is stopped and taxes are lowered.
>
> We will no longer attempt to kill one per week. We may kill one, we may kill more. We may skip a week. If we see changes in Washington, we may not kill for a month. We may stop altogether. Our actions are dictated by those in Washington.
>
> As voters, we tried other options. They all failed. We voted for people who said they would make changes. After elected, they changed. They went from being honest concerned citizens to being just as corrupt as the incumbent they replaced.
>
> This will be our final correspondence. Our goals are known. We are doing this for our childrens' sake.

Gary read the letter slow and methodically. When he finished he read it a second time. Convinced it was authentic, he looked at Tim and nodded an affirmative. It was so quiet in the newsroom you could hear a pin drop. Gary's nod caused a rash of whispers to break out.

Without speaking, Gary walked to the copy machine, lifted the cover, laid the document face down on the glass, lined it up with the marks for an eight and a half by eleven original, pressed the number for three copies and pressed start. The old Xerox clanked and grumbled, then hummed as it spat out the three requested copies.

Gary picked up the original and the copies. He looked up and was startled to see his entire staff looking at him. He handed one copy of the letter to Tim Brooks and the second letter to Hal, the mailroom clerk.

"This looks like another letter from the faction that killed the two Senators. I think it's legit. You may read it. You may talk about it among yourselves. You are not to make a copy. You are not to call anyone and talk about it. I mean NO one. If I find out you called home and told your wife, your husband, your dog, I will fire you on the spot. No questions asked. If you don't think you can keep it to yourself for the next 24 hours, until Tim's story is out, DO NOT READ IT. Have I made myself perfectly clear?"

No one said a word as they gathered around Hal who was reading the letter for the second time. They all squeezed in as close as they could so as many as possible could read the letter. As one would finish and back out, another would squeeze in his place. The scene reminded Gary of a bunch of young boys trying to get a glimpse of a Playboy magazine for the first time.

Tim had missed most of the commotion. He was back at his desk reading and rereading the letter. *I've got it, but how do I make a story out of it?* He thought to himself.

Gary stuck his head in Tim's office and said, "I'm calling the FBI. I'm sure they will be here in just a matter of minutes. I'll try to get something out of them. Front page is yours. Midnight deadline."

Tim, hardly looking up from the letter, gave Gary the "thumbs up" signal. He'd be ready.

* * * * * *

Russell and Kathy drove through the Jack-in-the-Box drive through and ordered two Jumbo Jacks, fries and Cokes. Kathy ordered Diet Coke.

"Greasy french fries and a Diet Coke. That makes as much sense as pizza and Lite beer," Russell said.

"You would love me just as much if I weighed 200 pounds, right."

"Of course I would."

"Yeah, maybe after a 12 pack of beer."

Russell was digging himself deeper. There was no way out. He made a mental note never to mention anything about her eating habits. The line moved forward and they were at the pay window. Russell paid, took the food and drinks from the woman in the head set, drove onto the main road and changed the subject with Kathy.

"I know we've been over it, but let's do it one more time. The more we hear it and think it, the better we should be prepared if something goes wrong."

"You are going to drop me off at the rodeo place. I go in and pretend like I'm looking for someone. I act frustrated and sad. Representative James hits on me. What if he doesn't hit on me?"

"If he's there, he will. Gene says he'll be there, evidently James calls it campaigning. Uses campaign funds to buy lots of shit and act important. Then takes a girl home. Gene's sources say he seldom misses. I guess girls that want to sleep with a U.S. Congressman go there and let him pick them up. I don't know what the deal is."

"What if he's already picked up?"

"If he's gone, we leave and try to come up with another plan. If he's there, but with another woman, he will drop her like a hot potato when he sees you. Guaranteed."

"So, I act drunk and loose. When he hits on me, I get him out of there. The less time I'm in the place, the less time people have to see me and identify me. He takes me to his car and you and Eric will follow. I suggest we go somewhere private, fast. There are lots of small private back roads around there and if he doesn't head that way, I'll suggest it. Nothing like a quickie in the back seat. You guys follow. He stops and I get out."

"That's important. Get out of the car fast. I don't want him pinning you in."

She gave Russell a, *you're damn right,* look.

"I tell him I want to do it on the hood or something. Don't worry, I'll get out. Then I maneuver him away from the car so he has no protection and you run over him with the truck."

"You got it. That area used to be rice fields. There are no trees and no other cover. Just be sure you get way away. I don't want him grabbing you for protection."

"You just run his ass down. I'll be all right."

"It shouldn't be a problem, Eric said he stole a Dodge Ram."

16

It took Agent Christian less than 10 minutes to get from the Blind Luck op center to Gary Stephen's office.

"This is the original, of course, I have a copy and I gave Tim Brooks a copy. It will be front page tomorrow."

The FBI agent nodded. He didn't expect Gary to sit on any news once the whole mess had become public knowledge. Christian studied the letter.

"I would have to agree, it's the same group. It looks like they're not as organized as we thought."

Gary gave the FBI agent a puzzled look.

"Off the record?"

"Sure."

"Two killings, one in Arizona and one in Illinois. A legitimate threat to kill one a week for an indefinite time period. We have been concentrating our efforts on known anti-government groups. Unfortunately, the United States is full of these groups. Many are armed and extremely dangerous. You are well aware of the guys that blew up the building in Oklahoma City. To me this letter says, if you read between the lines, that they are backing down. I'd be willing to bet that this is NOT the work of any sort of supremacist group or anti-government militia. Of course, until we are sure it's not an anti-government group, that is the direction we will continue to focus our investigation."

"We have assumed that you would be looking at those types of groups. Can I give it to Tim that you in fact are. I think they would be expecting it?"

The agent thought for a moment before saying, "I would prefer that you didn't. Not right now, anyway. But I will tell you, for the record, that Senator Abernathy of Florida has disappeared. He dismissed the agents assigned to him, then ran them all over Washington in an effort to lose them. It worked. We spotted him in Florida later, but lost him when he took off in a helicopter. With all the drug enforcement equipment we have in South Florida, I don't know how in the hell they lost him, but they did. That last part was off the record."

Gary Stephens smiled. He wasn't going to print anything that would jeopardize their relationship.

Christian continued, "that was late Thursday night. Normally, he would at least check in with his office. They haven't heard a thing from him. Again, off the record, he may just be shacked up with some sweet thing for the weekend. I don't know. If so, maybe you mentioning he is missing will flush him out. You heard it from an unnamed source."

"Of course."

The two men shook hands and Agent Christian left. Gary went to talk to Tim. There was finally something newsworthy.

* * * * *

Russell and Kathy had been at the truck stop only a few minutes when Eric pulled up.

Eric was beaming with pride over his commandeering of the truck. He was well aware of what was about to happen, but he could not help but smile as he parked the truck next to Russell and Kathy.

"I thought I would get here a little late, make sure that you were already here. I didn't really want to be sitting here any length of time in a stolen truck."

"I don't blame you, we've only been here a little while ourselves," Russell said.

The three discussed the plan again just to be sure they were all on the same page. Kathy was quieter than ever. The reality of the situation was beginning to sink in. Prior to seeing the hot truck, it was all still a fantasy. It had suddenly become very real.

"I would really like a beer," she said.

"Are you sure, I don't. . . " Russell said until Kathy interrupted.

"Please, Russell, I. . . " She bit her lower lip, "I really would like a beer."

Russell could see in her eyes that she was getting scared. Without another word he ran into the truck stop and bought a six-pack of Budweiser. One thing good about Texas, just about every gas station and truck stop sells beer.

Kathy was sitting in the Dodge Ram when Russell returned with the beer. He stopped briefly to talk to Eric. When he got in the cab of the pickup truck, Kathy was staring out the window.

"Are you sure you can go through with this? You can back out any time, I'll understand."

She leaned close and kissed him on the lips.

"I'm fine, really. I can do it," she said as she pulled a beer out of the six-pack, popped the top and took a long drink. Russell started the truck and slid the gear shift lever to drive. Using the old west signal to start the wagon train west, Russell motioned to Eric as he pulled onto Interstate 10 and headed east.

Kathy sat quietly and sipped her beer as they drove the 35 miles on I-10 to the Port Arthur exit.

"The rodeo arena is only about a mile from here. Are you ready?" Russell asked.

Kathy put on the baseball cap that Russell had given her. The cap looked like a Hawaiian shirt except for the patch on the front which was a divers flag. Underneath the flag were the words *Muff Divers* written in script. Kathy had asked what a muff diver was and Russell said he didn't know. At the moment she couldn't care less. Kathy pulled the visor down so she could look in the vanity mirror. She didn't like the hat.

"I don't think the hat goes with the romper," she said.

"It looks fine. You need it to hide your face. Remember to look down when you're not pretending to be looking for your friend," Russell said as he glanced at her.

She nodded as Russell slowed down to turn into the parking lot. The rodeo arena was a large rectangular sheet metal building. The main doors were facing a side street which Russell had turned onto in order to enter the parking lot. He drove slowly as he made one large lap around the parking area. He pulled the pickup in behind a large horse trailer near the middle of the parking lot close to the road.

"I can see the doors very clearly from here." He looked around the parking lot. Eric had pulled to the area closest to the main road and side street and had parked. "I will be able to see you no matter where you are except for this little spot right in front of me, and you will only be out of sight a few seconds if you have to walk through there. When I can't see you, I'm sure Eric can. If something goes wrong and you want to bail, take your hat off and hold it on your hip. I'm going to start the motor as soon as I see you walk out that door. If you take off your hat, I'll pull around and you can jump in here, or in the back, whatever you want to do."

Kathy pulled another beer from the six-pack and opened it. Russell looked at her, but said nothing. She took one big gulp then poured some into her hands and rubbed it on her neck and shoulders. She kissed Russell on the lips.

"I love you very much," she said as she opened the truck door and got out. He had a sinking feeling in the pit of his stomach.

Kathy took several deep breaths as she opened the door to the arena. The smell made her gasp as she walked in. The place looked much bigger from the inside than it did from the outside. There was a large arena in the center with rows of bleachers on both sides. An eight foot chain link fence surrounded the arena. At the far end were chutes with men in blue jeans and cowboy hats sitting on the top rail.

Kathy slowly panned the bleachers as if she was looking for someone. She walked down the narrow isle between the chain-link fence and the first row of bleacher seats. Occasionally she would stop and look around the bleachers. She could feel her heart pounding in her chest. It felt like every eye in the building was staring at her. They were. Not only was she probably one of the most beautiful women to ever walk in the building, she was certainly the most beautiful to ever walk in in a short white romper. Kathy sat on the front row, hoping James would find her.

She looked up when she heard the loud clank of the calf gate spring open. She watched as the tiny calf ran for its life as the man on horseback gave chase, swinging a rope over his head. With a flip of his wrist, the cowboy threw the rope perfectly around the calf's neck. Kathy was very impressed until the horse stopped dead in its tracks and the calf kept running until it reached the end of the rope. The baby cow grunted as its neck twisted violently when the rope went tight. The calve spun 180 degrees in the air and landed on it's back. As it laid there, the cowboy picked it up and slammed it back to the dirt. He took a small rope from his mouth, put the built in loop around one hoof, quickly wrapped two other legs, tied a knot and raised his hands in the air as if in triumph. The horse backed up, dragging the calf by the neck, until the cowboy climbed back on his horse and kicked him in the ribs with his spurs. There was scattering applause from the bleachers. Thoroughly disgusted, Kathy took one more look at the people in the bleachers and walked to the concession area she noticed at the area behind the shoots.

She looked at the menu, if you want to call it a menu, hamburger, cheeseburger, nachos, potato chips, popcorn, pickles, jalapeno peppers, Coke, Diet Coke and Sprite.

"Hello there!"

The booming voice made her jump. She turned to see a middle aged man, average height, slight beer gut, smiling at her. He wore blue jeans and brightly colored western shirt. Way too much starch.

"I'm sorry, I didn't mean to scare you."

"That's O.K.," she said letting her speech slur just slightly. She turned and looked up at the menu.

"I've never seen you here before," the man said.

Kathy glanced over her shoulder at the man, then looked up at the menu, then turned to face the stranger.

"No, I met this guy last night and he ask me to meet him here, but I'm late and I haven't seen him yet. I guess he figured I wasn't coming and left." Kathy's smile was genuine as she looked at his hair. He must have used a can of hair spray to get it that stiff.

"I'm Jack James," the man said as he held out his hand.

"I'm Sarah," she said, taking his hand and hoping he wouldn't ask for a last name. How did they forget to come up with an alias while they were planning. She wondered what else they had forgotten.

"Can I get you something?" The Representative from Beaumont, Texas asked as he nodded at the menu.

"No, uh, thanks," Kathy said with her sexy smile, "I don't think I'm gonna wait any longer. I was kinda hope'n they sold beer."

Jack James's eyes widened like a poker player who just drew a royal flush.

"I would absolutely be honored if you would allow me to by you a beer. I know a nice little ice house not far from here."

Kathy smiled as wide as she could, then frowned, drew away and said, "I don't know." She ran her eyes up and down the Representative. "I'm not sure, I mean, I don't know anything about you. . ." her speech was slowing and the pauses between the words were getting longer as she waited for James to interrupt.

He did. "I don't blame you one bit, ma'am. This place is just around the corner, not a lot of people, but they's good people, it's safe." He pulled a card from his shirt pocket, "here's my card, I'm Jack James, United States Representative from the ninth Congressional district. That's the Beaumont/Port Arthur area."

Kathy took the card, looked at it, smiled and said, "wow, that's cool." She hoped shit-kickers used the term "cool."

"I'd love to have a beer with you," she said as she took his hand and started toward the walkway that led between the arena floor and the bleachers. *Keep the head down and face away from the crowd* she thought.

"No, this way," he said as he pulled her toward a door in the back of the tin building. She could feel her heart in the pit of her stomach but said nothing.

It felt as though she were wearing lead boots as she followed James out the back door of the arena. She knew neither Russell nor Eric could see her behind the building. She leaned the direction she wanted to go, pulling James's arm, "walk with me, I need to get my purse from the car."

"You don't need your purse, believe me they're not going to card you."

Kathy smiled and leaned close to him, making sure he could feel her breasts pressing against his chest, "come on, it'll only take a second, I don't like not having my purse with me."

James gave in. It didn't occur to ask her why she didn't have her purse with her now if she didn't like not having it.

As they walked through the parking lot, around and between the rows of pickup trucks and horse trailers, Kathy chattered. She commented on what a beautiful day it was as she put her arms out and twirled in a circle, bumping into the Representative and giggling. She looked like Julie Andrews in *The Sound of Music* as she twirled across the parking lot.

With each twirl she would look at the Dodge Ram pickup parked ten feet behind the horse trailer. The driver was fixated on the main entrance door. Occasionally she would see him look down at his watch, then resume his stare at the front door.

Look this way, God damn you, she thought to herself. *I can't even take the hat off if you don't look at me.* They walked in front of the truck and trailer that was parked directly in front of the Dodge. Kathy walked far enough out so that Russell could not help but see her. The sight of her and James so close to the truck took Russell by surprise. He had been glued to the front door. Quickly gaining his senses, he turned the key in the ignition and the truck's engine fired. It idled perfectly quiet. Jack James did not notice the person in the truck, or the truck starting. Russell pressed his foot against the brake and eased the gear shift lever into reverse. He took a quick glance over his shoulder toward Eric. Eric was staring straight at him, he was ready.

Jack James said something that wasn't very funny but Kathy laughed anyway.

As she got even with the rear end of the trailer, but 15 to 20 feet to the left, Kathy stopped and looked toward the far end of the parking lot.

"Damn, it's further than I thought. I really need a beer. You were right, I don't need the damn purse, let's go." As she said it, James pulled her to him and kissed her on the lips.

Kathy was planning to walk James directly in front of Russell, *no way you won't be able to see me,* she thought to herself, pissed that she had to walk around the parking lot and then say she didn't want her purse after all. If she didn't let him kiss her, he might get suspicious. Jack slid his hand down her back and squeezed her ass. That was exactly what she was waiting for.

She jerked away, grabbed his hand and said, "Geez, not here, are you crazy?" She pushed him away and ran between the Dodge Ram and the horse trailer and stopped just on the other side of the Ram. She wanted badly to look at Russell. She could just image how he felt after seeing his fiancé being kissed and felt-up by another man. Even if it was for the cause, she bet he was pissed.

Russell was pissed. He looked around the parking lot and saw no one. He dropped the gear shift lever down two notches to drive and watched Representative Jack James strut toward his prey. As the Representative passed the first quarter of the Ram's hood, Russell slammed the accelerator to the floor. The big engine roared as the back tires spun, shooting gravel and shell as they dug for traction. James heard the roar and looked at the truck as it lurched toward him. He tried to reverse direction but his momentum had been carrying him forward. He started to jump in an attempt to get out of the way of the oncoming Ram, but there was no time.

The huge front of the Dodge truck hit just below his shoulders, lifting the Representative off the ground and slamming him into the horse trailer. The trailer bounced but didn't move. The pickup came to an abrupt stop, somewhat cushioned by Representative James' body. While the grill was crushing his chest, the front bumper flattened his waist area against the trailer causing a violent hemorrhage of bodily fluids.

Russell put the truck in park and stared at James lifeless body. "Shit!" He said as he looked toward Eric who was already on his way. He jumped out of the truck and scanned the parking lot. It was still empty. He went to the rear of the truck to wait for Eric who was closing fast. He expected Kathy to already be there. He looked to the other side of the truck and saw her standing, frozen in her tracks, staring at Representative James.

"Come on," he yelled. She didn't move. "Kathy, Come on." She still didn't move. Russell ran to her side and grabbed her arm, "Kathy," he said softly, "we have to go, please, come on, we have to go." She either didn't or couldn't hear him. She just stood there staring.

Eric slid to a stop on the soft gravel and jumped out of the car. "Let's get the hell out of here," he said as he pushed the back of the seat forward to let one of the two in the back seat. Russell grabbed Kathy and pulled her to the car. Eric helped and they managed to put her in the back seat where she immediately curled into the fetal position.

"You drive," Eric said as he ran to the other side of the car and got in. "Go! Go! Go!" he said as he slammed the door closed. Russell put the car in gear and stomped on the accelerator. The car threw gravel as it fish-tailed out of the parking lot. Eric kept an eye on the parking lot and the arena door as Russell drove the short distance to Highway 73. Russell stopped, looked both ways, no sense in getting stopped for running a stop sign, turned left toward I-10 and floored his Dodge 600.

"Speed limit is 70 through here," Eric said, still looking around for anyone that may have seen them.

Russell accelerated to 73 miles per hour and held it there.

"We'll be at I-10 in just a second. We should be all right then. How's Kathy?"

Eric turned around and looked at Kathy. She was lying on the back seat in the fetal position, white as a ghost and crying uncontrollably.

"I don't know," Eric said softly to Russell, "she doesn't look too good. Maybe you ought to get back there."

Russell strained to look over the seat, "we can't stop now. If somebody back there saw us, they could be just minutes behind." Russell took another look at Kathy and said to Eric, "get the hat, would ya."

Eric leaned over the seat and pulled the baseball cap from Kathy's head and handed it to Russell. Russell check the rear view mirror and saw no cars. He rolled the window down and threw the cap out the window.

"What about finger prints?" Eric asked.

"I don't know if they can take them off cloth or not. Maybe they won't even find the hat. I'd chance it rather than getting caught with it in the car."

Kathy's sudden scream scared the hell out of Russell and Eric. They both looked back to see her yanking at her romper. The zipper was in the back and she either could not get to it or forgot there even was a zipper. She ripped the spaghetti straps from the front and pushed the cotton romper down, over her hips and past her knees. She kicked the material like it was on fire to get it off her feet. When she was free of it, she threw the romper into the front seat. She pulled her legs up to her chest and rested her head on her knees. Her jaw shook violently as she continued to cry uncontrollably.

Eric looked at the romper and pointed at large spots of blood that had spattered against the front. While Kathy had been removing the romper, Russell had taken the west bound exit and merged on to Interstate 10.

"There's a change of clothes for her in that bag," Russell said pointing to a brown paper bag on the floor board. Eric took a sleeveless blouse out of the bag and handed it to Kathy. She slowly lowered her legs to the floor and reached forward to take the blouse from Eric. She put the blouse in her lap and held it with both hands. She appeared to be reading the label. Kathy sat motionless with her arms to her side, staring at the blouse, making no attempt to cover herself.

Eric looked a Kathy's naked breasts. A voice in his head was saying, "Eric, you are the scum of the earth! Stop looking at her," but he couldn't stop. He leaned over the seat and picked the blouse up and held it open like when dressing a child.

"Kathy," Eric said with his most gentle voice and all the compassion he could muster, "please, you need to put this on."

Like a child, Kathy raised her right arm and stuck it through the sleeve opening. Eric held the garment until she got her other arm through and began buttoning the buttons. As she buttoned, Eric looked at Russell. He knew he should say something, apologize for staring at Kathy while she was in such a way. All Eric could do was look at Russell, he was too embarrassed to say a word.

Russell said "thanks," and patted Eric on the leg. This was not a time for jealousy. Besides, Russell thought to himself, I would have looked too, she's the most beautiful woman I'VE ever seen.

Eric gave Kathy the shorts that were in the bag and turned back around as she put them on.

"I think she's doing better," Eric whispered.

Russell took a peak in the rear view mirror. Kathy's jaw had quit shaking and she was sitting upright, leaning against the back seat. They all rode quietly for the next half an hour. Russell turned the radio on softly and pushed the buttons until he found music.

Kathy eased forward and leaned on the back of the front seat. "Could you stop and get me a beer, please? I really want a beer."

"That sounds like a great idea," said Eric.

"There's an exit just ahead, right on the other side of the San Jacinto River bridge. There's a gas station that sells beer. Directly across from where we met earlier. I'll stop there." Russell wasn't sure why he went into so much detail about a beer stop. Probably because one does not think too clearly moments after they commit a murder.

Russell pulled into the parking lot and Eric jumped out and bought a six-pack of Bud. Everybody opened a can as Russell pulled back onto the freeway heading for Houston.

Kathy leaned back and sipped the beer. Eric and Russell both wanted to raise their cans high and toast to a mission accomplished. Neither thought it would be a good idea considering Kathy's state of mind.

Eric looked back at Kathy and she seemed to be doing fine. She was looking out the window.

"Rus, I don't want to sound like a chicken-shit, but if I am ever arrested and asked about this, I will swear I know nothing about it. I will deny I was here. That also means I have absolutely no idea what happened or who was here. I have no idea what you and Kathy did today. If they say you said I was there I will deny it. Obviously, I wouldn't be able to say you were there and you were trying to cover your ass, because I was not there. Are you OK with that?"

"I think that's a very good idea. None of us were there. Period. No matter what anyone says. I will mention it to Kathy too. As a matter of fact, I will tell everybody that, if they are ever questioned about the murders, they know nothing about James' murder. About any of the murders. We weren't at this one and Todd had nothing to do with the other two. Deny. Deny. Deny."

Kathy's touch of Eric's arm made him jump. He hadn't heard her slide forward in the seat. "Thank you, Eric, for what you did for me. I, . . . I really appreciate it." She looked at Russell and said, "that was the worst experience of my life. I don't want to ever,. . . no, . . . I will never do anything like that again. I want you to take me home and I am going to get drunker than I have ever gotten and I hope that in the morning I will not remember a thing. I hope nobody ever reminds me of this day. Eric would you give me another beer please."

Eric handed Kathy the remaining three beers from the six-pack. She took them, leaned back into the back seat and smiled for the first time since she watched Jack James, United States Representative from the ninth Congressional district, Beaumont, Texas get crushed by a Dodge Ram pickup truck.

17

Inside the rodeo arena, a cowboy sat atop a 2,000 pound Brahma bull and wrapped a leather strap around his hand. When he felt ready, he pushed the top of his black Stetson cowboy hat down on his head, and nodded. The cowboy at the back of the chute quickly swung the gate open. The bull snorted as it leapt out of the chute. Another cowboy jammed an electric prod into the bull's behind as a third man pulled a cinch tight around the its flanks. The enormous gray bull bucked and spun in a futile effort to kick free of the painful binding.

As the bull bucked, the cowboy, holding one hand above his head, tried to stay on for eight seconds. If he managed the eight second count, the difficult part then became getting off and away from the bull without being gored or stomped.

The bull made two spins left, stopped, bucked and spun right. The cowboy continued to spin left, landing head first into the soft dirt floor of the arena. His entire ride lasted less than five seconds. This cowboy didn't have to worry about getting off.

The rodeo clowns immediately moved in to distract the bull while the cowboy ran toward the chutes and safety. Except for the animals, the clown has the most dangerous job during the most dangerous part of a rodeo.

Bull riding is always the last event. Most cowboys participate in several rodeo events. A cowboy is most likely to be hurt during the bull riding so they make sure they have finished all the other events. Bull riding is also the most popular event. Probably because there is a better chance that the cowboy will be gored or have his head crushed by the animal's hoof. People always like to see disaster. Thousand of fans pack motor speedways every weekend just for the chance to see a spectacular automobile crash.

Outside the rodeo arena, in the deserted parking lot, Representative Jack James lifeless body lay pinned between the pickup truck and horse trailer. The few people that had meandered through the parking lot in the hour since the Representative's demise did not notice the head resting on the hood of the Dodge Ram. Had they noticed, it would have looked like he was sitting on the horse trailer resting his head on the truck. Without close inspection, the uninterested passerby would assume another cowboy had passed out on his truck.

The bull riding ended and the rodeo announcer thanked everybody for coming. Spectators strolled to their cars and left for home, an ice house or the local dance hall. It was 7:30 in east Texas. Time to start partying. Still, no one noticed Jack James's body between the truck and trailer.

Sammy West and Bill Conner led their quarter horses toward their trailer.

"God Damn it Sammy, look at that, some som-bitch parked right up against our trailer. How in the hell are we gonna load the horses?"

"Don't worry 'bout it Bill, I'm sure they'll move it in a minute. Let's get a beer."

Bill tied the two horses to a ring on the front of the trailer. Sammy opened the ice chest in the bed of his truck and retrieved two Lone Star beers. The two men drank and talked and spit, occasionally looking to see if the owner of the truck was near. Other cowboys wandered by and would accept the offered beer. They would talk and drink and spit. It was not uncommon for many of the cowboys to hang around the parking lot drinking Lone Star late into the night. Sammy and Bill were in no hurry.

Bill said to no one in particular, "I gotta piss," and walked toward the rear of the horse trailer.

"Fuck! Fuck! Fuck!" Bill yelled just as he disappeared behind the trailer.

Sammy and the other cowboys ran to the end of the trailer.

"God damn," said one cowboy.

"Son-of-a-bitch," said another.

Bill was pacing back and forth. "Fuck an A," he would say every time he paced to a point where he could see the body.

"That's Jack James," a voice from the slowly gathering crowd. The word "fuck" yelled very loudly three times usually gets attention. Even in the parking lot of a rodeo arena.

"I saw him leave though the back door with a really fine look'n babe," another voice said, "that must have been at least two and a half, three hours ago."

"I saw her too," Sammy said "she was wearing a little white dress type thing except the legs were sewn together. I remember thinking Jack was gonna have to wait till he got somewhere where he could take it all the way off. Couldn't just hike it up and slip'r the old snake." There were no laughs. How long it took to slip a woman the "old snake" was serious business among cowboys.

"Anybody call the cops yet?" A voice asked.

"He ain't gonna be snake'n anybody tonight," was the only reply.

* * * * * *

Having some serious investigative work to do revitalized the FBI agents at the Blind Luck Operational Center. Investigating the tiny shreds of evidence that would inevitably lead to another dead end was tedious and frustrating work. The disappearance of Senator Abernathy was a happening. It was now. He was somewhere in Florida, they were reasonably sure, and he was either dead, about to be dead or shacked up with some young girl. It didn't matter to the FBI. His trail was hot and they were going to find him. They shouldn't have lost him in the first place.

Agent Bates entered the room carrying several sheets of computerized printout with hand written notes on them. Agent Christian looked at him.

"The Great South Florida Land Development Company is a Cayman Island registered corporation licensed to do business in Florida. Their listed office is a post office box in Fort Lauderdale. The list of assets owned by the company includes undeveloped land in south and central Florida, an apartment building in Miami, a condo project near Orlando and a condo/resort type complex in Key West. We have found one airplane, two helicopters and four automobiles registered to the company. The airplane is in its hanger in Miami. One helicopter is in Fort Lauderdale. The helicopter that picked up Senator Abernathy has not been located. Neither has the pilot, we are still working on that. Also, no word on any of the vehicles owned by the company."

Bates paused to review his notes, then continued, "The Caymans have always been a place where people go if they have something to hide. The government there likes it that way. It brings lots of foreign money into the country. They don't like to give up information very easily, but we are working on them. We've got agents on the way to the condos and the apartment to see if they can find anybody that knows anything. It's going to take a little time though. It seems it's not the first time Abernathy has disappeared for a few days without checking in. I believe we had been misinformed. The locals seem to think he'll turn up in Washington on Monday morning. Our guys are pretty much on their own trying to check all these places out. They say they get the impression the Florida law enforcement agencies would rather not find the Senator and his weekend companion. If they found him, and he was banging a minor, they would have to arrest him, and they don't want to."

Agent Christian wished he hadn't reprimanded agent Bates earlier for wishing the Senator dead. He knew Bates wanted to say it now, and Christian, at the moment, would have liked to hear it.

"Thank you Bates," Christian said, "let me know as soon as you get anything else."

Bates nodded and left the room. He kept thinking of the joke a Dade County detective had told him earlier, "do you know why Senator Abernathy was kicked out of all the bars in Key West? They told him they wouldn't serve minors to liquors." Bates would save it for later.

Inside the Op Center the fax machine rang one time before it was automatically answered. The class 2 fax machine screeched as it attempted to connect with the class 2 fax machine on the other end of the line. The noise stopped as the two machines agreed upon a mutually acceptable data transmission rate. Seconds later paper began inching out the top of the Op Center machine until a full eight and half by eleven sheet of paper was sliced and ejected into the waiting tray.

Agent Christian picked up the fax from the Orange County Texas Sheriff's department and read it quickly. He sat in the nearest chair as he felt his knees give. Not a long fax, Agent Christian reread it slowly. He was hoping it would be different the second time. It wasn't.

"Fuck! Fuck! Fuck!" Agent Christian said rather loudly. The word "fuck" spoken three times rather loudly in an operations center of the Federal Bureau of Investigation gets a lot of attention.

* * * * *

Kathy Beck was as drunk as anyone had ever seen her. She had drunk four beers by the time she and Russell returned to her house.

They dropped Eric at his place so he could get his car. Both he and Russell thought it would be a good idea to hang out and talk about the affairs of the day. Once at Kathy's house, they decided to call the others. Julie Hanson was home and would be right over. Todd Evans could also make it. Messages were left with Mark Flanagen, Robert Green and Annie Simmons. Gene Thompson was in but had plans, he would try to change them and be over as soon as possible.

Russell, realizing that the Jack-in-the-Box hamburgers were the only thing he and Kathy had eaten all day, ordered pizza. He ordered plenty for anyone who might show. Kathy was busy with the stereo looking for "good-time music," as she put it, to play. She said no television or radio. She did not want to hear any reports about the death of Representative Jack James.

While Kathy looked for music, Russell and Eric discussed the events of the day trying to remember with as much detail as possible every single thing that happened and, if they screwed up at some point, what could they do about it now. They tried to determine if there was anything to tie them to the murder at the rodeo arena.

"What about Tony?" Russell asked, "won't he notice that the truck used to kill James was the same one you two stole?"

"I don't think so, first of all, he didn't get that good of a look at the one I took. I'm sure he could tell it was a Dodge Ram, they've got the awful looking front end, but he probably wouldn't remember the color or anything. He could figure it out easy enough, I would think, if he tried. After all, we steal a truck on Friday night, and Saturday night the same type truck is used to kill someone. But Tony would have to know what kind of truck killed James. That would mean he would have to watch the news, or, God forbid, read a newspaper. No, I don't think we have anything to worry about."

"That's good. I . . . "

The door bell rang and Russell stopped in mid-sentence. Logically, both men knew that there was no way they could be tracked, this quickly anyway, to Kathy Beck's dining room. Both knew they were expecting the others to be arriving any minute, and there was pizza being delivered. It didn't matter. The door bell scared the hell out of them. They sat in silence as Kathy bounced to the door.

"Hi Julie, come on in." Kathy said as she opened the door. Russell and Eric started to breathe again. A similar scene would be replayed several times before the night was over.

"Hi Kat," Julie said as she came in and hugged her friend. "Why was the door locked, you never lock the door when you're having everybody over."

Kathy didn't respond to Julie's question, but instead went back to the stereo where she was looking through stacks of compact disks and cassettes. Julie walked straight to the refrigerator pausing only long enough to acknowledge Russell and Eric's existence. She poured herself a glass of white Zinfandel and walked over to where the two men were sitting. She could see Kathy and could tell she was getting very drunk.

"What's wrong with Kathy?"

"Things didn't go exactly as planned today." Russell explained, "I don't know if it would have made a difference or not, but she was standing about a foot from Representative James when we, uh, I killed him."

Julie's smile disappeared as she bit her tongue. Her forehead wrinkled as she glared at the two men. "Damn you two!" She said in a surprisingly calm voice. "You shouldn't have got her involved. She is really sweet. I really care for her and I don't think either of you two do that much. This could really screw her up for the rest of her life."

"Julie, Kathy and I are going to get married next week, Don't tell me I don't care for her."

Julie's mouth dropped open. She stared at Russell, not quite knowing what to say. Her mouth hung open. Eric was surprised by the news as well. Not nearly as much as Julie, but very surprised.

Julie regained her composure and said, "so when did you all decide this, before you committed murder, or after, while she was in a state of shock?"

Russell didn't think Julie's comments warranted an answer, but he decided to give her one anyway. "We actually decided last Thursday night, after everyone had left. We haven't talked about it after. . . " he paused to think about what he was saying, "uh, after I killed him. I hope she will still marry me. I wouldn't blame her if she called it off. She was pretty upset. I am worried about her." As he was talking to Julie, he was looking at Kathy. He looked very sad.

"I'm sorry Rus, I'm sure it's hard on both of you," Julie said.

Russell smiled and nodded an "it's O.K." type nod. Julie left the two men to see how Kathy was doing.

"This is what I've been looking for," Kathy slurred as she found *The Best of the Loving Spoonful* cassette. "I love this tape. It's gotta be my favorite tape of all time. I just love John Sebastian. You know I saw him at Rockefeller's last year, for an old guy he was really good."

Kathy continued her drunken chatter as she put the cassette in the player and pushed play. The music started and she got quiet long enough to sing along:

> *Do you believe in magic,*
> *In a young girl's heart,*
> *How the music can free her whenever it starts.*
> *And it's magic.*
> *If the music is groovy,*
> *It makes you feel happy like an old time movie,*
> *I'll tell you about the magic and it'll free your soul,*
> *But it's like trying to tell a stranger about a rock and*
> *rooooll. . . . . .*

Kathy would sip beer during the instrumental portions and sing along with the words. Julie, Russell and Eric watched her and sang along too. The music put them at ease.

Todd, Mark and Annie all showed up within a few minutes of each other. Gene arrived about an hour later. It was only nine o'clock but Kathy was fairly well out of it. If anyone had been keeping track of the beer she had drunk, they long since lost count. Russell and Eric retold the story one more time to Gene. He looked at Kathy and said, "poor kid."

"I'm really surprised I didn't hear any thing on the radio about it yet. Are you sure you killed him?

"Oh yeah," Russell said.

Gene grunted and thought for a second, "are you sure you got the right guy? James was about 65, overweight, almost white hair."

Neither Russell nor Eric could speak. A lump the size of a Texas grapefruit became lodged in their throats. Their faces turned white as a sheet. Gene started laughing hysterically and said, "ah, I got ya." He continued to laugh and point at the two who were too much in shock to move. "It was on the radio just a few minutes before I got here. He is dead but the details were sketchy."

He laughed again.

* * * * * *

The phone rang in Gary Stephens office. He was sitting at his desk with his feet propped up looking at his copy of the letter from the killers. It was his direct line. He picked it up before it rang the second time.

"Stephens," he said.

"Hello, Gary. This is Agent Christian, FBI."

Something about the Feds, Gary thought to himself, *they always give their title and company*. He made a mental note to identify himself as Editor Stephens, Tribune next time he needed to call Agent Christian. He hoped it wouldn't be soon.

"Good evening, what. . . " he said before being cut off by the Agent.

"It's not our policy to do this, but I like the way you run your paper. I always have. Tim Brook's stories about Blind Luck have been right on the money. He has explained the facts, done excellent research on the victims, in fact, we saved some time by reviewing the information he had come up with. Nothing that I have found has been fabricated or sensationalized."

Gary liked the praise, but he was sure that this wasn't a social call. He noticed his hands were getting sweaty as he listened to Christian.

"Got a piece of paper?" the agent asked. Gary wanted to say that was the first really stupid thing that he had heard the Agent say since he had known him. Asking a newspaper man if he had a piece of paper. Gary was anticipating something hot or he would have made a sly comment like, "yea, I got a pencil too." Instead, he simply said, "ready."

"Approximately seven o'clock this evening, we received a fax from the Orange County, Texas Sheriffs' Department informing us that Representative Jack James of Beaumont was found in the parking lot of a rodeo arena outside of the town of Winnie, Texas. He had been crushed to death between a pickup truck and a horse trailer."

"Do you know what kind of truck?"

"I believe it was a Dodge Ram. . . "

"A Ram, you're kidding."

"No sir, I am not."

"I'm sorry, it was meant to be a rhetorical question."

"I figured it was. He was last seen leaving the arena with a young woman, according to an eyewitness, a very attractive young woman, wearing a very short white dress and a baseball cap. Dark hair, black or maybe dark brown, great breasts and great legs. Evidently the breasts and legs were verified by quite a few witnesses, but none could agree on what her face looked like. Our guys are on the way there now. We are going to work closely with the locals on this one. It could be that he tried something she didn't like and she ran him down. It may have even been an accident, but I don't think so. The truck was reported stolen in Houston last night. Until I am convinced otherwise, I'm treating it as another murder by the Blind Luck gang."

"One question if I may."

"Sure, go ahead."

"Twice you referred to 'Blind Luck' what's that all about."

"That's what we have named the operation "Blind Luck." I would appreciate it if you would forget I said that and when this is over, I'll buy you a beer and explain."

"I'll forget I heard it, and you can forget the beer, just keep calling me first."

"Deal," Agent Christian said as he hung up the phone.

Editor Stephens went to Tim Brooks office with the scoop. In a way he wished they were in the east instead of Arizona. A couple hours later and he might have been able to yell, "stop the presses." As it was, they may still have time to get a story on the AP wire in time for other papers, at least in the central time zones, to run it in the morning edition.

18

Kathy Beck got out of bed and stumbled to the bathroom. Russell could hear her hacking and coughing in an attempt to vomit again. *There is no way she could have anything left in her stomach to throw up,* he thought as he heard the sounds of something coming up and out into the toilet bowl. *Poor thing,* he thought as he got out of bed to try and help her, *I've been there.*

Kathy was leaning over the commode wearing nothing but panties. Russell had removed her blouse and shorts during the night. She either had not quite made it to the commode or had missed the bowl. He put her soiled clothes in the sink to soak. Russell stood at the bathroom door and watched her. She looked like hell. Vomit was matted in her hair, her face was absolutely white. Her makeup had rubbed off long ago.

Russell wet a wash cloth and wiped her face. He wanted to ask her if she felt better, but he knew what the answer would be, and right now he was sure she wouldn't appreciate the question. Russell was patient, when Kathy said she was ready to try to go back to bed, he helped her. When she was settled and as comfortable as possible, Russell went to the kitchen and filled a glass with ice water. He got two aspirins from the cupboard. He went back to the bedroom and gave them to Kathy.

"I really don't want them, I know they won't stay down," she said.

"You're probably right, but I've been in your position many times and some of it will get into your system. It will also give you something to throw up. I'm serious, it will make you feel better. If you throw them up, I'll get you some more."

Kathy didn't relish the idea of throwing up again, but her head hurt so badly she would try anything. She took the aspirin and drank half the glass of ice water.

"God, I feel like shit. What did I do? I don't remember anything about last night." She took a few more sips of ice water.

"I still remember James getting crushed, but it's nowhere near as vivid as it was yesterday." She put her hand in Russell's, "I'm really sorry if I acted crazy yesterday."

"Please, don't worry about it, nobody can blame you. I'm sorry, I should have waited, like we planned. It's just that I got so pissed when he grabbed your butt, and I saw where you were and that he would have to walk right in front of the truck to get to you, I knew that if I hit him then and there, it would be over and we could leave, so I rammed him. Gene heard on the radio on his way over last night that he died, but we didn't want to say anything to you."

"Thanks, but I could have told you he was dead." She closed her eyes and laid her head in the pillow. "Can we still get married next week?"

"I would love to marry you as soon as possible, if you still want me." Russell said with a smile.

"Of course I do," Kathy raised from the bed to kiss Russell too quickly and her stomach revolted. She headed to the bathroom once again. Russell went for more ice water and aspirins. It was going to be a long morning.

Five minutes is not a lot of time for the pain killer to be digested into the system. Russell decided to give Kathy three aspirins this time hoping a little more would get into her system before it came back up. Enough must have gotten into her system as she fell asleep after taking the three aspirins.

Russell laid on the bed, his back propped against the head-board. He looked around Kathy's bedroom while he tried to put the last few days into prospective. In a nutshell, he had become engaged and killed a United States' Congressman. It was very hard to focus on the details of married life, such as where would they live, should he find a steady job, what about children. If they have children, should they be told that their parents were two of the conspirators that killed three people. Would it only be three people. If it was up to Russell and Kathy, it would only be three, their killing days were over. What if they get busted? It was certainly possible, he knew nothing about criminal investigations. The FBI has tools that he couldn't even imagine. There was no telling what kind of evidence they would find in the truck.

Russell began to feel sick to his stomach as he thought about the Dodge Ram pickup truck. While waiting for Kathy, he had used a towel that was in the truck to wipe anything he may have touched. The steering wheel had been wrapped with a wool cover. He wondered if the FBI could get finger prints off the wool or the towel. He left in a hurry and didn't wipe any finger prints off outside of the door. He couldn't remember if he used his hand to close the truck door, or if he even closed the door. He buried his face in his hands as he remembered the beer cans left in the truck. He had bought the beer and Kathy had drank it, he couldn't remember if he had touched a can or not.

Russell looked at Kathy and she seemed to be sleeping soundly. He looked around her bedroom again at her off-white dresser and armoire, her stuffed animals looking down at him from the shelves, the lace curtains covering the windows and the off-white four poster bed he had slept in the past two days. This was not his bedroom, he couldn't live in this bedroom and it all wouldn't fit in his apartment. They would have to get a bigger apartment, or buy a house. He wondered if they give house loans to convicted felons? He thought convicted felons don't get bedrooms with four poster beds and lace curtains, they get four walls and bars with no curtains. Felons convicted of the premeditated murder of a Congressman get a lethal injection. Russell did not feel well.

Kathy, still sleeping soundly for the first time all night, didn't stir as Russell got out of bed. He used the bathroom then found a pen and a pad of paper near the telephone.

> My Love,
>
> I have gone home to clean up and change clothes. I will be back as soon as I can. I love you very much.
>
> Rus

Russell thought for a moment about where he could put the note to make sure Kathy would see it. The refrigerator was out of the question, he was sure she would not be eating for a while. He found some Scotch tape and taped the note to the seat of the commode. If she doesn't puke on it, she will see it. Russell took a front door key off of Kathy's key chain and left, locking the door behind him.

* * * * * *

At seven o'clock in the morning FBI agent William Dupree knocked on the office door of the Palm Court Condominium and Resort Complex. There was no answer. He walked around the office and a large stucco building which had "A 1-10" neatly stenciled on the side. Behind the building was an Olympic size pool with a Jacuzzi on one end and a waterfall on the other. To the left of the pool was a large fenced-in area which contained three tennis courts. The entire area was beautifully landscaped with palm trees of all sizes growing throughout the grounds.

Following every foot path throughout the complex would be too time consuming, the FBI agent determined as he retraced his steps back to his rented Ford Taurus. It took fifteen minutes of following driveways to bungalows and making U-turns and trying the next driveway before Agent Dupree spotted the 1996 Lincoln Town Car parked in front of bungalow 3C. He checked the license plate and it matched perfectly to a Lincoln Town Car registered to The Great South Florida Land Development Company.

Dupree used his cellular phone to call Blind Luck Op Center in Phoenix, Arizona. It was 5:15 AM in Arizona and the voice that answered the phone sounded wide awake and alert. It had been a busy night in the operations center. Dupree explained he had found one of the vehicles they were looking for and was preparing to enter the condo. Everything looked normal, the mini-blinds were closed and a Do-Not-Disturb sign hung from the door knob. The Agent said he would call back in a few minutes and let them know what he found.

Dupree hung up the phone and stared at the front door. There was a very good chance that a long-time United States Senator, one of the most powerful men in the country, was inside. This Senator was either dead, or, very likely contributing to the delinquency of a minor. The agent walked to the front door, took several deep breaths, and, ignoring the sign hanging from the knob, knocked very hard.

* * * * * *

As Russell drove from Kathy's house in West University Place to his apartment near the Galleria, his mind drifted from Kathy to marriage to prison and back to Kathy. He pictured Kathy looking at him through the glass window, crying, as they prepared to stick the needle loaded with a lethal combination of drugs into his arm.

Beads of cold sweat began to break out on his forehead and the sinking feeling in the pit of his stomach he had had all morning worsened. The feeling that someone was sitting on his chest also worsened when he spotted the police car in his rear-view mirror. He gasped for breath as he tried to stop his hands from their violent shaking. He knew the shaking had to be making the car weave. The small convenience store was only a block away when he saw it. Russell turned on his right blinker and pulled into the parking lot. The police car kept going. Russell sat in the car trying to compose himself, his hands covered in sweat, his knuckles still white from the death grip they had on steering wheel.

His heart rate seemingly back to normal and the shaking subsided, Russell went into the Stop-and-Go and bought a cup of coffee, large, a breakfast burrito, and the morning Houston Chronicle. He threw the paper in the seat next to him and drove the remaining distance to his apartment without another shaking spell. He was glad to be back in his own apartment with the beat up sofa, shadeless lamp and dirty dishes. He turned on the shower, as hot as he dared, threw his clothes on top of the pile already in the bathroom, and stepped in the tub. He let the hot water run over his head and down his back, it was invigorating. He let the water wash the events out of his mind and down the drain.

Russell felt like a new person as he stepped from the shower and dried himself off. It was amazing how hot running water could cleanse the mind and freshen the soul. He shaved and actually hummed a few bars of a Lovin' Spoonful song, although he wasn't sure which one, he had heard them all many times last night. He grabbed the Styrofoam cup with what was left of the coffee from the Stop-and-Go, the newspaper and reclined on the sofa. The headlines made the beads of sweat reappear on his head and hands: REPRESENTATIVE JAMES FOUND CRUSHED.

* * * * * *

Gary Stephens woke up at 7:30 A.M. Later than usual even for a Sunday morning, but not that late considering he was at the office until way past midnight the night before. He still had plenty of time to make his 9:40 tee time at the country club. The club was only a five minute golf cart ride from his condo.

Gary loved golf. It became his passion once he became disenchanted with the pressured lifestyle of an investigative reporter. Gary bought the decent sized, two-bedroom condo, overlooking the 16th fairway of The Burning Desert Golf Club, before the real boom of desert golf courses hit. His condo had more than quadrupled in value since he bought it almost twenty years ago. He kept his golf cart in the other half of the two car garage along with his four or five sets of golf clubs. He knew he would be much better off spending five hundred dollars on golf lessons instead of a new titanium headed, graphite shafted, oversized driver, but it was much easier to go out and buy a new driver than take lessons.

Every Sunday at 9:40, weather permitting, Gary and his three partners played golf. In Phoenix, that meant that they played golf just about every Sunday. He could not, off the top of his head, remember the last Sunday he had not played golf. He tried to play as much as he could during the week, and some weeks he managed to play several times, some weeks he didn't get a chance at all, but on Sunday, they played, no matter what.

Gary was sitting on the balcony watching the early morning golfers. From where he sat, a good golfer should be hitting his second shot from a point directly across from him. Gary spent many afternoons sitting on his balcony watching the golfers hit their third, and sometimes their fourth shots.

At one time, a majority of the members of the club had been good golfers. Mostly before they retired and moved to Arizona. Some had been excellent golfers. Age had taken it's toll, and now, hardly one in four hit their second shot across from Gary Stephens' balcony.

Sipping his coffee, the editor looked over the morning newspaper that was waiting for him on his door step. He had read most of it the night before from his computer terminal. Gary could only shake his head as he read the bold print on the front page: Texas Representative Found Dead, Florida Senator Missing, Gunman Kills Children in Scotland, Women and Children Bombed in Bosnia. *What is the world coming to?*

As he glanced at the paper, something buried deep in his subconscious, many years ago, began pounding at the brain door wanting to be let out. Gary could feel it, way down in the billions of bytes of storage in his brain, there was something important that had to do with something that he would want to do something about. It was there, but he didn't have a clue what it was. He had read it, he was sure, if he only knew what "it" was. "It" would come to him. It might take a while as his brain began to search the database that consisted of everything the newspaperman had read over the past 30 or 40 years.

The feeling of *deja vu* passed and Gary shook it off. Whatever was hidden in the depths of his brain was still down there. He stared out across the golf course for a few minutes, still nothing. Whatever it was had reared it's ugly head and winked at Gary Stephens then disappeared. A glimpse was all it took, his intuition told him he needed to bring "it" back. He would bring it back, it would take time, but he would bring it back.

19

Agent Christian sat reading the Sunday Tribune. He was now positive the Blind Luck gang was involved in the death of Representative James. Twenty four hours ago he knew nothing about Jack James of Beaumont, Texas, and now he knew more than enough.

If information is needed on a public figure, ask the newspaper. Even if the newspaper is a thousand miles away from the person the information is needed on, it doesn't matter. Newspaper people have friends who have friends. Agent Christian doubted Gary Stephens or Tim Brooks knew anybody that worked for the Beaumont newspaper, but he bet that they knew people in Houston or Dallas, who would know someone who worked at the Beaumont newspaper. And someone at the Beaumont newspaper would know everything there was to know about Representative James.

There is always at least one employee of every newspaper in the country that doesn't like a particular public figure and keeps a file of every piece of dirt he can dig up on that person. If you need information about a public figure, all you have to do is find the person at that newspaper and the last page of section A.

Representative James had joined the army two years out of high school. Most of his enlistment was spent in South Carolina and Germany. A mix-up landed him in Viet Nam for seven days where he managed to parley ten minutes under enemy fire into a Silver Star, which he repeatedly presented to himself at public ceremonies.

After the Army he used the G.I. bill to get a recreation degree from Lamar University. James discovered the recreation curriculum by accident. Needing an elective, he took "Camping and Outdoor Education." He was one of four men in a class with thirty-five women. He knew immediately he had found his calling.

Upon graduation he landed a job as recreation director with Club Med. He loved the work and the fringe benefits were outstanding, but the pay left something to be desired. At Club Med, James met many public servants who, after several very strong rum drinks, disclosed the opportunities available in Washington. It became top priority for James to be sure the visiting Congressmen were given preferential treatment. He also made sure all their desires were fulfilled.

In less than a year, James had more friends on Capital Hill than most legislators. When he suggested that he would make a good Congressman, his friends were happy to support him. He won his first attempt at Congress by a landslide. The voters of East Texas were extremely impressed by the powerful contingent of current Senators and Representatives who supported the twenty-seven year old "beach bum," as those who opposed him referred to him. James hand picked a successor as recreation director at Club Med and moved to Washington.

In twenty years as a member of the House of Representatives, Representative James went from "beach bum" to multi-millionaire. He sold a large tract of land for a substantial profit after a federally funded bridge was conveniently located near it. Though never proven, many people believed the legislation allowing large oil companies and chemical plants to dispose toxic waste in east Texas netted James a good portion of his fortune. A fortune the newspaper estimated to be at fifteen to twenty million dollars, safely deposited in a Cayman bank account.

Most voters were aware of their Representative's exploits, the worst of which were bribery and questionable land deals, but also included alcoholism, acceptance and use of illegal campaign contributions, and over two hundred junkets to various Club Meds throughout the world. But James remained close with the influential Congressmen who helped him get elected. The city of Beaumont benefited from these ties and the voters knew it. James was never seriously contested in any reelection attempt.

Agent Christian was just finishing the newspaper article as Agent Berg entered the room.

"Alex," agent Berg said, "we may have a break."

Agent Alexander Christian put down his newspaper as he thought, *finally, a break.* "What do you have?" he asked.

"Orange County Sheriff found a guy who had been videotaping the rodeo. During the calf roping, there is a shot of the woman they believe left with James. It's a very quick shot and it's not very good, according to the deputy that saw it, but we've got an agent from Houston on his way to pick it up. They will digitalize it and send over the modem to us. Diana in computers is one of the best we have with graphics. She will look at it frame by frame and digitally enhance the best shots. With a little luck, we'll have a face in a few hours."

The agents were absolutely giddy about the prospects of having a face to put on the front page of every newspaper in America. They would have a name within 24 hours and the person in custody soon thereafter. The other dominoes would fall just as quickly, as soon as they got the first one.

The ringing telephone interrupted the minor celebration in the Op Center. Agent Christian picked it up. He listened intently for several minutes before thanking the caller and hanging up. The look on his face attracted everyone's attention while he was on the phone, now they were waiting to hear the information that had made the agent pale.

"That was agent Dupree in Florida. Senator Chuck Abernathy was found dead this morning at approximately zero seven thirty eastern time in Key West, Florida. He immediately notified the local authorities and sealed off the area. Reporters were the first to arrive on the scene, like in every other city, the reporters in Key West have police scanners. This was the first chance Dupree had to call us back, said it wouldn't have made much difference as Abernathy was beginning to smell. He'd been dead awhile. A single, small caliber bullet to the head. No sign of a struggle, the door was locked so whoever did it left with a key. Dupree had to wake the manager to open the door and then he almost had to arrest him before he would open it, kept wanting to see a search warrant. When Dupree explained that he had reasonable cause and that he was going to get in the building even if he had to kick it in, the manager still refused. It wasn't until he was handcuffed that he finally agreed to open it. Dupree is sure the manager knew whose condo it was and had been given strict orders not to go near it, especially when the do-not-disturb sign was out."

Every agent in the room came down to earth as quickly as they had gone up with the news of the video. Two murders within the past twenty four hours, twelve hours to be more precise, a total for four in the past three weeks and, other than a video tape, they were no closer than they were after the murder of Senator Carson. As much as anything, Agent Christian was mad at himself. He had hardly seen the light of day in over a week. He had worked relentlessly on bullshit, following every lead no matter how minor or insignificant. He was now nearly exhausted, just as some hard evidence was beginning to surface.

The first two murders, both by poison had left virtually no clues. Even though several eye witnesses saw the killer of Carson, none took enough notice to give a decent description. The murder of Abernathy was with a gun inside a condominium where the killer had to have been for a while.

Whenever a person is at a place for a while, clues will be left. No matter how careful they are, they inevitably leave clues. There would be fingerprints, hairs, strands of thread, possible foot prints in the carpet or outside in the dirt, and, in this case there's a bullet. If the weapon had ever been used in a prior homicide, ballistics would match it up.

The murder of James was the one everyone was excited about, they had a truck, eyewitnesses and a video. Just mentioning the video shot the adrenaline levels up dramatically around the Op Center.

Agent Christian picked up the phone and punched the numbers for the computer center.

The phone rang twice before it was answered. "Berg here."

"Harry, this is Alex, what's the ETA on the video?"

"Here or enhanced?"

"Both."

"Should be here in an hour and a half, two hours max, enhanced, another two to three hours. Total, five hours at the latest."

"Thanks, let me know as soon as you have something."

Alexander Christian hung up the phone and looked at his watch. "The pictures won't be ready for several hours, Dupree from Florida shouldn't have anything for several hours. I don't expect much more out of Texas till this afternoon at the earliest. I need one volunteer to stay and anybody that is not working on something hot, I suggest you take a few hours off. Go take a nap, take a walk, play golf, go make love to your wife or. . . , just get some air. This afternoon, we hit it with everything we've got. Any volunteers to stay?"

"I will," said Agent Bates.

"Great, thanks. Let's all plan to be back no later than thirteen hundred hours. I won't have my pager, anything that happens can wait four hours. See you at one."

* * * * * *

Occasionally Russell Lewis would bartend at banquets and private parties. The base pay wasn't that bad, anywhere from fifty to a hundred bucks a night, usually three or four hours of work, plus tips. He had a good memory so he was able to tell the drinker what he wanted when he came back for his second drink, and he always made them strong. At an open bar, the patrons liked to see the booze flowing freely. Pouring stiff drinks always led to big tips.

Russell bought a Sentry 1170 fire proof box years ago to keep important papers in. Birth certificate, passport, certificate of authenticity for his Mickey Mantle autographed baseball and the best pieces of his modest coin collection. For the past couple of years, Russell had been putting all his tip money in the fireproof box. Occasionally he would take a twenty from his wallet and put it in the box and take out ten or fifteen ones. On a rare occasion, usually some sort of an emergency, he would take money out of the box.

Russell dug out all the envelopes from the box that contained various sums of cash. He laid it out on the floor in separate piles of ones, fives, tens, twenties, fifties and one hundreds. He was surprised that he had as many hundreds as he did. He added all the stacks, two thousand seven hundred fifty five dollars. He put it all in one large manila envelope. He found his passport and two Krugerands he had been given as gifts, and put them in the envelope. He spread the metal clasp to secure the top and put the envelope on his bed.

The dark green sports bag he was looking for was under his bed. It was not too large where Kathy might think he was trying to move in, but it was big enough, if packed just right, for at least a weeks worth of clothes. A weeks worth of clothes in the south meant one pair of Docker slacks, neutral color, five polo shirts, mostly white, two button up shirts, at least one of Hawaiian nature, three T-shirts, four pairs of shorts and seven pairs of underwear. No socks and no extra shoes.

Russell put the envelope and his checkbook in the bottom of the bag and packed the clothes on top of it. Everything fit in the bag, snugly, but it all fit. A pair of blue jeans would have been nice, but they would take up too much room in the bag and it was too hot to wear them. Hopefully they wouldn't be missed. He wore a white Polo shirt with an American flag and America3 over the pocket, from the 1993 America's Cup race, and charcoal colored shorts. The only shoes he needed were his boat shoes.

Russell looked around the apartment, no animals to put out, no fish to feed, no coffee pot to turn off. He turned the shadeless lamp off and locked the door as he left. He had no idea what he was going to do or when he would be back, it could be as soon as this evening if Kathy told him to go home, it could be never. The rent was paid for two more weeks, he didn't have to worry about it until then.

The two hour nap he didn't mean to take on the couch made Russell feel a thousand percent better. He hadn't realized how tired he was until after he napped. The murder had taken more out of him than he thought it would, and being up most of the night with Kathy had completely exhausted him. Sleep depravation can do strange things to a person's mind, missing just one night of sleep can begin to have an effect. It had definitely affected Russell this morning.

Russell was worried about Kathy as he drove back to her house. She hadn't called so she probably hadn't gotten up, unless it was to vomit, in which case she would have found the note. There was really no reason that he could think of to be worried, but he couldn't stop thinking about her. She had a very rough night and it was his fault. He made a promise to himself that he would never give her a reason to get in that condition again.

For no reason, the brown paper bag on the floorboard caught Russell's attention. He could not think of what could be in it. As he drove he kept looking at the bag. Slowly it came to him as he pieced the events of the previous day together. Kathy ripping her clothes off and Eric giving her clothes from the bag to put on. It had totally slipped his mind, but it had to be the white romper. The blood stained white romper. Eric must have stuffed it back in the bag.

Russell debated on what to do with the bag. Kathy said she liked the outfit, but she did rip it when she took it off and it was stained with Representative James' blood. The debate didn't last long as Russell decided he must dispose of the bag and the romper, and he now wanted to do it quickly. Russell pulled behind a strip center where every store had their own dumpster. He thought for a moment about which one he should put the bag in and realized that he had become too paranoid. Any dumpster would be as good as any other. Nobody would be going through the garbage looking for little white rompers wadded up in brown paper bags. Russell decided on the dumpster behind the Chinese restaurant, it was the most disgusting, nobody would ever dig in it.

Kathy was still asleep when Russell returned. He looked in the bathroom and his note was badly stained. He pulled the note off the toilet seat and wondered if she saw it, he also wondered if she had even missed him. Russell laid the note on the counter top next to the sink. He found a large sponge and a bottle of pine cleaner. He scrubbed the toilet seat and the bowl area to removed the dried remains of Kathy's late night and early morning visits. It looked pretty decent and smelled considerably better when he finished.

Russell walked into the den and opened the curtains that covered the double glass sliding doors that led to the back yard. The sunlight brightened up the room instantly making the carnage from the prior evening much more noticeable. He found a large black trash bag and began filling it with pizza boxes, beer cans and wine bottles. Trying to remember how many people had come over, he was amazed at the number of beer cans, most of which Kathy had emptied.

When the house looked more like Kathy's place instead of a bachelor pad, Russell checked on Kathy again. He stood in the door looking at her. The color had returned to her face and she looked peaceful. He closed her door and went into the kitchen to look for something to eat. The microwaved burrito from Stop-and-Go had not stuck with him and he was beginning to get hungry. Russell was amazed at the small amount of food that was in the house. He began to wonder about his future wife's cooking ability. He was beginning to realize how little he actually knew about her.

The lunch decision was quickly made by the lack of food in the house. Russell grabbed his keys and left. He seriously considered going to a grocery story and actually buying food, completely stocking the refrigerator, but then he wasn't sure how Kathy would react. In Russell's mind they were now living together, he just didn't want to seem to obvious until she suggested it. Russell opted for a Burger King instead of the supermarket, where he ordered two Whoppers, large fries and onion rings. He stopped at a convenience store, the Pick and Get, and bought a bottle of orange juice, a six pack of Pepsi and a can of tomato juice.

Kathy was awake but still in bed when Russell opened the bedroom door.

"How ya doing?" he asked sympathetically.

"I feel like shit!" she said, trying to smile.

"I know the answer is going to be everything, but really, what hurts?"

"Everything," she managed a bit of a smile, "actually, compared to a few hours ago, I feel O.K., I guess. My stomach still feels real queasy and my head hurts a little, I think the aspirin you gave me helped. Thanks. I love you."

Russell was very happy to hear the words, after what she had been though, he would not have blamed her for never wanting to see him again. "I love you too," he said as he leaned to give her a quick kiss on the lips. "Do you think you can get up? A hot shower and some food will make you feel a lot better."

"I don't think I can eat."

"Come on, I'll help you to the shower."

Russell helped her out bed and to the bathroom. She leaned on Russell as he turned the water on and waited for it to get hot. He adjusted the temperature and she stepped in, still wearing panties. Russell watched her a few minutes, until he was sure she was stable and she wouldn't fall and hurt herself, then left.

It was fifteen minutes before Russell heard the water in the shower turn off. Several times he thought about checking on her but he didn't want to seem like the mother hen type. Kathy appeared with a towel wrapped around her body and one on her head. The towel around her body hung from her arm pits to just below her hips, not quite low enough to hide the fact that sometime during her shower, she removed her panties.

The food was on the kitchen table waiting. Kathy thanked him for cleaning and said she would try to eat after she got dressed. She walked to her bedroom and closed the door. Kathy was still moving very slowly so Russell assumed he had some time. He turned the television on and changed the channel to CNN. Sports was just ending, Greg Norman was the leader of the Greater Greensboro Open going into today's final round. Headline News was next after Joe Slick tries to sell you a Toyota Land Cruiser for sixty thousand dollars.

The CNN anchor person said they were going to Beaumont, Texas for a live update on the murder of Representative James, the latest victim in a plot to kill Congressmen that had now reached four. Russell heard the word four, but it didn't register.

"I'm here with Deputy Trent Lake of the Orange County Sheriff's Department. Deputy Lake, I understand you have some developments in the James killing."

"Yes, ma'am. Late last night it was discovered that a videotape had been shot of the rodeo. During the calf roping, we believe we caught the woman Representative James left the building with, on tape. We sent a copy of the tape to the FBI office in Houston this morning."

The camera zoomed in on the female reporter. "The investigation is being conducted by the FBI. We have not yet been told when, or if, they are going to release a copy of the videotape to the media. This is Sheila Burke, reporting live from Beaumont, Texas."

Russell turned the television off and sat in silence, too stunned to move. The FBI had a video of Kathy at the rodeo arena. Russell tried to think, but his brain had froze, his only thoughts were, NO, NO, NO, this cannot be happening. NO, NO, NO.

Kathy appeared from the bedroom wearing a long, loose fitting white sundress. Her hair was pulled back but still wet, she had put make up on. She looked stunning. "I'm ready to try and eat something," she said.

"Great," Russell said managing a smile, hoping he could eat and keep it down.

Russell was assuming that the live interview he just witnessed was the first mention of the videotape. Hopefully none of the other members of the group saw it. He had to tell Kathy, and he would, but he wanted to pick the best time. He did not want the phone to ring and have Julie or Gene tell her about it. They ate in relative silence, the phone didn't ring.

* * * * * *

The white golf cart offered little relief from the early afternoon desert sun. Gary Stephens took a drink of water and tried to guess the temperature. It seemed to be too hot for April. He looked at the dry desolate hills surrounding the lush green fairways. *It's going to be a hot summer, hotter than usual,* he thought to himself.

"That's the worst I've seen you play in a long time Gary, what's up?" Ed Emminger asked.

The comment startled Gary. He had been staring off into the distance and not heard his partner walk up.

"I guess my mind has not been really on the game. This morning I had a feeling of *deja vu*. I can't put my finger on it, but I know it has something to do with the letter I got yesterday from the Congressman killers."

"What letter?"

"I'm sorry, that slipped, no letter." Gary smiled at his golfing partner.

"I saw they got another one yesterday. I read the bio's you all printed, these guys were not saints. If I was a Congressman, and a sleazy one, which of course I wouldn't be, but if I was, I'd be scared shitless right about now."

"Ed, you're an insurance salesman for crying out loud, if you were a Senator, you probably would have been the first one they went after."

Both men laughed as they rode to the green where the two other members of their foursome were waiting.

"You're away," one of the others called to Gary Stephens.

Gary chipped from the fringe to within two feet of the cup and Ed kicked the white golf ball back, meaning that it was close enough, a gimme. Gary continued though the motions of the golf game with little improvement. He would make a good shot followed by a bad shot. He was not playing well, but he wasn't bothered by it. What bothered him was a little voice deep inside his brain that was trying to find its way out so it could tell him something. Something important.

* * * * * *

It took all afternoon and Russell still hadn't found the right time to tell Kathy about the video. He knew there really was no "right" time, he was just delaying the inevitable.

He would have to tell her. He didn't want to tell her during lunch. She needed to eat and telling her would have just made her ill again. She seemed in much better spirits after she had eaten, even smiling on occasion. Russell decided not to bring her down by telling her about the video.

They spent the evening laying on the couch watching videos on television. Russell had run to the video store and rented four movies, all comedies. He felt Kathy needed to laugh. The movies worked. Even Russell had gotten into the movie and had forgotten about the video of Kathy Beck. It was nice to see Kathy laughing and smiling again.

As the movie ended, Kathy rolled over to face Russell and said, "that was great. I really needed some escape. Thanks for going out and getting the movies, I didn't want to watch regular TV tonight. You know how they always do those news breaks. I was afraid I would see one about James."

Kathy put her hand behind Russell's head and kissed him. They held each other tight as their kiss became more passionate. "I really love you," Kathy said as she began kissing his neck.

Russell pushed Kathy back so he could look into her eyes. Kathy smiled as she looked back into his eyes. "O.K.," she said as she smiled.

"What?" Russell said with a confused look.

"I can tell by your eyes. You want to go make love but you aren't sure how I feel. You know I've been sick all day and you don't know if it's a good idea to suggest we have sex. Actually, I feel pretty good. I love you and I know you love me. You have asked me to marry you and I have said I would. We haven't set a date, but I got the impression it would be soon. So, O.K. Today has not been one of the best of my life, but making love to the man I love is not a chore for me. As a matter of fact, feeling you inside me makes me realize why they call it making love. It really is special."

Russell laid beside Kathy quietly listening to her. He couldn't bring himself to say a word.

"Am I rambling?" Kathy said after a moment of awkward silence. "What I am trying to tell you is that I enjoy making love with you. And I want to do it, a lot. They say a girl shouldn't tell a guy that, but I. . . Yesterday was wonderful."

Russell pulled Kathy's head to his shoulder and stroked her hair. "Kathy, I know what you are trying to say, as well as what you are trying not to say. You've heard that if the woman initiates sex, she's a slut. Well, personally, I kinda like the idea of having a slut for a wife."

Kathy screamed as she jerked back to see Russell smiling at her. Her lower lip began to quiver as she said, "I. . . I poured my heart out to you and you make a joke. I. . . "

Russell's heart pounded in his chest as he looked at Kathy. He swallowed hard and began to beg her forgiveness when she could no longer hold her frown and began laughing.

"Two can play this game." She laughed again. "I guess I showed you."

Russell put his hand over his heart as if to check if it was still beating. "You did indeed." He managed a smile.

"You know, I never realized how difficult it was to talk about sex. I think we should save the rest of this conversation till later. You wanna go make love?"

Smiling, Russell kissed Kathy on the lips and said, "I don't think so." His smile disappeared. His face looked cold and rigid.

"Russell, you're scaring me. Did I say something wrong? I've only been with one other guy. I. . . " Tears began to roll down her checks.

"Shrrr," Russell said as he pulled her close to him. "That's not it. Please, I love you. That's not it."

"What's wrong then?" Kathy pulled back far enough to look at Russell. She bit her lower lip as she cried.

"I've been trying to think of a way to tell you all afternoon."

"You want to call off the wedding?"

"No damn it. Please just let me finish. This isn't easy." Russell paused looking for the right words.

"Please Russell, just tell me. You're scaring me."

"Kathy, I was watching TV while you were in the shower. There was a news report from Beaumont. They said that someone was shooting a video inside the arena and they have a picture of the woman that James left with."

Kathy stared at Russell without speaking. Russell didn't know what else to say. He hadn't watched any more television so he had no way of knowing if the video had been shown or not. He had nothing more to add. He now felt he should have waited, found out more about the video, then told her. It was too late now.

"Did they show me on television?" Kathy's voice was weak and faint.

"I don't know, not while I was watching. All I saw was the one report. It was live, so I guess that was the first report. I don't know anything else."

Without saying a word, Kathy got up and went into the bathroom. She closed and locked the door. Russell followed her to the door and stood outside, listening. He couldn't hear a thing. He wondered if she was just going to the bathroom, if she was getting sick again, or, if she was considering something worse.

The few minutes he stood outside the locked bathroom door seemed like an eternity. He imagined the worse, that she was taking pills or slashing her wrists, and he became scared. Russell twisted and pushed the door knob. It wouldn't budge. He pounded on the door and yelled, "Kathy, please open the door." He kept pounding until the door opened.

"Damn it! You scared me. Are you O.K.?"

Kathy nodded. Her face was white. Russell tried to hug her but she pushed him away and walked to the kitchen. Expressionless, she picked up a glass and filled it with ice, then walked to the sink and filled the glass with water. Taking a small sip, she walked to the kitchen table and sat down. Russell sat down beside her.

Kathy stared at the glass, making a design in the condensation which had already formed. Showing no emotion, she looked at Russell and said, "I'm going to turn myself in."

* * * * * *

"First I'll run the video at full motion, then I'll run it again and explain why we have named the woman 'the luckiest bitch on earth'." Agent Bates was sitting at a computer in the operations center. Agent Christian was sitting next to him, as many agents that could squeeze in were behind them, vying for a look at the screen.

Agent Bates clicked the icon for the media player, loaded the file and pressed play. In a few seconds the agents watched a cowboy rope a calf, jump off his horse and tie up the animal. Bates pointed to the small figure of a person dressed in white in the background.

"Now I'll replay it in slow motion." He restarted the file and ran it to a point where the cowboy was throwing the rope and pressed pause. "Right here you can see her," Bates pointed to Kathy Beck sitting on the front row of the bleachers. "As you can see her head is down and we can't see her face because of the hat she's wearing. As I move on a few frames, you can see her head start to lift as she watches the calf being roped. Just as her head comes up enough to see her face, she raises her hand to her mouth. It's a split second after the calf gets jerked back by the neck, I imagine she didn't like that."

Agent Christian interrupted, "she is about to kill, or at least lead a human being to his death, and she hides her face when she sees a cow get clotheslined. Go figure. Why did you call her 'a lucky bitch'?"

"Just watch." Bates continued the video. "She's looking up but has her hand in front of her face. Here she starts to bring her hand down. At the exact same time, the cowboy finishes tying the calf's feet and raises his hands, that's a signal that he is finished and they stop the timer. Notice as her hand comes down, his hand comes up and covers her face. As his hand comes down, she looks down again, covering her face with the hat."

"Damn, she is lucky," someone in the back of the room said.

"There's more." Bates kept clicking the mouse moving the video one frame at a time. "She gets up to leave and looks back across the arena, almost directly at the camera. . . right. . . here," he froze the frame.

"What the hell is that?" Christian shouted.

"A fence post. She looks right at the camera as she walks in front of a fence post. The arena is surrounded by a chain link fence, posts every ten feet. By the time she clears the post, she is looking up toward the bleachers and all we get is the back of her head until she's out of the video. That's why we called her lucky. If she's the one who led James to his death, we assume she's a bitch."

The Blind Luck operations center filled with disappointment. The agents that had been standing went back to the tasks they were performing before Bates entered the room.

"Diana took the best frames and digitally enhanced them. Just a second, I'll show you what we have." Bates slid and clicked the mouse as he started a new viewing program and loaded the enhanced files. Agent Christian waited and watched, it was hard for him to show any enthusiasm.

Agent Bates explained the enhancement process as he loaded the photo files. "This is the first one, it's just as she was raising her head to look at the calf roping. The bill of the hat covers the top half of her face, but you see her mouth and chin clearly.

"Wow," said Christian, "that's incredible, that is very clear considering." Those that heard the comments were coming back to watch again. "But it's not a lot to go on."

"This next frame she has her hand over her mouth. We enhanced it hoping we could see the upper part of her face, but the hat shaded the overhead lights and we got nothing but black. Every other frame was pretty much the same, something either covers her face or the hat shades it. The next frame is when she gets up." Bates clicked the mouse and the image appears on the screen.

"Wow, no wonder James left with her," an agent said.

"No wonder none of those cowboys could remember her face, she is fine," said a different agent, emphasizing the word "fine."

Agent Christian felt compelled to remind his agents that the were talking about a murder suspect, but as he watched each computer enhanced frame of Kathy walk, he had to agree with the other agents, the woman they were looking for was exceptionally well built.

"How true is the color in this picture?" Christian asked Bates as they looked at a profile of Kathy at the widest part of a step.

"The lights in that arena were very bright and it looks like the tape was shot with a high quality camcorder, I would guess the colors are fairly accurate." Agent Bates answered.

"At least we know our girl is from the south. She spends a lot of time wearing shorts in the sun. Not necessarily sunbathing, just out in the sun. Look at anybody from the north that wears long pants most of the year, their legs are usually as white as a piece of paper. Look at her legs, they aren't a deep tan that you get from sunbathing, but a natural tan than comes from years of normal everyday walking around in the sun wearing shorts. This girl is from the south and I would be willing to bet Houston."

One of the agents from the back of the room spoke up, "I've been to Houston, and I have to admit that I can't recall seeing more attractive women in one town than in Houston, not even Los Angeles, it must be something in the water. However, Houston is full of topless bars, most of which have several girls that look like that. It wouldn't surprise me that this girl was recruited to lure Mr. James out of the rodeo and is not involved with the other killings."

Agent Christian thought for a second. "I disagree, not about Houston, but about the girl. I think she was involved all the time, otherwise, I think we probably would have found her body by now. I don't think our gang would let her watch them kill a U.S. Representative and live to tell about it."

"That makes sense," another agent agreed.

20

Gene, Julie, Annie, Eric and Todd met at Pappasito's Mexican Cantina for dinner Monday night. It was Todd who made the arrangements, he thought they should talk about the future of their group. Russell had told him that he and Kathy wanted out, were out, and wanted no part of any future plans. They were all still friends, of course, but they would not attend any planning sessions or post murder congratulatory celebrations.

Nobody at the table could blame Russell or Kathy, especially Kathy. They all had watched CNN sometime during the day Sunday, and they all saw the replay of Deputy Lake telling about the videotape of Kathy.

"You all heard the news, somebody killed Senator Abernathy and we got credit for it. Today the Senate voted down a bill that would have limited the liability of tobacco firms in smoking lawsuits," Todd said.

Gene took over the conversation. "That bill was all set to pass, it was a sure bet, several major tobacco companies had paid, or donated, millions of thousands of dollars to make sure it passed. Do you remember back in the eighties when Charles Keating gave five Senators over a million dollars to intervene with federal regulators on his behalf when his Savings and Loan was in trouble? Well, I imagine that million pales in comparison to the money that was paid by the tobacco industry.

"The Senate gave some bullshit reasons why they changed their minds, said the recent killings had absolutely no bearing on the decision. Yeah, if you believe that. They changed their minds because they are scared to death. We've got'em on the run."

Pappasito's chain of restaurants in Houston are among the most popular. They are always crowded and they are always loud. You can sit in the middle of Pappasito's, drink margaritas and talk about killing people. No one would hear.

"I agree," said Todd, "I think we should sit tight and watch.

They are scared and they are trying to do what is right, on one bill anyway. So we should think about who we could get to next, if we need to, and wait. If they pass another wasteful spending bill or raise taxes, we try to kill whoever we think we can, and get away with it."

"That's assuming they don't bust Kathy and the rest of us before the weekend," Julie said.

It was not a subject anyone at the table wanted to bring up.

Gene leaned in toward the group. "Before Todd did his first deed, we all knew the risks. We all talked about it, I know we thought it was just talk, nothing would happen, but as we got closer, any of us could have said 'bad idea, we shouldn't do it' and we wouldn't have. But we did it, and I for one am glad. I could not believe what I saw on C-span today. Those guys were friendly, working together, talking about putting politics aside, talking bipartisan, and actually meaning what they said. Yes, we have committed crimes of dramatic proportion, but today, at this moment, the United States of America is better because of it." Gene paused while his four friends quietly applauded.

He smiled, nodded and continued, "I am going to tell Russell and Kathy the same thing, they did something that will make the world a better place. Killing a person is serious and some people can't, or won't, understand that sometimes it is necessary. Adolf Hitler, Saddam Hussein, and Benito Mussolini, just to name a few. They all gradually came to power, got more powerful, and wouldn't stop until they were dead. Just watch, Hussein is going to keep pushing until he is dead. They should have killed him during the Gulf War. They are going to wish they had. Look how long Castro has been in Cuba. They should have killed him in the sixties. Can you imagine how different the world would be today if someone had killed these men as soon as they realized what kind of people the really were."

Gene took a sip of wine and said, "I'm sorry, I started rambling a bit." He paused to regain his train of thought. "You know I was against this when we started, but the men we, Todd, Russell, Eric and Kathy killed, although I wouldn't compare any Congressmen with Hitler, but Carson, Williams and James, and Abernathy for that matter, would have destroyed this country had our constitution not limited their power. We have done a great thing." Gene raised his glass and toasted with his friends sitting around the table. They all took a drink. "To Todd, Russell, Kathy and Eric, may no one ever know what you did." Their glasses were raised again.

* * * * * *

Kathy had only gotten out of bed to use the bathroom. When she finished, she would walk slowly back to her bed, lay down and pull the sheet up to her neck. Russell tried bringing her food, but she refused to eat. He finally got her to drink a glass of orange juice. She spent the day staring at a wall until she fell asleep.

Russell spent the day channel surfing, looking for any information on the video of the woman who left the rodeo arena with James. Most of the reports mentioned the video, but none showed it.

Russell had convinced Kathy that they should wait and look at the video before she turned herself in. He tried to tell her that there was a chance no one would recognize her, but she was sure the FBI had a perfectly clear video of her with Representative James.

Becoming irritable himself, Russell decided to try a different approach to knock Kathy out of her depression. He had tried sweet and understanding, and she only seemed to be becoming more depressed.

Russell looked into the bedroom at Kathy. She was awake, staring at the wall. She noticed him looking in at her, but did not acknowledge his presence. Russell stepped back from the door, took off his clothes, walked back in to her bed, yanked the sheet off and jumped on top of her.

Kathy yelled "No," as she put her hands up to stop the naked man from falling on her. Russell wiggled his body against hers as he kissed and bit her on the neck.

"What are you doing?" Kathy asked, almost smiling.

"I decided if my wife was going to go to jail, I was gonna get a little before she went."

Russell pulled Kathy's loose white dress up above her waist and forced his knees between her legs. She spread her legs to give him room as she looked at him and smiled.

"That's better. You look much better when you smile."

"Russell, darling, I am so scared I can't get out of bed. It has given me a lot of time to think about it though, and you were right. I might as well wait and let them find me. I doubt if they will go any easier on me if I turn myself in."

"I won't let them find you. I haven't seen that tape yet, but they are bound to show it soon. If we think you can be recognized pretty easily, like by someone that doesn't know you, but happens to see you on the street, we'll take off. We'll go to Mexico or South

America or somewhere. We may not be free, but we'll be together."

"You promise. You won't leave me?"

"I will never leave you."

They held each other and made love all night. Each, silently thinking that they could be arrested at any moment. Both felt it might be the last time they made love, with each other, for a very long time.

* * * * * *

"I can't believe it," Agent Christian said to begin the night briefing being held in the makeshift conference room away from the distractions of the operations center. "The videotape was a disappointment. We are now sure that an attractive woman lured Jack James from the rodeo arena. We already knew that from the descriptions the cowboys gave us. It is good evidence, however, if, when we catch these people, we can match up the chin and mouth and make a 99 percent positive ID. The things they can do with computer graphics are amazing. What's the latest on Senator Abernathy?"

Agent Robbins stood up to address the room. "Senator Abernathy was killed by a single, small caliber gunshot wound to the head. The bullet entered through his left eye, it did not exit his head." Even the most experienced agents in the room felt the hair on the back of their necks rise as they pictured the Senator looking at a bullet coming straight for his eye. The thought was especially distressing to the lone female agent at the briefing. She had seen and heard as much as any man in the room, but she had a phobia about eyes. Anything to do with the eyes made her skin crawl. Her stomach would begin turning and her body would start trembling. Luckily, Agent Robbins did not dwell on the subject, and Ms. Anderson was soon back to normal. She took several deep breaths to send as much oxygen as possible to her brain and tried to focus on what the agent was saying. She hoped he would not bring up the gunshot again.

Agent Robbins continued his report, "the Senator was on the bed, completely nude except for his socks, I guess he must have been in a hurry. His pants were in a pile at the foot of the bed, almost as though he stepped out of them and on to the bed. His shirt was not far away, but the buttons had been ripped off. Either he was in a big hurry, or someone did it for him. We found several black hairs on his body and on the bed around him. They have been sent to the lab for analysis. A single .22 long-rifle shell casing was found in the corner, obviously from the murder weapon, which was probably a small semi-automatic hand gun. The killer either did not look for the casing or did not care if we found it. There were no finger prints found on the casing. There were very few prints at all found in the bedroom, but quite a few in the kitchen area. My first guess was the area was wiped clean after the Senator was shot. But then I thought about the casing being left behind, not very professional. So I think the Senator and the killer came in together, went straight to the bedroom, ripped his clothes off and hopped into bed. She may have ripped his clothes off, leaving her own on, thus concealing the weapon, then shot him. If they arrived together, someone had to pick her up when she left, the Senator's car was out front. Which, by the way, only contained the Senator's finger prints, no other sets were found. Nobody we talked to saw any other cars, or the Senator's for that matter, around the condo. 3C is on the far end of the complex, as far away from the other units as you can get. It was a perfect little hideaway for Senator Abernathy."

"So, what you are telling us," Agent Christian recapped, "is that once again, we have virtually nothing to go on."

"We do have the hairs, which, by the way, are long and black, same as our Lucky Bitch."

Christian hated the name they had given Kathy Beck, but it did fit and the other agents, even Ms. Anderson, seemed to like it. "We know she was in Winnie, Texas Saturday afternoon around four o'clock. Do we have a time on the Senator's death?"

"The coroner's initial estimate was sometime late Friday or early Saturday morning," Agent Robbins said.

"I think it would be very difficult for our girl to kill Senator Abernathy, even if she did it very early on Friday afternoon, in Key West, Florida and be in Winnie, Texas on Saturday afternoon. Check all flights from Key West and Miami to Houston. See if anyone was booked from Key West to Houston. Find out if Beaumont has an airport with flights to Miami or Key West? Check the flight logs of every private airport within a hundred miles of Winnie, Texas for flights to south Florida. Until we know who we are dealing with, we have to assume they are capable of anything.

"Will do. We are also still looking for the helicopter pilot that picked up Abernathy at the airport. He has disappeared. If he wasn't involved, I would think that he would come forward and answer our questions."

"He may be in the Caymans by now. The death of Chuck Abernathy may have closed the South Florida Development Company. Anything else?"

"Yes, there is," Agent Robbins said as he picked a stack of papers from the desk and passed them out. "This letter was found in Senator Abernathy's brief case. The case was closed and locked. There are two locks, one on each side, both combinations. Neither of the locks look like they had been tampered with. But that doesn't mean the case wasn't open, the letter put in and the case closed and locked. Abernathy's finger prints were the only prints on the case and they were on the snaps. They had an expert in Miami look at the original and he verified the signature. I personally don't think the killer knew about the letter and it's just a coincidence."

"It's ironic isn't it, that if the Blind Luck gang killed Senator Abernathy, they did it only days before his resignation from the Senate," Agent Christian said.

The room was quiet as the agents read the letter signed by Senator Abernathy:

> For personal, as well as health reasons, effective immediately, I am resigning my position representing Florida in the United States Senate. It is my opinion, the Senate should appoint my aide, and soon to be Harvard Law school graduate, Lisa Thompson as my interim replacement. Pending a special election for a permanent replacement. At this time I am also extending my fullest support for Ms. Thompson in the special election.
>
> Charles D. Abernathy
> United States Senate

Agent Robbins broke the silence. "Lisa Thompson was in Florida last weekend at her home in Winter Haven. She flew back to Boston on Sunday morning, she still has a few weeks of law school left. She heard about Abernathy's death yesterday, and, seemed to take the news pretty hard. Two agents talked just briefly with her this morning. They didn't ask about the letter, but they hinted at it. They don't think she knew about it, however, she was very reluctant to tell of her whereabouts Friday night. She landed in Tampa on Thursday morning, her brother picked her up and took her to her parents home in Winter Haven. She said she left Thursday and came back Saturday afternoon. She volunteered that information quite easily, but when asked where she was, she said she would rather not say. Key West is a long drive from Tampa, but easily done in the three days she would have had. The agents pushed her, threatened to take her into custody if she didn't answer the questions. She finally said she was staying with a friend, an old boy friend, not far from Winter Haven. Agents are on their way now to check him out."

"What color hair does she have?" Christian asked.

"Blond, long blond."

* * * * * *

It didn't take Russell long to become stir crazy. By Tuesday afternoon, he had grown tired of fast food hamburgers. He wanted to go out and get a large steak, medium rare with sautéed mushrooms and cold beer. Kathy would not leave the house. She was sure every policeman in the United States, and most foreign countries, had a picture of her. She kept the doors closed and locked and the curtains drawn.

"Kathy, if they had a picture of you, it would be on every news channel and in every newspaper. They would not rely on spotting you driving down the street. We haven't heard any more about the video and they haven't shown it on TV. I don't think they really have one. I'm sure it's safe to go out, let's go to a small quiet steak house and have dinner. We will come straight back, I promise."

Kathy was tired of staying inside, but her fear of going to jail and being in a cell for years made sitting inside her house for a few days much easier. "OK, Steak and Ale for dinner, then right back home."

"I promise." Russell liked the way she said "home," as if it was "their home."

Kathy put on a sun dress and Russell changed to his one pair of long pants. Almost every restaurant in Houston allows short pants, especially in the summer, but Russell wanted to make the evening seem special, so he opted for the long pants. No socks.

As they drove, Russell could tell Kathy was glad to be out of the house. She was apprehensive at first, but she soon relaxed. Russell wanted to talk about what they would do if, by chance, they got caught. He wasn't necessarily thinking about getting caught, but what they should do, or say, if they were someday unexpectedly arrested. He felt this was not a good time to bring it up, maybe over desert.

By the time they arrived at Steak and Ale, Kathy was like a new person. She was beginning to smile again, with consistency, for the first time in several days. The two ate like they hadn't eaten in weeks. Russell had a beer while Kathy had water, she was still not ready for beer, that would take awhile. They talked about their future, when and how and where they would get married. Kathy said maybe in a few weeks they would fly to Vegas and get married. She wasn't ready to go that public too soon. Russell said he understood. They decided they would both call their parents when they got home and give them the news.

Kathy suggested to Russell that he give up his apartment and move in to her house. He wanted to say "yes" so fast, but he said he thought he should keep his apartment, but still live with her. That way, if her parents asked, he still had his apartment. She wouldn't be lying to them. Kathy agreed. She wasn't sure how her parents would react to them living together in their home. After they were married, it would be OK, but not before. Russell said after they were married, he would really like to find a place that was "theirs." Again, Kathy agreed, saying that it would be nice to have a place of their own.

Russell had another beer while they ate. The waiter removed their plates and brought the dessert tray. Kathy picked out a chocolate cheesecake, Russell didn't want anything. In a few minutes, the waiter returned with the dessert and two spoons. Russell took a taste but mostly watched Kathy eat.

Russell looked around the dining room. Steak and Ale is broken into several small rooms throughout the restaurant. Russell and Kathy were in a room by themselves.

"We really need to talk about something, Kathy," Russell finally got up the nerve to say.

"Yes?"

"I don't, or I didn't want to bring it up, but I think we should talk about it."

"O.K., what is it?" Kathy had an idea, and she didn't want to drag it out any longer than necessary.

"What to do in case we get arrested."

Kathy didn't look at Russell, she looked at the cheesecake and picked small pieces off to eat.

Russell put his hand on Kathy's free hand and said, "if by some chance we get arrested, either one of us, or both of us, it is very important that we say absolutely nothing."

Kathy looked up at Russell. "But why?"

Russell ignored the question and continued with his train of thought. "There is no way of knowing what they know. If they arrest us, then we have to assume that they at least have a clue, it may only be the video." Russell didn't want to bring up the video, but found no way around it. "They certainly aren't going to pick us up for no reason and question us about the murder of some Congressmen. If they think one of us did it, they may try to make the other confess by saying that the other already confessed. Remember, that will be a lie. I will never say you were involved in any way, no matter what. I will never tell them anything. And you have to promise to do the same thing, don't tell them a thing."

"Of course, I promise, I would never tell them you killed James."

"Or that I was even involved?"

"Or that you were even involved."

"Good, that is important. If they came to me and said you told them the whole story, how I did it and everything, and I thought you really told them, I might crack and confess. But if I know they are lying, trying to trick me, I can hold out."

"But how long can we not say anything? Sooner or later they will figure out how to make us talk."

"They can't question you without an attorney. I guess we hold out until we talk to an attorney, privately, and he tells us the best thing to do. He can talk to us both, if they won't let us talk to each other, and he'll tell us what to do. I really don't see how they can pin this on us. I personally don't think we will ever get caught."

"Famous last words." She said and managed to smile.

* * * * * *

Gary Stephens looked at the clock on the night stand next to his bed. It was 2:15 in the morning. The dream had been so vivid he thought it had really happened. All the Senators and Representatives were lined up single file and someone was shooting them. After each shot the shooter would ask if they were going to clean up their act, cut spending and lower taxes. The Congressmen would say "no," and another shot would ring out. Another body would fall into a bottomless pit.

Gary went into the bathroom and urinated. He washed his hands then splashed water onto his face. He looked in the mirror. "What is it, what in the hell am I missing? What is it I can't remember?" he said out loud to no one.

"Line them up and shoot them, line them up and shoot them." Gary was talking to himself in the mirror. "That must have something to do with it. Line them up and shoot them. I've heard that before." *But where?* he thought to himself.

Gary walked in to the den and turned on the light. He picked up a legal pad and sat in his favorite recliner. On the top of the legal pad, he wrote in all caps LINE THEM UP AND SHOOT THEM! He stared at the legal pad trying to remember where he had seen those words. It wasn't from the letters from the Blind Luck gang, they said they would kill, not shoot. He could not remember where he read the words, or why? Why were they going to line them up and shoot them? Did they want wasteful spending stopped and taxes lowered as do these terrorists, or maybe it was to stop the Vietnam war, or maybe it was to stop abortions. Whenever a group wants another group to stop killing, they threaten to kill them. It makes absolutely no sense. Gary still could not comprehend "pro-life" groups killing abortion clinic doctors.

Gary fell asleep in the recliner convinced he had read the words written on the legal pad somewhere before this current mess started. Having been in the newspaper business almost forty years, he had read a lot of words.

* * * * * *

The plain black Chevrolet pulled on to the shell driveway and stopped in front of the trailer. The FBI agent checked the odometer and calculated the distance from Lisa Thompson's home to Bubba's trailer. Larry Thompson had given the agents the oil change receipt showing the oil had been changed in his sister's car the day before she arrived. The mileage was written on the receipt. The agents had subtracted the mileage currently on Lisa's Toyota from the mileage on the receipt.

"Exactly double, almost to the tenth," the agent said as he checked the mileage.

"Maybe she rented a car from here and drove to Key West." Both men looked at Bubba's inventory of heaps for rent and laughed at the thought of one of them making the trip to the end of Florida.

Bubba was washing his Ford Ranger as the two men approached him. By the time he shut off the water, they were beside him holding badges in front of his face.

"I am Mickey Childress and this is John Atkins," the older of the two said. "We're with the Federal Bureau of Investigation. We'd like to ask you a few questions."

"Sure," Bubba said, trying desperately to think of anything he may have done wrong.

"Do you know a woman named Lisa Thompson?" the older man was still asking the questions.

Tears welled up in Bubba's eyes. He didn't want to blink as he knew it would send the tears rolling down his cheeks. It wouldn't be the first time he cried since Lisa left.

"Uh, no, why?" he managed to say, totally unconvincingly.

The two agents looked at each other. It was hard to keep from laughing.

"Are you absolutely sure?" It was the younger agent's turn.

Bubba stared at the ground. He couldn't say anything.

The young agent continued, "can we go inside? It's very important that you tell us the truth."

Bubba nodded and pointed toward the front door of the trailer. The agents motioned for Bubba to lead the way. "No wonder she was reluctant to tell us who she was with. You think she slept with this hick?" The older agent whispered to the young agent. Inside the trailer the younger agent, Atkins, asked the questions. "Bubba, this is very important, was Lisa with you recently?"

Bubba was nowhere near as stupid as he let people think he was. He liked it that way. He thought for a minute while bobbing his head back and forth. Bobbing really makes a person look stupid. Bubba thought about the two FBI agents, a dead U.S. Senator in Key West, and Lisa renting a truck and putting the exact miles on it as it would take to get to Key West and back. Bubba did not believe that Lisa killed Abernathy, but if she did drive to Key West, it would not look good for her. He decided to tell the agents that she had spent the weekend with him. If she had told them she had only spent the day with him, he would say he was just trying to brag, because, they were right, she was only here Saturday. On the other hand, if Lisa had told them she was with him the whole time, and he covered for her, she may come back. It was worth the risk.

"Bubba?"

"Yea, she was here. She left Saturday afternoon while I was asleep."

"Had she been asleep too?"

"Yes."

"With you?"

"That's kind a personal."

"It's very important."

"Yes, we were sleeping together. She must have woken up, got dressed and left without me hearing her."

"Do you expect us to believe you were sleeping with a woman who was chosen by Senator Abernathy as his successor to the United States Senate?"

The surprised and confused look on Bubba's face assured the agents that he didn't know about Abernathy's letter endorsing Lisa. If she was aware of the Senator's letter of resignation and request that she take his place, she didn't tell her boyfriend.

"You didn't know Abernathy was planning on resigning and had named Lisa Thompson as the person he thought should replace him?" The letter was not public knowledge, yet. There would be no way Bubba could have known about it. Bubba could only shake his head.

"So how long was she here?"

Up until this point Bubba had told the absolute truth. He could pass any polygraph. "She got here a little after noon on Thursday." Again, the truth.

"And she was with you until Saturday?"

"Mostly, yeah," just stretching the truth.

"And have you talked to her since?"

"No." The tears built up in Bubba's eyes again.

"Have you known her long?"

"No."

"I've seen pictures of Lisa. You are telling us she flew down here spend a few days with you and then left? I'm finding that a little hard to swallow." Agent Childress knew he was being hard on Bubba. Actually, he believed the story. It was his job to push.

"She loved me," Bubba said, "and I love her. And she said we could never see each other again."

"Why did she say that?" The agents knew why. Bubba knew why. The question the agents really wanted to ask was why she ever wanted to see him in the first place.

Bubba had dug a deep hole. He knew it. His brain was working double overtime trying to come up with an answer for questions like, "where'd you meet, how long have you known each other? Did she say could never see you again because she had just off'd a U.S. Senator and she was planning to take his job and you would cramp her style in Washington?

"I asked her to marry me and move in here and help me run my business. She said 'no'." Bubba figured if Lisa's goal was to be a U.S. Senator, she probably would not want to live in a trailer with him. Bubba let the tears loose.

The two agents were almost in tears themselves. Neither could figure out why, but evidently Lisa and Bubba had been in love. The two agents left. Lisa Thompson was no longer a suspect in the death of Senator Abernathy.

21

Wednesday, April 17th was a beautiful day in Washington D.C. Funerals are synonymous with dreary, gray, overcast days, but this day was gorgeous. "A great day to be alive," someone said before they realized what they were saying.

Lisa Thompson stood crying next to Mrs. Charles Abernathy. The tears were real, they were not for Mr. Abernathy, but for his wife. Lisa sincerely felt bad for what she did. She had no idea if Senator Abernathy's wife was aware of his activities, surely she must have been. How could someone be married to a man like that for so long and not know what he was doing?

The flags around Washington had been flying at half staff since the death of Senator Carson. They would continue to fly at half staff until May 14th, thirty days after the documented date of the death of Senator Abernathy. Everyone attending the funeral, mostly Congressmen and their spouses, hoped the flags would be raised on schedule, that they would not remain at half staff to honor yet another victim.

As had been with Carson and Williams, Abernathy enjoyed a very nice send off. The division of the government that was in charge of state funerals had received more practice than they wanted. Representative James was buried in a private ceremony in Texas.

A procession to Arlington Cemetery was followed by a short grave side service. The United States flag which had draped the coffin was folded by an honor guard made up of members of each branch of the armed services. No matter how bad a person is in life, they always have nice funerals. It was the same for Senator Abernathy. "He was a good man." "He will be missed." The mourners said as they passed in front of the coffin and said their respects to the family and Lisa Thompson. She was considered family. His only aide that was.

As the crowd thinned out, Lisa was thinking about getting a cab back to her Washington apartment. She was tired, the funeral had saddened her. She felt sorry for Mrs. Abernathy. Fortunately, they had no children. Lisa also felt for the older Congressmen. She knew some of them and they were good men. They were scared. They had just attended the third funeral for a colleague and every one was worried that he might be next. Sure, Carson, Williams, James and Abernathy were no saints, but they shouldn't have been killed. What happens if they run out of "bad" Congressmen? Will they start killing just to be killing? Most Congressmen at the funeral said their good-byes and went straight home and locked their doors. Body-guards in tow.

"Excuse me, Miss Thompson, I know this is not the time or the place, but we would like to speak with you for a few minutes, would you mind?"

Lisa looked at the three men who had approached her. All three were wearing dark suits, one had an ear piece in his ear. She recognized one man as the lone remaining Senator from Florida. One of the other two was doing the talking. "I am Scott Harrison and this is Leonard Chives, we're with the FBI, and Senator Mayes tells us you two know each other."

"Yes, hello Senator."

"Hello Lisa, I'm very sorry, I know you and Chuck were close."

Lisa nodded but did not say anything.

Agent Harrison continued, "if you don't mind, we need to ask you a few questions. Again, I know this is a bad time, if you would rather wait until this afternoon, we will, but this is very important."

"It's O.K. I was just going to go home. Did you want to go somewhere?"

"Do you have a car?" the Senator asked.

"No, I was going to catch a cab."

"Why don't you come with us, it won't take long and we will drop you."

Lisa agreed, and the four got in the rear of a black limousine. Lisa looked around at the inside of the limo.

"It's for the funeral, they put me in one because I'm from Florida," Mayes said as though defending the cost of the limousine. In recent weeks the members of Congress had become very careful about how and why they spent government money.

Agent Harrison opened his brief case and removed the letter written by Senator Abernathy and handed it to Lisa.

"Are you aware of this letter?"

Lisa read the letter. Tears began to flow from her eyes and down her cheeks. Mayes handed her a tissue and she wiped her eyes as she read the letter. Of course she was aware of it, she had typed it, on Chuck Abernathy's computer. She printed it out and left it on his desk for him to sign. She had completely forgotten about it. She only wrote it to make Abernathy think she really thought he would resign and appoint her his successor, even though she knew it would never happen. Obviously, the Senator had signed the letter just in case she asked about it. He could always tear it up after they had their sex filled weekend. Too bad he never got the chance.

"Where did you get this?" she asked, her bottom lip quivering.

"We found it in his briefcase in Key West. We believe that is his signature."

Lisa looked at the signature and nodded.

"Lisa, I need to know," said Mayes, "if the Senate appoints you interim Senator, are you going to accept? Will you run for the seat in the special election?"

"Mr. Mayes," she said, her voice stabilizing, "I would like to. You know I have worked for Mr. Abernathy for almost seven years with the intention of becoming politically active. However, I can't."

The three men in the car seemed stunned. They each thought she would jump on the opportunity in a minute.

"I am only twenty-six years old. The constitution requires all Senators to be at least thirty." She looked at Senator Mayes, "unless you think they would make a special exception for me." Lisa smiled for the first time, the three men seemed to relax.

"Before his death, the Senator and I talked about me running for the House. I will probably do that, and maybe in four years run for the Senate. I really haven't given it much thought. All I really want to do is pass the Florida Bar this summer. Look what happened to John Kennedy Jr. when he didn't pass the bar on his first try, everybody in the world knew about it. Whoever you're running against will make sure everybody knows about it." She was beginning to ramble and she knew it. What she really wanted to do was go back to Boston and disappear for a few weeks until the death of Senator Abernathy was old news.

"Because it was almost like a last request, we will have to make the letter public. If you run in November for the House, I imagine you will be a shoo-in. If you don't screw up, you will probably win the Senate in four years, that's when Chuck's term would have been up." Senator Mayes was very glad he was not up for re-election in four years. Here was a very intelligent, very attractive, Harvard law graduate that had been hand picked by one of the most popular Senators in the history of Florida to succeed him. She would beat just about anybody she comes up against. Senator Mayes was going to stay on her good side.

"Thank you Ms. Thompson, I know this was hard," Agent Cheeves said. "I would also like to mention that our agents talked to your friend Bubba. He confirmed your story. I can see why you were reluctant to tell us who you were with."

Lisa began to cry again. This time it was for Bubba, she really had fallen in love with him.

* * * * * *

Two days of relentless investigative work had turned up nothing. The mood in the Blind Luck Operations Center was at the lowest level since the investigation began. Everyone, from the President of the United States, on down, was on the Director of the FBI's ass. He in turn was on the deputy's ass, who was on Agent Christian's ass. The buck stopped there, however. He knew how hard everyone had been working. It is very hard to investigate a murder when there was just nothing solid to investigate. Not everybody in the world has been fingerprinted. It's great to have fingerprints from a crime scene, but unless the perpetrator has a prior arrest, or a job that requires fingerprinting, the prints are not in the computer. Until there is a suspect to match the fingerprints to, they are worthless.

The five p.m. briefing was worse than usual. Not only was there no new information, Congress had rushed through a bill that would make it more difficult to catch terrorists. It was unbelievable. At a time when the FBI needed every possible resource, Congress had limited their power. No one would dare say it, but Agent Christian knew what his agents were thinking. *Let's let these people kill them all. Here we are working 18 hours a day and they limit our resources*. Agent Christian was very glad none of his agents said it out loud.

Agent Christian cleared his throat to start the briefing, "it's been four days since the last two killings, what do we have?"

Agent Robbins was the first to speak, "the lab verified the hairs found in bungalow 3C belonged to a white female. The hairs were natural, there was no hair coloring, and they showed traces of marijuana and cocaine, both substances had been used within the last week. Here is something interesting, I don't think it will help, but it is interesting. The numbers from the shell casing indicate the bullet was at least ten years old."

Another agent spoke up, "so now we know that the killer is a dope addict that uses very old ammunition. We will all be needing hair color before we solve this one."

The agent's comments lightened the spirits in the room, slightly.

Agent Bates began his report. "Drug use doesn't fit our psychological profile. I can't imagine your average coke-head being too concerned about rising taxes. Most old bullets come from the bottom of closets. People who bought a gun for home protection and never fired it. That would fit our profile better. But these are the types of guns that are most often stolen in household burglaries. The guns are then sold or traded for drugs and end up on the street. We are checking the records for every stolen gun in Florida and Houston over the past year. Maybe we'll get lucky. Agent Scott Harrison talked to Lisa Thompson after Abernathy's funeral. She was very surprised by the letter, and he said it noticeably touched her. Senator Mayes asked her if she was going to accept the interim position and she reminded him that she could not, she is only 26. You must be 30 to hold a seat in the Senate. They confirmed her alibi for the weekend, I don't think she was involved. I'm not 100% convinced it was our Blind Luck gang, Senator Abernathy had a lot of enemies. Any one of which could buy a drugged up hooker to put a bullet in his head. We are looking at every Jane Doe that turns up in South Florida very closely. If someone had the Senator killed, they would kill the killer for sure."

"That's good, what about James?" Agent Christian asked.

"We covered the truck with a fine tooth comb. No good finger prints on the truck, but a very good set on two beer cans found inside the truck. We ran them through the computer, but came up empty. You saw the video Sunday, that was a disappointment. We weren't going to release the tape in hopes we could scare something up, so far, no luck. I heard that the man that shot the tape has hired an attorney to get us to release it back to him. Evidently the tabloids are offering big bucks for it. Even though you can't see her face, I'll bet they show it a million times. That son-of-a-bitch is going to make a ton of money off Representative James' death."

Agent Bates comments did nothing to lighten the mood in the room. They all knew as soon as the tape was aired, the "Lucky

Bitch," would know they didn't have her.

"Thanks, anything else?"

"Yes sir, one other thing. We found out today the chemical used to kill Williams was Anszoid. It's some very nasty stuff, made by a company in Houston. We are checking now to see who they sell it to and how they transport it, and also, who would have access to it," an agent said.

"That's great, thanks. Lori, check with Houston and find out what their offices are like, and check on hotels close by. We may very well be moving the Op Center to Houston soon. That's all I have, anything else? Good. Thanks."

Although every agent was in the same building and most of the time they were in the same room, they all agreed the nightly briefing was a good way to get together and talk out loud about what they were doing and what they had found. Just to be sure everybody was on the same page.

* * * * * *

Gary Stephens had added nothing to the legal pad with the words, LINE THEM UP AND SHOOT THEM! written across the top. The deaths of James and Abernathy had been big news. Bigger than Carson and Williams because of the way they had died. People cannot understand poisonings. They don't show many people in the movies dying a violent death from a poisoning. People can get a mental picture of a bullet through the eye because they've seen it on television. In fact, both Carson and Williams died a much more violent death than Abernathy.

The news from Capital Hill was just as big. Was Congress giving in to the terrorists, or did the terrorists just open their eyes to the fact that they were spending money like crazy and taxing the hell out of the citizens. Every interview with every Legislator said neither. They were only doing what they thought was best for the country, like they always have. It's just a coincidence that some of the more outlandish spending bills were not passed this week. It did not matter that newspapers were getting letters addressed to the "Congress Killers" hinting at who should be next. Polls showed most Americans were happy that spending was being cut, but America was still divided on the methods used to get those results.

Gary would think about the words on his legal pad as time allowed, which was usually when he was in bed trying to fall asleep. He hoped he would remember where he read it, or at least what newspaper, or even when, would be a big help. Just knowing the decade would be a big help. It was hard to believe, that in a country as good and as strong and as powerful as the United States, people have always been dissatisfied with the government. With the possible exception of George Washington and the first Continental Congress, someone or someones have always been trying to change the way the government is run by killing it's members, usually it's the leader they go after. John Kennedy, Abraham Lincoln, James Garfield and William McKinley were killed, while assassination attempts on Reagan, Ford, Truman and Roosevelt failed. Usually, killing the leader only made matters worse.

There was no time in his lifetime when Gary thought that the words he was looking for might not have been written. If he had read the words in a newspaper or magazine story sometime in his life, he had a lot of work to do to find the article. He thought about recruiting some help, but then he thought, *what if it was only a dream?*

22

Annie Simmons was 25 five years old. Very athletic. She met Todd Evans at the downtown Houston YMCA while playing racquetball. Todd invited Annie to the Pizza Inn where the group was holding another Thursday beer and pizza night. Annie instantly hit it off with the group and became a permanent member.

Annie's personality was the type that loved to be the center of attention, she loved to tell people how much fun everybody had on a given night because she was there. Had she not been there, nobody would have had fun. She wasn't pushy, but it didn't take long to notice the trait. She had a very well shaped body, small but firm breasts, thin waist and muscular, but very shapely legs. At one time she was very much in love with Todd. The two were an item for a few months, and would have been forever except for the fact that, as Todd put it, "after you look at her face for a while, you see a strong resemblance between her and Grampa Munster, from the old television show, *The Munsters*."

Annie Simmons was jealous. She had sat and listened to Todd talk about how he had poisoned Senators Carson and Williams, and how Kathy and Russell had done in Representative James. She sat quietly and toasted them at the restaurant and listened to Gene talk about how they had already changed the world. Annie wanted to be involved. She was the one that had suggested James, but nobody remembered that, they only remembered who was actually involved in the killings.

Now there was talk that they would not kill again. Congress was making changes and as long as they were trying, the gang would not kill another Congressman. The consensus was that if they were making changes and the gang killed again, Congress might decide that no matter what they did, this crazed faction was going to kill, and then they would stop trying to change their old ways.

Gene's idea was to be ready. Have a victim in mind and a plan in mind that would, hopefully, work. If Congress passed a bill that was wasteful, or passed a new tax or increased an old one, they would then execute whatever plan they had, as quickly as possible, and somehow notify Congress, and the world, who did it and why.

Todd and Annie, no longer lovers but still friends, said they would be willing to do it, kill a Representative if necessary. They agreed to work together to come up with a good, safe plan. The longer they had to wait, the better. Gene had heard that most legislators were scared and staying very close to the FBI and Secret Service agents assigned to protect them. As time went by, the cockier ones, typically the ones the group was after, who had felt themselves invincible all along, would begin to feel safe again and venture out without protection.

Todd and Annie decided to talk about it over margaritas at Todd's apartment. They discussed a list of names Gene had given them of notably corrupt politicians and some of their known habits. The only name on the list they recognized was Representative Babineaux of Louisiana, whom they had discussed before. This list was different from other lists and discussions because it contained the name of a woman. Representative Margaret Oliver of California.

According to Gene's notes, Representative Oliver had, as did Carson, Williams, Abernathy and James, made a great deal of money while a member of Congress. Like the other members, she managed to purchase parcels of land, with very favorable financing from a Savings and Loan, just prior to an announcement which made the land's value skyrocket. She promptly sold the land for a substantial profit.

She was also, according to Gene's notes, a lesbian and very sexually active. Annie had consumed several very strong margaritas during the impromptu planning session. Todd had made them strong for a reason. Tequila made Annie horny. She would do almost anything to get laid when she was drunk on Tequila, and Todd knew it.

One night, after the two had stopped dating, the gang had been out for Mexican food and margaritas, Todd and Annie were the last to leave. They were sitting in his car in the parking lot talking when Annie leaned over and began performing oral sex on him. Of course Todd did not resist and, in fact, enjoyed it very much.

When she finished, Todd had been totally satisfied. The combination of total satisfaction and alcohol left him in a condition where he could do nothing more, while Annie was now ready for reciprocation. Unfortunately, Todd had little desire as Annie tried everything she could think of to arouse him again. Nothing Annie tried worked, and, after an hour of trying, she and Todd left for their respective homes. Todd felt bad about it, he definitely had the most fun that night, but there was nothing he could do about it, at the time.

They never talked about the night and had never had any form of sex together since. Todd thought maybe she was drunker than he thought she was, and didn't even remember the night. It didn't matter, it was water under the bridge for both of them, it hadn't affected their friendship.

Todd was feeling the effects of the margaritas and he could tell Annie was too. Her eyes were beginning to droop and her speech was beginning to slur. Todd caught himself looking at her breasts and becoming very aroused.

"I think we should concentrate on this Representative from California, uh, Oliver, Margaret Oliver. According to what Gene says in his notes, she is as corrupt as any of the others. We shouldn't omit her because she is a woman, she can do as much damage as any man in Congress can," Annie said.

"That's true, I'm sure she can. We will have to do some research and find out the best way to get close to her."

"She's a lesbian, I bet I could get close to her."

"Then what? Could you kill her?"

"I think so, or I could keep her busy while you did it. Kind of the opposite way Russell and Kathy killed James. I would lure her out and you could run her over." She thought about it a second, "or, I could get her to come back to a hotel with me and you could be hiding in the closet and while she was preoccupied, you could hit her on the head or stab her or something."

Todd could tell the booze was doing a lot of the talking, but it wasn't a bad idea, if she could go through with it.

"But what if you," he stopped to think of the right words, "have to keep her interested?" Todd asked. It wasn't exactly the right words, but he got the point across.

"You mean what if I have to let her kiss me?"

"Well, yeah, or more."

"I really wouldn't have a problem with that."

"Are you sure, you could let her kiss you, or. . ." Todd couldn't bring himself to say it.

"Let her go down on me? Sure, it's not like it would be the first time." Annie was enjoying this.

Annie's first experience with another woman had begun innocently enough. She had met her while playing racquetball. They played several games together and really hit it off. After they showered, Annie suggested they go for a drink. The woman suggested they go to her place, she needed to feed the cat, they could have a glass of wine there, then go to a bar if she wanted. That sounded fine to Annie, she had no reason to suspect the woman was being anything other than friendly. They got to her apartment and she fed the cat, she did have a cat, and poured two glasses of wine. They talked and drank more wine until very late.

At some point it suddenly hit Annie that the woman was interested in more than talk. Once it dawned on her what the woman was doing, it was obvious. Annie wondered how long it had been going on before she noticed. Her first thought was to leave, but she couldn't. She thought about having sex with a woman, and it began to arouse her. She then wondered how she was supposed to let the woman know she was interested. Obviously the woman was going very slow, she didn't want to scare Annie.

They were dressed similarly, both wearing mid-thigh shorts and sleeveless blouses. Annie pulled her legs up under her and sat crossed-legged. It didn't take long for her leg to go to sleep and she uncrossed her legs and complained that it had fallen asleep. Her new friend took the hint and began rubbing her leg. When she asked if the rubbing helped, Annie said "yes," but higher. The woman kept rubbing her leg, slowly inching higher. Annie leaned back and closed her eyes and the woman took it from there.

Annie did not relate the entire story to Todd, but enough of it to convince Todd that, yes, she could keep Representative Oliver interested while they killed her. She also related enough to get Todd very aroused.

"She was a very beautiful woman and we made love. I enjoyed it very much. She knew exactly how to please me, and I tried to please her." Annie looked at Todd and knew he was about to explode. She could never figure out why 100 percent heterosexual men love to hear about, and watch other women making love. It must be a penned up fantasy to be with more than one woman or something. She continued her story, "I still prefer men and I guess I'm still like 99% straight, but if I'm not interested in a guy, and I'm horny, and an attractive woman hits on me, then I'll go home with her."

Annie remembered the night in the parking lot very well, she had not been too drunk. She remembered pleasing Todd to the "ultimate," then being ignored by him. It was pay-back time. "I guess it's settled then, we go after Margaret Oliver when, and if, it becomes necessary. I will lure her to a private place and we will kill her."

"That's right," Todd agreed.

"Good." Annie leaned over and kissed Todd, "let's go to bed."

Todd did not hesitate. He was off the couch and leading her to the bedroom almost before she finished her sentence. They wasted no time removing their clothes and getting in bed. They had been kissing and caressing only a short while when Todd gently pushed down on Annie's head, a subtle hint telling her what he was wanting.

Annie let Todd push her until she reached his chest where she kissed and sucked his nipples until they were erect, then she leaned forward and kissed him gently on the mouth and said, "you do me first." Annie laid on her back and spread her legs as Todd performed oral sex on her.

Todd was wonderful, and Annie layed back and enjoyed his work. She held out as long as she could, much too long for Todd, until she had a violent orgasm, nearly crushing Todd's head between her legs.

"That was fantastic, thank you so much," she said as she caught her breath. Todd stretched out beside her to rest his neck, which she had nearly twisted off, and to give her ample room to reciprocate. Annie turned the opposite direction and said, "Good night," leaving Todd to take matters into his own hands. Todd realized she had just evened the score and didn't press it. Annie fell asleep smiling.

* * * * * *

Gary Stephens took off his glasses and rubbed his face and eyes. He had been staring at the computer screen, reading articles for four straight hours. He had spent days trying to remember where he had read the words he wrote on the top line of the legal pad: LINE THEM UP AND SHOOT THEM!, but kept coming up blank. He was absolutely sure he had read the words, somewhere.

Gary started with the CD-ROM of the Phoenix Tribune. Everything that was ever published in the paper since 1986 was on CD-ROM. It had been suggested to him that they go even further back and put the entire history of the paper, 75 years, on CD, but it would have to be input manually and Gary couldn't justify the expense. Now he wished he had. If he didn't find what he was looking for on the CD, he would have to go to microfilm. That meant instead of entering key words, such as "Shoot," "Senator," "Waste" or "Taxes," then reading only the articles that were selected in the search, he would have to read every page of every paper in an attempt to find one article that may not even be in the Tribune.

Several times Gary thought about giving up this exercise in futility, then the little voice would pop into his head and tell him, "it's out there, just keep looking," and he would read another years worth of articles.

After reading another fifty or so articles about Senator's killing time on junkets or Congress shooting down line item veto power, Gary tried different key words to sort on. Whatever he tried, there were usually 20 to 30 articles, none of which had anything to do with lining them up and shooting them.

Tim Brooks knocked on the open door to Gary's office and came in as Gary turned from his computer. "You've been sitting at that computer for two days, what the hell are you up to?"

Gary decided he had held it in long enough. Sometimes talking about it will cause something to ring a bell or saying it out loud it will sound different and he would catch something he'd been missing. He told Tim how the words had been plaguing him, he couldn't get them out of his head, but he could not remember where he heard or read them.

"I know I've seen them somewhere," he said. "I could be doing all this for nothing, because, if I find it, it could be something that has absolutely nothing to do with what is happening now. But I have this gut feeling that it does. I have to find the article."

Tim thought for a moment and looked at the words on the legal pad, "it sure doesn't ring a bell with me. You have no idea when it might have been?"

Gary could only shake his head no.

"You know, you might run this past your friend at the FBI, they may keep files on people who write threatening letters. Maybe it was a letter to the editor you read and then tossed, you would never find it if you threw it away."

"I might call Christian, I didn't think about that, thanks."

Tim nodded good-bye and left. Gary Stephens had a sinking feeling in his stomach. Letters to the editor. He had read thousands, and thrown most of them in the trash. He was always getting letters from crack-pots. What if this was what he was trying to remember? He would never find it. He closed his eyes and tried to think about golf, but a little voice kept saying "line them up and shoot them, line them up and shoot them. . . ."

* * * * * *

"That's wonderful news sweetheart, when's the wedding?" Kathy's mother said after Kathy told her about Russell.

"Well, since you and daddy are in England and his parents are in Vermont, we thought about just going to Vegas, maybe in a couple of weeks."

"No, honey, you don't want to do that, this is your wedding, it should be the most memorable day of you life. We will be happy to fly home for it. We'll pay for everything too. It's the bride's parents responsibility, you know. You really should have a nice wedding, it should be your only one."

"You're right, mom, I'll talk to Russell about it and if he agrees, we'll set a date. What would be a good date for you? We want to get married soon."

"Don't get mad at me dear, but you don't HAVE to hurry, do you?"

"No, mother, I don't," at least she didn't think she did, with falling in love and killing people, she hadn't really thought about getting pregnant. She wasn't on the pill and they had not used protection. Russell must have assumed she was on the pill. She made a mental note to get on the pill, ASAP!

"I didn't think so, I thought I knew you better than that. You just pick a date and we will be there. Can you make all the arrangements or do you want me to come home and help?" Kathy's mother said.

"I just want a small wedding, you know, family and a few of my close friends. I'm sure I can handle it."

They talked about marriage and life in general before her mother said they were running up too much in long distance and they should hang up. Kathy promised to call back as soon as she talked to Russell and they set a date for the wedding. Her mother was very happy for her. Kathy began to cry, she didn't know why, she just needed to cry.

It took her several minutes to regain her composure. Russell was watching a baseball game on the television when Kathy came out of her bedroom. Her eyes were red and swollen.

"What's wrong sweetie?" Russell asked when he saw her eyes.

"I just talked to my mom and I guess it upset me. She really trusts me, you know," she said as she sat on the couch next to him and leaned on his chest. He put his arm around her shoulder and held her tight.

"She asked me if we had to get married, and I said no, and she said she didn't really think I would, she thought she knew me better than that. Russell, I just helped you kill someone, and I don't know, I could be pregnant."

Russell had to swallow hard to get the lump out of his throat. This day and age, you think about protecting yourself from HIV, he never thought about pregnancy. "I'm really sorry, baby, I never thought that we should be using protection. Have you felt all right lately?"

"I don't know, I was really sick and throwing up the other morning."

The lump came back to Russell's throat and his face went pale.

"I was hung over," she laughed and Russell soon managed a laugh. "What if I was, you know there is a chance, I haven't had my period yet."

Russell thought about it, he had to make sure it wasn't a trick question, "I want to have kids with you, but I think we need to enjoy our youth first. You're just a kid yourself, I still have to buy your beer."

The two laughed again and she said, "I'll call the doctor tomorrow and see when I can get in to get on the pill. I want to have kids too, but not right away." She was thinking that she wanted to be sure she was not going to spend the rest of her life in prison before she had children, but Russell was happy and she didn't want to spoil it.

"I'll call my parents and see if they want to come to the wedding. I'm sure they will, why don't we set a date?" Russell said.

Kathy jumped off the couch and got a calendar. Russell noticed the bounce was back in her step. She was happy they were going to have a real wedding. Every little girl always dreams about her wedding day. He hoped hers would be perfect.

She came back with the calendar turned to May. "Today is April 17th, we should be able to do everything we need to do in three weeks, so how about May eleventh, it's a Saturday. If we can't book a church, I could live with doing it somewhere else, maybe we could have it here. The living room is big enough, I don't really want a lot of people anyway, what do you think.?"

"You decide, just give me a starting time and I'll be there. I do love you Kathy Beck."

"I love you too."

That night they made love using protection.

23

Tim Brooks put his head in Gary Stephen's office and said, "damn it Gary, you've hardly moved from that computer all week. It's late, it's Saturday night. Why don't you call it quits and we'll go get a beer. I could sure use a cold one. The FBI hasn't released a thing since Monday and I've exhausted all my angles. If it weren't for Congress passing all the right bills and defeating all the wrong ones for a change, instead of the other way around, I could have just taken a vacation this week."

"It's a damn shame somebody has to kill four of them to get them to do the right thing, isn't it?"

"Yeah, it is. But a Democrat wasn't about to let a Republican get a bill passed that would make him look good. And visa versa. They'll help them get a bad bill passed just so that at the next election they can say, 'look at the shit Joe Republican pushed last year,' or 'look, Moe Democrat sat on his ass all year and didn't do a thing.' The only thing they could agree on was to give themselves a raise."

Gary shook his head in disgust. "Maybe I shouldn't even be looking for that article. What if I'm right and I give the FBI a name and they catch these people. Congress will go right back to their old ways."

"You are looking for it because you're a decent person and killing is not the way to change things."

"Oh yeah? Well, I'm finished. My eyes hurt, my head hurts, I've read twenty years of the Phoenix Tribune, twenty five years of the New York Times and close to twenty five years of The Washington Post. I've had it. I must have dreamed the article. I would like to go get a beer and forget about this. Then tomorrow, I'll play my usual round of golf and I won't even think about it anymore. I gave it my best shot. I came up empty. Like you said last week, it was probably a letter to the editor I read and tossed. It would make sense, the letters that started this were basically letters to the editor. Had Carson not been killed the day I received the first one, I probably would have tossed it too. I can't believe I just wasted a week of my life on this God damn thing. It wasn't my job anyway, that's what we have the FBI for."

Gary seemed to be rambling, but Tim didn't mind. He knew his boss needed to let out some frustration. "You're right," Tim said, not exactly sure what he was agreeing to, but he knew the man needed to hear it. "Let's go, I'm thirsty."

"I'm ready, let me stop by the can, and we're outta here."

The two men walked toward the men's room, Gary still complaining that Congress should work together toward a common goal - the good of the United States of America and the American public - not for their own personal gains. "And you know what else," Gary said, but did not wait for a reply from Tim, "the son-of-a-bitches keep talking socialized medicine. That's NOT what we need, what we need is socialized LAW! Way too many God damn lawyers anyway. Just about every lawmaker is a lawyer, sounds like a conflict of interest to me. Somebody ought to make an amendment to the Constitution that if a person holds a law degree, or is a member of the Bar in any state, that person cannot be a member of Congress. I bet you would see some changes then, and you wouldn't have to kill any of them."

Tim just kept agreeing, the man was definitely on a roll.

* * * * * *

Sunday morning Russell called his parents and told them of the wedding plans. May eleventh was fine with them, they would be there. They were very happy he was marrying Kathy. His parents had met her several times and thought she was a very nice girl, they wondered why he had never mentioned that they were dating. Russell told a few white lies to hide the fact that they had never really dated, only slept together and killed a United States Congressman.

Kathy smiled all day Sunday as she called friends to tell them about the wedding. Julie Hanson said she would be honored to be the Maid of Honor, but there was lots to be done. She would come over Monday night and they would start planning. Julie was as excited as Kathy was.

Russell drove back to his apartment to check it out. Everything seemed to be as he left it. He dropped a check for the next month's rent off at the office, which was busy with prospective renters. He had brought the green sport bag with him to take more clothes back to Kathy's. It had been a week and he no longer felt that he might have to leave town in a hurry. The FBI didn't seem to have anything to link them to the James killing, and the video was not much. The rights were finally negotiated and *Hard Copy* was the first to show it Friday evening. Some local news stations aired it and some didn't, saying there wasn't really anything there to view.

Russell put his passport and the money he had taken with him back in the Sentry fireproof box. His plan was to grab Kathy and run at the first sign of trouble, and he fully expected trouble. Mexico was close, but they would have expected him to try and cross the border so Russell was going to drive to Florida and try to bum a ride on a sailboat going anywhere out of the country. There were always cruising boats leaving Florida, and when the skipper looked at Kathy, pictured her in a bikini for most of the trip, they would have no problem getting on. Russell was a decent sailor, so it wasn't as if they would have been a burden. Russell daydreamed for a moment about Kathy and him alone on a sailboat somewhere in the Caribbean going nowhere slowly. At the moment, he could think of nothing he would rather be doing.

He filled the green sports bag with another pair of long pants, several pairs underwear and some shirts. Enough to last him, he thought, until he could ask Kathy if he could use her washing machine. He knew that when he finally asked, Kathy would probably volunteer to do his laundry. He just felt awkward about having her do it. Maybe it was his last bastion of bachelor-hood, and he didn't want to give it up too soon.

Russell grabbed his bag and took a final look around the apartment, it was the same as he had left it last week. It was amazing how clean the apartment stayed when no one was in it. As he walked to the door he noticed the answering machine flashing. He rewound the tape and listened to the messages.

"Jesus!" Russell said as he listened to Gene Thompson warn him about Representative James. The second call was Gene telling him to be sure and erase the tape. Russell listened to two other messages before he pushed the rewind/erase button. He watched the tape rewind then pressed play again. The only noise from the machine was a barely audible hiss. Russell sat on the couch and waited for his heartbeat to return to its normal rate. He tried to put his mind back on the sailboat in the Caribbean, but he couldn't, he could only think about what might have happened if the wrong person would have gotten a hold of the tape.

After rewinding and listening to the tape hiss several more times, Russell was satisfied that he had in fact permanently erased the message. He went to the bathroom and relieved himself. *Nothing like having the piss scared out of you,* he thought. As he flushed the toilet he noticed the *Sail* magazine on the top of the tank. He took the magazine, stuffed it in the green sports bag, and left his apartment. He would make a point to call several of the sailboat charter companies later from Kathy's.

* * * * * *

"Nice putt, Gary," his partner said as he sank a 15 footer with an enormous left break on the eighth green.

"Thank you. It's funny, usually if you hit a putt like that and leave it two or three inches away, they say 'nice putt.' But if you make it, they say 'yeah, lucky putt'."

"No, that was a good putt. You had it lined up all the way and stroked it perfectly. Well done." He held his arm up for a "high five" and Gary slapped his palm.

Gary's partner said, "you've been driving the ball well and putting great. This is just about the best I've seen you play, if you keep this up I bet you will knock at least fifteen strokes off last week's score."

"I feel a lot better this week. Last week I couldn't keep my mind on the game at all. You know about the Congressional killings the last few weeks, right?"

"Of course."

"Well, I read something, somewhere, sometime, that I am sure was related. I just cannot remember where, or when, I read it. I spent almost every waking minute last week looking for it and I came up empty. I've accepted it. I tried as hard as I could and that's it, the FBI will have to find the killers without Gary Stephen's help."

The two men laughed and the talk reverted back to golf as they drove to the next tee box. Gary's putt had been for a birdie so he had the honors. He hit his Taylor Made titanium driver dead solid perfect and the golf ball shot down the left side of the fairway, then gently faded back to the right, landed and rolled to a stop 285 yards away. The other three members of the foursome teed off and they drove down the cart path toward their balls.

"Gary, I hate to ask this, but I've got a nephew, my sister's son, who is majoring in journalism at the University of Washington, he graduates in May. I was wondering if you would take a look at his résumé and samples, and, well, if you have a place for him, that would be great, or maybe if you know somebody he could talk to."

Gary was driving the cart and staring straight ahead. His friend was beginning to wonder if Gary heard him, when Gary looked at him and said, "would you mind finishing alone, I have to go to the office. Just put the cart in my garage when you finish."

Without waiting for a reply, Gary stopped the cart and got out started walking across the fairway toward his condo.

"Gary, I'm sorry, you don't have to look at his résumé," his partner yelled, half joking, not sure what set him off.

"Pick up my ball, would you please," Gary said as broke into a jog toward the sixteenth fairway and his patio door.

He was out of breath when he reached the patio, but he was so pumped with adrenaline he hardly noticed. In a daze, he took off his golf shoes and put on an old pair of sneakers. Without changing clothes Gary grabbed his car keys and left. On the way to the office this time Gary did not notice the beautiful Phoenix weather or anything else for that matter. He reached the office in record time, for him.

The personnel files were kept in storage boxes in the area between the parking garage and the first floor of the Phoenix Tribune building. Gary used the steps to go up the one level to the archives. He scanned the massive room looking at the boxes stacked from the floor to the ceiling on steel shelves. Walking up and down the isles, he tried to remember where the old personnel records were kept. He could have called the librarian to come down and show him, but it was Sunday and he didn't want to wait for her come in. She probably could have told him where to look, but it didn't dawn on him to make a call. The system started to make sense as he looked at the content's description written on the side of each box.

It wasn't long before he found the personnel records. They were boxed chronologically by departure date, the active employee files were kept in personnel. He quickly glanced at the labels. Many companies will destroy their records after seven years, but the Tribune had a policy to keep them indefinitely. That meant when the entire storage space was full, they would throw out the oldest to make room for the newest.

There was one 24 inch by 15 inch storage box with a tie-down lid for every year. Everything about the employee was in the box, from résumé to termination. Gary pulled the box labeled 1995 from the shelf and looked for a comfortable place to sit.

Gary opened every folder in the box and read every clipping attached to every résumé. He knew he was on the right track and he kept reading. After the first box was finished, he stretched, got a drink of water, and started on box number two.

Total elapsed time was over three hours, but it only seemed like minutes when Gary pulled the folder belonging to Eric Moore from box number twelve. Long ago he had stopped reading the names on the résumé and was going straight to the submissions.

Gary thought he was having a heart attack his heart was beating so rapidly when he saw the article. He was finally holding it in his hands, it wasn't a dream. He read it out loud to himself:

> . . . With a budget of over a trillion dollars, an amount so astronomical most people can't comprehend, Congress cannot manage to run the government within the budget. Maybe we should take all the Senators and Representatives, line them up and shoot them, one by one, until the remaining members of Congress wake up and start doing what is right for the country. . .

That was all Gary needed to read. He left the box open, lying in the middle of the floor, and walked to the elevators. The elevator seemed to take forever to get down. Gary was glad it was Sunday and the administrative workers were not in the building, it would have taken even longer for the elevator to reach the archive level. When the doors opened he entered and pressed the floor for his office. Gary was finishing the article when the doors opened.

"I got it!" he yelled as he passed Tim Brooks office on the way to the copy machine. He pressed "2" and began making two sets of copies of everything in the folder.

"What have you got?" Tim asked as he caught up to Gary at the copy machine.

"The name of the person responsible for the Congressional killings."

"You're kidding, who?"

"No, I'm not kidding. He was a fucking employee! I fired him several years ago. Read this. I have to get over to the FBI office." Gary handed Tim a stack of copies from the copier and took the second set to his office. Tim followed hoping for more of an explanation but got none. Gary left the folder with the originals on his desk headed for the elevator. "I'll be back in a few minutes, we'll talk then."

The elevators closed as Tim Brooks stood watching. He had never seen his boss, a very laid back, the never gets excited type, buzzing through the office. Tim went back to his desk to look through his copy of the documents Gary was so excited about. Tim read through them once then began typing on his computer, he paused, thought, and decided to wait. Gary Stephens may have found the killer.

Gary pressed the large red button next to the front doors of the office building. On weekends the front doors required a pass card for entry but anyone could exit by pressing the red button. Gary hit the sidewalk at a pace somewhere between a fast walk and a slow jog. He never slowed when he came to the street, oblivious to the light and the "Don't Walk" sign.

It was the high pitched squeal of rubber and the sound of someone leaning on a horn that snapped Gary out of his daze just in time to see the Ford Explorer coming at him. He jumped straight up, mostly out of fright, as the front bumper of the Explorer slid into his legs. The impact pushed Gary forward and to his hands and knees. He stayed motionless several seconds as he took inventory of his body. He hurt, but there was no severe pain.

"Are you all right?" the driver of the Explorer was asking as she came to Gary Stephens' aid.

Gary nodded and said, "yes, I'm sorry it was my own fault, are you all right?" The woman was visibly shaken. She thought she had just killed someone.

"I'm fine. Do you want me to call an ambulance? I have insurance."

"Please, it wasn't your fault, I'm fine. Thank you, but I have to be going."

Gary didn't wait for a response as he walked past the small crowd that had gathered. He was more embarrassed than hurt, and very glad it was Sunday. Monday through Friday and there would have been two hundred people around him rubber necking.

By the time he made it to the FBI headquarters, his knees had begun to swell and he was having trouble walking. He tried the front door and it was locked. A small plaque next to an even smaller button read, *After Hours, Ring Bell*. Gary pressed the button several times.

"Yes?" Gary had not seen the speaker and the voice startled him. He was expecting someone to come to the door.

"My name is Gary Stephens, I'm the editor of the Tribune. I would like to see Agent Christian, he knows who I am, it's urgent."

"One moment please."

In a few minutes Agent Christian was opening the door. Gary stepped in and the two shook hands.

"What the hell happened to you?" the Agent ask as he looked at Gary. His pants were ripped at the knees and blood was beginning to seep though the material. His hand were badly scraped and also bleeding, Gary had not noticed.

"Uh, I just got hit by a truck."

"What, are you OK?"

"Well, I thought so, I don't know. It's not important, I think I know who your killers are, at least one anyway."

"Let's go upstairs to the infirmary, we can talk while they bandage you."

Gary was limping badly by the time they got upstairs. It felt nice to sit down. Lori volunteered to help with the wounds and another agent brought ice. Gary gave the copies of Eric Moore's personnel file to Agent Christian and began telling his story as the two agents cleaned his cuts and wrapped his knees in ice. His knees felt much better by the time he had gotten to the part of the story where he found the folder in the storage box.

"It's really a well written article. It may have even been the reason I hired him in the first place. I imagine that's why I remembered it, or at least thought I remembered it. He was a good, aggressive reporter, just a little too aggressive for my newspaper. He really pressed a woman who had just been through a horrible tragedy. I have never liked that kind of reporting."

"It could be just a coincidence that he mentioned killing Congressmen and now, almost six years later, somebody starts doing it." Christian said.

"Every writer has a style, it's almost like a finger print. I've been in this business so long I can pick up a paper and nine times out of ten tell you who wrote an article just by reading it."

"And you think this Eric Moore wrote the letters you received?"

"I can't tell about the first two, there just wasn't enough to go on. But I would bet on the third, it was longer and had his style."

"Is he still in the area?"

"I saw a note in the file that the Houston Post called for a reference. I don't know if he got the job, but the Post was bought out and closed recently, so I don't know."

Agent Christian jumped to his feet and said, "Jerry, can you be sure Mr. Stephens gets back to his office safely, and home if necessary, then back here ASAP. Lori, you've got a contingency plan for Houston, correct?" She nodded affirmative. "We leave as soon as possible. There will be a briefing in twenty minutes. Let's get on it."

Agent Christian had almost left the room when he realized he hadn't said anything to Gary, "I'm sorry I almost forgot to thank you."

"I fully understand." Gary said as he attempted to stand. "One more thing, can you give us some time before you let them know we're coming?"

"Nothing will be printed until we hear from you. Please don't forget us."

"Don't worry, I'll pay the long distance personally."

The two shook hands and Agent Christian left in a hurry.

"Do you need a ride back to your office?" the agent with Gary asked.

"Just get me down the stairs, I'll be fine."

"Are you sure?"

"Yes, I'm sure, you have work to do."

The Agent showed Gary Stephens out the front door and Gary walked slowly back to his building. His knees and hands hurt, but his back felt great, a heavy load had just been lifted off of it.

Precisely twenty minutes after Agent Christian said goodbye to Gary Stephens, he was entering the makeshift briefing room. "How long will it take to be completely operational in Houston?" He asked.

Agent Lori Anderson was the first to respond. "In as few as twelve hours we all could be functioning. In 24 hours, it will be like we never left Arizona. The Houston office has a large training facility inside their building downtown. Communication links are being set up as we speak. As soon as they are established we will start a download of everything on the computers presently located in the Blind Luck Op center to the computers in Houston. When we arrive in Houston, everything that is on our computers here will be waiting for us. All hard material, maps, papers, photographs, everything, is being boxed and will be overnighted to Houston tonight. The boxes will be waiting for us when we get there. We will have to unpack because we are the only ones who know what we want to do with the material. They have secured a private office for each agent that is coming and several other offices have been turned into emergency sleeping quarters. Rooms have been reserved for us at a hotel very close to the FBI building, so we will have a place to go if we have time. A caterer has been lined up to be sure food is available whenever we need it. The Houston office does have full workout facilities and showers, so we could work around the clock if necessary. Their lab is state of the art, probably better than ours. They have quite a few more agents than we have here, all at our disposal. Of course they have a full complement of wire tapping and surveillance equipment. The Houston Police Department and Harris County Sheriff's office will be notified when we deem appropriate. Houston says we can expect full cooperation if we need the locals. Since we don't know who we are dealing with, I didn't want the locals notified, the Blind Luck gang could very well have someone on the inside. America West and Southwest Airlines both have numerous flights from Phoenix to Houston. When you are packed, go to the ticket agent and they will put you on the next flight. Even if it's full, they will bump someone, so you'll be on the flight. A stack of paper is on the table. It contains a list of things you need to know, such as the address and phone number of the office in Houston. The name of the hotel where you are registered, the names of the Houston Agents who will be working closest to us, and city maps of Houston. Any questions?"

"Lori," asked Agent Robbins, "what about vehicles?"

"I'm sorry, Bill, they have a fleet there that should accommodate us. I almost forgot, we will draw a cash advance when we get to Houston. If anyone needs cash to get there, see me and I will see what I can do. Anything else?"

"Thank you Lori, this is good." Agent Christian said, "let's plan to get acclimated to Houston tomorrow. Remember there is a two hour time change, we will have another briefing at 1700 Houston time tomorrow. When you pack, I would plan for two or three weeks, minimum. Just because we think we know who we're after, doesn't mean, one, he did it or is involved, two, we can prove it if he did, and, three, we know he isn't alone, we want to get the whole gang, not just one. Plan on a lot of field work, I hope you all are tired of being in the office. One other thing, don't forget that you are carrying a weapon through the airport. The FAA has most of the checkers jumpy as hell, be sure to follow proper procedures and don't move too fast. We don't want to cause a scene. Anything we've forgotten?"

The room was quiet, the agents were looking forward to a new location. They may still be in a room with four walls, telephones, faxes and computers, but it would not be the same room. A change of pace always helps an investigation that is going nowhere. Before Christian could dismiss the group, Agent Bates said, "sir, I would just like to add that, for the hell of it, I called Houston information and there are several Eric Moores in town."

"That's good to know, at least we know we have one suspect in Houston to check out. Gary Stephens finding that article is about as "blind lucky" as you can get. Now let's use our investigative skills to find Eric Moore and the Lucky Bitch!"

24

As the Agents were packing their personal belongings for the move to Houston, it was the general consensus that each agent wanted to see their boxes loaded onto the truck that would deliver them to the airport. It was late when the truck left the operations center and the agents decided there was no need to fly all night when the equipment wouldn't arrive till sometime after ten in the morning. The best thing to do was to go home, get some sleep, catch an early flight and be fresh when arriving in Houston. The logistics officer was able to put every agent on the same flight, which made it easier for all concerned.

Two vans met the team at Bush Intercontinental Airport and drove them directly to FBI headquarters downtown. Agent John McBride was the director of the Houston Federal Bureau of Investigation office. Agent Christian knew McBride well, they had worked together on several interstate cases.

The two vans pulled into the underground parking garage and stopped at the guard station. The guard, hardly glancing up, recognized the vans and the drivers and waved them through. The vans parked in the tow-away zone next to the elevators.

"I'll drop you off here and you can either leave your bags here, or carry them with you. I can take you all at once to the hotel or one at a time as you are ready, it's totally up to y'all," the driver of the lead van said.

The agents had work related items that they didn't trust the freight company with, so they had packed it in their bags. They all needed their bags, and decided it best to take them up to their temporary offices, take out what they needed, then, when, and if, they ever made it to the hotel, they would take the rest of their things with them. It was going to be a hectic day, nothing needed to get misplaced.

Upstairs, Agent McBride greeted Alexander Christian and his team. Each person was introduced as a formality. Many had met before, if not in person, over the telephone.

"Alex, you are Operations Center Commander, Operation Blind Luck has been given top priority by Washington," Agent McBride said, "so every person in this office is at your disposal. I assumed you would want to operate in two-man teams as usual, so I thought the best thing to do would be to have one of my people and one of your people on each team, at least until your people become familiar with Houston. Your people know the case and mine know the area, it should work out well. We have all the information from the James case, and I'm sure you do too, so we will have one team assigned to that case to make sure neither of us has missed anything."

"Thanks John, I can't imagine how we could have missed anything, but it's happened before. What about Moore?" Agent Christian asked.

"There were quite a few Eric and E. Moores in the phone book. We ran the social security number you gave us from his old employment application and cross checked with the Department of Motor Vehicles and the Texas Employment Commission. Both agencies had him on file and both had the same address. As of nine this morning, we have had someone watching the address, photographing anybody that goes in or out. The Agent checked in at one and there has been no activity, in or out. It's twenty after now, so unless it's happened in the last twenty minutes, we still don't know what he looks like. We thought about calling The Houston Chronicle, they're the ones that bought the Post, and find out if they have a photo on file, but he may be working there and we didn't want to warn him. Even if he is not working there, if we call them and ask for a photo, you know they are going to ask questions. I know you don't want any press. If the 'Blind Luck Gang' is here in Houston, and they read that you were moving your investigation here, they would figure you are getting close and split."

"Good, what we want to do is identify him and tail him. We know there is more than one person involved, but we don't know how many. We need to find as many as we can before we make any arrests. Once they know we are on to them, some, or all, could run. It could take years to round them up. Once we have as many as possible identified, we will hit them all at the same time. We can't give them a chance to warn each other. What about electronic surveillance?"

"We have a scanner listening for portable and mobile phone

calls, but no wire taps yet. We need a court order to put in the taps or wire his apartment. I have a time set for nine in the morning with a judge to get wire tap permission. I hoped that would give you enough time to prepare your case." Agent McBride smiled at Christian. He knew the chances of getting a tap were slim, there just wasn't much evidence yet. A search warrant would be next to impossible.

"Thanks," he said facetiously, "we need to get started. I understand our boxes have been delivered and the communications are all up and running and the computer downloads have been completed. Is that correct?"

"Correct. It's almost one-thirty now, why don't you all unpack here, get checked into your rooms at the hotel and unpacked there, grab a bite to eat and plan on a briefing here at five. At that time we will make the team assignments. I have one team relieving at Moore's residence right about now and another on standby in case he has visitors. We plan to follow everybody he comes in contact with. I sure hope you are right about this guy."

"Me too. If I am wrong about this, not only have we wasted a lot of manpower and money, but we are dead in the water. Every other lead has been a dead end. We would have to sit and wait for the Lucky Bitch to walk by."

"The who?" Agent McBride was caught off guard by the comment.

"Let's go to the OCC, I'll tell you on the way." The two walked toward the new Blind Luck Operations Command Center with the other agents following along. The agents from Arizona were making mental notes of landmarks around the office. Nothing is worse than being in a hurry to go from one office to another and getting lost for five minutes.

Agent McBride had turned the training room in to the Operations Command Center. There was more room than in Phoenix, but the lighting wasn't as good. The room seemed much darker. McBride had added extra phone lines and computers from the original request, the room could handle it and he felt it would be better to have too many than not enough. Not knowing the number of people they were after made their work even more difficult. It could be two, or three, or ten, or fifty, they could not even make an educated guess at this time. If it was only ten, it would tax the FBI personnel. Following ten people 24 hours a day is not an easy task, period. If the surveillance drags on several days or weeks, reinforcements would be needed.

Agent McBride was amazed at the luck of the as of yet unidentified Kathy Beck. She really was lucky, but McBride was still a little bit surprised by her moniker. Christian explained that he didn't exactly approve of it either, but it just fit her perfectly. It was hard not to use it. "Lucky Bitch," had indeed become the code name for the unidentified woman in the video.

The agents did not wait for orders or instructions. They had jobs to do and they got on it. The boxes were unpacked and materials set up exactly as they were in Phoenix. The extra room was a blessing, there would be more maps and diagrams to go on the walls, every inch of floor and wall space would be utilized. A list of the phone numbers and radio frequencies were passed out. All mobile phones and radios were secure. Even if the bad guys had a scanner, they would not be able to understand the conversations. Everything was ready. In less than twenty four hours, the FBI had packed up the Operations Command Center and moved it 1200 miles and was again fully operational.

Each agent checked the computers to be sure all the data was downloaded without any fatal errors. Agent Berg showed the video and the computer enhanced pictures of Kathy Beck, the Lucky Bitch, to the Houston agents. They all agreed, she was lucky. They hoped her luck was about to run out.

* * * * * *

It obviously takes a certain personality to run for public office. Politicians must have enormous egos in order to campaign for months on end telling anyone who will listen how great they are. They cannot be afraid of public ridicule, as their opponents will try anything in order to win. No politician likes to lose or give credit to anyone else.

For the past week, the press had been praising Congress for banding together, passing good bills and defeating bad ones. But every radio and television newscast, magazine and newspaper article that praised Congress, eventually made a point of mentioning the fact that it took the killing of four Congressmen to get things started.

No matter how much they pled their cases, the American public did not believe that the about face by Congress was a coincidence. The Congressmen knew it was true, but their egos prevented them from admitting it. Instead, they attempted to prove that they were not being blackmailed by passing one of the worst bills in the history of the United States.

The bill would give Congressmen a twenty percent salary increase and a fifteen percent per diem increase. The bill also included a provision to dramatically increase the benefits for retiring legislators. To pay for the increases, the bill imposed a three cent per gallon gasoline tax and a five percent tax on air travel.

The bill didn't fool anyone. As soon as the reports of the bill's passage began circulating, journalists began writing the editorials describing how insane the leaders of our government must truly be. The politicians had a myriad of reasons for passing the bills, none of which made much sense.

The evening newscasters pointed out in editorials that it was obvious Congress passed the bills in an attempt to prove that they were not afraid of the threats upon their lives, that they, in their own words, "would pass the laws they deemed necessary to keep America strong."

It had been suggested that the retirement package was included in the bill because many of the current Congressmen were planning to retire at the end of their current term. By retiring, they would be eligible for the benefits. If they were not re-elected, they would not be eligible.

Eventually, the President would veto the bill and Congress would succumb to public pressure not to override the veto. But Congress had done what the Blind Luck gang would have never been able to do, they slit their collective throats. The voters were outraged. Less than one third of the incumbents would be reelected in the following election.

Public opinion was now swayed in support of the terrorist faction. Some call-in radio talk shows were now allowing callers to choose, by name, who they felt the next target should be. The host would always discourage violence and the caller would inevitably agree, but nevertheless, if they strike again it should... Most of the owners of the stations did not like having callers suggest which Congressmen they felt should be murdered, but free speech was a constitutional right and ratings were sky high, so it was allowed to continue.

* * * * * *

Annie Simmons worked for PFC Travel Network, one of the largest chained travel agencies in the world. While most major cities had several offices, Houston had one huge franchise. The original owner bought the rights to all of Houston while the network was still in it's infancy. He had only one location, on Post Oak Boulevard near the Galleria. Timing had been perfect and the agency grew with the early 80's boom. The company was in the process of doing a feasibility study to determine if they should open more, smaller offices throughout town. Then the oil bust hit.

Many companies, including travel agencies went out of business. PFC picked up as many clients from closed travel agencies as clients they lost from failed businesses. When the economy began to get better, PFC added personnel and added office space in its single location. Most of their business was corporate and tickets were mailed or delivered by PFC drivers, so a single convenient location only meant additional overhead in the form of phone systems, secretaries and rent.

Annie joined PFC after she had technically been kicked out of Sam Houston State University in Huntsville after her second year. She was fine her first year, but she soon discovered drinking and having sex was much more fun than studying and going to class.

She was a trainee at minimum wage, but she was able to take trips to Mexico and the Caribbean at either a very reduced fare, or for free, as often as she could get off. If a free trip to Club Med came up, she would not hesitate to take time off, without pay, and go. At minimum wage, she would have had to work for a year to pay for it. Playing racquetball and working out at the YMCA kept her in excellent physical condition. When she hit the beach at a Club Med, she would easily meet men.

It was almost nine in the evening, Monday, when Annie made the call to Todd Evans. He answered the phone on the second ring.

"Hi Todd, it's Annie, did you hear what Congress did today?"

"Yeah, I did, It's been on the radio and that's almost all they're talking about on the news."

"Well?"

"Well, what?" He knew what she meant, but he wanted to make sure she was serious, if she couldn't say it, she sure as hell couldn't do it.

"I think we should kill Oliver."

Not only could she say it, she could say it very coldly, it gave Todd the chills.

"I agree, as a matter a fact, I talked to Gene just a little while ago and he said he found out about a club in San Francisco where she hangs out at a lot. It's a gay bar." He waited to see if that brought a different response from Annie. It didn't.

"I knew she lived in San Francisco, so I already got us two passes on Continental. They're good anytime, but it's standby, which shouldn't be a problem. I usually get bumped up to first class anyway. When do you want to leave?"

"Don't you think we should have an idea of what we want to do?"

"Find out where the club is and I will see if I can get us a cheap hotel close. I'll hang out at her bar until I meet her. I will bring her back to the hotel and we will kill her."

Todd felt a chill run up his spine again. He never realized she was so cold, or maybe it was just a game to her. Using the word "kill" was no different than any other word. Whatever it was, it gave Todd a bad case of the chills. He was very glad he did not get more deeply involved with her.

"And how are we going to kill her?"

"I don't know. Do you have a gun? I know, didn't you kill Senator Carson with cyanide? Do you have any left? I'll bring her back to the hotel for a drink and we'll have set up so I can put the cyanide in her drink, and *voilà*, we grab our bags and catch the next flight home."

"Annie."

"Yes." Annie was on her bed with her feet in the air. She was acting like a 15 year old girl who had just been asked to the Junior prom.

"We will have checked into the hotel using our own names, or at least yours, so we get a discount, right?"

"I guess, why?"

"The hotel is gonna be kind a pissed, us leaving a dead person in the room, we will probably have to pay the full rate if we ever want to stay there again."

"Oh, I guess there's more to this than I thought. I can book the room with a fake name, they don't check ID's, we'll pay with cash."

"And you don't think they will remember what we look like?"

"You aren't making this any easier."

"Annie, murdering someone and getting away with it isn't supposed to be like getting laid during spring break."

"OK, do you have any ideas?" Annie's excitement level had

come down a couple of notches, but she was still pumped up about murdering the Representative.

"The cyanide part is good, and I do have some left. You let her take you to her place for a drink. I'm sure there will be some point in the evening when she leaves the room, maybe to go to the bathroom, or to put on something more comfortable, then you slip the cyanide in her drink. After she drinks it, you get the hell out of there and walk to the nearest pay phone and call me. I'll come get you, we'll go back to the hotel and wait until morning, then check out and fly home."

"Wow, Todd, that's a good plan. When do you want to leave?"

"Let's see if Gene can find out if she is going to be in San Francisco or not this weekend and, if she is, we'll leave Thursday."

"That sounds good to me, do you know where the bar she goes to is? I'll see if I can get us something close."

"I think he said it was Angie's, near Fisherman's Wharf."

"That's good, I know we can get into the Hyatt there. Call me as soon as you talk to Gene."

The two continued to talk about different scenarios that might come up. If necessary, Annie said she could probably get the tickets switched to Washington D.C., Margaret Oliver probably had a favorite bar up there too. They could use the same plan, just change the location. Todd agreed and said goodbye. He hung up the phone and felt another chill rise up his spine, Annie Simmons was a scary woman.

Todd called Gene Thompson to discuss the conversation he had just had with Annie. Gene agreed that she was cold, but he wasn't surprised. He always felt she had the type of personality that would do anything, even kill, if it would get her more attention at the next party. What did surprise Gene was fact that she was willing to have sex with Representative Oliver and that it would not be her first lesbian encounter.

"That's an incredible story," Gene said after Todd told him of Annie's homosexual fling.

"It surprised me. I always said she would fuck anything that walked, but I meant men. I have to admit, I thought about asking her if she had a friend and we could get together for a *menage a trois*, except she would probably bring a guy."

"You had better be very specific, that's for sure. I'll call Oliver's office tomorrow and tell them I would like to set up an appointment in D.C. My guess is they will tell me that she is going to be in San Francisco, or wherever, if she is not going to be in Washington - they usually do."

"Why do they tell you?"

"I tell them I'm a lobbyist for the NRA or tobacco industry, her secretary would tell me the last time she peed if I asked."

"Not only would she tell you, she probably would do it all over herself. Let me know what you find out."

"See ya."

Gene hung up the phone and pictured Representative Margaret Oliver's lesbian secretary peeing all over herself.

* * * * * *

Eric Moore had been laid off from the Houston Post almost a year and his unemployment benefits were about to expire. His 1990 Acura Integra was paid for and still ran fine. He lived in a nice apartment very close to the Southwest Freeway, U.S. Highway 59, south of Houston, that was far enough out so the rent was reasonable, yet close enough to be only 15 minutes from the Galleria area, "uptown," as it's commonly referred to.

The combination of unemployment and unreported proceeds from freelancing, Eric found he could live quite well. Having only rent, telephone and electric bills to pay each month left him with plenty of spending money, which he spent freely.

Eric spent half the day Monday determining how long he could live if he did not earn anything by freelance, once his unemployment insurance expired. The findings were not pleasant. He now wished had not personally delivered the second letter to Gary Stephens in Phoenix. But that was done, no reason to worry about it now.

Freelancing was what Eric enjoyed, but he also liked having a steady paycheck. Editors were fickle, one day they may love your work and the next you couldn't pay them to print it. Eric spent the second half of Monday updating his résumé and selecting articles to send with it. He selected a dozen or so publications from a database he kept on his hard drive which contained the name, address and phone number of almost every publication in the United States and Canada.

He typed what he thought was a good cover letter, briefly explaining his qualifications and achievements, imported the editor's name and address from the database, and sent the letter to his laser printer. In minutes, Eric was holding a stack of perfectly typed and addressed résumés and envelopes.

The three articles Eric picked out, were, in his own opinion, some of his best work. With this résumé, and these articles, he was sure he would have a job before the unemployment ran out. It was late when he was satisfied with the letter, resume and sample works, but he didn't have anything better to do and he wanted to get them in the early mail. Kinko's Copies were open 24 hours a day, so he decided to go out and make his copies and drop the finished product in the mail.

As Eric Moore opened his apartment door, FBI Agent Curt Wright brought the Nikon F with a 90 - 250 zoom lens to his eye. Eric closed the door and walked down the single flight of steps. By the time he reached the ground, Agent Wright had used half a roll of film. He and his partner, Agent Sam Zimmerman watched as Eric started his car and drove out of the parking lot toward the freeway.

Zimmerman drove as Wright radioed in that they were on the move, the suspect had been spotted and was going north on the Southwest Freeway in a white Acura Integra. Agent Wright photographed the car and Eric in the car. Eric took the first exit from the freeway causing Zimmerman to accelerate in order to keep from losing him. The agents were worried that somehow Eric may have spotted them, it's very unusual for someone to enter a freeway then immediately take the first exit. Eric pulled in to the parking lot of Kinko's and parked. The two agents pulled into the second entrance of the strip center and circled back. Eric was already walking into the copy store, he had not seen the two agents following him.

Wright continued to snap pictures of Eric Moore in the brightly lit store while Zimmerman called in the updated location. A second team consisting of one Houston agent and one Arizona agent was on their way to help in the surveillance. It is always better with two teams when following somebody, if one gets cut off or is forced into making a wrong turn, the other team can cover until the first team can get back into position.

Eric made his copies, paid and left. He had no interest in the man behind the counter and no desire to chat with him. Eric sat in his car and folded the copies and stuffed the envelopes. For all practical purposes, he was oblivious to his surroundings. Zimmerman and Wright were trying their best to be nonchalant, but it didn't matter, Eric wouldn't have noticed them anyway.

FBI team two arrived at the same time Eric was backing out of the parking space and radioed to team one that they had him. Team one waited until both cars were out of sight before giving chase. Eric was listening to Nine Inch Nails on the radio and was in no hurry. He was driving the speed limit of 35 miles per hour, which was horribly slow to every other driver on the road. The two FBI teams were having a hard time going slow enough to stay a safe distance behind but close enough to follow.

Team two reported the subject had turned into a post office parking lot. The parking lot was empty so they would continue on and turn around. Team one stopped at another strip center close enough to see the post office parking lot. Eric drove up to the mail drop, stopping long enough to deposit his résumés in the blue and red box, then exited the parking lot going the same direction from which he had come. Team one pulled in behind and followed him back to his apartment where he parked his car and went inside.

Team two parked next to Team one in the parking lot. From their vantage point, they could clearly see the door of Eric's apartment and the steps leading down. Visitors would most likely park much closer than the agents to the apartment and not notice the two suspicious men in the dark Chevrolet watching and photographing them.

Team two, consisting of Agent Harry Berg from Arizona and Guy Holland of Houston took over the surveillance of the apartment. Team one returned to the office to have the film developed and distribute pictures, the first identifiable pictures of a member of the Blind Luck gang.

As team one left the scene, they passed the plain white van which was arriving to set up the electronic surveillance. Without permission to wire tape, the FBI had to rely on free-air snooping. When using portable or mobile phones, the signal is broadcast from a high frequency transmitter, the phone base, to the receiver, the phone. That signal is broadcast over the air waves and is available for anyone with a receiver tuned to the same frequency to listen. Since the signal is being broadcast, it is not illegal to tune in via a scanner and listen to the conversation. If Eric Moore uses a portable phone, the FBI was now ready to listen in. If not, a warrant was required to install a phone tap as well as other listening devises inside the apartment.

Eric used a portable phone. So did several hundred other people with in the apartment complex. Without a tape of Eric's voice, recognition was impossible. The agents monitored as many calls as they could, listening for anything that would identify Eric, while the computers digitally recorded every call within its range.

Eric opened a beer and turned on the television. He channel surfed the dial before deciding nothing very good was on. He settled on a Los Angeles Dodgers, Atlanta Braves baseball game. He watched the game until he finished the beer and went to bed. He was happy with what he had accomplished today. The FBI agents settled back for a long and uneventful evening.

25

Agents Christian and McBride sat in Judge Malcolm K. Winter's chambers as the Judge read the three letters received by Gary Stephens at the Phoenix Tribune and the article written by Eric Moore when he was a student at the University of Texas at Austin. Judge Winter was very deliberate as he read the letters. Agent Christian would have sworn he saw the Judge's lips move.

The judge laid the letters on his desk and continued to stare at them through the bottom half of his bifocal glasses. He stared at the papers so long that the agents began to get antsy, they crossed and uncrossed their legs, glanced at each other with facial expressions that said, "what in the hell is this guy doing?."

With a pained look on his face Judge Winter finally looked up at the two agents and said, "what else do you have?"

Again the two agents looked at each other, this time hoping one or the other would have an answer for the Judge.

It was Agent McBride's jurisdiction, but it was Christian's case, so after a moment or two of awkward silence, Agent Christian said, "that is all we have linking Eric Moore to the Congressional murders, your honor. We have partial pictures of a woman we cannot yet identify, finger prints we have as of yet been unable to match, and we have linked the chemical used in one of the deaths to a plant located just outside of Houston. Eric Moore may not have been involved in the actual deaths, but I think the article written by him definitely links him to the killings."

"You say he wrote this article his senior year of college, 1992 while at UT, correct?"

"Yes, sir."

"Have you read anything else written by him since then?"

"Yes, we have every article he wrote for the Tribune and every article he wrote while he was at the Houston Post. He has been doing some freelancing lately and we have found some of those works. We are still looking for the rest."

"Did you bring anything that he has written lately that may link him to your case?"

Both agents knew where Judge Winter was going and they didn't like it. Agent Christian hesitated before he said, "we could not find anything in any article he has written since the article you are holding that would tie him to the case."

The Judge paused and looked at the letters and the newspaper pieces again, as though he was trying to read something into them that was not there. "I'm sorry. You have one newspaper article out of three, all of them written almost six years ago, that is similar, very similar I must admit, to the letters received by a newspaper editor claiming responsibility for the murder of four United States Congressmen. I'm very sorry, personally I think he may be connected, but this is not enough for me to grant you permission to set up a wire tap or to search his home. Even if I did grant it, and you found evidence, his attorney would have it thrown out because the warrant was granted without due cause, and anything you found would not be admissible."

"Although I hate to admit it, you're right. We could jeopardize getting convictions." said Agent McBride.

"Bring me something substantial and I'll give you your warrants. But I need enough so it won't get tossed at trial."

The agents shook hands with Judge Winter and watched as he put on his black robe for court. The agents left the office first and were almost out of the court room when they heard the bailiff announce "all rise," as the Judge entered his court.

"I knew what we had was pretty lame, but I hoped he would do it so we would have a fighting chance. We could be following this guy for week, or months, or what if he is the wrong guy, what if it is a coincidence that the ideology is very similar? How long do we follow Eric Moore until we say 'uncle' and look somewhere else?"

"Alex, we've been watching him less than 24 hours, let's give it a chance."

Agent Christian laughed and shook his body, he looked like a dog that had just gotten out of the water, "we've been on this for over three weeks and this is the only thing we have. I just needed to blow off a little steam, sorry about all that. I honestly think this guy is involved, and search warrant or no search warrant, we will nail him."

"That's better, let's go find something 'substantial'."

* * * * * *

"I'm not sure I understand. They let us take a sailboat and sail anywhere we want to?" Kathy Beck had just been informed of her future husband's idea for a honeymoon.

"That's right, it's just like renting a car. You get in the car and you can drive anywhere you want to. We can find a small deserted island and snorkel in the crystal clear water and make love on the beach in the pure white sand. It's the perfect honeymoon. No lights, no telephones, no motor cars. . . "

Kathy interrupted, "if you break in to the theme from Gilligan's Island, the wedding is off."

"I know the words, you know, are you sure you don't want me to sing it?"

"I'll wait. Back to this sailing thing, are you sure you can sail?"

"Of course, I've been sailing for years on Clear Lake and Galveston Bay. You don't have to be that good, anyway, there's a motor on the boat so you could just motor from place to place. They give you regular charts plus maps for idiots with all the islands and the best anchorages on them. All you have to bring is booze and clothes, they supply everything else."

"Are you sure you don't want to take a regular cruise? Maybe through the Panama Canal, everybody says that is real boring, we could stay in our cabin and make love all day."

"Kathy, I love you, but we could stay here and make love in my apartment all day, staying on a sailboat would be an adventure too."

"Russell, I love you too, but I have had enough adventure the past few weeks to last a lifetime." She kissed him gently on the lips and said, "maybe it would be relaxing to be on a boat with no place to go and nothing to do, why don't you go ahead and check on it."

"I'm glad you said that," Russell said with a smile. He went and got his *Sail Magazine* from his green sports bag. "There are a bunch of yacht charters all over the Caribbean, Antigua, St. Croix, Bahamas, just about any place you want to go."

"Wherever you want, except the Bahamas, that's pretty common, if I'm going to spend time on a sailboat, I want it to be someplace exotic."

"I can do that, let's pick out a place and I'll make some calls, maybe I'll call Annie and see if she has heard anything about the islands."

"I'm sure she has."

"Ooh, Kathy, my love, did I detect a bit of sarcasm in your voice?"

"I just get tired of hearing her favorite line, 'been there, done that', I don't know if she's chartered a sailboat before, but I bet she's spent all day fucking in the sand."

* * * * * *

When Eric Moore's apartment went dark early Monday evening, team two knew they were in for a long night. Agents Berg and Holland spent time walking around the complex and telling old war stories. One agent would keep watch while the other napped or drove to McDonald's for a snack and a bathroom break. Whichever agent was on watch, would stay in position to watch the apartment door, without being too conspicuous, which was difficult when standing alone, late at night, with a portable radio. The agents had "police" written all over them, luckily, nobody came or went to notice. Team one arrived as the sun was beginning to come up. It was none too soon for agents Berg and Holland.

The four agents talked about the non-events of the prior evening before team two was officially relieved. The only excitement of the night came when the communications van called the agents over to listen to someone who had made a 900 call. The woman on the 900 end of the call explained in graphic detail what she would do to the poor schmuck who was paying by the minute to listen. It was certain all the agents would listen to the tape before the investigation was over. It was perfectly legal, the tape had been made over public airwaves.

With a newly printed and distributed 8 X 10 photograph of Eric Moore, the two agents sat and waited for him to make an appearance. Every hour they would check in with the command center to let them know they were alive and well and everything was fine. Several teams were standing by in case Eric had visitors. Everyone who came to the door, with the exception of the postal carrier, would be followed and photographed.

Agent Christian debriefed team two along with Agent McBride. They were hoping for something, anything, to at least suggest they were on the right trail. Team two could give them nothing.

Christian leaned back in his swivel desk chair and looked at the picture of Eric Moore that had been thumb-tacked to the wall in the command center. It was an excellent photograph. The high speed, low grain film had plenty of light inside Kinko's to produce a very detailed likeness of suspect number 1. Plenty of space had been reserved on the wall for other suspects, unfortunately, Eric Moore was not cooperating.

Eric was in his money-saving mode. He had no reason to go out and he had no reason to invite anyone over. He spent most of his time at his computer working on articles. He had several in various stages of completion and he was determined to finish them and send them to editors. Eric promised himself if he finished them, or at least most of them, he would take a beer and go to the pool for a while.

From his bedroom window, if he pressed his head real close, he could see the pool and most of the concrete patio that surrounded it. Occasionally, Eric would check the pool grounds to see if anyone, anyone female, was there. If there was, he might reconsider his goal of finishing the articles and go to the pool earlier than planned. For whatever reason he was up and moving around the apartment, he would look out, then disgruntled, go back to work.

Agent Wright sat at a large round table with a bigger umbrella next to the pool. Agent Zimmerman had made the noon run to McDonald's for hamburgers, French fries and soda. Wright sat at the pool with his radio and camera under a beach towel. He wore a white polo shirt, brown shorts and tan boat shoes. When Eric Moore checked the pool area for nubile young women, the agent was the only person he saw. Eric went back to work, never giving Wright a second thought.

* * * * * *

The telephone on Todd's desk made its annoying high pitched warble and Todd picked up the handset before it could make the sound a second time.

"This is Todd," he said into the mouth piece.

"Good afternoon Mr. Evans."

"Well, good afternoon to you Dr. Thompson, how are you this bright and beautiful day?"

"I am just fine and dandy Mr. Evans." The two chuckled into the telephone. They didn't call each other often, but they had just gone through a typical exchange. Gene Thompson continued, "I talked to, who I presume was a young woman, it was very hard to tell by the voice, who was Representative Oliver's secretary. The

209

Representative is going to be in her office in Washington the
remainder of this week and also through Wednesday of next week.
She would be happy to see me this Friday or next Monday or
Tuesday. She is tied up Wednesday and is leaving late Wednesday
for San Francisco. She will be back in her office the following
Monday."

"That's great Gene, did you set up an appointment with her?"
Todd laughed after he asked the question.

"I told her I would have to call back, I was tied up this week and
next with several Senators, but I really wanted to meet with her. The
secretary said she would be happy to set up an appointment with Ms.
Oliver for the week after next. I couldn't tell if she peed in her pants,
but I'll bet she was wearing pants."

After the picture of the dyke peeing in her pants had faded from
their memories, Todd said, "thanks Gene, I really appreciate that.
Annie has some comped stand-by tickets we can use at any time, but
I think she has to make hotel reservations in advance."

"Are you sure you want to do this, I mean she may have some
security with her. Be careful and don't be afraid to bail and come
home."

"Don't worry, I know Annie is fired up about doing this, so I
am going to explain many times that she doesn't have to do it. The
first sign of trouble and she is to get the hell out and we will come
home."

"I hope she doesn't let her ego carry her away and get her, or
us all, in trouble."

"Yeah, me too. Listen, I've got to get back to work, are you
going for pizza Thursday night?"

"Most likely."

"Good, Annie and I are too, I don't know about Russell and
Kathy, but everybody else will be there."

"See you Thursday. Bye."

"Bye." Todd hung up the phone and thought about what Gene
had said. Just about everything Annie did was so she could brag, or
at least talk about it, later on. This is one event she would never be
able to talk to anyone outside of the group about. This worried Todd.
He could picture her with some Studly Wellhung at some resort,
listening as he told stories about his great run on Wall Street or how
in college he intercepted a Troy Aikman pass and ran it back for a
touchdown. Annie would listen until she couldn't stand it any more
and precede to tell him how she and her friends, mostly she,

masterminded the murder of five United States Congressman. Annie would say five, she would definitely take credit for the timely murder of Senator Abernathy.

After much thought, Todd decided to go ahead with the plan. If he decided at any point that it was too big of a risk involving Annie that closely, he could call it off. At least he was going to get an inexpensive trip to San Francisco out of the deal, he had always wanted to go there. He tried to remember what they called Frisco, "the city for lovers," or "the most romantic city," or something like that. He knew it had to do with romance. He just wished he was not going with a woman that looked a little like Grampa Munster, who was planning to seduce and kill another woman.

Todd prepared a vacation request form for April 30 through May 3 and sent it to his boss for approval. He then called Annie Simmons to tell her it was on and to make the reservations.

26

Eric Moore grew up on television. He could sit and watch reruns of Hogan's Heroes, Bewitched and The Beverly Hillbillies for days, and, much to the chagrin of the FBI agents stationed outside his apartment, he did. There had even been speculation among the agents that he had slipped out, unseen by the team on duty, and that he was not even in the apartment. His car had not moved in two days, so he must still be in there, they reasoned. Each team would suggest, only half jokingly, that a different team had blown their cover and Eric had skipped town, never to be seen again.

Even Eric was feeling the need to get out after being inside for the better part of three days. He was convinced he needed to find a new apartment and he would check out the pool first. If there were attractive women around it, he would look at the apartment. In his complex, there obviously were no attractive women that didn't work during the day.

Eric called Russell at Kathy's to see if they were going for pizza, it was Thursday. Russell said Kathy was busy planning the wedding, but he was going to try, she might, it would depend on what she was doing when it was time to leave. Eric said he would see him around seven and hung up the phone.

Russell and Eric had been friends for years and knew each others voices well. There was no need tell the other who was on the phone. The FBI communications van recorded the conversation and filed it as another unidentified call. The FBI had well documented evidence that an enormous amount of pizza was consumed by the residents of The Forum Park Apartments.

After showering and shaving for the first time in two days, Eric left his apartment for Chuck's Pizza on Richmond Avenue. He wore tan shorts, a white polo shirt and hiker sandals. He preferred boat shoes but sandals were "in" footwear, so he wore them. Agent Zimmerman pressed the shutter release on his Nikon and the motor drive advanced the film. They had a couple of very good shots of

Eric, but here was a chance to take a few more in broad daylight. These would be even better than the ones he had taken at Kinko's.

Agent Zimmerman kept the camera handy as he called in the team's position on the radio. Another team immediately scrambled to intercept and help follow. The agents had no trouble staying a safe distance behind, but not losing track of Eric. Traffic was heavy enough so the agents could keep a couple of cars between themselves and the white Acura, but still have no trouble changing lanes or turning if Eric did.

The second FBI team pulled into the parking lot of Chuck's pizza a few minutes after Zimmerman had radioed their position. Team two got out of their dark Chevrolet and into team one's dark Chevrolet for a strategy session.

Chuck's pizza was a free standing building on the corner of a busy intersection in Uptown Houston. The building had several tall, thin windows that were dark tinted and impossible to see in. The agents were positive Eric was not inside eating pizza alone, but they could not see in from the outside. Being a public restaurant, numerous people would be coming and going, they had to have a team inside.

The choice was between going inside the air-conditioned building to eat pizza or staying outside and waiting for the signal to photograph and follow someone leaving. Technically, team one was still in charge, they took the inside duty. Wired with the standard FBI short-range communication system, Agents Zimmerman and Wright entered Chuck's Pizza and found a perfect position to watch Eric Moore.

The waitress was bringing a pitcher of beer to the table, with seating for eight, where Eric sat alone, as the two agents found a booth and sat down. They had found a booth along the wall with high backs that, if he leaned just a little, Agent Wright could see Eric's table. When sitting inside the booth, the agents could not be seen by anyone who might join Eric. Everybody, however, would have to walk past the agents to get to the table.

The agents looked at the menus as they watched Eric to kill some time. It was a good guess that Eric was expecting several people, and a large group meant they might be there a while. The same waitress that had brought beer to Eric waited on the two agents.

Wright and Zimmerman had been partners for over two years and knew each other well. Zimmerman said, "give us one large special and I'll have an iced tea."

"And I'll have a Coke," said Wright.

As the waitress wrote the order a second person sat at the table with Eric Moore. Wright leaned just slightly to get a better look. It was Russell Lewis, he was alone. The waitress retreated to the kitchen to give the cook the newest pizza order, then to make the agents their drinks.

When he was sure the waitress was out of sight and no one could see him, Agent Wright put the small ear piece in his ear and whispered into the microphone he was hiding in the palm of his hand. "Team two, this is team one," he paused and waited for team two to respond. Again, he spoke into the hidden microphone, "team two, we have a second subject just joining the party. He is a white male, 25 to 30 years old, around 6 feet tall, 175 to 185 pounds, brown hair, clean shaven. He will be wearing blue shorts and a polo shirt."

Team two repeated the description and reported that they had seen the subject enter the building. Since there was still plenty of light, they were photographing everyone who entered the building. Agent Wright acknowledged and informed team two that he was out. He put the microphone and ear-piece back into his pocket.

"They've already got a picture of number two, they are taking everybody that comes in as long as they have light. Let's hope they all get here before dark."

Agent Zimmerman agreed.

The pizza came quicker than the agents would have preferred. They ate slowly and drank way more iced tea and cola than one should when on a stakeout. They had watched the apartment all day and they would probably be watching someone all night.

The process of pulling the ear piece and microphone out and describing subjects happened three more times as Annie, Todd, and Julie arrived. All three had been photographed as they entered the building.

"Damn, I wish we could get a bug on that table, I would love to hear what they are talking about." Agent Zimmerman said.

"Me too, but we can't even do that legally any more," answered Wright.

"You can't legally kill four Congressmen either, but they may have. I wish we had a snooper with us, we could point that little dude at the table and hear everything they're saying, no one would ever know."

Zimmerman agreed, but there was nothing they could do about it now. They sat and watched as Mark Flanagen and Gene Thompson showed up. Wright radioed the information to team two who responded by saying it was too dark to get pictures, they would have to try again later.

By easing just a little to his right, Agent Wright could see Todd and Annie at the end of the table, leaning in toward each other, involved in a private conversation.

"I have a reservation at the Hyatt Fisherman's Wharf for Wednesday through Saturday night." Annie said. "The best rate I could get was 99 dollars a night, but that's good for San Francisco. After New York City, San Francisco is one of the most expensive towns in the country. We should be pretty close to Angie's, or whatever the name of that lessie bar is, so I can walk to it every night if I have to. I sure hope I don't have to, I would like to see a little more of the town." She thought for a second and said, "but if I find what's her name the first night, then we're coming home, right?" Todd nodded but didn't say anything. "So, no matter what, I am going to spend whatever nights I'm in San Francisco, trying to get picked up by a woman. Damn, I'll have to go back for a real visit sometime."

Todd sat drinking beer as he listened to Annie talk about how smoothly it would go. Gene picked up his wine and joined the two at the end of the table. He sat with his large back to Agent Wright, effectively blocking the agent's view. Gene pulled some folded papers from his shirt pocket and slid them along the table to Annie.

"These are from a magazine article I had about Representative Oliver. There's a picture of her and it mentions her likes and dislikes. The name of her favorite bar is in the article, and it says she goes there quite often. I don't know if she will be there this trip or not, but that's the only place I know of. If she doesn't show, you might mention that you're from San Antonio or Dallas or New York, anywhere but Houston, and you met her there last year and you would like to see her. Start by asking if anybody knows her, and if they do know her, ask if she is in town. Act like you didn't know she was in town or they might get suspicious. Just something you might try if she's not there, I'd hate to think you wasted your trip. But be careful, the more people you talk to, the more people that will have a chance to recognize you and identify you."

"Thanks Gene, but I know that. I can handle it." Annie said.

Without the luxury of being able to drink several pitchers of beer, Agents Zimmerman and Wright were having a hard time staying inside the Chuck's Pizza without looking suspicious. The waitress refilled their drinks whenever they were low, but she was taking longer and longer to come around each time. It didn't look like the group was about to disband any time soon, so Wright brought out his radio kit again.

"Team one to team two."

"This is team two, go ahead team one."

"It doesn't look like the party is going to be breaking up any time soon. You all come in and get the booth directly in front of us and we will come out."

"That sounds good to us, team one, we were just thinking about getting something to eat."

"How much back up is out there?"

"Besides us, we have five, one team for each subject, if you all are up to an all-nighter."

"No problem here. It must look like a convention out there."

"That's a Roger."

"Team one out."

Agent Wright tried to picture the seven dark Chevrolets all parked in a row in the parking lot. They wouldn't be together, he knew, but it was fun to imagine.

Team two came in and seated themselves in the booth next to team one. Zimmerman and Wright left a very generous tip, paid the bill, used the restroom and left.

Agent Guy Holland situated himself near the end of the booth so he could see the end of the subject table. By leaning out just a little, he could see the entire group. Being one booth closer gave them a much better view to see the table but was of no help with hearing. Agent Berg carried the radio because he was totally hidden from view of everyone at the table.

Berg tested the radio and reported they were in position. If the waitress was the slightest bit suspicious, she did not let on as she took the order from the agents of team two.

Berg and Holland were digging into their mushroom and black olive pizza when Holland noticed Gene Thompson stand up and start shaking hands. "I think we have one leaving," he said to Berg who relayed it to team one, who radioed team seven to stand by, one suspect was on his way out. The description of Gene, white male, early 40's, 5'6" or 7", 200 pounds, balding, brown slacks and a tan dress shirt, sleeves rolled up, followed and was relayed to team seven.

Gene hugged Annie and Julie, put a ten dollar bill in the middle of the table and waved goodbye as he left. Team seven pulled to the rear of Chuck's, turned around, and waited. Gene Thompson walked outside and got into his truck. Zimmerman radioed that subject number seven was entering a white 95 Ford Ranger pickup truck, Texas license number X ray, Charlie, Tango, Charlie, six, six. XCTC 66. Five minutes later as team seven was following the white Ranger, Zimmerman radioed that the truck was registered to Gene David Thompson, Houston, Texas. No outstanding warrants.

Todd drained the heavy glass beer mug and sat it hard on the table, making a resounding clank. He announced that it was getting late and some people had to go to work the next morning. Annie agreed, she was also getting tired and was ready to go. Todd put a donation toward the tab on the table and left with Annie. Agent Berg notified team one that subjects three and four were on their way out. Zimmerman relayed the message to teams three and four, "you're up."

Eric, Russell, Mark and Julie moved closer and ordered another pitcher of beer. The subject of conversation immediately turned to Annie and Todd. Julie managed about half a mug of beer before she was thoroughly disgusted with the conversation. She added her contribution to the check fund and left. Team five was dispatched to follow the red Camaro, registered to Julie E. Hanson.

The three people still at the table seriously considered ordering one more pitcher of beer, but Mark said he needed to get up early for work. Russell said he wasn't in a big hurry, Kathy's mother was coming into town to help her with the wedding plans. Kathy had told her mother she could handle the arrangements, but her mother insisted. In less than a week the wedding had gone from an elopement in Las Vegas to a church wedding with attendants, flowers and ushers, followed by a reception with a cake, a meal and booze. The booze part was the only part Russell and his friends were interested in.

With Kathy's mother coming to Houston until after the wedding, Russell was going to have to move back to his apartment. From the way Kathy talked earlier in the evening, he may not even see her for a while. "Kathy said 'her mother had a thousand things for them to do until the wedding' and I don't think they involved me," he told his friends.

Eric was not in a hurry to leave either. He would just as soon stay at Chuck's and drink beer, then sleep late in the morning. He had nothing planned for the day.

Russell waved at the waitress, who was beginning to sweep the floor around the empty tables. So that she wouldn't have to make an extra trip across the room, Russell held up the empty beer pitcher and waived it. She nodded and disappeared toward the kitchen. She soon reappeared with beer and three new frosted mugs. Mark decided that it wasn't that late after all, he would stay and help them finish the new pitcher of beer.

Agent Berg pressed the transmit button on the small transceiver and told the Agents waiting outside that it might be a while, the three remaining subjects just ordered another pitcher of beer.

Eric wanted to talk about the wedding. He felt his friend was rushing into it. Sure, he thought Kathy was stunning, even more stunning after he saw more of her, and yes, he thought she had a wonderful personality. She was indeed perfect, but he thought they should date a while. Eric couldn't come up with a single valid reason Russell and Kathy should not get married. A "gut" feeling was not good enough for Russell.

Gene had been married and divorced before he met the group, no other member was married. Russell and Kathy would be the first. The longest either of the three men still at the table had spent under one roof with a woman was about a week. Russell had just surpassed that record and his friends wanted details. Every guy in the group, at one time or another had a crush on Kathy, but she never gave any of them, other than Russell who seem oblivious to it for a year, the slightest hint that she was interested romantically.

And now Russell was living with her and was about to be married to her. Another pitcher was ordered, this was a special occasion, it might be the last Thursday night at Chuck's Pizza that Russell would spend as a bachelor.

Other than the three men sitting at the far corner of the long table, Agents Berg and Holland were alone in Chuck's Pizza Place. Berg radioed that the subjects were the only ones left and there was no need for them to stay inside.

Agent Berg left enough money on the table to cover the check and a tip and the two men joined the other agents outside.

Russell discussed the wedding plans Kathy had made and his idea for a honeymoon. Eric and Mark were much more interested in the sailing trip than in the type of cake Kathy had ordered for the reception. Russell left out the part about making love on the beach in broad daylight, even though he badly wanted to mention it.

The waitress came and politely suggested they leave, it was

past last call and she needed to pick up the pitcher. Eric poured the beer that was in the pitcher evenly into the three mugs. Eric made one last toast to Russell and Kathy, "may you live happily ever after."

The three added up the pot and tossed in enough money to pay the bill and leave a nice tip, said goodbye to the waitress and left. Having too much to drink and knowing they were way beyond the legal blood alcohol level, they each drove the speed limit and made sure to signal every turn. Teams one, two and six had no trouble following.

Agent Christian tacked the last of the six pictures on the wall next to the picture of Eric Moore. He sat in his swivel desk chair and leaned back as far as it would allow. Alexander Christian studied each picture and the name that was attached to it. "She's not here."

There were several people in the room, but Christian was not speaking to anyone in particular. Agent Lori Anderson said, "I'm sorry, did you say something?"

Without moving his head from the photographs on the wall, he repeated, "she's not here, the Lucky Bit. . . uh, the Lucky B., she's not here. Damn it!"

Agents Wright and Zimmerman let team three take surveillance on Eric Moore's apartment when it was obvious that Annie and Todd were only going to require one team for the night. They came back to the command center with the film for developing and to brief Agent Christian on the evening. Annie Simmons was the only picture on the wall without a name. She had come with Todd and left with him. Two teams of agents followed just in case Todd dropped her somewhere and continued. One team would have stayed with the woman while the other team took Todd Evans. The apartment Todd and Annie went to did not match the address returned by the Department of Motor Vehicles. Either they were at the woman's apartment or Todd Evans had moved and not changed the registration of his vehicle. Both teams stood by until team three got the orders to relieve Zimmerman and Wright.

"What about Jane Doe?" Agent Zimmerman asked, pointing at the picture of Annie Simmons. "She could have been wearing a long black wig under the hat at the rodeo arena."

Christian stared at the picture of Annie. "Nope, her legs are more muscular. Look at the calves, this girl works to keep her body like that. Lucky is younger, I'd guess five or six years, and it's all natural. The mouth is all wrong too. Look at Jane, she's got a longer nose and tiny lips, she looks a little like Grandpa Munster. 'Lucky', on the other hand has a beautiful mouth, full bottom lip, wide lower jaw bone, high cheeks, even when her mouth is at rest, it looks like she is smiling."

"Damn it, why weren't you there?" Christian said to the pictures of Kathy as he leaned back in to his chair and fell asleep.

27

Kathy spent the morning cleaning the house. Kathy was not a slob, but she was not as clean as her mother. Every generation seems to be a little less clean than the prior generation. Someday it is going to be a very filthy world. Russell had helped some the day before and it was his responsibility to make sure all the beer cans, wine bottles and pizza boxes were in the trash.

Kathy ran the vacuum sweeper and fluffed all the pillows on the couch. Her main concern was that she would miss evidence that Russell had been living there. She did not want her mother to find a man's sock stuffed behind a pillow.

Satisfied the house looked good, as good as a 20 year old girl living alone should be expected to keep it, Kathy sat down to watch the news until it was time to leave for the airport to pick up her mother.

She flipped the channel from the local all news channel to CNN to CNBC looking for updates on the Congressman killers. She was still timid about being seen in public. Whenever she was out, she had this horrible feeling people were looking at her. In fact, people were looking at her. From the time she was 13, she could turn heads, men and women would look at the beautiful woman entering the restaurant or walking through the mall. Until she had become wanted by almost every law enforcement agency in the world, she didn't notice the people looking at her.

The news didn't mention the killings. It had been almost two weeks since the deaths of Senator Abernathy and Representative James. It was old news. The FBI had not held a press conference since they reported Abernathy's death. *Hard Copy, Inside Edition, EXTRA* and The Fox Network aired the video tape from the rodeo arena, but public response was underwhelming. The video was soon old news as well.

The effect the deaths had on Congress and passage of the "spite" bills, as the press had labeled them, the recent bills which had been passed only to spite the "Congress Killers," were the only things still actively being discussed by the media.

Kathy was glad the media had stopped talking about the deaths. She tried to avoid the news during the first days after the death of James, but she inevitably would see or hear a news report on how Representative James died. The reports would bring the picture of Jack James being crushed between the Dodge Ram and the horse trailer rushing back to her memory. The image she would see in her head was as clear as the day it happened. She would begin shaking and sometimes the feeling that she would vomit was so strong, she would go to the bathroom and kneel by the toilet.

She thought about the incident less and less every day. In her opinion, she was dealing with it very well, considering the circumstances. Kathy looked at the clock and realized it was past time to leave for the airport. She called Russell to see how he was and how the evening had gone at Chuck's. Russell said he had a slight hangover, but was fine. She said she had to leave to go to the airport to get her mother, and would try to call later. Russell said he would be home, it was Friday night and he missed her terribly, but understood that she needed to spend time with her mother. They both said "I love you," and hung up the telephones.

Kathy left for the airport while Russell took another Tylenol. He hadn't missed her the night before, the first night in over two weeks that they had not been together, but he missed her desperately now. Russell couldn't make himself do anything, he laid on the couch and channel surfed. He never expected he could miss anyone as much as he missed Kathy. It was going to be a long weekend.

The FBI did not have enough resources to put a complete communications van at the location of everybody Eric Moore came in contact with. Team two, still outside Russell's apartment waiting for relief, had a hand held scanner that could pick up most portable telephone frequencies. On a Friday morning, there was very little air traffic, which made it possible for the Agents to monitor, at least for a short while, every phone conversation that took place within the apartment complex over a portable phone. Russell Lewis still used the old fashioned type phone which was connected to the wall by a cord. His conversations were private.

* * * * * *

The FBI had called for all available personnel. They currently had seven teams in the field following persons believed to be involved with the murders of four U.S. Congressmen. Each team of two were given a second vehicle to make the surveillance easier. One agent in one dark colored Chevrolet kept the subject, or the subject vehicle in sight at all times.

Annie Simmons worked in a large office building so it was impossible to keep her in visual contact. The travel agency Annie worked for was a retail operation even though most of their business was handled over the telephone. The building also housed a small deli as well as many other businesses. Houston agent Howard Weiss cautiously followed Annie up the elevator to the main entrance of PFC Travel and watched her enter the large double glass doors. Two receptionists sat just inside the doors to accept visitors. Those visitors needing a travel agent, waited for the agent to come to the front and escort them back to the cubicle they called an office. Those visitors wanting to pick up tickets or travel brochures were helped by one of the two receptionists.

Agent Weiss studied the area long enough to determine there was no place he could watch the large glass doors from without being overly conspicuous. He returned to his dark Chevrolet and reported that they could only watch her car. That was acceptable, the FBI now had a name and address after checking her license number with the DMV. The orders were to watch her, but don't get too close. If she was involved, or even if she wasn't involved, if she thought she was being followed, she might mention it to one of her friends, a friend that very well could be involved, and the entire gang would be alerted.

The FBI's policy, at the moment, was to treat everyone of the seven that were with Eric Moore on Thursday night as highly possible suspects. If possible, every person that came into contact with the original seven would be identified.

The work at the Blind Luck command center had become fast and furious. All seven photographs now had a name attached to the bottom of it. The one remaining picture, a computer generated print, was merely labeled "Lucky."

The files on the seven were getting thicker by the minute as more information came into the command center. Two sets of files were being kept, hard and computer. The hard file, a simple manila folder with every single piece of paper on that person, was kept in a topless box on a large table in the center of the room. One person was in charge of the box. That agent would review every single document and log it before filing it in the folder. It was his job to be sure no duplicates got into the folder.

The second set of files were kept in the computer. Every piece of paper and photograph was scanned and stored under the suspect's private directory. The files were tagged as "read-only," anybody on the system could access any document and view it or print it, but they could not modify it or erase it.

Once the names were known, several agents worked around the clock gathering every single piece of public information about Eric Moore and the people he had come in contact with. There is an enormous amount of information about each individual that is public information. Once the FBI had a name, address, driver's license number and social security number, it was easy to obtain a wealth of knowledge about the individual. By checking their credit history, they could find out where they worked, where they liked to eat, where they liked to shop, where they banked, even where they usually filled up their car with gas. As long as they used a credit card, it would show up. A check of the state records would report anyone on unemployment or welfare. Eric Moore showed up on unemployment, a printout of his record went into the file. By accessing the county courthouse records, it could be found out if they were married and if so, to whom, if they owned a house or not, or if they were about to be married.

The names of Russell Lewis and Kathy Beck did not show up during the check of Harris County marriage records. The license had been purchased on Wednesday, but it would be weeks before the information was properly processed and entered into the computer. The Government really couldn't care less if the young couple were married or not, or if either one was already married, or if one had ten spouses. The Government only wanted the 20 dollars for a license and a record to notify the IRS to expect a little more money this year. Another couple was about to agree to pay Uncle Sam a little more in order to live together without "living in sin." The twenty dollar piece of paper, which took only minutes to obtain, also guaranteed at least two lawyers, in the event that the happy couple decided they were not so happy, a future income. If the divorce involved children or property, the lawyers would be able to send their child to college for a year on the fees.

With every passing minute in the command center, the lives of seven friends were becoming very well known to the FBI Agents. Unfortunately, there was still nothing in the files to connect any of the seven to the four dead Congressmen, other than being an acquaintance of a person who once wrote an article about shooting Congressmen, one at a time, until ones which remained alive acted responsibly. Every agent connected with the case knew they were grasping at straws, but at the moment, it was the only thing they had.

* * * * * *

It was a long weekend indeed for the Federal Bureau of Investigation surveillance teams. Saturday night Todd picked up Annie and took her to Pappasitos' Mexican Cantina for dinner. The purpose was to discuss the plan to kill Representative Oliver. Todd was apprehensive about killing a woman, even if the woman acted more like a man. He wondered if Annie could go though with it. What if Oliver saw her putting the cyanide in the drink? Could Annie overpower her and kill her by some other means? Todd realized he knew nothing about Representative Oliver's physical abilities. Annie worked out regularly and was in excellent condition, but what if Oliver spotted her putting poison in her drink and attempted to subdue her? Could Annie, at the very least, escape?

Todd wanted to ask Annie the questions, but couldn't find the proper way to say, *Annie, let's say Oliver sees you putting something in her drink and tries to call 911. Can you take the phone away from her and beat her in the head with the nearest blunt object until she's dead?*

He felt he had planned his murders very well, and had gotten lucky when none of the witnesses could agree on a police sketch. He thought Russell and Kathy had also had a good plan, and maybe they even got lucky the way it happened, but he didn't like the fact that his and Annie's plan was to have Annie slip poison in a drink sometime during the night. Too much could go wrong.

Annie assured Todd everything would be fine, she would be able to do it. She was going to go home with her and surely they would have something to drink. The woman would have to go to the bathroom sometime, and there would be plenty of time to spike her drink. The Congresswoman would not be expecting it, Annie had the element of surprise on her side.

Annie was very convincing. She spoke with extreme confidence. She stared him straight in the eye, her gray eyes never moving from his. Her voice never once cracked, there was absolutely no evidence of indecision. Todd now believed she could handle any unexpected situation which might arise.

Todd and Annie raised and touched their salt-rimmed margarita glasses in a toast to the success of the mission. They laughed after the toast at the word "mission." Neither had thought much about what to call what they were doing. Todd firmly believed what they were doing would ultimately benefit the country. The murder of corrupt politicians would send a message to the rest of the politicians, albeit a harsh message, but nevertheless, a message that it was time to shape up. Until the past Monday when Congress passed the spite bills, the country was already better off. Newscasts were reporting that Congress was reconsidering the spite bills following the public outcry observed the past week.

Todd believed Annie was ready to take a human life only because she had felt left out. He wondered how she would feel after she watched Representative Margaret Oliver's convulsions as she died from cyanide poisoning. It would not be a pretty sight and he was sure Annie would be changed for life. He just didn't know how she would be changed.

The two continued to drink margaritas and laugh as they discussed a better word then "mission." "Adventure" was considered, they felt they were definitely headed for an adventure, but it wasn't quite the right word either. Their train of thought wavered quickly as the alcohol took effect, and the conversation didn't stay on any subject very long.

If any one of the four FBI agents who were watching Todd and Annie have dinner could have read their lips, the whole Bureau would have been toasting. Unfortunately, stained glass, crowds, smoke and distance made it all but impossible for the agents to pick up a single word. The agents spoke often on how they needed to be able to use their electronic surveillance equipment. Without the equipment, they couldn't get the evidence needed to get the equipment.

The two FBI teams were delighted to see Todd arrive at Annie's apartment. It meant the two would be together for at least a few hours, possibly all night. They spent the night together Thursday, why wouldn't they sleep together on a Saturday night?

Both teams, four agents watched while Todd and Annie had dinner. The agents discussed who would have the night off if the two did spend the night together. It would only take two agents, and although the team which was not watching would be on call, they could go home, or to the hotel, and sleep or just take it easy until a call came for backup.

Each of the four agents were sure there would be no call for back up and wanted the time off. Team four promised to cover an extra few hours the following evening, Team three agreed and relieved them for the night, assuming the two stayed together. Todd and Annie had enough Tequila not to disappoint Team four.

While Annie and Todd were having dinner, Eric Moore was alone in his apartment more bored than usual. Friday afternoon, he had noticed a woman at the pool he had met before, so he grabbed a beer from the refrigerator and went to talk to her. She remembered him and they ended up talking for over an hour. Eric was rehearsing in his mind how he should ask her out when she said she had to leave, her boyfriend was coming over soon. Eric lied, saying he had to leave too, it was nice seeing her again, etc., and he went back to his apartment. Another team of two FBI agents were assigned to the woman and another team to her boyfriend when he left her apartment late that evening.

Being disappointed that the previous day at the pool didn't go better, Eric wanted to get out. He thought about calling Russell, but didn't really want to hear about how much he missed Kathy. After all, it had been a whole three days since he had seen her. The image of Kathy, sitting in the back seat of Russell's car holding her blouse in her hands, wearing nothing but sheer panties, came into Eric's mind. He couldn't really blame Russell for missing her.

Eric decided to call some friends he hadn't seen in a while. Some were close friends that were never part of the group and some had been close friends, but they hadn't seen each other in a while. He found four that didn't have much to do and would love to meet for a drink. They decided on Grif's, a small sports bar in the Montrose area of Houston.

They sat outside on the deck, away from the crowd of regulars, rugby players who meet at the bar after a contest. They talked about old times and old friends. Two knew Russell and were surprised he was getting married. One knew both Russell and Kathy and was very surprised the two of them were getting married.

The talk eventually made its way to the subject of the Congressional killings. Eric tried to change the subject several times but the other three seemed obsessed with it. Eric decided to sit quietly and say nothing. It was better to be quiet than to risk saying something that might tip the fact that he knew more about it than his obsessed friends who were arguing theories that were, for the most part, not even close to the truth.

This time it was distance and darkness which prevented the agents from making out any of the conversion by reading lips. Another four teams were called in to continue surveillance on Eric's friends. The agents, all dressed casual for undercover work, decided the reward outweighed the risk and attempted to get closer in order to listen to the conversation at Eric's table.

Two Houston agents went inside and ordered a beer. They stood near the door and watched one of the many small television sets hanging from the ceiling. It didn't appear that Eric nor any of his friends noticed the agents enter the bar, so they would not know that they had not been inside long. The agents casually walked onto the patio and mentioned how nice it was outside and that there sure was a lot of smoke inside. They sat at a table one over from the subjects and talked about how they thought the Astros would do this year.

When the agents heard a lull in the conversation at the table near them, they would immediately find something to talk about. When Eric's table would get loud, the agents would listen. Although they couldn't hear everything, the agents knew they were talking about the Congress killings. Unfortunately, while inside Grif's for only a few minutes, they heard several conversations about the Congress killings. Eric's table talking about it meant nothing.

28

Agent Christian called a Monday morning briefing to be attended by all the agents who had been on the case in Phoenix. As many Houston agents as were necessary to continue surveillance were to do so and the remaining were to attend the briefing.

Alexander Christian looked at his troops. None had slept more than four hours at any one time in the nearly four days since the gathering at Chuck's Pizza Place. The two women looked the best of the lot. Make up covered the dark circles under their eyes and they didn't have the stubble from lack of shaving their male counterparts were sporting.

Agent Christian began the briefing. "We have watched these seven people for almost four days. We know their names, where they live, where they work, what kind of car each drives, who they are sleeping with, what they eat, we've followed them and we've dug through their garbage. Still, the only thing we have linking them, and it only links one of them, to our investigation, is a newspaper article written six years ago. Has anyone seen or heard anything that might make us think we are on the right track?"

Agent Christian paused and panned his audience. He did not see a lot of hope in their faces. He was just about to continue when Houston Agent Jim Bond sat up in his chair in a manner that got everyone's attention. Jim Bond's real name was indeed James. He was known as "Jimmy" in high school and college, and still by his friends, but shortened it to "Jim" when he joined the FBI.

Bond put his hand to his mouth and stared off into the distance. It was obvious by the look on his face that the wheels were turning in his head, it just wasn't clear why they were turning. Christian waited, sure Agent Bond had something to say. He was about to give up on him when Bond said, "I'm Jim Bond, I was on surveillance last night at Grif's Bar. My partner and I bought a beer and tried to sit close enough to hear the conversation. What we heard was basically the same stuff we hear wherever we go. As a matter of fact, we heard similar conversations at several different locations inside the bar. But it just occurred to me that Eric Moore was not active in the conversation. For some reason, and I didn't think about it until just now, but as he was the one who wrote the article, it seems to me that he would have had some opinions on the subject. I was facing his table and I don't remember him saying anything while they were talking about the killings. They talked about other things and he joined right in, but never when they were talking about the Congress killings."

The room was silent while the agents who weren't at the bar let the agents who were think about it. Slowly, each agent agreed that, even though they couldn't hear the conversation, there were times when Eric Moore seemed to appear uninterested in the conversation. One remembered it well because Eric kept looking in his direction across the street.

The room again got quiet as all the agents thought about what had just been said. Agent Christian thought it would be a good idea to think out loud, to brainstorm. "It could mean he has talked about it so much he just didn't want to talk about it any more. Or, he didn't want to talk about it with these guys because he knows way more than they do, and he didn't want to say something he shouldn't know. Or, the other four are the ones that have actually done the killing and Eric Moore only wrote the letters and feels like an outsider."

"Sir," Agent Bond said, "from what I heard, I don't think they were involved. One suggested it was an FBI plot to get rid of undesirable Congressmen. Anything is possible, but if the FBI is behind this, I would like to know so I can go home and go to bed."

Jim Bond's comments brought some light laughter from the agents, but most of them just wanted to go home and go to bed.

"I can assure you Mr. Bond," Christian had been waiting all morning to say "Mr. Bond", "the FBI is not behind this."

Bond smiled and nodded as if to say "I know."

Agent Christian said to Agent Bond, "do you think, from what you heard, we should end the surveillance on the four from the bar?"

"Yes, sir, I do. Unless they knew we were agents and were putting on an act for us, which would have been an Oscar performance, I don't think they were involved with the murders. But I also think just as strongly that Eric Moore is very involved."

"I agree with you. We will call off surveillance on the four from last night. What about the six from Thursday night?" Christian was not asking anyone in particular. No one answered.

The agents looked at one another and whispered their opinions and ideas. Agent Christian said, "Moore could not have done this by himself. He had to have had help. We don't think the four from the bar are involved, we have the names of three of them from the DMV and addresses of all four. We should have a name for the fourth very soon. We will check them out as time allows. The only other contacts he has made was at the pizza place Thursday night. We have also come up empty there, should we call off surveillance on them too? Again, we have their names and addresses. We can find them if we need them.

"Friday afternoon Moore spent some time at his apartment pool with a woman who could have been the Lucky B. The body was very close but the digitized photographs of the lower face didn't match up. She went out with a man who is on probation for causing a disturbance at an abortion clinic. We are keeping an eye on them, although from the report of the surveillance team, I don't think they were involved with our case. We will watch them a few more days just to be sure.

"We could not hear the conversations that took place last Thursday at the pizza place, for all we know, they may have sounded exactly like the conversations from last night at Grif's bar. If they were, we might have decided to drop our surveillance of the six people that were with Moore that night too.

"We know that one of the six, Gene Thompson, is very active politically, a card carrying Democrat. We have found nothing to indicate any of the others have strong political ties at all. A couple of them aren't even registered voters. I believe Eric Moore is involved and knows the Lucky B and the driver of the truck that hit Representative James. The Lucky B is our only hope, if Moore is involved, sooner or later he, or one of his friends will meet up with her, and we will be there to take her picture.

"Once we get a picture of Lucky, and match it to the picture from the rodeo arena, we will get our warrants and wrap this thing up. Any other questions or comments?"

"Just for arguments sake, let's say we don't find Lucky, how long do you plan to keep up surveillance on Moore and the six from last Thursday?" A Houston agent asked.

"Good question." Agent Christian had been thinking about that very same thing for some time. "I can't answer it. If we have absolutely nothing more in a week than we have right now, we would have to consider dropping surveillance on some of them. As of this moment, I am prepared to follow Eric Moore indefinitely, I feel strongly that he is involved and sooner or later he will slip and we will be there to catch him."

The briefing officially ended, but most of the agents stuck around to bounce ideas off one another. Agent Christian returned to the command center to see if anything new had come in while they were at the briefing. There was nothing new. He sat in his swivel chair and looked at the photographs on the wall. The number of pictures had grown to almost 40. Anyone that any of the main seven came in contact with were photographed and put on the wall. Lines were drawn to identify who was seen with whom. The wall was beginning to look like a huge family tree with Eric Moore as the Great Great Grandfather.

* * * * * *

Unlike the slow, laid-back weekend most members of the group experienced, Kathy Beck had been busy. She and her mother bought a wedding dress and booked a small church. Friday afternoon was the only time available, so, after checking with Russell, they moved the wedding plans up one day. They ordered flowers, hired a caterer for the reception, to be held at the Beck home, hired a photographer, picked out tuxedos for Russell and his father, Todd and Kathy's father and set up appointments for them all to be fitted.

Russell had bought a wedding ring set for himself and Kathy. Kathy had suggested, rather strongly, that she wanted to be with him when he picked out rings, but Russell convinced her that she was too busy and he could handle it. She finally relented and told him to go ahead and buy them, she was a size 5. Russell tapped out one credit card on the ring, he was sure his bride would be happy.

Russell was not as pleased with his ability to book the honeymoon. The month of May was the start of the summer season for charter services and many were booked. He was finally able to make a reservation on a 40 foot Benateau in St. Marteen for the week of May 27th. He made plane reservations for May 24th, thinking they would stay in a hotel a few days before boarding the boat. It would give them a chance to explore the island so they could sail to other islands and not feel they need to stay around St. Marteen. For the two weeks between the wedding and the honeymoon, Russell booked nights in Galveston and San Antonio. A one month honeymoon sounded wonderful to Kathy.

Russell calculated how many days he would have to work contract or bartend to pay for everything, and he was satisfied he wouldn't have any trouble. Besides, his father had suggested there was a very nice cash wedding present waiting for him.

It was going to be a small wedding. Todd Evans was best man and Julie Hanson would be maid of honor. There were no brides-maids or groomsmen. Kathy and her mother spent Saturday addressing the forty invitations. Most of the invitations went to out-of-state relatives who were not expected to attend. Many of the invitees were single friends who probably wouldn't bring dates. Kathy expected, including the wedding party, only about thirty guests.

Russell called Kathy Monday afternoon. Kathy's mother answered the phone. Russell was never very comfortable talking to girlfriends' mothers, but he muddled through a brief conversation with his future mother-in-law until Kathy took the phone away.

"Hi honey," she said.

"Hi, I've missed you."

"I've missed you too. Hang on a second while I go into the other room."

Russell waited and listened to another phone pick up, then a few seconds later the click of a phone hanging up, and finally Kathy was back on the line.

"I'm beat," she said, "I've been running since my mother came in Friday."

"How's everything going?"

"Great, I think we have most everything done. As far as I know, we got everything booked. I'm glad we're having a wedding, but I'm also glad it's less than two weeks away. If I had to worry about all this for two or three months, I'd be a wreck."

"You would be fine no matter how long it took. Can we get together tonight? I really miss you."

"I'm sorry Rus, Mom and I are going to the formal shop so I can try on my dress tonight. And you can't see me in it until the day of the wedding, otherwise it's bad luck. But let's plan on going out tomorrow night."

"O.K., I guess I can wait one more night. Dinner and a movie sound good?"

"Only if we can see the movie from your bedroom. I miss you

too." Russell couldn't see her, but he could imagine the naughty smile she was smiling on the other end of the telephone line.

"Are you sure you don't want to wait until after the wedding? You know, anticipation," Russell said, only half joking.

"That's a sweet thing to say, even if you don't mean it. No, we are going to be busy the week before the wedding and I don't think we will have a chance, so that will be long enough. I miss my silver tongued fiancé."

Russell knew exactly what she meant by "silver tongued," and it had nothing to do with the way he talked. He laughed and talked for another hour about the wedding and life in general. Kathy said she hated to, but she had to get off the phone, it was time to leave for the formal store. They told each other how much they loved each other and said goodbye.

Russell laid back on his couch and thought about Kathy. He felt he was the luckiest person on earth to be marrying her. He fell asleep and dreamed about making love with her.

* * * * * *

Annie called Todd and suggested that he spend Monday night with her. The plane left at 10:30 in the morning and she thought they needed to talk about some things.

The two had spent Thursday and Saturday nights together and it was beginning to seem like old times. They were very comfortable around each other, even kissing occasionally when they were not making love. Todd could tell by Annie's mannerisms that, to her, it was more than two horny people having sex. She had loved him once and the feelings were returning.

Todd was feeling differently toward Annie as well. When he left her, he would feel melancholy. He wasn't sure if he was falling in love, but he felt the two of them were way past just being friends. He wondered how he would feel when she left the hotel room to go to a lesbian bar to pick up a woman. Even though his feelings for Annie were changing, he still fantasized about being with her and another woman for an evening.

On the phone, Annie told Todd what he should bring. They were flying standby, so it was always better to only have carry-on luggage. It's horrible to be stranded somewhere and be without a change of clothes because your bags made the plane and you didn't. Todd added that it might be a good idea not to bring anything she couldn't afford to lose. They may be leaving San Francisco in a hurry. Annie didn't ask Todd, but she wondered what she should wear to a lesbian bar to pick up a woman.

Todd decided against taking his overnighter suitcase, a small bag that was the exact size allowed as carry-on, the type all the flight attendants and pilots pull through the airport, because it was somewhat expensive and he didn't want to lose it. He found an old nylon sports bag he used to keep tennis and racquetball rackets in. He packed one pair of pants, four pairs of underwear, several T-shirts, a swim suit, a polo shirt and a light pull-over sweater. He would carry a light jacket with him. Annie had said that San Francisco nights could get chilly.

From the refrigerator, Todd retrieved the small clear unlabeled glass jar. Several wrappings of Scotch tape covered the lid to prevent accidental use. He took the jar to the kitchen table where he had laid out three glass tubes. The tubes looked like miniature test tubes, each with a small plastic top which secured the contents. Todd had discovered the little tubes by accident. One day while walking through the men's section of a department store, a salesperson handed him some cologne samples. Without paying much attention, Todd put the samples in his pocket. Later, when he was looking at the samples, he noticed the little glass tubes would be perfect if he ever need carry very small amounts of something.

When searching for a small container for his rendezvous with Senator Carson, Todd remembered the samples. The little vials worked perfectly.

Todd had emptied the cologne and washed the little glass tubes and left them open to air dry. Being very careful, he filled the tubes with the white powder from the small glass jar he had taken out of the refrigerator. When all three vials were full, he laid them on the plate he was using to catch any powder that might escape the tube. He took the plate and vials to the sink where he used a dry paper towel to wipe any residue from the little tubes and rinsed the plate and put it in the dishwasher.

Very carefully, Todd wrapped tape around the little caps to prevent them from falling off in transit, put all three in a zip-lock bag, and dropped the bag into a sock, which he put with it's mate in the sports bag. He put a couple of fresh wraps of tape around the original jar and put it back on the bottom shelf of the refrigerator door. The jar was still half full, a little bit of cyanide goes a long way.

After checking his wallet to be sure the money he had put in it after leaving the bank didn't somehow disappear, he took a quick look around the apartment checking everything was as it should be. Coffee pot off, telephone answering machine on, air conditioner turned up to 90 degrees. He opened the apartment door to the warm and humid Houston April afternoon. A cold chill rose up his spine as he walked to his car. It was the same feeling he had had twice before. He was glad he did not enjoy what he was doing.

Todd put his sports bag in the seat beside him, turned on the local head-banger rock station - loud - and drove to Annie's trying not to think about what they were going to do. A dark Chevrolet followed.

He didn't notice the FBI agent following. In fact, he didn't notice much of anything. He drove to Annie's as if he were a zombie and the car was on auto pilot. It seemed to Todd that he had just left his apartment and he was at Annie's. When he snapped out of his trance, he had to look around to be sure he was where he wanted to be.

It was like Annie had been waiting at the door. As Todd started to knock, she opened the door to let Todd in.

"How do I look?" Annie asked as she did a 360 so Todd could look at her ensemble. She wore a black T-shirt, no bra, blue jeans and shoes that looked more like hiking boots.

"Like a dyke," Todd answered.

"Great, that's the look I was going after."

"I don't know much about lesbians, but I've heard there are two types, femme, and butch. I guess you are the butch, right?"

"Not necessarily, I've done some research. I had heard the same thing you have heard, about femme and butch. I didn't want to go in femme if Oliver was femme, or butch if she was butch. So I found out that a lot of lesbians dress kind of manly. It doesn't mean they are butch or femme. I think it is just so that other women will know they are gay. I don't know, I don't really understand them anyway. I can't imagine a woman that doesn't ever want to be with a man, just like I can't imagine a man that would never want to be with a woman. But, hey, different strokes, right?"

Annie didn't wait for Todd to answer. "So, anyway, if I'm dressed like this, I should be considered open to go either way. I'm thinking about changing to a pair of black slacks instead of the blue jeans, it'll make me look more classy.

Todd and Annie talked the plan over and over again, trying to think of things that might go wrong and what they would do if something did go wrong. Todd finally brought up the question of what she would do if Margaret Oliver got suspicious and tried to overpower her. Annie said she used to work out at the Y several times a week and felt she was in excellent condition and could handle the Representative. Annie thought she could, without hesitation, whack her over the head with a frying pan if necessary.

Todd showed her the three little vials and explained that the amount of cyanide in one vile should be enough to kill a large man rather quickly. Getting the cyanide into a drink was the only real concern Todd had. He went so far as to suggest that if there was an opportunity at the bar, put it in her drink then stand near the door. As soon as she drinks it, get the hell out of there.

Annie reassured Todd that she could handle any situation that might occur, and if she had to, she would hold the Representative down and pour the shit down her throat.

"Just be careful," Todd said, "remember, in alcohol this stuff is tasteless and odorless. In water there is a bit of a almond taste and odor, she may not notice it, but be careful."

"I told you, don't worry. I'm sure I can handle it. Now why don't you shut up and take me to bed?"

"I don't know," Todd said with a grin, "I've never slept with a dyke before."

"Well, if you are really good, I'll share my girlfriend with you." Annie smiled at Todd, knowing he would not know for sure if she was serious or not.

They made love while Todd fantasized about Annie and another woman in bed with him. When they finished, sleep came easier than he had expected.

29

The motion Annie made as she got out of bed woke Todd from his dream. He looked at Annie as she walked, naked, to the bathroom and closed the door. He looked at the clock, it was 6:15. He closed his eyes in hopes the dream would return, but he couldn't even remember what it had been about. It had been so vivid just a few short moments ago.

Todd normally got up for work between 6:00 and 6:30. He didn't use an alarm clock, he would tell himself what time he wanted to get up in the morning, and he would always wake up around that time. As often as not, he would wake up at exactly that time. He was always amazed with himself that he could do it. Even when he had been out drinking until two in the morning, he would tell himself he needed to be up by six, and he would wake up.

He heard the toilet flush and the water in the sink running. Annie came out of the bathroom, walked to the dresser, to the closet and back to the dresser. Todd laid in the bed admiring her body. She worked hard to keep in shape and it showed. More than anything Todd wanted to call out to her and tell her to come back to bed, that they should make love until they had to get ready to leave, but it looked like Annie had other plans.

She was walking back and forth across the room putting items in her flight bag, taking things out and exchanging them for other items. Obviously happy for the time being, she picked up what looked to Todd like a pair of shorts and panties, and disappeared back into the bathroom. When Todd heard the water in the shower start, he got up and went into the kitchen for a drink of water. He wished he had gotten up while Annie was packing her bag and gone to the bathroom.

Todd was seriously thinking about using the sink when he heard Annie coming into the living room.

"Good morning," she said with a smile. Annie was wearing the tan shorts she had taken to the bathroom with her, but no top. Todd got up to kiss her and caress her breasts. "Is this what you are planning to wear on the plane?" he said laughing.

"Yeah, do you think they'll let me on?"

"I doubt it, you know what they say, no shirt, no service."

Both laughed at his comment. Todd explained how long he had been waiting to use the toilet, and that he had to go.

"You should have come in, I wouldn't mind," she said.

"I guess I didn't think you would want me to pee in front of you." Todd was talking on his way to the bathroom.

"So you don't want me to hold your dick?"

"Wait till we get to San Francisco."

"Promise?"

Todd said "sure," but it wasn't heard as he had already closed the bathroom door.

Annie tried on several blouses before she found the one she wanted, a short sleeve loose fitting Hawaiian print. She put it on and tucked the bottom into her shorts. She looked at herself in the full length mirror. It looked like a good traveling outfit.

Being a seasoned traveler, Annie knew how to pack light. Her favorite destinations were in the Caribbean. She would take two bathing suits, two nice sun dresses for the nights, several pairs of shorts and blouses, and enough underwear for the duration. She hated spending travel time at a laundry mat. Anything other than underwear she could wear several times, but not underwear. If it was absolutely necessary, she would wash her panties in the sink and hang them in the shower to dry.

Packing light for a trip to San Francisco was much harder. The days are usually warm, but could be chilly. The nights were almost always cold. Add the fact that she needed to dress to impress a woman at a gay bar, and it became very difficult.

While Annie was packing, Todd showered and got dressed. He wore a white polo shirt and brown Docker's. His bag was already packed so he killed time channel surfing while waiting for Annie.

It was still early when Annie entered the living room and announced she was ready. The small bag she was carrying looked like it was about to burst. The zipper seemed to be stretched to it outer most limits.

"I'm ready," she said, as though it was a major accomplishment.

Todd looked at his watch and said, "it's only eight, you wanna go back to bed for an hour?"

"Let's go get something to eat. How 'bout IHOP, I'm in the mood for pancakes." She ignored his "back to bed" comment.

"Sure, that sounds good, there's one on the Loop not far from here."

Annie went through a routine of checking the stove, curling iron, air conditioner setting and coffee pot to be sure everything was set as it should be. When Todd was sure she was ready, he picked up both his and her bags and waited for her to open the door. She opened the door and held it as Todd carried the bags out. Annie took one last look around the room before closing and locking the door.

"They're moving," Agent Howard Weiss said into the microphone.

"My ETA is about two minutes. Are they together?" Agent Lori Anderson asked. Just moments earlier she had notified Weiss she was on her way to relieve him. Because of the length of time, and the number of people under surveillance, the FBI had gone to a four on, four off, watch routine.

Agent Weiss followed Todd's car and passed the direction to Agent Anderson, who was now only a block away. She pulled in front of Weiss so that he could fall off. Anderson would follow until she felt she may have been spotted, then she would turn or pass and let Weiss take over again.

Traffic was heavy, but Agent Anderson had no trouble following. Todd felt he had plenty of time and would change lanes early to be sure he would be able to make the next turn without cutting someone off. Lori would ease in one or two cars back.

Todd parked the car and he and Annie went inside the International House of Pancakes. Agents Weiss and Anderson parked in the far corner of the parking lot. They had a clear view of the front door as well as Todd's car.

"I guess they are taking the day off," Agent Anderson said to Weiss.

"They're obviously not dressed for work." Agent Weiss said, trying to look alert. He had worked four hours the night before, but instead of getting rest, he went to the command center to review any information that had come in during the previous eight hours. He still had time for a nap when he realized that there was not much new information, but his wife had mentioned she wanted him to pick up some things for her, if he got a chance, so Agent Weiss spent the next hour and a half at the 24 hour Wal-mart.

It was now catching up with him. He asked Anderson if she

needed help, and she said no. It looked like another dull day. She didn't think much would happen at the IHOP. Agent Weiss said goodbye, if she needed him, he would be at home, sleeping, but could be back in twenty minutes, don't hesitate to call. He drove away thinking there was something he needed to tell Agent Anderson, but he couldn't think of what it was, it must not have been too important. Nothing about this surveillance had been very important.

Todd and Annie finished their breakfast and were enjoying the coffee until Annie suggested they should leave. They still had well over an hour to make the 30 minute drive to the airport, but they were flying stand-by and Annie wanted to get there early. Besides, you never know what kind of traffic you might encounter on the way. It was better to be early than late.

Todd paid the bill and they walked to the car. It was only a little after nine in the morning, but the temperature had already reached 80 with the humidity above that. As the two got into the already hot car, Annie pulled on her blouse, which was sticking to her chest. "I hope it's cooler in California, I can't believe how hot it's going to be here today."

Todd heard, but didn't respond. He was busy backing the car out of the space.

"You have to go to the first entrance over there," Annie said as she pointed to the first of two entrances from the frontage road into the parking lot, "if you go out the second, you can't get on the freeway. See, the ramp starts there, between the two exits."

"Yeah," Todd said as he looked at the parking lot exits and the freeway onramp. "It's a good thing you saw that, if I had gone out the other exit, we would have had to go a long way up before we could get on the freeway."

"There's lots of traffic though, you will either have to haul-ass across three lanes, or turn into the close one and take the long way."

"I'll do it." Todd said as if crossing the three lanes of frontage road to the on-ramp was a challenge.

A small gap appeared and Todd stomped on the accelerator. The car shot through the small opening between cars and on to the onramp of the freeway. He never saw the obscene gestures expressed by the motorist who thought he had cut it a little too close.

Agent Anderson had not noticed the ramp to the freeway until Todd was on it. She was sitting at the second exit waiting, assuming they would ease into the traffic and continue up the frontage road.

She sat in her car and watched them disappear over the overpass. Lori thought about backing up and going to the first parking lot exit and trying the same maneuver Todd had to enter the freeway. Instead, she saw a sufficient gap in traffic and thought she would go ahead and get on the freeway at the next entrance ramp. It couldn't be that far, she reasoned.

"Well, Toto, this isn't Arizona," Agent Lori Anderson said to herself as she sat at the second red light since leaving the IHOP. It had been nearly five minutes and she had traveled less than a mile. She had lost them.

She had become familiar enough with Houston to know that if they were going back to Annie's apartment, they would probably be taking the second exit off the freeway. She would check the apartment, then Todd's apartment before radioing in that she had lost them. There was no sense in being the only agent to lose a tail on this case. The two had done nothing important to the case in five days, there was no reason to think today would be any different.

The road construction had not gone up yet and Todd had an easy drive to Bush Intercontinental Airport. Normally he would have parked in one of the satellite parking lots and taken the shuttle, but they both decided it might be a good idea to be able to get to the car in a hurry. They probably would not want to be standing on the curb waiting for a bus when they returned.

Todd carried the bags as Annie led them directly to Gate 21B. Annie talked to the gate attendant, told him who she was and who she worked for and that they had stand-by tickets. The attendant looked at the tickets and began typing into the computer sitting on the counter.

He watched the screen flicker and pressed a few more keys. "Coach is pretty full," he said without looking up from the screen. "But I can go ahead and put you in first class." The attendant wrote the seat number on their ticket envelope and handed two boarding passes to Annie. "Have a good flight," he said as they left the check-in counter.

"This is great, I've never flown first class before," Todd said.

"You'll like it, that's one of the few perks I get for working for such a crummy salary, I almost always get bumped to first class."

Annie proceeded to tell Todd of some her more memorable experiences in first class. It was beginning to dawn on Todd why he stopped dating Annie the first time, when he heard the pre-boarding call. "That's us," he said, interrupting one of her stories that had already drug on way too long.

They boarded the plane and found their seats. The flight attendant came by before Todd had barely buckled his seat belt.

"Can I get you anything?" she said.

"I'll have a Bloody Mary," Annie said, looking at Todd for his order.

"Me too," he said, surprised that the attendant was taking drink orders. In a few seconds she returned with the two glasses of Bloody Mary mix and two one and a half ounce bottles of vodka. Todd took a drink of the Bloody Mary mix to make room for the Vodka, opened the small bottle and poured about half into the glass. He stirred and sipped the concoction while he watched the other passengers still boarding. It took less than five minutes for Todd Evans to realize he enjoyed first class travel.

Agent Lori Anderson drove to Annie's apartment, then to Todd's apartment, then back to Annie's looking for Todd's 1993 Ford Thunderbird. It had been over an hour since she lost them at the IHOP and she felt sure they would show up. She knew if she reported that she had lost them and they turned up back at one of their apartments soon after she reported, she would be the butt of many jokes for a long time. The male agents would not claim she lost them because she was a woman, but neither would they pull any punches because she was a woman.

On the other hand, if she did not report that she had lost them, and another Senator or Representative was killed, she might lose her job. She decided to report that she had lost them.

She radioed the command center and explained what happened and when. She explained that she felt she could handle any situation and had told Agent Weiss to go home. It probably wouldn't have made any difference how many agents were at the IHOP, no one could have followed them on to the freeway, there was just too much traffic.

She blamed herself for not reporting it immediately. Another agent might have been close, or maybe even on the freeway, that could have picked them up, but she was sure she could get on the freeway and catch them. She didn't count on the traffic, the lights and the lack of entrance ramps.

Agent Christian told her not to worry about it. It could have happened to anyone, especially an agent from out of town. He said that Todd Evans and Annie Simmons had not done anything exciting in the past five days, there was no reason to expect that things would change. Christian notified all units to watch for Todd's Thunderbird.

Christian asked Agent Anderson via the cellular line, "did it look like Todd Evans was aware of your presence and was purposely trying to lose you?"

"No, sir, I am sure they did not see me. I think they just wanted to get on the freeway, and when they saw a gap, they took it. I watched them from the ramp until they disappeared over the overpass, it didn't look like they were in a hurry."

Special Agent in Charge Christian assured Agent Anderson that the couple would turn up either at one of their apartments or at one of the friend's apartments.

Lori thanked him and continued her search. She was glad she reported losing them but was not reassured by her bosses words. There was an empty feeling in the pit of her stomach that told her she had really screwed up.

30

The dark ominous clouds moved slowly from the north bringing lightning, high winds, rain and tornado warnings. Blocking the sun, the line of thunderstorms made the beautiful spring afternoon look more like midnight. The wind picked up, slowly at first, until it reached near gale force, swirling dust and debris high into the air. The rain followed with a fury, pounding the ground and reducing visibility to only a few yards.

Russell Lewis stood at the window watching the rain pelt the small patio outside his front door. He looked at the black clouds, lined with an eerie dark green and knew that Houston was in for a downpour. Before he called Kathy to cancel their date, he turned on the weather channel to be sure this was not a passing storm. In Houston, there's a saying, "if you don't like the weather, wait ten minutes, it will change." According to the radar, the weather was going to change, it would get worse. Tornado and flash flood warnings were up for Harris County as well as all of the surrounding counties.

Russell reluctantly picked up the phone and pressed auto one. The telephone automatically dialed Kathy's number, which had been programmed in only recently. The previous auto-dial number one was now history.

The phone was answered on the third ring by an unhappy sounding voice. Kathy was following the "cool rule", never pick the phone up before it had rung at least twice.

"I was afraid you were calling to cancel," Kathy said after Russell had told her the roads were beginning to flood and that they shouldn't go out. "How about if I come over to your apartment, that way it will save time and you won't have to make two trips?"

Russell thought about the offer, but then he pictured his soon-to-be wife being swept down a bayou and said, "you better not, it's supposed to get even worse. It's not worth losing you forever for one night together."

"That's sweet Russell, but it's not that far, I don't think I'll have any problems, then I'll just stay till it clears, that could be in the morning, you know."

Russell loved the way she said that, and it almost swayed him to her side, but the bright flash and deafening crack of thunder jolted him back to his senses. "No, we'll get together tomorrow night, it's just not worth the risk."

A similar lightning bolt struck near Kathy's house and its ensuing thunder convinced her that she shouldn't be out this night. "You're right, I guess, but I can't go out tomorrow, Mom and I are going to pick up my dress and have some pictures taken."

The news hit Russell like another bolt of lightening, but he weathered it. "Then we'll make it Thursday, I'll see if anybody is meeting at Chuck's and we'll get some beer and pizza. Then we can come back here."

"That sounds great, I haven't seen the gang in couple of weeks. But I don't want to stay at Chuck's long, I really miss you."

Kathy and Russell spent the next two hours on the telephone discussing their lives. This was the first chance they'd had, since becoming engaged, to really talk. When they had been alone, it was difficult to talk about the future. They were sure a videotape of Kathy was going to be broadcast nationwide at any moment. They spent the time together kissing, making love or just holding one another close. Conversation seemed inappropriate.

The beginning of their conversation was very normal, chit chat about who was doing what and, of course, the weather. As the two talked, it began to dawn on them that things were different. It was no longer a boyfriend talking to a girlfriend, but two people who were about to promise to live together for the rest of their lives talking.

The longer they talked, the more they realized that the things they were talking about would affect them both. It was no longer "I," but "we." In a very short time two kids grew into adults. Talk went from beer and pizza to houses, jobs and babies. By the time they said "good-night," they had laughed, cried, fought and made up. The raging storm which had kept them apart had brought them closer together than either had thought possible.

Outside Russell Lewis's apartment the lone FBI agent sat in his dark colored Chevrolet Blazer. He tried the windshield wipers but the rain was too hard even for the high speed to keep clear. Assuming only an idiot would be out in this kind of weather, he gave up and turned the wipers off. He got as comfortable as possible and sat watching the rain, occasionally looking the direction of Russell's front door, completely obscured by sheets of rain.

* * * * * *

The weather in San Francisco was beautiful. Clear and cool with low humidity. Annie went in search of brochures of things to do while Todd went to the car rental booth. Todd had just finished signing the rental agreement when Annie walked up. She was carrying a handful of travel pamphlets which contained everything from tours of the wine country to boat tours of the bay. Todd noticed the brochure for Alcatraz and pulled it from the stack.

"I don't think we'll be needing this one," he said as he threw it into a nearby wastebasket. "I don't particularly want to see the inside of a prison any time soon, even if it is only a tour." They both laughed at the gesture even though, in the back of their minds, both were thinking it was not very funny.

Todd drove while Annie navigated the streets of San Francisco. Like most tourists, they found Lombard Street, "the crookedest road in America" and drove down it, twice, before going to the hotel. Todd parked the rented Chrysler Cirrus in front of the main entrance to the Hyatt Hotel and handed the keys to the attendant who in turn handed Todd a parking receipt.

Annie checked in while Todd wandered the hotel lobby trying to look like he was not with Annie. Though the hotel desk clerk couldn't have cared less, Todd felt uncomfortable having Annie check in. He felt it was the man that should do those kind of things. Todd made a note of the sports bar in the corner of the lobby. Several large screen televisions were broadcasting a baseball game from the east and horse racing live from some track somewhere that someone in the bar probably had a wager on. Todd felt the bar would be a good place to spend time while Annie went in search of Ms. Oliver.

Annie's poke in the ribs startled Todd who had become engrossed in the baseball game. "Let's go," she said as she gave him a slight tug to get him started toward the elevators. "We got the discount rate since I work for a travel agency, and they upgraded us to a better room. We get a view of the street instead of the roof top, and one king bed instead of two doubles."

"That's great." Todd said even though he really hadn't given it much thought. The view might be nice, but Annie would be going out in an attempt to be picked up by another woman. Todd would just as soon had the two doubles, at least he wouldn't be disturbed if she came in late and he was asleep. He decided it wasn't worth commenting on.

It was only 4:30 in San Francisco, but Todd and Annie's stomachs were still on Houston time where it was 6:30, and they were hungry. Pier 39 was only a short walk from the hotel and Annie suggested the walk would do them good. As they walked through the myriad of small shops selling overpriced little plastic cable cars, Todd Evans and Annie Simmons looked just like the millions of young lovers who had walked the streets of San Francisco before them.

They held hands as they walked, occasionally stopping to look at the post cards, T-shirts, coffee mugs and chop sticks that every shop sold. They wondered how all the shops could possibly stay in business. Every shop sold the same crap and nobody ever seemed to buy anything. Annie mentioned that she liked to buy a coffee cup from every place she visited, but Todd reminded her why they were in San Francisco. She might not want anything to remind her of the trip. Annie agreed.

The young couple strolled to the end of Pier 39 and watched the sea lions play on the special platforms built just for them. No one knows why, but one day sea lions appeared at Pier 39 and began living on the boat piers which filled the small protected harbor. Being a protected species, it was illegal to harass the sea lions. Boaters and dock owners were upset because they couldn't use their piers. Technically, a person must stay at least 100 feet from any protected animal.

After months of debate, it was determined that the city would build special floating platforms away from the boat docks just for the sea lions. The arrangement made everybody happy, including the sea lions who would sleep or bark all day and all night throughout the winter and spring until they left for the outer islands to breed and bear their young, returning to the same docks every winter.

Todd and Annie stood and watched the animals play. They laughed at how they would pile on top of each other on one platform while another platform was empty. Two sea lions would fight, the winner staying on the crowded float while the loser was forced to move to an empty platform.

When Todd and Annie could no longer ignore their increasing

hunger pains, they found a small romantic restaurant overlooking San Francisco Bay.

The clam chowder was "to die for," but, as hungry as he was, it was hard for Todd to eat as he looked out across the bay at Alcatraz, sitting out there dark and cold as the last cruise boats left to bring the tourists back to the mainland. Todd could not keep from looking at the small island and wondering how horrible it would be to spend the rest of his life in prison, never again having the chance to buy a coffee mug or watch the sea lions frolic.

It was too late for him, but Annie had not yet done anything illegal, other than possibly conspiring to murder someone or associating with a known felon, neither of which should call for an extraordinarily long prison sentence. Annie chatted like a school girl on a field trip, but Todd didn't hear much of the conversation. He needed, somehow, to convince Annie that they should enjoy the four days in San Francisco and go home. Forget about Representative Oliver.

As fog and darkness reduced visibility, Alcatraz was soon only a memory. Todd's appetite improved when he could no longer see the island, and he became much more aware of the woman sitting across from him. He had at least another day before Representative Oliver would be in town, he would convince Annie by then that they had done enough to change the world. She should not risk spending the rest of her life in prison for murder.

With each glass of wine Todd's mood improved dramatically. By the time they had finished the main course he was feeling extremely passionate. Before he could suggest they have dessert back in the hotel room, Annie said, "I think the bar that Representative Oliver goes to is real close to here. I was thinking I might go by there and hang out for a while, you know, have a few drinks, meet some people, so that when I go back tomorrow night, I won't look so suspicious."

The wine had clouded Todd's thought process enough that he was having a hard time coming up with a reason for her not to go to the bar. He didn't want to tell her that he thought they should scrub the whole plan and just enjoy San Francisco, because he knew Annie. She was prepared to go through with murder, and he would have to be very coy in order to convince her otherwise.

"Do you think it's a good idea, you don't want anybody to remember you?" Todd said.

"I thought about that, but I really think I need to be seen in there at least once before I meet Oliver. I don't really know how it works in a gay bar, who is suppose to hit on who. So I may have to hit on her, and if she gets suspicious, like maybe I don't act enough like a lesbian, then I've blown the whole plan."

Todd wanted to say that would be fine with him, but he realized Annie had made up her mind that she was going to the bar tonight, no matter what he said. He also wondered if maybe she was hoping to meet a woman and have sex with her. Todd put his hand on top of Annie's and said, "I was hoping we could go back to our hotel now, this is our first night in San Francisco together."

"I'd love to, but I really think I should stop by the bar. You go back to the room and I'll be back real soon. I promise I won't stay long."

There was no changing her mind, so Todd decided to make the best of it. He paid the bill and walked out with Annie along the wooden pier to the street. Neither said a word as their minds were preoccupied with the coming events.

When they reached the street, Annie said, "I think I know where the place is, I should probably walk alone. Can you find your way back to the hotel?"

"Uh, yeah, I guess. Are you sure you want to go alone?"

"Yes, I don't want to even get close to the bar with you with me, if somebody just happened to see us together, it could screw up the whole thing."

Todd didn't like it all. He had lost control of the situation and Annie was about to walk off, alone, to a gay bar. He knew there was no sense in arguing with her, so he told her to be careful and that he would see her back at the hotel. He would be in the bar for awhile. If she needed him and he wasn't in the room, have the hotel page him in the bar. Todd did not say it, but he hoped that she would not need him. He was feeling the effects of the wine from dinner, and he had already decided he would switch to beer when he got to the hotel bar. It would not be long before he would be totally useless.

Annie put her arm around Todd's neck and pulled him close to her. She kissed him on the lips then turned and walked off. Todd thought about following her, but if she spotted him, she'd be pissed. He watched her walk around the corner and out of sight before he left, in the opposite direction for the hotel and a cold beer.

Annie was wearing pleated shorts which were cuffed at midthigh, a loose fitting blouse and white sandals. It was not what she thought to be a lesbian outfit, but she didn't want to go back to the hotel and change. She knew if she went back, she would end up in bed with Todd and never make it back to the bar. The dinner wine was having its effect on her too.

The outside of the bar looked much like any other bar in San Francisco, part of a larger brick building that was too narrow and too tall. There were windows in front, but they had been painted black many years before. "Angel's" was painted in white script letters on one of the black windows.

Except for a homeless person sitting on the steps of a locked door, the sidewalk around Angel's was vacant. Music could be heard but not identified coming from the bar. Annie slowly opened the door and walked inside. The music was louder, but not deafening as it usually is in bars. The lighting was subdued, almost dark, not much lighter than the street Annie had just walked in from. It was not what she had imagined.

Annie had pictured a much bigger place with lots of women with very short hair dressed in men's clothing. Angel's was not very large, a long bar with stools lined one side while the opposite side was lined with booths. There was a small stage at the far end fronted by a small Parquet dance floor. Round tables with wooden chairs were placed in no particular order throughout the bar.

Annie sat at the corner of the bar and ordered a white wine. The bar was not crowded at all. A couple of women sat at the bar and there were a few in the booths and at the tables, but even for a small place, it could hold a lot more people.

Annie studied the bartender and the other patrons. They were not at all what she had expected. The bartender was an attractive woman in her late thirties, light brown shoulder length hair, wearing black slacks, a white blouse and a white apron. She could have been a bartender at any bar Annie had ever been in.

Annie sipped her wine as she looked around the bar. The women seemed to range in age from their late 20's to mid to late 40's. A few looked like what she thought a dyke might look like, but most of them seemed very normal. If there had been men in the club, Annie would never have guessed the women were lesbians.

Her glass almost empty, Annie was debating if she should have another drink or go get Todd out of the hotel bar, take him up to the room and make mad passionate love to him. She didn't notice the two women get up from a table near the end of the bar.

The two women, both in their late 30's walked toward the door. They stood at the door talking a few moments, then kissed each other on the cheek and said goodbye. One of the women left the bar while the other walked over and sat on the stool next to Annie.

The bartender immediately asked the woman what she would like.

"A glass of Chablis," she said as she looked at Annie and her near empty wine glass. "Hi, can I buy you another wine?"

"Hi, uh, sure." Annie said, she had been caught a little off guard by the woman's offer.

The bartender filled two glasses with wine and sat them on the bar, removing Annie's old glass before disappearing to the other end of the bar.

"My name's Maggie," the woman said, extending her hand toward Annie.

"I'm Annie," she said taking her hand but immediately wishing she had used an alias. The woman, Maggie, looked to be in her late 30's, average height, around 5'4", average looks although her dark complexion gave her an exotic look. She was very trim and quite shapely. She wore a polo shirt tucked into pleated slacks. Even after studying her picture for nearly a week, Annie barely recognized Representative Margaret "Maggie" Oliver. The fact that Ms. Oliver was not supposed to be in town made Annie wonder if this Maggie was another woman who happened to bear a strong resemblance to the Representative.

"I haven't seen you in here before, are you from San Francisco?" Maggie asked.

The wine had clouded Annie's brain and she knew it. She had already given Maggie her real name and if she tried to B.S. too much she was sure she would end up contradicting herself. She decided she would stick to the truth the best she could, and hopefully, remember anything she would be forced to ad-lib.

"I've never been here before. I just flew in from Houston today and a friend of mine told me I should come by here. She said it was a nice place for a drink." Annie put a little extra emphasis on "she."

"Are you in town on business?" Maggie asked.

"Not really, I'm a travel agent and one ticket became available, so I thought, why not? What about you, do you live here in San Francisco?" Annie was particularly interested in the answer to this question.

"Part time, I live in Washington D.C. part time. I'm a Representative from the area." Margaret Oliver paused while she took a drink of wine and said, "would you like to go sit at a table or booth?"

"Sure," Annie said picking up her wine glass, "the booths look comfortable."

The Representative led Annie to the last booth in the darkest part of the bar. Annie was surprised but not shocked when Maggie sat on the same side of the booth with her. The two sat sideways in the booth, facing each other, talking and drinking wine. Annie liked to talk, especially when she had been drinking, but Maggie was a professional. She knew when to speak and when to allow Annie to speak. The conversation was never at a lull.

Before Annie realized it, it was past midnight and Margaret Oliver had positioned herself so that one of Annie's bare legs was draped over the Representative's leg. Part of Annie's brain was trying to pay attention to Maggie and carry on a conversation while the other part was trying to work on a plan to murder the woman.

Annie wished she had brought at least one of the vials of cyanide with her, but she hadn't expected to have a need for it. She thought about making up an excuse to go back to the hotel, but she was afraid Maggie would either want to come along, or would not wait for her to return.

There was a possibility Maggie might suggest they go back to Annie's hotel. Annie had tried several excuses in her mind, none of which sounded too good. She realized she should have said she made the trip with a co-worker, a straight co-worker, and they couldn't go back to her hotel room.

Annie assumed Todd would either be drunk or asleep by now. Either way, it would not be a good idea to show up at the hotel with Maggie. She thought about calling Todd and warning him they were coming, but he had made it clear that it would not be a good idea to murder the Representative in the hotel room. The only thing Annie was sure of, was that they could not go back to the hotel. She decided to play it by ear. Sometime during the night, somehow, when she got her chance, she would kill the woman herself.

When Representative Oliver casually laid her hand on Annie's leg, Annie hardly noticed. She noticed a little more as the Representative began rubbing her leg from her knee to thigh. It really got Annie's attention when the hand slid up the baggy shorts leg to her pubic mound.

Instinctively, Annie stopped the Representative's hand and looked around the bar to see if anyone was looking at them. No one was.

"Relax," Maggie said as she rubbed Annie between her legs, "this place is very discrete." She pulled Annie close and kissed her on the lips, slipping her tongue into Annie's mouth. Annie kissed Maggie as deeply and as passionately as she had ever kissed a man. Frankly, she quite enjoyed the way the Representative kissed.

While they kissed, Annie pushed Maggie Oliver's hand from beneath her shorts. "I'm sorry, not here." Annie whispered.

"Would you like to come back to my place?"

"I would like that." Annie said with a clumsy smile, it was her attempt at a sexy smile that didn't quite work. Maggie didn't notice.

It was strange, had Annie been in a straight bar, she would have never, or at least almost never, let a guy slide his hand under her shorts like Margaret Oliver had. And although she very likely would go home from a bar with a guy, she probably would not have agreed to it so easily. But this was a gay bar, and Annie was there by herself. To Representative Oliver, it was obvious the reason Annie was there was because she wanted company for the night. Oliver, abandoning her political savvy, didn't feel the need to beat around the bush.

The Congresswoman paid the tab and took Annie by the hand, leading her behind the bar, through the storeroom and out the back door.

"I have to be very careful," Maggie said as she held the door to her Buick open for her new friend, "it's no secret that I'm a lesbian. In fact, it's the gay and lesbian vote that got me elected, but my opponents, even the gay ones, say I should have a monogamous relationship and not have affairs. Even if they didn't care, I think what we do is personal and it's nobody's business, so for your sake, if not my own, we have to be very discrete.

"This is the employees' parking lot. Very few people know it's here so I can come and go with out being seen from the street. I hope you don't mind, but I have a secret service agent that almost lives at my house, so I thought we would go to a hideaway I've got near Chinatown. It's small but we won't be disturbed."

Annie leaned across the seat, kissed Maggie on the lips and said, "that's fine with me, I don't care, as long as it's safe. Why is there an agent at your house?"

"You've heard about someone killing Congressmen recently, haven't you?"

"Yea, two of them were from Texas, did you know them?"

"I didn't know the Senators at all, but I knew James pretty well, he was always trying to 'reform' me. Said I 'should try Jack and I would never go back'. I asked him what he preferred, men or women. He made a big deal about how much he liked women and how he thought being with a man was disgusting. I told him I had a bisexual male friend and the three of us would get together. If he would suck my friend's dick, he could have his way with me. I would do anything he wanted, oral, anal, anything." Representative Oliver began laughing as she remembered the story.

When she caught her breath, she continued, "I'm sure he wanted to make a comment about gay men being fags or something, but decided he had better not. It was the first time I had ever seen him speechless. He didn't know what to say. I know he wanted me, especially after I said 'anything'. But as much as he wanted 'to reform me', he would never consider giving a guy a blow job. It was quite a dilemma for him. Kinda like free ham to a Jew. He never suggested I sleep with him again."

Annie was surprised by the Representative's language. She had used similar language before, but never in front of someone she just met. She couldn't even recall a guy, even ones she performed oral sex on, being so explicit. They certainly made the suggestion, but never said it outright. It didn't seem to bother Ms. Oliver at all.

The two women laughed at the story as Maggie drove up and down the hills of San Francisco. Annie was beginning to get nervous. She was here for only one reason and the perfect opportunity was staring her right in the face. At the bar, only the bartender got a really good look at her. She might be able to identify her, but a lot of women go in and out of the bar every night. She probably would not remember who Oliver left with.

They had left through a back door and were on their way to a 'hideaway', as Maggie had put it. Most likely there would be no one there to see them. It would have to be tonight. If she waited until tomorrow night, the chances were good that Representative Oliver would tell someone, or maybe write a note on her calendar or something, that she was meeting "Annie from Houston," that evening. Nope, Annie convinced herself. It had to be tonight. It was now or never.

31

It was after midnight in Houston when Agent Christian put out the call for all agents, except one that would continue surveillance on Eric Moore, to come to the command center for a special briefing. It was still raining intermittently, but the major portion of the storm that had pounded the city for most of the afternoon and evening had drifted off toward Louisiana.

Most of the agents were awake, either on surveillance, just getting off surveillance or about to go on surveillance. Those who weren't doing either were following up other leads that had come into the office. Most of which were more dead ends. All of the Arizona agents were available and only three of the Houston agents were at home asleep. Christian decided not to bother those that were actually getting some rest.

It took less than 45 minutes for all of the agents who were coming to assemble in the conference room one floor above the Blind Luck Command center. Agent Christian started the briefing by asking if anyone had anything new they would care to share with the group. No one did.

"As you know," Christian said when no one else volunteered any information, "we are no further along on our investigation than we were two days ago, or two weeks ago, for that matter. I am still convinced that Eric Moore is involved and we will stay with him for as long as it takes. I also think that most of you are aware that we lost Todd Evans and Annie Simmons this morning."

Lori Anderson did not look around the room even though she could feel everyone in the room staring at her. She kept her eyes glued to Agent Christian, who never looked directly at her.

"I wasn't too concerned this morning, I was sure they would turn up at one of their apartments, but they have not. Is that correct?" Christian asked the agents who had just come from Todd and Annie's apartments. The two agents nodded an affirmative. Lori felt a knot appear in the pit of her stomach.

"It could be the storm, they may have gone somewhere and decided to wait for it to pass. They could have gone to Galveston, or anywhere for that matter. Then again, they may have gone off to kill another Congressman."

Lori felt the knot in her stomach pull tighter as her boss speculated on where Todd and Annie might be.

"It might be a waste of time, but I would like," Christian paused and scanned the room, "Harry, would you check the list to see if any Congressmen are within, oh, about 100 mile radius of Houston."

Harry left the room to go back to the command center where, stored in a computer data base, was the location of every U.S. Senator and Representative. If any Congressman travels more than 25 miles, someone, either the Congressman himself, the secret service or the FBI was to call in the new location to the command center. The information is to be updated as soon as it arrived so that the whereabouts of everyone the FBI is trying to protect is known.

Unfortunately, with over 600 members of Congress, many of whom felt they didn't need protection, the database records were not as accurate as the FBI wanted. Harry Berg set up the parameters to select an area 150 miles from Houston. He took it upon himself to increase the distance to 150 miles, if too many showed up, he could always redo the search with a new set of parameters.

The cursor blinked while the computer server, somewhere in the bowels of the FBI building searched the database for the information. Moments later a list of seven names appeared on the screen along with the location and miles from Houston. Although it was the name of the town that was input into the database, the computer retrieved the location's longitude and latitude, then, by subtracting the minutes and seconds from Houston's coordinates, could print the exact number of miles each person was from the FBI building in downtown Houston.

By using the Congressman's name as a key field, Agent Berg requested the state and Congressional district for each of the seven names on the list. He reviewed the list one final time to be sure it was what he wanted, then clicked the print icon. Fifteen seconds later a perfectly printed list rolled out of the Hewlett-Packard Laser Jet printer.

Before returning to the briefing, he decided to print the list of "hot" Congressmen, members of Congress who fit the profile the Blind Luck gang seemed to be targeting. Simply put, the most corrupt of the lot. Berg pulled up the database, highlighted the top twenty five names and pressed the print icon again. The list promptly rolled out of the Laser Jet printer.

Agent Berg made five copies of each list, five happened to be the number on the copier keypad he touched first, and returned to the briefing. Keeping one copy for himself, Berg handed the other four plus the original to Agent Christian explaining that he decided to use 150 miles instead of 100 and that he also had the top 25 from the "hot" list.

Christian passed out the four copies and took a few minutes to study the lists. "We've got three in Houston, two in San Antonio, one in Austin and one in Beaumont. Don't these guys ever stay in Washington? None of the names are on the hot list, but let's check them out anyway. Would somebody find out which agency is watching who and find out if they are in fact watching them."

"I'll do it," Houston Agent Curt Wright said as he left the briefing room.

"Annie Simmons is a travel agent, there's always a possibility they took an airplane somewhere. I want you all to divide up the airlines and find out if those two flew out of Houston today. That's all I have, if no one else has any comments, let's get on it."

As the Agents gathered to split the commercial airlines among themselves, Christian decided it would be a good time to take a nap. The cot in his temporary office felt as good as the most expensive mattress he had ever laid on. He was sound asleep seconds after his head touched the pillow.

It was after 3:00 A.M. when the Continental Airlines representative said to Agent Sam Zimmerman that, yes a Todd Evans and an Annie Simmons were on flight 233 from Houston to San Francisco. The flight arrived in San Francisco at 1:05 P.M. Pacific time. Zimmerman made the announcement to the other agents in the command center and immediately began accessing the database to see which Congressman, if any, were in the San Francisco Bay area. Only one name appeared on the list, Representative Margaret Oliver, who was also number eleven on the target list compiled by the Federal Bureau of Investigation.

"Do you think we should wake Alex? He will probably want to know about this." Agent Berg asked Zimmerman as he looked at the list.

"Not yet, I'm going to call California and see who's with Representative Oliver. If she's O.K., we will warn her that two possible suspects are in the area and they should take the necessary precautions. We'll give Alex a little more time to sleep. I can't remember the last time he slept more than an hour or two at a time. It's gotta be catching up with him."

Another access of the FBI database revealed the Secret Service was in charge of protecting Ms. Oliver. Zimmerman called Washington, and by using a series of codes and passwords, was promptly connected to the Secret Service agent assigned to protect Representative Oliver.

"Panetta here," the groggy voice on the other end of the telephone line said.

"Tony Panetta?" Zimmerman asked knowing there would not likely be a different Panetta watching the Representative, but it also gave Panetta an extra few seconds to wake up.

"Yes."

"This is Special Agent Sam Zimmerman, FBI, I am a member of Operation Blind Luck."

"Yes sir, Agent Zimmerman, what can I do for you?"

"We have information that two of the suspects in the Congressional murders are in the San Francisco area and that Representative Oliver may be a target. Do you have her under surveillance at this time?"

The long, silent pause answered the question. Zimmerman impatiently waited for the official response.

"No sir, we don't. She left this evening around seven, after giving specific instructions that she was not to be followed. You see, she has as much a sexual appetite as any man I have ever known, and she also enjoys the same company as the men I know, you follow?"

"I think so, she's a lesbian and very amorous."

"That's a very nice way to put it, yes. Well she believes we cramp her style, so she goes to a bar and meets other women then takes them to a little hideaway she has. She's also been very careful about it, we have tried but we haven't found the place yet. It actually belongs to a constituent who lets her use it."

"And you think that she is at this hideaway now?"

"I'm sure she is. As far as I know, she is not very sexually active in Washington, but as soon as she gets back here, she goes crazy. She had an appointment in Washington canceled today, or yesterday I guess it was, so she moved her plans up a day, probably so she could get laid."

"So she wasn't due to be in San Francisco until today?"

"That's correct."

"That might be a good sign. It could be a coincidence that our suspects flew into town yesterday. Does the Representative publish her travel plans?"

"No, most of the Congressman don't since the killings started. But anyone that wanted to know could have called her office and asked, the secretary there would tell them."

"I really don't like it, too much of a coincidence. I'm going to get in touch with our office there and have them call you. We need to find Oliver, and we need to find our suspects, Todd Evans and Annie Simmons. I'll send digital photos to your office so you'll have them on hand. Also, this may change, but we only want to keep the suspects under surveillance, do not attempt to arrest them. We don't know for sure who, or how many, are involved and we don't want to spook any of them. Call me immediately if Oliver turns up, I hope I'm wrong, but I have a gut feeling about this and it's not good."

Zimmerman gave Agent Panetta the necessary phone numbers should he need to get in touch with the command center. He then called the San Francisco regional FBI office and briefed them on the situation. He sent a large file via the modem containing biographies and pictures of Annie Simmons and Todd Evans.

Agent Lori Anderson had been listening to Agent Zimmerman's side of the conversation. The knot in her stomach, which had just recently gone away, came back with a vengeance. As gracefully as she could, she excused herself and went to the ladies' room. It was her fault and no matter what anyone said, she would still feel that way. Sitting on the small padded bench against the wall Lori kept going over what had happened in her head. The only thing she could have done differently was to call it in immediately, maybe another agent was on the freeway and could have picked up the tail.

Agent Anderson splashed water on her face and looked at herself in the mirror. In a way, she felt like crying, she felt like screaming, she felt like she should just resign and go home and then she would tell herself over and over again that there was nothing she could have done. She looked in the mirror and vowed that this would not get the best of her. If Representative Margaret Oliver dies, she would be sorry, but she did the best she could.

Lori left the bathroom and went to the commissary and made herself a cup of coffee, black, and picked a cherry filled and a plain glazed donut from the fresh box. The sudden sugar rush made her feel much better.

32

Representative Margaret Oliver unlocked the door and pushed it open, allowing Annie Simmons to enter the small apartment first. Maggie followed, closing and locking the door before turning on the light.

The apartment was small. There was barely room in the living room for the love seat and 19 inch portable television. Annie knew the Representative only used the apartment for sex, she wondered why she even had a television. The kitchen too was small, but very modern, with a fairly new refrigerator and microwave. Again Annie wondered why have a microwave.

Maggie gave Annie the full tour showing her the kitchen, pouring two glasses of white wine from the refrigerator, the living room, the bedroom and the bath, accessible only from the bedroom.

In each room, Annie looked for a weapon. There were no pots or pans on the stove. No fireplace, so there were no fireplace tools. She didn't even see an umbrella with a sharp pointed end. The bedroom was also void of blunt objects. Next to the bed was an alarm clock and a desk lamp. Annie studied the lamp and decided it was not heavy enough to do any damage.

Maggie was speaking, but Annie had not been paying much attention. Her mind was set to kill the woman in the room with her and she needed a weapon. Annie had been looking around the room and did not see Maggie reach for her glass of wine. It gave her a bit of a start as Maggie took the glass from her hand. At first, Annie thought the glass was slipping out of her hand and tightened her grip on it.

"I'm sorry," said Margaret Oliver, "I was going to set it down for you."

Before Annie could say anything, Maggie took the glass and set it with her glass on the night stand next to the bed. Annie stood watching, her mind still trying to come up with a way to kill the woman.

After setting the glasses down, Maggie put her arms around Annie and kissed her. Annie responded and kissed her back, as passionately as she was being kissed. As they French kissed, Representative Oliver applied just enough force with her body to move Annie backward a step and on to the bed. As they lay there kissing, Margaret unsnapped Annie's shorts and slid them off. Annie raised her behind off the bed so her shorts and panties would slide off easily. It was more of a reflex action than a concerted effort to help the Representative remove her clothes.

Annie was still thinking about how she was going to kill Representative Oliver. It was another reflex action that caused her to spread her legs when Maggie's hand began exploring her. The same reflex caused Annie to moan as Maggie's fingers found her more sensitive areas.

Annie was beginning to get extremely excited as Margaret Oliver began to inch her way down Annie's body. Stopping only momentarily to kiss the nape of Annie's neck, breasts and navel as she moved to the garden spot. Keeping focused was becoming more and more difficult as Maggie began performing oral sex on Annie. Annie tried to ignore what was happening to her and think about weapons. There must be a knife in the kitchen, she would get it after they made love. Sometime during the night Maggie was sure to have to use the bathroom. Annie would get a knife and hide it under the bed. The next time they made love, she would stab her. Annie thought of the wine bottle in the refrigerator. It was certainly heavy enough, she would go for a glass of wine, then hit her over the head with the bottle.

U.S. Representative Margaret Oliver was undoubtedly the best at oral sex Annie had ever enjoyed. Whenever Annie tried to think about a plan, Maggie's tongue would dance across an area that would make her entire body quiver. Annie's mind was soon only aware of the pleasure she was receiving from the woman she intended to murder.

As Annie felt the first signs of an orgasm, her body began to have uncontrollable spasms. Annie moaned with pleasure as Maggie began to work her tongue and fingers harder to give Annie one of the greatest climaxes she had ever experienced.

The orgasm rushed though Annie's body and Annie could not keep from screaming out loud as Maggie worked on her G-spot to make the "O" last longer. Annie's stomach muscles jumped and her legs tightened around Maggie's head. The orgasm became so violent that Annie tried to pull away, but the Representative kept her mouth attached to Annie, making the orgasm last longer and longer.

It wasn't until Maggie said "easy" that Annie opened her eyes and realized she had Margaret Oliver's neck in a vice grip between her legs. The Representative was smiling and patting Annie's legs, motioning for her to ease her grip. Annie, still breathing hard, locked her ankles and squeezed Maggie's neck between her thighs.

By the time Margaret Oliver's brain comprehended that her neck was no longer being squeezed from a reflex action of the love making, it had been deprived of blood and oxygen a full minute. Margaret twisted her head in attempt to free herself from the grip of Annie Simmons' muscular thighs. The twisting only made matters worse as pressure from Annie's legs crushed the trachea, obstructing the vital passage through which air could reach her lungs, while continued pressure on the jugular prevented oxygen from reaching her brain.

Margaret's twisting became more violent as her gag reflex, and the human will to survive stimulated a rush of adrenaline. Annie squeezed her legs with all her might, not only to keep up pressure, but to keep Margaret from breaking free of the death grip.

The closer Representative Oliver came to death, the harder she fought. She dug her finger nails deep into the superficial muscles of Annie's legs. Annie felt nothing as she squeezed the fragile neck between her legs. Soon Margaret Oliver's body became motionless except for the heaving of her chest cavity as it tried in vain to fill itself with life sustaining oxygen.

Only when Representative Margaret Oliver had laid perfectly still for several minutes did Annie open her eyes to look. Annie kept from screaming by taking numerous deep breaths, almost to the point of hyperventilation before she got a hold of herself. She had not expected to see blood, but it was everywhere, and it was her own blood. Maggie's finger nails had made deep gashes in Annie's upper thighs. The bleeding had already stopped, but violent movements had splattered the blood everywhere. Annie's blouse was covered.

Annie finally looked at Maggie for the first time, her head still being held tightly between Annie's legs. After all the movies where the victim jumped up after being strangled, Annie was taking no chances. She looked at Maggie's face, her eyes were open, staring off into the distance. Annie looked at the eyes, looking for any sign of life. There was none. Annie searched her soul for remorse, regret, sadness, for any feelings. There were none.

As Annie released the pressure of her legs, she felt the effects of nearly five minutes of total exertion. For a second, she didn't think her legs would come apart. Her muscles hurt and she was now becoming aware of the stinging from the cuts. Annie swung her legs off the bed onto the floor. She stood slowly, supporting much of her weight with her hands until she was sure her legs could indeed support her entire body weight.

Annie stood and looked at Maggie Oliver on the bed. Her eyes were still open, staring into forever. She was dead. Killed up close with Annie's own hands, or in this case, her own legs. Not like when Todd had killed, with poison, miles away in one case, but right here and now. Annie Simmons only wished that Representative Margaret Oliver knew why she had died. She had been one of the most corrupt politicians in history. She had stolen, lied, cheated and did not care who she hurt. Annie actually felt rejoice. This woman needed to be stopped and now she was. Annie wanted to tell the world.

She made her way to the bathroom and looked in the mirror. Her legs, blouse and stomach were covered in blood. Annie found a wash cloth in the small linen closet and wet it. Slowly she cleaned the dried blood from her legs, being careful not to reopen the wounds. She took off her blouse and wiped the blood from her waist and stomach.

The blood came off easily and in no time Annie had cleaned herself up. She found a small tin of Band-aides and, although she was not bleeding, put a bandage over each puncture in her legs. It was better to spend the time putting bandages on now than to have her legs start bleeding on the way back to the hotel.

It surprised Annie that the bedroom had no closet. She looked in the living room and again, there was no closet. She couldn't wear her own blouse and Maggie had not taken hers off, so it was out of the question. Annie noticed the tall thin chest of drawers in the corner and checked the top drawer. It contained sheets and pillow cases. There was no clothing in the next two drawers. The fourth drawer held three neatly folded men's polo shirts and several pairs of women's underwear.

Annie chose a plain white shirt and checked to be sure it had no identifying words or initials on it. It would not be good for her if she was picked up by the cops wearing a polo shirt with the initial's "M.O." on it. There were no distinguishing marks, it was a very plain shirt. Annie put the polo shirt on, found her shorts and panties, checked them for blood stains, and, finding none, she put them on.

It was nearly 2:30 in the morning and Annie felt she had already been in the apartment longer than she should have been. She thought about changing the sheets and putting Maggie in the bathtub and rinsing her off, but decided she would be better off just getting the hell out of there. Even though the police would have blood stains, they would have to have a sample from Annie in order to match it up. Annie had no intention of them ever getting a sample.

Quickly, Annie checked the kitchen and found a brown paper bag in which she put her bloodied blouse. She went back to the bedroom and looked around the room one more time, then at the Representative's lifeless body and said, "Goodbye Maggie, you did give me the best orgasm of my life. It really was wonderful, had it not been so good, you might still be alive." She turned and walked to the door before adding, "and I would still be planning to kill you."

Representative Margaret Oliver's hideaway was the perfect spot to commit a murder. The entrance was from an alley off a small side street. The side street, where apartment owners parked their cars, was secluded itself, making the alley a place where only people with a reason went. At almost three o'clock in the morning, no one had a reason to be there.

Annie walked down the alley and out the side street, staying in the shadows the best she could. Having not seen another living soul, Annie reached the main street and looked around in an attempt to get her bearings. On the way to the apartment her mind was preoccupied with the murder of Ms. Oliver, as well as clouded with wine. She knew she was somewhere in the city of San Francisco, presumably near Chinatown, but other than that, she was totally lost.

A light fog had settled over the city giving a Londonesque look. It reminded Annie Simmons of how she pictured London when she read stories about Jack the Ripper. How ironic, she thought.

No city in America is absolutely safe for a woman, or a man for that matter, alone, walking the streets at three A.M. For a large city, San Francisco is probably one of the safest. The street crime associated with drugs had moved to Oakland and the suburbs. The city itself is a peninsula which has seen its property values increase so dramatically, criminals simply cannot afford to live there. The run down neighborhoods which would have housed the drug users, drug dealers and street gangs had been bought by developers and turned into $250,000, one bedroom condo's.

Annie decided to turn left on the main street, simply because that way was down hill. The gouges in her legs stung and her leg muscles were extremely sore. She didn't think she could walk up hill at all.

She walked several blocks, looking up and down each side street for landmarks that would give her an idea of where she was and which way she should be going. No cars passed in either direction and the fog reduced the light of the street lamps to a soft glow. If anyone had seen her in the street, they would never be able to recognize her again.

A green sign attached to a stop light read "Fisherman's Wharf," with an arrow pointing to the right. Being sure no cars were coming from any direction, Annie darted across the street, moving as fast as she could make her sore, stiff legs move.

Three more blocks and Annie found herself in the heart of Chinatown. Even at three in the morning, it was still somewhat busy. Less that two blocks away Annie saw several cabs lined up in front of a large restaurant. Staying as close to the buildings as she could, she covered the distance as quickly as she could and got in the cab. As she sat, she cried out as the pain shot from her legs when they bent and stretched for the first time in over an hour.

The cab driver turned and looked at her as she tried to rub the stiffness out of her thighs.

"Just sore from walking," she said keeping her head down, hoping to prevent the driver from getting a good look at her face. "The Holiday Inn at Fisherman's Wharf please," she said before the driver could ask.

The ride was short, but there was no way Annie could have walked it. The use of adrenaline had zapped her and she was now exhausted. The cab pulled up to the front of the Holiday Inn and Annie paid and tipped the driver. She waited until the cab was out of sight before walking across the street to the Hyatt.

33

Agent McBride stuck his head into the office where Alexander Christian was sleeping. The sound of the door opening and the flood of fluorescent light woke Christian. He held his hand in front of his eyes to block the light. He looked around the office trying to determine where he was.

He saw John McBride looking at him from the doorway. "Wow, I was dreaming I was playing golf in Arizona, this was sure a rude awakening," Christian said.

"If you think it's bad seeing me, wait till you hear what I've got to tell you." McBride wanted to grin, his comment was meant to be humorous, but he just couldn't force a smile.

"Bad?"

"Not sure yet, it's beginning to look like it."

"Can it wait five minutes?"

"It's already waited two hours, we didn't want to wake you. This is the first time you've slept more than an hour in quite awhile. Another five minutes isn't going to make too much difference."

"Good, let me run to the head and clean up a little, I'll meet you in the command center."

McBride was surprised Agent Christian didn't want to know what was up immediately. In fact, Christian did want to know, but he knew that the cobwebs left from the deep sleep would have prevented him from following anything at the moment. It was better to wait a few minutes, until his brain was completely awake and alert.

Christian walked to the men's room still in a half sleep state. He urinated, washed his hands and splashed cold water on his face. He studied his face in the mirror. He thought his eyes looked pretty good, considering, but he definitely needed a shave. He rubbed the stubble on his face trying to remember the last time he shaved. He decided he wasn't sure what time it was or even what day it was, and he sure as hell couldn't remember the last time he had shaved.

On the way to the command center Agent Christian stopped by the commissary. He poured himself a large cup of coffee and put two kalochies on a napkin. The kalochies were gone by the time he reached the command center, had the coffee not been so hot, it would have been gone as well.

Agent Christian stood outside the door of the Blind Luck command center and sipped his coffee. He knew something was up and he wanted to be as awake as possible when he was hit with it. After two more sips, he opened the door and went inside.

The room became quiet as he entered. Christian was taking another drink of coffee as he walked in, he had to look over the edge of the Styrofoam cup to be sure he was in the right room. He stood and looked around the room. Nobody looked at him, and yet they were not working, everyone seemed to be staring off into space.

"Come on people, unless they assassinated the President, it can't be as bad as you all make it appear."

Agent Lori Anderson stood and faced her boss. She did not look good. Her face was pale except for the dark circles under her eyes, which were somewhat blood shot. Her makeup had faded and could no longer add color or hide the dark circles. She said, "I guess I should be the one that fills you in. It was my fault. . ."

Christian interrupted, "I assume this has something to do with Evans and Simmons. I've read your report and there is not an agent in this room, including myself, that would not have lost that car. If I wanted to put blame on you, I could say you should have radioed the second they got on the freeway. However, we've had surveillance on these people for five days and none of them had done anything to suggest to us they we would not be able to pick them up again either at their office or home. Lori, I think most of us would have done exactly what you did."

Christian looked at Agent Anderson and wished he could do more to make her feel better. He had a good idea what she was going through. Even though he had just told her it wasn't her fault, and he knew she had told herself many times that it wasn't her fault, a little voice in the back of her head was telling her she screwed up big time. That it was indeed her fault. It was that little voice that kept telling the brain to release the acids into her stomach which made it difficult to eat or sleep.

Another problem, Christian felt, was that Agent Lori Anderson was one of only two female agents assigned to operation Blind Luck. The two women were never assigned together and seldom were even in the same building at the same time. If one of the guys had a problem, he would get together with one of the other male agents and talk it out, usually with extremely colorful metaphors. Even though every male agent considered Lori an equal, there was a difference, and it was difficult to get around it. They all talked to Lori and tried to help, but none of the men knew her well enough to treat her as one of the guys. Whenever the conversation got colorful, the male agents would retreat. The fear of saying something Lori would consider sexual harassment was always present in their minds.

Lori thanked Agent Christian for his words of encouragement then briefed him of the situation. It didn't take long as there were not many facts to tell. She saved the speculation for a later discussion.

Christian listened closely to Lori, then asked, "and there is still no word on Congresswoman Oliver?"

"That's correct. I talked to the Secret Service agent at her home a few minutes ago and he told me he had heard nothing. He said they were in the process of waking some of her 'friends' that might know where her secret hideaway is located. They are getting a lot of 'I don't knows', and they are not sure if it's because they really don't know, they don't like being woken up at three in the morning or if Oliver has instructed them not to say anything."

"Have they located Evans and Simmons?"

"No sir, they did rent a car from Dollar and we are checking hotels now. There are a lot of hotels in the Bay area," Agent Bates answered.

"Did you inform the FBI in San Francisco to follow, but under no circumstances make contact?"

"Yes, but what if they find Oliver dead, should they pick them up?"

"No, and I think it would be a good idea to reiterate that. Especially if they find Oliver dead. Then we know for sure this group is our gang and we want to get the whole group. And I don't give a flying fuck if a judge thinks it's a coincidence that two of our suspects were in the same place at the same time a U.S. Representative was killed, we will use every means available to make sure we get every one of these people."

* * * * * *

The sound of water running in the bathroom woke Todd Evans from a sound sleep. He had sat in the bar waiting for Annie until he was so drunk he was afraid he wouldn't be able to make it back to his room. His head hurt so badly it was difficult to focus on the red numbers glowing from the small digital clock next to the bed. It was 3:45 in the morning.

Todd pressed a pillow over his head trying to snuff out the pain and noise. It didn't work. He fumbled to turn on the lamp which was on the stand next to the digital clock. He made a slightly audible moan as the light shot through his eyes and burned the front of his brain. Finding his travel bag, he took out three extra-strength Tylenols. Before going to bed, Todd had set a glass of ice water on the night stand next to the bed. The ice had melted but the water was still cool and tasted wonderful as he washed down the Tylenol tablets.

He sat on the bed, leaning against the headboard, hoping everything would stay down long enough for the pain killers to do their thing. He closed his eyes and tried to imagine what Annie had been doing for the past six hours. He pictured her making love with a beautiful young woman with long blond hair. He wished they would have come back to the hotel so he could have joined in on the fun. He wondered if there actually were any beautiful young women with long blond hair at lesbian bars.

Annie appeared from the bathroom wearing long baggie slacks and a short tight blouse which stopped two inches above the waistband of her slacks, exposing just enough skin to be incredibly sexy. She had a very cute "innie" navel. She was surprised to see Todd sitting up.

"We need to get packed and leave," she said as calmly as if they were going to breakfast.

"Why, have you decided against killing Margaret Oliver?" Todd asked, wishing he hadn't said anything about it. She must have changed her mind and it saved him from having to change it for her.

"I've already killed her." Again Annie spoke with no more emotion than a person ordering a beer.

Todd heard what she said, but he was hoping the pain in his head had turned what she said into something different. "What?" was all he could say.

"I said it's done. I killed her last night, or this morning, whenever, I don't remember what time it was. She was at the bar last night, said a meeting or something was canceled and she came into town a day early. She said she was glad because she met me."

"Geez Annie, how, uh, where, uh. . ." Todd's head hurt terribly and Annie's confession had thrown him for a loop.

"Calm down," Annie said. She could tell he was having a hard time comprehending what she was telling him. "Listen, Representative Oliver introduced herself to me and we talked awhile, then she kissed me, and then she asked me if I wanted to go home with her. I said 'yes,' so she drove me back to a hideaway she has. I don't think it was her place, I got the impression someone else actually owned it, but she said she was the only one that had a key. It was like it was hers, but it wasn't. She told me she loved sex and had to be discreet because she was a public figure."

Todd wanted to interrupt and tell Annie he didn't care who owned the apartment or what it was used for. He wanted to hear what happened. Todd decided she would get to it sooner or later and sat quietly listening.

Annie finally got to the part Todd was waiting for. "We had only been there a few minutes, long enough for her to pour us both a glass of wine, when she kissed me and pushed me onto the bed. She made love to me and then I strangled her with my legs."

Todd stared at his friend in disbelief. She spoke with absolutely no emotion. It was like she did this kind of thing everyday. Going over what she had just said in his mind, Todd felt like he should ask something, but she had explained it in no uncertain terms. He wanted more than anything to run to the bathroom and vomit, and it was not the beer that made him feel the need.

Knowing that it had hit him hard, Annie said, "we really should get ready to go to the airport. We need to check in the car and be there early enough so we can get standby on the first flight out. I think one leaves at six-thirty or seven."

Leaving town was suddenly the best idea Todd had heard since arriving in San Francisco. A hot shower also sounded like a good idea. He made his way to the bathroom and turned the water on as hot as he could stand. He stood letting the water hit his head and run down his body. The steam generated by the shower helped to relieve some of the pressure of his swollen brain. The pain killers were taking effect and by the time he turned the water off he was feeling much better. Still not good, but much better.

Todd dried himself, combed his hair and walked into the main room to get his clothes. When he had gone into the bathroom, a change of clothes was the furthest thing from his mind.

Annie had turned every light in the room on and was sitting on the bed watching television. She watched Todd walk across the room and said, "Umm, I wish we had time for a little hanky panky."

Todd didn't say anything, he really didn't know what to say. He was glad they didn't have time as he definitely was not in the mood. Annie watched as Todd put on a pair of boxer shorts, tan Dockers and a white polo shirt.

"Aren't you going to ask me how I did it?" Annie asked.

The shower did wonders to clear his mind and he did in fact have a lot of questions he wanted to ask. He just wasn't too sure he wanted to hear the answers. There is an old saying, if you don't want to hear the answer, don't ask the question. "If I remember correctly, you said you strangled her. Of course I want to hear the details, I'm just not sure I'm up to it right now. I've got to be honest with you. Last night at dinner I decided this wasn't a very good idea and I was going to try and talk you out of it today. It's obviously too late for that."

"You wouldn't have talked me out of it. I believe in what we are doing and I think it will make the country a better place to live. You read the things she was doing, and nobody else was going to do anything about it, so I did."

"Are you prepared to spend the rest of you life in prison for it?"

Prison was a consequence she hadn't considered. "We have to get caught first, and we won't. Then they would have to convict us. All we have to do is hire O.J. Simpson's lawyers and we would get off scott free."

"We can't afford O.J.'s lawyers. They'll fry us."

"Naw, this would be the biggest case since the O.J. trial, we could get really good lawyers who would do it just for the publicity. Remember, a lot of people are on our side. They think we are doing the right thing. They just have to pick a good jury and we'll walk."

Todd had to agree that there would be lawyers lining up to defend them, but he really hoped it wouldn't get that far. "What about evidence, do you think you left any evidence, like finger prints or anything? What about people at the bar, do you think anybody will recognize you?"

These were questions Annie was hoping he would not ask, but she had already decided if he asked, she would tell him the truth. "The bar was pretty dark and the only person I think might recognize me would be the bartender, but she didn't pay too much attention to me." She hesitated to collect her thoughts before continuing. "I probably left a lot of evidence at her apartment though. I knew if I was going to kill her, it had to be then and there. If I tried to meet her later, like tonight, she would probably ask my name and where I was staying. If I gave her the information, she might tell someone. So I had to do it. I didn't have your poison, so I was trying to think of how I could do it when she went down on me."

Todd really wasn't sure he wanted to hear the rest of the story and thought about stopping her. He had a feeling he wasn't going to like it, but he didn't interrupt.

"She was really good, I mean really, really good."

"O.K., she was a good. . . " Todd decided not to finish his sentence.

"Anyway, I couldn't think about anything but what she was doing. She REALLY was good, and I had the most incredible orgasm. I didn't even realize it, but I was squeezing her neck with my legs. She said something like ease up, or something, I can't remember, but I thought, this is perfect, and I locked my feet together and squeezed my legs as hard as I could. Obviously, I didn't plan it so I didn't know what to expect, but she fought harder than I thought she would. I have these gashes in my legs where she dug her fingernails into my legs.

"It's strange, but I didn't feel anything until she was dead, then it really began to hurt. My leg muscles were real sore too, they still are. I could hardly get out of her bed. I bled a lot on the sheets, it's still there, and I'm sure I left finger prints. My legs hurt and I was in a hurry to get out of the apartment. I figure if they never find me, and I don't know how they will if we catch the early plane, they won't be able to use the evidence."

"You've never had your fingerprints taken?"

"Not that I can remember."

"Let's just hope the bartender can't remember what you look like. If she does, and they get a decent composite drawing, you will be on the front of every newspaper in America."

Annie didn't tell Todd, but she actually hoped the police or the FBI would come up with a drawing they thought was good enough to give to the press, but was not good enough that someone would recognize her. She would have to find a book store that sold many different newspapers so she could get a copy of every one that published her picture.

"Just in case, as soon as we get home, I'll get my hair cut so I will look totally different. At least that way it would have to be someone that knows me in order to identify me. I won't have to worry about some clown at the Stop and Go turning me in," she said.

Todd had finished packing while Annie was finishing her story. He still had questions, but he decided they could wait. "Are you ready?" he asked as he closed the zipper on his sports bag.

"Yeah, if I can walk. Every time I sit for a while, my legs tighten up. I don't know if I'll be able to get off the plane after a four hour flight." She laughed but Todd failed to see any humor in it. He thought about how she had squeezed his neck during sex and pictured Representative Margaret Oliver dying between Annie's legs. If he ever performed oral sex on Annie, or any woman, again, he most certainly would think about Margaret Oliver.

Todd picked up both bags as Annie checked all the drawers one last time to be sure that nothing had been left behind. He stood at the door and looked around the room they had spent less than 24 hours in. It felt like he was leaving a home he had lived in 20 years.

Annie walked like she had a limp in both legs as she tried to work the soreness out. By the time she reached the front desk, she was moving much more comfortably. Todd went to get the rental car and left the check-out duties to Annie. He would reimburse her for the hotel when they got home.

Check-out went smoothly and Annie joined Todd as he waited for the Valet to bring the Chrysler Cirrus to the front door. They stood silently and looked at the skyline, traces of daylight were beginning to brighten the eastern sky. A front had blown through taking the fog, that was so thick only hours ago, out over the Pacific.

The valet arrived with their car and Todd helped Annie in the passenger side. After paying for one night's parking and a tip, almost as much as the car rental for a day, Todd got in the car. He started to ask Annie if she remembered how to get back to the airport, but she was sound asleep. Using a very generic street map, plus the fact that traffic at five o'clock in the morning was very light, Todd had little trouble finding the airport.

When he gently shook Annie awake, she couldn't believe they were at the airport and she had been asleep close to an hour. They stayed together as Todd checked in the rental car and Annie inquired about availability on the next flight to Houston. There were plenty of seats available and, just as on the flight out, they were given two seats in first class.

34

Agent Berg hung up the phone in the Blind Luck command center and swung around in his swivel chair. He was looking at Agent Christian, but speaking to the room. "They finally found somebody that knew the location of the hideaway. There's a team on the way to check it out right now. There's also an Annie Simmons registered at the Hyatt Fisherman's Wharf Hotel, which is not far from the apartment location and very close to the bar where Representative Oliver was last seen. There's a FBI team on the way to the hotel, they will call us as soon as they check it out."

"That's good work," said Agent Christian, "be sure the FBI teams, as well as anyone else involved, Secret Service, local police, know not to attempt to apprehend Evans and Simmons. I want the whole gang and if we bust two of them, we may never get the rest."

Christian thought for a moment then added, "and if they find Ms. Oliver dead, remind everyone out there not to let the news media know we have suspects, we want these two to think they got away clean."

Agent Alexander Christian was working on the assumption that Representative Oliver would not be found alive. He preferred to get the ball rolling and stop it if he was wrong, and she was alive, rather that wait until she was found, and if she was dead, start the planning process.

Agents Christian and McBride found an empty office and went over their resources. McBride assured Christian that they had plenty of listening devices and homing devices, which would be placed on every person's car so they would not lose anyone else. Personnel was the only problem. The agents assigned to "Blind Luck" were exhausted after only one week of around the clock surveillance, if it took another week, or two, to gather the necessary evidence, the agents would be beat.

McBride was reluctant to spread his agents too thin as there was other work in Houston that could not be ignored. The two agreed the best idea would be to ask Washington for all available support. The phone on the desk rang and Christian picked it up.

"Christian," he said into the handset.

"This is Berg, sir. We just received word that Annie Simmons checked out of her hotel around five this morning. The desk clerk also ID'd her and was pretty sure she was with Todd Evans. We checked with Continental Airlines to see if they were booked on a flight back to Houston, but they said their computers were down, we would have to check back later. The same team that went to the hotel is now on their way to the airport. There's a flight that leaves San Francisco for Houston at six-forty. That flight will probably be airborne by the time the agents get there, but at least they will be able to find out if our suspects were on the plane."

"Thanks, Harry. Any word on Representative Oliver?"

"No sir, not yet. Should be hearing something soon though."

"Good. We will be coming back to the command center in just a few minutes."

Agent Christian hung up the phone. "Evans and Simmons checked out of their hotel at five this morning. That does not bode well for Ms. Oliver. I just can't figure out why Simmons used her real name at the hotel. Maybe I'm way off base and they checked out to drive up to the wine country. If we go busting in on Representative Oliver and a lesbian friend, we are going to look real fucking stupid."

"No, Alex, I think your instincts are right on. Those two flew to California and killed a U.S. Congressman, or, Congresswoman in this case, and are now on their way home. Had you not gotten a tip and been following them, we wouldn't have a clue. And unless they left a calling card with Oliver, we would be just as in the dark about her death as we were with the other four."

"You're right. I'm surprised they didn't stay in San Francisco and see the sights for a few days, they've been so lucky this far." Alexander Christian was battling mixed emotions. He didn't want Representative Oliver to be dead, but if she was, there would be no doubt who did it.

"We better be getting back, something should be coming in on Oliver soon," said McBride.

"Go ahead, I feel like hell. I'm going up to the gym to shower and shave real quick. If Oliver's dead, it'll wait ten minutes. If she's not dead, then I've got all day, we were wrong."

"If I were you, I'd be quick."

Agent Christian nodded at McBride as he headed toward the showers. McBride arrived in the command center as the report on Representative Margaret Oliver was coming in. The agents stood silently, listening to the speaker phone as the FBI agent described the carnage.

"Forensics is saying the probable cause of death was from strangulation. However, it looks like she did not die without a fight. There was blood everywhere. We also have an enormous amount of tissue under her fingernails and she has no lacerations. The blood had to come from the murderer. Representative Oliver is on her way to the coroner's office. As soon as we get the details, we will pass them on to you."

Agent McBride asked several questions. As the agent in California was answering them, Lori Anderson quietly excused herself and went to the ladies room. She laid down on the sofa in the lounge and began to cry. A little voice in the back of her head said, "it's not your fault."

Todd Evans and Annie Simmons found their seats on the Boeing 737 bound for Houston and were asleep before the coach passengers were finished boarding. Todd woke up somewhere over Nevada and ordered a Bloody Mary. He considered holding the vodka, but then thought, *what the hell, a little 'hair of the dog' would do me good.*

By the time lunch, burritos and guacamole, was served, Todd was feeling pretty good. He ordered Annie a lunch and when she didn't wake up, ate it as well. He ordered another Bloody Mary and leaned back in his chair. He could definitely get used to flying first class.

Even the drinks could not erase the picture of Annie strangling Representative Oliver between her legs. Todd had performed oral sex on Annie a number of times and remembered how she would squeeze her legs together when she had an orgasm. On more than one occasion he had to get her attention and have her ease up on his neck. He never realized it could be so lethal.

As he thought about it, it brought a smile to his face. What an incredible way to kill a person. The smile disappeared as Todd felt the cold chill over take his body. He thought of all the evidence left at the scene. Blood, fingerprints, gashes in Annie's legs and witnesses at the club. And that was only what he knew about. There probably was more he didn't know of. If the police ever found

Annie, they could prove she was the killer with little effort. Todd was very glad they were out of San Francisco.

By the time the pilot made the announcement that they were on their approach to Houston's Bush Intercontinental Airport, Todd had drunk enough where he was feeling quite well. He hoped Annie would be able to drive as he nudged her awake.

"We're about to land, you might want to wake up."

"Already?" Annie said as she stretched in an attempt to loosen her stiff muscles. "I don't even remember us taking off. That is really strange, I usually don't sleep well on airplanes."

"I guess you don't usually stay up all night the night before you fly."

"Maybe I will next time, it sure makes for a quick flight."

The plane jerked as the wheels touched the ground, squealing as they attempted to slow the speed of the airplane. The roar of the air hitting the fully extended flaps, deafening in coach, was hardly audible in first class.

"I really like flying up here," Todd said as they taxied to the gate.

"Yeah, I know. It's really the shits when I have to fly in coach. It's real easy to get spoiled."

The voice of the Captain thanking everyone for flying Continental interrupted their conversation. The two sat quietly waiting for the fasten seat belt sign to go out. Annie rubbed her legs trying to work the stiffness out.

The plane was still rolling when the first click of a seatbelt unbuckling was heard. Soon after the plane sounded as if it was full of crickets as the passengers unbuckled their seatbelts and reached for their carry-on luggage. Very few heard the ping as the seatbelt light was turned off.

Coach passengers were held back as the first class passengers were allowed to exit the plane first. Todd held Annie by the arm and tried to support her as she attempted to walk up the ramp. Over four hours in the plane had pulled her muscles tighter than a drum. Pain raced up her back with every step.

It took awhile, but the couple reached Todd's car in the parking garage. Todd opened the passenger side and helped Annie slide in. He didn't even suggest that she drive, he knew it was out of the question.

Todd walked around the car and let himself in. "You OK?" he asked.

"My fucking legs hurt. It feels like someone is sticking ice picks in them."

Todd was sorry he asked. It was supposed to have been a rhetorical question.

"I know it can be serious if a human bites you, I wonder if it the same with fingernails?"

"That would be just my luck, the bitch probably gave me AIDS or something. Geez."

"I'm not really sure that lesbians have AIDS, I think it's mostly the gay men."

Annie just glared at Todd. She knew he was right and she had only said what she did to make a point, but she was in no mood to discuss it. Todd sensed it was not a good time to tease Annie so he started the car and drove toward the exit in silence.

Just as he did not notice the two FBI agents who were waiting as they got off the airplane, Todd paid no attention to the dark Chevrolet Lumina as it followed him from the airport.

* * * * * *

"They're mobile." Agent Berg shouted as he monitored the radio traffic between agents in the field.

"Good, who's on them?" Agent Christian asked.

The Blind Luck Command Center seemed deserted compared to the past few days. All available agents were now on the street, leaving only Agents Christian, McBride and Berg in the Command Center.

"Holland and Zimmerman."

"They're good, they won't be made," McBride said, aware of Christian's concern that everyone involved be arrested simultaneously, if possible, and that if just one suspect was tipped, the whole lot would probably disappear across the country, or the world for that matter. It could take years and thousands of man-hours to find them all.

Agent Christian closed his eyes and pinched the bridge of his nose. He sat quietly with his eyes closed as he tried to put everything that was happening into perspective. Satisfied that everything that could be done was being done, he opened his eyes and looked at Agent McBride. "Let's go see Judge Wopner and see if he'll give us those fucking warrants!"

McBride knew he was talking about Judge Malcolm Winter but

did not offer the correction. He assumed "Judge Wopner," was meant as an insult toward the judge. He also knew why Christian was upset with the Judge. McBride had known Judge Winter for some time and had always liked and respected him. He did not appreciate Agent Christian's comments or tone toward the Judge, but he certainly understood. The Judge had refused to issue search warrants and another person was dead. But it was the Judge's job to protect citizens from illegal search and seizure. He felt there was not enough evidence to justify wire taps and searches, so he made his ruling and a United States Representative died because of it. *Very ironic*, Agent McBride thought to himself.

McBride called the courthouse and an aide said that the Judge would see them in his chambers as soon as they got there. During the short walk to the court house, the two agents talked about the Judge's refusal to issue warrants and the resulting consequences. McBride was reluctant to bring it up, but thought it would be good for Christian to unload some baggage before he got in front of the Judge.

By the time they reached the court house McBride was happy he brought the subject up. Christian did unload, and by the time he finished he was actually agreeing with the Judge's original decision. Had they gotten warrants, accumulated the evidence and made arrests, only to have it all thrown out of court on a technicality, it would have been disastrous.

A clerk showed the two FBI agents into Judge Winter's chambers. He was sitting at his desk reading the morning newspaper. He did not look up until the two agents were standing directly in front of his desk. He nodded at the two chairs as he folded the business section and laid it on his desk.

Judge Winter knew why the agents were in his office and could assume they were in a hurry. "Yes?" He said without exchanging pleasantries.

Agent Christian began. "Since we were last here to see you, we have had several people we believe are responsible for the murder of five United States Congressmen under surveillance. Under surveillance to the fullest extent allowed without breaking any laws. Unfortunately, one of our agents lost two of the suspects. It was later determined that those two suspects flew to San Francisco Monday morning and returned very early this morning. Last night, Representative Margaret Oliver of San Francisco was murdered. Ms. Oliver was last seen leaving a bar with a person who has been identified as one of our suspects. We would like you to issue a warrant for the arrest of Ms. Annie Simmons and Mr. Todd Evans, as well as permission to install eavesdropping and surveillance equipment as we deem necessary." Christian paused to catch his breath. He wanted to add that this was a matter of national security and how the President of the United States had personally told the Director of the FBI that this case should be top priority, but Judge Winter interrupted.

"Granted," Judge Winter said as he straightened the already straight papers on his desk in order to buy some time as he thought about the latest victim. He continued, "I am sure I know how you feel and I am sorry. I. . . "

It was Agent Christian's turn to interrupt, "your Honor, I didn't agree one hundred percent with your earlier ruling, and I still don't, obviously, but I understand why you had to make it, so if it's OK with you, I would just as soon forget about it." Christian knew that when the Judge said he was 'sorry', that he was sorry that a person had been killed, not that he was sorry about his decision. He also felt, and he was correct, that the least said, the better.

Agents Christian and McBride left the Judge's chambers with the necessary paperwork which would legalize the various surveillance devices which had already been installed. It was only a matter of time now until their job would be finished, except for testifying at the trial. Agent Christian was sure that by the time they made their arrests, they would have enough evidence to get a conviction, no matter how high-priced a lawyer was hired for the defense.

During the walk back to the command center, the subject of the trial came up. Agent McBride did not agree with his counterpart's optimism. "Of course it will go to trial, we could have a video tape of the murder and they would plead 'not guilty'. It's bad enough that a person has to commit a crime, but I wish just once somebody would say 'yes, I did it. This is why I did it, and I got caught, so I'm ready to accept my fate'. But no, they get a lawyer and plead 'not guilty' and tie up the courts, and occasionally walk. Lucky for us, most are found guilty and sent to prison. Why don't they just plead guilty?"

"Everybody has the right to a fair trial," Agent Christian said, mostly to rile his friend, but it was true, no matter how guilty a person was, they had the right to a fair trial.

"I know, and I agree with it. But when it was placed in the Constitution, they were strapping women to poles and dunking them in the water. If they did not drown, they were considered witches and burnt at the stake. If they drowned they said 'whoops' and tied another one on. Think about the time we spend preparing a case before we make an arrest. How many times do you think we've arrested and charged an innocent person?"

Christian thought about the question but McBride continued before he could answer.

"Never, that's how many times, never. And that's not just me personally, I can say that for this district office. There are enough bad guys out there that we don't have to make an innocent one look bad. Yet, even though we have a very good conviction record, some have walked. And some of those who walked we have caught again for a different offense and got a conviction. It's crazy."

The debate could have continued indefinitely, but the two men were back at the command center and decided to save their thoughts for another occasion. They were anxious to be updated on any reports from the field agents.

Agent Harry Berg looked rattled as the two senior agents entered the room. In their haste to see Judge Winter they didn't realize they had left Berg, a rookie agent, alone at the command center during a crucial period of an investigation.

Berg looked up at his boss as he entered the room. "All teams have checked in and all prime suspects are accounted for. Wire taps are in place in the homes of Todd Evans and Annie Simmons. Eric Moore is in his apartment but we have installed a tracking and listening device in his car. We decided to wait for warrants before going any further."

"We have the warrants on Moore, Evans and Simmons," Agent Christian said, "we had those ready, the others will be over soon. We can go ahead and install them at the Thompson, Flanagen, Lewis and Hanson residences. And by the way Harry, sorry about abandoning you this morning, I didn't even realize you were alone in here."

Agent Berg nodded and went about forwarding the instructions to the field agents waiting to install various types of listening devices. Christian looked at the wall of pictures and mentally noted which ones were now, or would very soon be under total observation by the FBI. These people could not go to the bathroom without someone listening in. It would not matter if they were at home, work or in their car, someone would be listening, and taping. Even if they walked a dog, a long-range listening devise would be monitoring their every sound.

It was not only a matter of time, but a matter of patience as well, until enough evidence had been collected to put the whole lot away for a long time. Agent Christian looked at the single photograph on the wall without a name and wondered how long it would be until they found the Lucky Bitch.

35

Annie Simmons had taken the week off from work as she didn't know how long she was going to have to spend in San Francisco. She slept most of Wednesday and spent Thursday morning lounging in her apartment. She wore a flower print sundress which hung loosely from her shoulders.

Just before noon, Todd called to see how she was doing. He told her that Russell had called and wanted everyone to get together at Chuck's Pizza around 7:30 P.M. Annie said that sounded great, and Todd said he would come by and pick her up at seven.

Much to the chagrin of several FBI agents, nothing was said during the conversation about the murder of Representative Oliver. Though disappointed they did not have an admission on tape, they were excited that the whole gang may be planning to meet that evening, possibly for a victory celebration of sorts. It was quite possible the arrest of the Blind Luck gang was less than ten hours away. The information was relayed to the command center.

Annie was happy to hear about the gathering at Chuck's. It had finally dawned on her that she had killed another human being, and even though she could justify it, she was beginning to feel guilty about it. She was going to go out and get extremely drunk and come home and have sex until she could not stay awake, sore legs and all. If Todd didn't want to have sex with her, she would find someone that would.

She pulled up the sun dress and looked at her legs. Her muscles were still a little sore but it no longer hurt to stand. The gouges had scabbed over but the surrounding area was badly bruised and showing signs of infection. Annie thought about going to a doctor for some antibiotics but was afraid the doctor might become suspicious of the wounds and notify the police. Though she had not turned on a television or read a newspaper in two days, Annie was sure the murder of Representative Oliver had been in the news.

The hours preceding the murder Annie could only think about

collecting the newspaper clippings and videotaping the news broadcasts. Now she didn't want to hear about it or even think about it. She had no desire to call other members of the gang and tell them of the details. She knew they were all aware of it and would be interested, but she had no desire to make a call. She decided on a nap. The evening was going to be long, she hoped.

* * * * * *

Chuck Renning graduated from high school in 1969 and somehow had avoided the draft. After high school he spent his time working odd jobs, surfing and taking drugs. Mostly surfing and taking drugs. He had shoulder length hair, above average looks and build, and a terrific tan. Although prone to exaggerating the truth at times, he had a charming personality. He was married as well as divorced in 1970, but was never without female companionship.

The combination of drugs and sun took it's toll and by the time he was 30, he looked 40. His entourage of young, healthy, and extremely attractive women turned into tattooed topless dancers. Chuck left the surfer crowds for the biker gangs and sold drugs and women to earn a living. Not having the true "biker mentality," he decided bikers were not his type after he witnessed his first stabbing. The cold indifference to a dying human being was more than he could stomach.

Chuck continued to use and sell drugs which kept him with enough income to afford a small, rundown apartment and an old beat-up van. One afternoon he was scheduled to meet someone for a drug deal. Having nothing better to do, he arrived at the appointment early and saw his contact talking with several policemen. Realizing it was obviously a bust, Chuck left, found another buyer for the dope he was carrying, and, miraculously, as he had been using drugs of some kind for nearly 20 years, went straight.

Having limited education, no skills and no work experience, Chuck Renning accepted a job at a Pizza Hut for minimum wage. He actually enjoyed the work, making pizzas, washing dishes and occasionally waiting tables. A man of simple means, minimum wage was plenty. It paid for his apartment and gas. He couldn't remember the last movie he had gone to and he didn't own a television or VCR.

The 18 and 19 year old girls who worked with Chuck were infatuated with the stories of 60's and 70's, drugs and biker gangs.

Mostly, he just became friends with the girls, but enough were eager to share his affections, which made for a nice bonus for flipping pizzas.

Pizza Hut employees were not known for their longevity. Chuck liked the work and worked hard. He was made assistant manager after his first year and began making a decent salary. He moved into a better apartment, bought a television and eventually a VCR. It seemed the girls really enjoyed going to his apartment to watch movies.

While assistant manager, Chuck performed all the managerial tasks. He trained several "manager trainees" only to watch them get their own stores. As capable and more dedicated than anyone, Chuck was not what Pizza Hut considered corporate material. His past was no secret and he still had the look of an anti-establishment type. He still referred to cops as "pigs."

A neighbor of Chuck's owned a small pizzeria on Richmond Avenue. He and Chuck would often bump into each other late at night after closing their respective stores and sit together and talk about the business. The neighbor did not consider Chuck a threat to steal trade secrets. One evening Chuck was depressed about seeing another "trainee" promoted to his own store, he wasn't complaining, just depressed.

The neighbor, sensing Chuck's discouragement, offered him a job as manager of his pizza place. Without hesitation, Chuck accepted the position and started the next day. Two years later, the neighbor ready to retire, sold the business to Chuck for next to nothing. He said he would only have to pay taxes and he had already paid too much tax and it was now time he got his share back from the government. The name was changed to "Chuck's Pizza Place" and has enjoyed a faithful clientele for many years.

Chuck's early exploits did not go unnoticed by the Houston police department who still maintained a file on him. According to the file, which had not been updated in over 10 years, Chuck Renning was involved with drugs, prostitution, motorcycle gangs and possibly linked to a murder.

Agent Alexander Christian looked though the file on Chuck Renning he had just received from the Houston police department and reviewed the information his own agents had put together on him. He said to Agent McBride, "it looks like this guy has been clean for over ten years. I'm surprised HPD still had a file on him. Nevertheless, I don't think we will let him know what we are doing.

I think our Blind Luck gang just likes to go there, I don't think Renning is involved, but why take the chance. If he spots us putting in a bug, we will then show him the warrants."

Agent McBride agreed. "I'll notify the team of our decision. I would like to be in the sound truck, what about you?"

"I wouldn't miss it."

Several agents reported that the suspect they were assigned to had been informed of the gathering at Chuck's Pizza Place and were planning to attend. Agent Christian peeled a piece of yellow paper off the pad and stuck it on the picture of each of the suspects who was confirmed to attend.

The first generation of what looked like Eric Moore's family tree had yellow stickies stuck to them. Only Robert Green and the young woman from the pool were not marked. No longer a suspect, the later remained on the first row only because she was one of the first contacted by Moore after the surveillance began.

Christian had one yellow sticker left. Russell Lewis had spoken to an unknown female and they were both planning on being at Chuck's. Christian held the sticker for the unknown female and stared at the photographs of the Lucky Bitch. He wanted to put the sticker on her picture, he wanted the sticker to belong to her.

As he held the yellow sticker and looked at the pictures, Agent Christian tried to reason why the FBI had not yet identified her. After all, every other member of the group had been in contact with one or more of the other members several times in the past few weeks. Where was the Lucky Bitch?

Christian thought about the many different scenarios. She could have left town after setting up Representative James. She could be so scared that she has gone into hiding and may not surface for a long time. She may have gone to Florida and was involved with the death of Senator Abernathy. Not likely, the FBI had found no evidence to support it. And the scenario the Agent most hoped for, that it was just a coincidence she hadn't been around any other members of the gang yet. She would be tonight. Alexander Christian stuck the yellow sticker on the picture of Kathy Beck.

Agent McBride looked at the wall of pictures. A yellow sticker was stuck to the photographs of Eric Moore, Todd Evans, Annie Simmons, Julie Hanson, Gene Thompson, Mark Flanagen, Russell Lewis and the Lucky Bitch. The only member of the group without a sticker was Robert Green.

"So you think she will be there?" McBride asked.

"I think Lewis is bringing her. I also think we can forget about everybody else. I think that the meeting tonight is strictly for those who are directly involved, those who have been a part of it since the beginning. Had anybody outside their tight little group known about the murders, I think word would have spread and someone would have tipped us. I only expect to see one new face tonight." Christian nodded toward Kathy Beck's picture.

"If she's there, and Evans and Simmons are there, should we go ahead and make the arrests? We've collected enough evidence from Representative Oliver's loft to convict Simmons, but I'm not sure we have anything, other than association, on any of the others."

"I've been thinking about that. I'm hoping that we will find more evidence after we arrest them. Once we get a chance to go through their homes, I'm sure we will turn up more evidence. I'm also hoping they talk about it tonight. At least we would have conspiracy."

The conversation between the two agents was interrupted by Agent Berg shouting into the telephone. "What? You're kidding. Shit! Give it to me again. Damn it!" Berg hung up the phone and looked at the legal pad he was using to take notes.

It only took a few seconds for the Agent to realize Christian and McBride were silently looking at him, waiting for an explanation of what they had just heard. Berg looked up, his face slightly pink from embarrassment. "They just monitored a call from Julie Hanson to Eric Moore. It seems as though Russell Lewis and Kathy Beck, not sure who she is, are getting married next week. Hanson wants to give them a surprise party tonight. She is going to call all their friends and have them meet at Chuck's tonight."

The silence in the room made Agent Berg uncomfortable. He continued, "Moore thought it was a great idea and they are both making calls as we speak."

Agent Christian thought for a moment while looking at the photographs on the wall. "At least we are now assured that the Lucky Bitch will be there. I assume that Kathy Beck is the person Lewis is bringing. If she isn't 'Lucky', we will soon find out who is. Unfortunately I don't think we will hear many details of the murders."

"I agree, but we will have a listening device in every nook and cranny of that building. I don't care if two people crawl into the freezer to talk, we'll hear it. If you need me, I'll be in my office," Agent McBride said.

A phone rang and Agent Berg answered and began scribbling quickly on his legal pad. Alexander Christian looked at the wall of suspects and tried to determine exactly how much evidence they had on each one. He was sure the fingerprints and DNA samples would implicate and convict Annie Simmons. But other than a few smudged finger prints taken from the Dodge Ram and the video of 'Lucky,' they had no other concrete evidence on any of the others.

There was a very good chance they would find more evidence, but what Christian really wanted was taped conversations by members of the gang as they discussed who killed who, how and why. He knew 'why', according to the letters sent to the newspaper, but did they truly expect Congress to change just because a few members were murdered? And did they truly believe that they could murder members of the United States Congress and get away with it?

There would be no answers to the questions this evening because of a last minute party. The growling in his stomach reminded Agent Christian that he hadn't eaten all day. Agents had been coming and going and it looked like there were plenty to cover for him. Disappointed and frustrated, he decided to take a walk and get a bite to eat. There was not much more he could do at the command center at the moment.

36

Julie Hanson and Eric Moore arrived at Chuck's Pizza Place at exactly the same time. Eric saw Julie drive in behind him and met her at her car door. "Right on time. I thought I might have time to have a beer before you got here," he said.

"I told you I would meet you here at 6:30, it's 6:30." Julie said as she looked at her watch. Eric thought about making a comment about how women are usually late but he wisely thought better of it and said nothing.

"Help me with this stuff," Julie said, as she opened the trunk of her car. "I talked to Chuck earlier to be sure it would be O.K. if we hung up some signs and ribbons and balloons and he said 'no problem'."

Eric picked up the two grocery sacks of party supplies from the trunk and followed Julie into the building. Chuck greeted them at the door and led them to a room adjoining the main dining area. "I usually only use this room during lunch when we're real busy, but I thought you all might like some privacy."

"Thanks," Julie said, "this will be great."

Chuck smiled at Julie before looking at Eric. "Would you like a beer?"

"You might as well bring a pitcher."

"Two mugs?" Chuck asked as he looked at Julie.

"Yeah, I'm in a beer mood."

Chuck disappeared after the beer.

"Beer? I can't remember the last time you drank beer," Eric said.

"My best friend is getting married next week. I don't know why, but it's put me in the beer mood."

"You don't approve?"

"I guess it's all right. I don't know. I like Russell well enough. I don't know, maybe it's him or maybe I feel like I'm losing a friend." Her voice lowered, "maybe it's the killings. I don't know if we should have ever started that."

"I know what you mean. But that may be all over now. I haven't talked to Annie or Todd about it, but I have a feeling they have done all they want to do. . ."

Eric stopped in mid-sentence as he heard someone call Julie's name. He turned to see two of her friends whom he had only met a couple of times. The three women hugged and began hanging party favors. Chuck brought the pitcher of beer and left it on the table. He stood for a second to see if Julie's friends wanted anything. Being ignored by the women, Chuck said to Eric, "Juanita is going to wait on you tonight. Tip her well, the beer and pizza is on the house."

"Are you sure? We may be drinking a lot tonight," Eric said.

"You all have been coming here as long as I can remember. It will be my wedding present to the happy couple."

"Thank you very much. I'll let them know." Eric held his mug of beer up in the air as a toast to Chuck. Chuck nodded and went back to the kitchen. Eric emptied the mug, refilled it and sat and watched the three women stringing crepe paper and balloons.

FBI Agents Lori Anderson and Sam Zimmerman sat in the main dining area and also watched the three women hanging decorations. They looked at each other in disbelief. It had taken most of the day and nearly every available agent to place a listening device near every booth and table in the main dining area of Chuck's Pizza Place.

Had they wanted to place bugs in the adjoining room, the braided rope blocking the entrance would have made the task extremely difficult. Surely Chuck, or another employee, would have questioned anyone trying to enter the roped off area. It was decided that the room would not be used and they should only be concerned with the main dining area. Specifically the end tables which were pushed together the last time the group met.

So, throughout the day, a pair of agents came into Chuck's and had lunch, each pair sitting at a different table or booth, and placing small sensitive electronic transmitters somewhere on, under or around the table. The last pair of agents, Anderson and Zimmerman, also placed transmitters in the men's and lady's restrooms.

Lori Anderson walked to the ladies room in order to get a better look at the area Julie and her friends were decorating. The room was about half the size of the main dining room with booths circling the entire area. Several square tables had been placed end-to-end to form one long table in the middle of the room. The room had no windows. In the back corner there was an emergency exit.

Lori walked as slowly as she could without looking conspicuous. She studied the room trying to think of a place, and a way, to bug the room. She walked into the ladies room and washed her hands. As she rubbed her hands together under the blower, she looked into the mirror. She caught herself just before she talked to herself, remembering that everything said in the room was being recorded by FBI agents in a van parked outside.

Desperately wanting and needing the pep talk she started to give herself before realizing the room was bugged, Agent Anderson looked in the mirror and thought about Representative Margaret Oliver. No matter what she had been told, there was no denying the fact that Simmons and Evans had been her responsibility, and she had lost them. And because she lost them a person was dead.

It didn't matter that she was not the one that decided not to try and bug the adjoining room, Anderson felt she needed to be sure that it did get bugged. It also didn't matter that the agents were in agreement that there probably would not be much said about the murders since the gathering was changed from "just the group" to a large party. Lori Anderson wanted to be sure at least some of what was to be said in that room would be heard.

As Lori left the restroom and walked past the smaller room, she noticed another man and another woman had joined the party. She did not recognize either one of the two. The woman was already busy making a sign wishing the happy couple the best and the man had joined Eric next to the pitcher of beer. A smile came over Lori's face as she reached her table.

"What are you smiling about?" Zimmerman asked.

"A thought just struck me."

"Call an ambulance, there's been an accident. A thought struck Lori."

Lori ignored the remark. She was looking at the Agent across from her but talking to the agents who were listening in the truck. Trying to sound as if she was talking to Zimmerman, she said, "there has got to be a florist shop or a supermarket close by here that sells flowers. Buy three small bouquets and put a transmitter in each. Get a small card and write, 'Best Wishes from your friends' on it. Wait until a few more people get here for the party, then have someone bring in the flowers. Give them to the waitress and tell her they are for the party. She will take them to the party and I bet they will spread them along the big table. We should be able to hear just about everything."

"That's good Lori, I hope they aren't asleep out there. Did you get that guys?"

The two agents looked at each other and smiled. "Why don't we go find out? There isn't much else we can do in here," Lori said.

While Zimmerman paid the bill, Lori stood beside him trying to think of anything they may have forgotten. As she opened the door, Lori's stomach tightened into knot. It was everything she could do to stand straight and appear calm as she held the door open for Annie Simmons and Todd Evans.

"Thank you," Todd said as he passed Lori.

Lori was frozen. She could not move. Todd didn't notice that she did not acknowledge his "thank you."

Zimmerman was also taken back by the appearance of Todd and Annie, but quickly recovered. He realized Lori was still holding the door, standing as if frozen in time. He kissed her on the lips and said, "thanks dear, let's go."

The kiss was as big of a surprise as seeing Todd and Annie for the first time since she had lost them at the IHOP Monday morning. She snapped out of her trance, regained her composure and walked out behind Sam.

"Cute," she said as they got outside.

"Hey, it worked."

Todd and Annie were greeted with hugs and handshakes as they entered the room adjoining the main dining room. Juanita was barely a step behind Todd with another frozen mug. Eric took the mug and filled it with beer from the pitcher. He filled his own mug with the little amount remaining and handed the empty pitcher to the waitress. She knew to refill it.

Eric handed the mug to Todd then picked up his own mug and held it up to Todd. Todd, knowing exactly what was meant, held his mug up to Eric's. Without saying a word, they touched the glasses together and took hearty drinks.

Eric then walked to Annie and hugged her. "Good show," he whispered into her ear.

"Thanks."

"Are you all right?"

"Sure, thanks."

Eric gave Annie a kiss on the lips then rejoined Todd at the long table. Annie knew nothing more could be said with the three "non-gang" friends present. Someday she may want to talk about it, but for now she was happy the other friends were here. She picked up an unused mug and held it as Todd poured for her from the newly arrived pitcher. She watched as the beer circled the bottom of the mug and began forming a head as the glass filled. Todd quit pouring and let the head continue to rise almost to the point of overflowing before beginning to subside.

"Perfect," Annie said as she took a drink and returned to the girls who were finishing the decorations.

Several more people arrived and joined the party. Though they had broken into smaller groups, the main topic of conversation was how surprised Russell and Kathy were going to be. When Juanita carried the three small flower arrangements into the room, the men didn't even notice. The women said, "how nice," looked at the card and wondered who actually sent the flowers, then went back to their gossip.

"Well done, Anderson," Agent McBride said as he listened to the scanner tuned to the frequency of the three listening devises which were placed in the flower arrangements.

* * * * * *

Russell purposely left his apartment a little bit late as to arrive at Kathy's a little bit late. He liked Kathy's mom but he did not feel like getting into a long conversation with her. He hoped Kathy would be ready by the time he got to her house and they could leave immediately.

He wore a striped Beach Boys style shirt, green shorts and boat shoes with no socks. Unless he was working, it was his typical summer outfit. He pressed the button mounted next to the door on Kathy's house and listened for the ringing inside. As he waited for an answer to the bell, Russell stood on the front of the small concrete porch and looked up and down the street.

The afternoon sun reflected off the windshield of the dark green 1998 Chevrolet Blazer hiding the occupants from detection. Unaware of the sun's glare, the two FBI agents froze in their seats as Russell looked directly at them.

The sound of the door opening prompted Russell to turn and walk back to the door. He did well at hiding his disappointment when it was Kathy's mother who opened the door. In one continuous motion she pulled him inside the house and hugged him as though he was a long lost son.

Mrs. Beck continued to hold Russell's hand as she explained how happy she was that he and Kathy we going to be married. She could tell that Kathy was very happy and that also made her happy. Russell stared at his future mother-in-law and smiled and nodded but was actually only hearing a small portion of what she was saying. It had been well over a week since he had seen Kathy. He missed her terribly.

In a way, he was glad they had been apart. He was absolutely convinced now that he wanted to spend the rest of his life with her. Any doubts he may have had vanished over the past week.

Russell's heart pounded in his chest as Kathy entered the room. She looked more gorgeous than ever. She was wearing a loose fitting white blouse which hung just to her navel, light blue shorts and sandals. Russell broke away from Mrs. Beck's grasp and hugged Kathy, his hand holding the small of her back. He caressed the area of bare skin between her blouse and shorts.

Kathy wanted to stand and make small talk with her mother even less than Russell did. Rather than giving her mother a chance to start a conversation, Kathy pulled Russell toward the door and out. She said goodbye as she closed the door.

They were in the car almost before Russell realized they had left the house. He started the engine and headed up the street.

"Turn here." Kathy said as they made it to the first intersection.

"What?"

"Turn here, now!"

"That's not the way. . . " Russell said as he made the requested turn.

"I know, now pull over. Quick!"

Russell did as he was told. The car had barely stopped when Kathy pushed the shift lever into park. Before he could speak Kathy put her lips on his and slipped her tongue into his mouth.

Russell immediately understood what was happening and returned the kiss.

Kathy slowly backed away from Russell and looked him in the eyes. "I really missed you," she said as she kissed him lightly on the lips.

"I missed you too," he said as their lips rubbed together. "Why don't we skip Chuck's and just go back to my apartment?"

"I'd love to, but Julie called to see if I, we, were coming. She said it had been a while since we saw each other and she would come only if I did. I told her we were coming. So let's go and have a beer.

Then I'll say we have to go, I'll make up some reason, and we'll go back to your apartment. Actually I told mom I would be home very late."

"That sounds wonderful," Russell said as he kissed Kathy deeply one more time before attempting to compose himself to drive.

Kathy rested her head on his shoulder and her hand on the bare skin of his leg just below the leg of his shorts. She noticed that Russell had gotten excited, either during the kiss or the discussion about going to his apartment, and she thought about relieving him. The tinted windows would conceal anything her hand was doing in his lap. It would probably even hide her if she put her head into his lap, which would be much cleaner and probably wouldn't take much more than a minute of two, if that long.

She decided she would wait and do that for him sometime after they were married. Maybe even save it for a time when the sex was beginning to seem old, if that ever happened. Kathy kept her head buried in Russell's shoulder so he could not see the smile on her face. It was everything she could do to keep from laughing out loud as she imagined her husband's reaction to unexpected oral sex as they drove down the road.

Curt Wright started to use the cellular phone to call the Blind Luck Command Center to be sure the message was received loud and clear. He thought for a second and said to his partner, "I think I'll use the radio, I want everybody to hear this."

He made sure the very high frequency radio was positioned on the correct channel and keyed the microphone. Using proper procedures he hailed the command center and waited for a response. It came shortly thereafter.

"We have the Lucky Bitch in sight. I repeat, we have the Lucky Bitch in sight. She has just been picked up by Lewis."

There was a pause while Alexander Christian made his way to the radio. "Curt, this is Alex, are you sure it's Lucky, over?"

"Yes, sir. I would say at least 99% sure. We have pictures to bring in as soon as we get a chance, but we saw her walk from her house to her car and you can't miss that walk. She is an incredible looking woman."

"Curt, this is McBride. I'm at Chuck's Pizza, are you en route here?"

"I believe so. They stopped a block away from her house for a few minutes, I thought they were going to get it on right there, but they are mobile again and in your general direction. I'll keep you posted if anything changes." Agent Wright signed off and listened as the other agents signed off.

Agent Christian decided to remain at the command center when he realized that the gathering at Chuck's was going to be a crowd rather than the small group he believed responsible for the Congressional murders.

Christian picked up the phone on the first ring.

"Christian," he said into the hand piece.

"Alex, this is McBride, if that is indeed "Lucky," what do you want to do?"

"There's not much we can do. Right now we don't know who is involved and who isn't. We could pick up everyone at the party and still miss one or two. We will have to just wait, watch and listen until we are sure we have them all. We can now pick up "Lucky," Simmons, Moore and Evans at any time. They aren't going to be going anywhere."

"That's a Roger. As long as they don't know we are on them, somebody is going to talk."

"And we will have it on tape. Keep me informed."

"Will do. Bye."

Agent Christian hung up the phone and looked at the wall of photographs. He was sure everyone involved was on the wall, but how many were involved? He added a yellow sticker back to the photo Kathy Beck, a.k.a. "The Lucky Bitch," and pulled the stickers off the pictures of Flanagen, Hanson and Thompson.

"Those are for sure," he said to himself, loud enough where everyone in the room heard. *How many more?* He thought to himself.

Russell Lewis and Kathy Beck pulled into Chuck's parking lot. Kathy was still smiling from the thoughts of what she had planned for her future husband.

"Chuck's kinda busy tonight," Russell said as he looked for a place to park, "usually I can park right in the front."

Kathy did not respond to his comments as she tried to compose herself. Her thoughts had given her a case of the giggles and she did not want Russell to ask her what she was laughing about.

Russell parked the car and gave serious consideration to taking up where they had left off on the side street near Kathy's house, but he didn't want to have to get out of the car with a bulge in his pants.

He opened the car door and quickly slid out, holding the door open while Kathy slid across the seat, under the steering wheel and out of the car. They walked arm-in-arm into Chuck's Pizza Place as nearly 20 Federal Bureau of Investigation agents looked on.

Not only were the agents who were assigned to suspects which were at Chuck's watching, but just about every available agent that had access to the VHF frequency and heard that the infamous "Lucky Bitch" was on her way, made their way to Chuck's Pizza Place.

Agent McBride made the call to Alexander Christian at the Blind Luck Command Center. The Lucky Bitch had arrived.

Russell Lewis and Kathy Beck had not noticed the crowd in the smaller dining room when Julie Hanson shouted "surprise." The flash of the camera froze the utterly stupid expression on their faces as they realized they had walked into a surprise party for them.

"This is wonderful," Kathy said as tears welled up in her eyes.

"Yeah," was all that Russell could add, more embarrassed than surprised.

Todd Evans handed Russell a mug of cold beer, raised his own glass and said, "here's to the happy couple. May their lives be long and prosperous."

Cheers came from the crowd as everyone raised their glasses to toast the couple. Russell wasted no time in downing half of the beer in his mug. His embarrassment soon faded.

After all the women made their way to Russell and all the men made their way to Kathy to hug and congratulate them, most of the people divided into smaller groups. There were people who had not seen each other in a long time and there was a lot of catching up to be done.

By 9:30 some of the people began saying their good-byes. The first to leave were the married couples, who had once been close friends with Kathy or Russell, but over the past few years had drifted into another lifestyle. By 11:00 the party had dwindled down to the main group and just a few of the closer friends the couple had not seen in awhile.

Outside, the FBI contingent had also dwindled to only those agents who were on duty. For the most part, the conversations inside Chuck's were quite boring. Occasionally a microphone would pick up some hot gossip about another person present at the party, but nothing had been said that would help the agents determine who was involved with the Congressional killings.

John McBride was unusually upbeat however. He was sure, sooner or later, most of the non-regulars would leave and the only people left at the party would be those who were involved in the murders. With all the beer and wine that was being drunk, the talk would soon turn to the killings, and he would have everything he needed.

Inside, Russell was staring across the room at his fiancé. She looked gorgeous and the beer he had consumed made him want her all the more. He was sitting with Eric Moore and Todd Evans at the end of the long table. There were still several people at the party in addition to the regulars, and Russell knew it would be rude to leave. But he also knew that Kathy could not spend the night with him. If they were going to have any time at all alone, they would have to leave soon.

Russell was still looking at Kathy when Todd said, "I guess you heard about Oliver in San Francisco?"

Outside in the plain white van the FBI agent lurched upright in his seat. "We've got something on mike six," he said as several other agents, including McBride tuned their headphones to the correct frequency.

"Russ?" Todd said as he leaned closer to ask the question again when he realized Russell had not heard it the first time.

"I'm sorry," Russell said before Todd could repeat the question, "I was just looking at Kathy. You know we were only going to stay a little while then go back to my place. I haven't seen her since her mother got into town. It might be rude, but if you guys don't mind, I think I'll see if she wants to go make nookie."

Russell got up from the table and walked up behind Kathy. He put his arms around her waist and whispered into her ear, "I'm going to go to the bathroom. Why don't you say your good-bye's and we'll go back to my place and make mad passionate love for an hour or so."

Kathy stood silently as she listened to Russell's proposition. When he finished his speech and walked off toward the men's room, Kathy immediately began saying her good-byes.

"What is it you have?" McBride asked the agent who had made the announcement.

"God Damn it! Just before the guy said he was going to go see if his girlfriend wanted to go 'make nookie', one of the other guys asked if they had heard about Oliver."

"Who did the asking?"

"I'm not sure. We'll have to wait until they match all the voices with names. But damn it, they were going to start talking about it and now they're leaving."

Agent McBride took the headphones from around his neck and hung them on the console. "I am too," he said.

37

One agent for each suspect was left on surveillance while all others were summoned to the command center for a staff briefing. Alexander Christian sat in front of the wall of suspects and looked at each of the photographs. He paid particular attention to the clear picture of Kathy Beck, which was taped next to the original digitally enhanced photograph taken at the rodeo arena.

Agent Christian certainly understood why Representative Jack James had followed her out of the arena, but he could not understand how she could have been involved with his death. She certainly did not look like a murderer. None of them did.

With every available agent scheduled to attend this morning's briefing, it was to be held in the larger conference room instead of the command center where the most recent briefings had been held. Christian glanced over his notes one last time before going to the briefing. It would also allow everyone a chance to get there so he could start the briefing immediately.

Special Agent in Charge Alexander Christian closed the conference door behind him as he entered the room. He walked straight to the podium and without a greeting, started the briefing.

"It has been one week since we identified Kathy Beck, the individual we believe lured Representative James to his death. We have monitored every movement and conversation of everyone we suspect to be involved with the Congressional murders. We have taped evidence linking eight individuals to the killings. We are sure that these eight knew about the murders, but we do not know to what extent they were involved.

"We do know for sure that Kathy Beck, who some of you still refer to as, 'The Lucky Bitch,' Todd Evans and Annie Simmons were directly involved. We do not know who else is directly involved. If we could wait long enough, I'm sure we would hear exactly who did what. One of these persons has to talk to someone about it sometime.

"Unfortunately, we don't have the time. Everyday we have these suspects under surveillance we increase the chance of being spotted. If we are indeed spotted, there is a chance that they could destroy evidence inside their homes before we could make the arrests. I would prefer to arrest them all at the same time, and if possible, away from their homes so they would not have a chance to destroy any evidence before we can do a thorough search.

"Most of you are aware that Lewis and Beck are getting married tomorrow evening. I would prefer we not have to follow them all around Texas, and I definitely do not want them leaving the country. I understand they plan to drive to Galveston Island and San Antonio before flying to the Caribbean. They plan to be gone three to four weeks. Obviously, we cannot let this happen.

"The wedding is tomorrow. All of our suspects are planning to attend. We will make our arrests at the wedding." Agent Christian paused to let what he had just said sink in. The agents had gotten to know these suspects extremely well. They had listened to their most intimate conversations. They knew them as well, if not better, than any friend or relative knew them.

As the top eight suspects began to emerge, the agents would talk about them using their first names. Almost like they were friends themselves. The agents realized these people were murderers, but unlike other criminals, the agents did not hate them.

All conversations were heard by at least two different agents, sometimes more, just in case something was said that one agent might have missed. At one time or another, almost every agent in the room had listened to Kathy talk about her wedding. She was bubbling with excitement.

Kathy Beck had a wonderful personality. Even over the telephone the agents could see her smile as she talked. Her conversations were monitored extremely close in hopes she would mention who actually killed Representative James, but she never mentioned it. Had it not been for the video, she probably would not even have been a suspect. Most of the agents wished there was no video. She had won the hearts of the Federal Bureau of Investigation.

That was why SPIC Christian's announcement that the arrests would happen at Kathy Beck's wedding caused a stir at the briefing. Christian knew it would, he felt the same way about Ms. Beck.

Christian continued, "I don't see that we have an alternative. If we go to the homes and attempt to make arrests, we risk losing evidence. You all know lots of things can be flushed down the toilet in the time it takes to kick a door in. We certainly cannot let our number one suspect fly to an island in the Caribbean for a honeymoon.

"Why not?" asked Harry Berg, the youngest agent in the room, "I'll volunteer to tail them."

The comment was received with a few chuckles in the audience. After weeks of surveillance in Houston, *most* of the agents would have volunteered to follow the couple to the Caribbean.

Alexander Christian smiled at Berg's comments. "Me too," he said, "I haven't done much field work lately, I could use a refresher."

The mood in the room lifted, but every agent in the room knew that this was no laughing matter. The eight people they were going to arrest were in some way responsible for the deaths of five United States Congressmen. No matter how nice they seemed, they were murderers and should be considered extremely dangerous. Christian took the opportunity to remind the agents of that fact.

"Except for the agents on surveillance, everyone will meet here tomorrow at 1500 for final instructions and we will issue M-16's at that time. We have notified the Houston Police Department and they are going to assist us with traffic control. They are also loaning us their SWAT team."

Christian paused and took a drink of water. "You may be wondering, and John checked with the D.A. here in Houston, it will not make any difference to the them, so I plan to make the arrests after the ceremony. There are no windows in the church, it will be very easy to move into position during the wedding. We'll go over the details tomorrow. Are there any questions or comments?"

Every agent had a comment, but all wisely kept them to themselves. Christian was going by the book. He had no choice. If he left the SWAT team out and an agent was killed, he would never forgive himself, or be forgiven by the Agency. After all, Ted Bundy was an attractive, eloquent man, who killed an untold number of young woman.

The agents filed out of the briefing room to return to their duties. Most had mixed emotions. They were about to end a grueling investigation that had been going on around the clock for nearly two months. They were about to savor the fruits of their labor, but that also meant arresting eight people whom they had come to know extremely well. In a very short time, those eight people would meet the agents.

John McBride waited with Christian as the other agents left the room. "I met with Judge Winter last night and got the arrest warrants signed. He wasn't overly impressed by the evidence we have on five of the eight. I have to agree with him. I reread all the transcripts and, although it does implicate the five, it sure doesn't convict them."

"I know, and quite frankly, if they just knew about it, and were not actually involved, either with the planning or execution, I don't care what the judge does with them. I want the person who put in the poison, pulled the trigger, drove the truck, and, Annie Simmons. Forensics says Representative Oliver's neck was probably crushed between someone's legs. I don't want to know how Annie Simmons got her legs around Oliver's neck."

"What about The Lucky. . . , Kathy Beck? I'd say she was an accessory."

"Honestly?" Christian looked at the other agent.

"Sure."

"I would have liked to have known her before she met this guy she is going to marry and before she was involved in murder. She is as charming as she is beautiful. She is going to make a lot of women at the federal penitentiary very happy."

Agent McBride knew his friend was not being facetious. It hurt Alexander Christian to even think about it, but it was the truth. Kathy Beck would be passed around by both the inmates and guards until she committed suicide, became so used up that no one wanted her, or until she became so hardened that she would not allow herself to be passed around. There would be no pleasant options for her in prison.

McBride thought about mentioning the fact that Representative James was not having a good time right now either, especially considering where he probably is, but decided logic was not what Agent Christian needed to hear at the moment.

* * * * * *

Although there was nothing, that she knew of, to be nervous about, Kathy Beck was a nervous wreck. Everything was running smoothly, which was part of the problem. Had there been things to do, Kathy would not have had so much time on her hands.

Every few minutes Kathy would ask her mother the same questions, and her mother would reassure her that everything was taken care of. Finally, out of desperation, her mother told her to call

Russell and have him come and get her and take her somewhere, anywhere, just get her out of the house.

It took an enormous amount of coaxing, but Kathy relented and called Russell. He said he would be right over, they would go to a movie. A movie would be a good idea, Kathy thought. One reason she had been so reluctant to call him was that his performance last Thursday night, dampened by all the beer, had been less than spectacular.

Never being overly sexually active, Russell had opened her to new horizons which she was more than ready to begin exploring. Now she was determined only to explore them only with Russell as a husband. She could wait one more day.

Russell rang the door bell and waited for the inevitable encounter with Mrs. Beck. He did not know why he didn't like talking to her, she was a very pleasant woman, he just didn't. He had experienced the encounter every evening the past week and was happy to endure it in order to spend time with his beloved. He was afraid she would be too busy again this week to see him, being the week before the wedding, but they had been able to get together every night.

The door knob twisted and Russell braced himself for the inevitable hug as he stepped toward the door. Kathy pushed him backward as she closed the door behind her.

"Let's go," she said as gave him a peck on the lips.

Russell put his arm around Kathy's waist as they walked to his car.

"What's wrong?" Kathy asked, noticing a glazed look in his eye.

"Nothing, you surprised me, that's all. I was expecting your mother."

"Oh, yeah, she does like to greet you at the door. I don't think she could wait to get me out of the house. I've been bouncing off the walls."

"Would you like to go back to my apartment and use up some excess energy?"

"I would love to, but not until tomorrow night."

Russell opened the side door of his car and held it for her. She started to get in then stopped and kissed Russell.

"I love you," she said, then turned and got in the car.

"I love you too," Russell said as he closed the door and walked around to the driver's side. He got in and looked in the rear-view mirror. He continued looking into the mirror until Kathy said, "is something wrong?"

"I don't know. Do you know anyone that has a green Chevy Blazer?"

"I don't think so, why?"

"I know UTE's are very popular now, but I seem to be seeing them a lot. There's one down the street now, and it wasn't there when I pulled up."

"What's a 'UTE'."

"A sport utility vehicle. I've noticed one behind me several times after I've picked you up, and I don't remember ever seeing it when I pulled up. It's kinda like it's following me."

"Russell!" Kathy said, her voice cracking, "do you. . ." Russell put his hand over her mouth to quiet her. He turned the radio up and leaned close to her ear. "If they're following us, we may be bugged. Don't say anything." He kissed her on the mouth before straightening up. He looked at her and could see she was scared. As he winked at her he said, "I really don't want to go to the movies, why don't we just go to the park and talk?"

"O.K.," was all Kathy could say. She had put the death of Jack James into a dark corner of her brain and it had just come roaring back. She sat quietly, her shoulders heaving as she took deep breaths. Russell drove them toward a small neighborhood park.

"This is Weiss, we've been made. Repeat, we've been made. Get another tail here as soon as possible, and be sure they are not in a Blazer."

As soon as Russell and Kathy turned the corner, Agent Weiss turned the opposite direction.

"Just in case they circle back around to look for us, we better be going in the opposite direction," Weiss said to his partner.

"Weiss, this is Zimmerman. We were watching Beck's house from Thoreau Street, about two blocks away. We are in a Lumina, but we don't have a directional finder. You will have to keep us informed of their location."

"We can do that. They are out of range for our listening device, but the direction finder is strong. They are eastbound on Bellaire."

"We're on our way. Stay back at least a mile. Don't take a chance on them spotting you again."

"Roger, out."

Russell turned left on Montrose Avenue heading toward Bell Park. Kathy stared straight ahead, afraid to speak. As they neared the turn for the small park, Kathy said, "Griff's is just up the street, let's go have a beer."

"Are you sure?"

Kathy just nodded. Russell had been checking his rear-view mirror and had not seen the Blazer since leaving Kathy's house. He turned off Montrose two streets early, then overshot Griff's by a street, and circled back. He parked on the side of the road across the street from the neighborhood bar.

As he crossed the street, Russell looked for any suspicious vehicles. Not only were there no suspicious vehicles, there were no vehicles at all moving in the area. In another half hour or so the place would liven up with the lunch crowd, but for now Kathy and Russell had the bar to themselves.

Kathy sat at a small round table in the corner as Russell ordered two Budweisers from the bar. He put the bottles on the table and sat down.

"I watched all the way here and I didn't see anyone following us. I guess I shouldn't have said anything. Maybe I'm just being paranoid. I don't see how anybody could know we were involved with James' death. I'm sorry. Are you all right?"

Kathy held the bottle of beer to her lips and took several swallows.

"I've been a nervous wreck all day. That's why mom told me to call you and have you get me out of the house. I was driving her up the wall. When you said you thought we were being followed, I started remembering James getting squished by the truck. I thought I was going to be sick. I feel a lot better now." She took several more long drinks of beer. "Get me another beer please."

"You're kidding? You've never finished a beer before me."

"I may have a lot of surprises in store for you. Still want to marry me?"

"Try and stop me."

The two laughed as Russell went to the bar for another beer. He decided to get two while he was there. When he got back to the table he said, "we had better take it easy, aren't we having dinner with our parents tonight?"

"I'll be O.K.," Kathy said as she picked up the new bottle of beer and took a drink.

Both consumed their second beer much slower than the first.

Russell ordered lunch and they ate, drank and discussed the future. They watched the normal lunch crowd come, and go, before they decided they too should leave.

Both Kathy and Russell thought a nap would be a great idea. They thought about going to Russell's apartment, but they knew that they had had too much to drink. The combination of the beer and a bed would lead to a much more physical activity than sleeping. They were determined to wait one more day. Waiting would make their wedding night even more special.

Russell walked Kathy to her front door and kissed her goodbye. As he walked back to his car he continued to look for suspicious vehicles. He had convinced Kathy they were not being followed, but he had not convinced himself. Driving home he watched his mirror, but saw nothing out of the ordinary. When he got to his apartment, he went straight to the bedroom and passed out on the bed.

"Weiss to command. Lewis is home and it's sounds like he is asleep. Everything is normal."

"Weiss, this is command, thanks. We had everyone on red alert in case we needed to move. I will send the signal to stand down."

In the command center Agent Christian breathed a sigh of relief. "We are so close, I can't believe we almost blew it on the last day. Remind everyone to be very careful this evening. I don't want to have to chase these people all over the city."

38

Kathy Beck woke up and looked around her room. It had been two weeks since she had woken up with Russell in her bed and she missed him. She laid on her back and looked at her stuffed animals, lace curtains and fluffy comforter, wondering if she would miss those things.

Her parents had suggested Russell move into their house, at least temporarily. They would be going back to Europe and there was no sense in the couple renting an apartment, especially since neither was gainfully employed.

Russell still had his apartment and they were going to be gone for almost a month, so they decided to put off making a decision about where they would live until they got back from their honeymoon. Neither cared where they lived as long as they were together. The housing situation would work itself out.

Kathy lay in the bed reminiscing about the past and dreaming about the future. She had been awake over an hour when she heard the light tapping on the door.

"Come in," Kathy said as she sat up on the bed, pulling the sheet up with her.

Her mother stuck her head in the door. "Your father is cooking. He wanted to make you breakfast one last time. He was doing very well until this morning. I guess it's finally sinking in that he little girl is no longer a little girl. I think I even saw some tears in his eyes earlier."

Tears built up in Kathy's eyes as she got out of bed and ran to the kitchen where her father was cooking. "I love you, daddy," she said as she hugged him. Both of them started crying. "I'm still your little girl," she said between sobs.

"You'll always be my little girl," he said as he wiped his eyes and went back to his cooking. "Get dressed, I'm making French toast, hash browns, scrambled eggs and bacon. Is there anything else you want?"

"No, that sounds great daddy, thank you."

She kissed her father on the cheek and went back to her room to get dressed. She passed her mother who was standing in the hall with tears in her eyes. Kathy kissed her on the cheek as she passed. Kathy put on an extra large T-shirt and white shorts and walked back to the kitchen. Her father was just putting the eggs on the table. They all sat and ate and talked about the past and told funny stories from the past 20 years. It was one of the happiest times the Beck family had spent together in many years.

Alexander Christian looked at the alarm clock next to his bed. The red digital numbers read 9:15 A.M. He had left the command center just after eleven the night before, after the field agents reported that all suspects were safely tucked in to their beds.

Knowing that today was going to be busy, Christian went to his hotel and enjoyed the first good night's sleep in many weeks. The telephone had not rung and his beeper had not gone off. He figured all was well.

Agent Christian took a long, hot shower and shaved before putting on gray slacks, white shirt and red tie. He laid the .357 magnum revolver on the dresser while he put on the shoulder holster. He opened the cylinder of the pistol and looked at the end of the five bullets. He repositioned the open slot so it would be under the hammer, closed the cylinder, checked the safety and placed the weapon back in its holster. He hoped he would not have to remove it again.

The phone woke Russell Lewis from a sound sleep. He moaned, stretched and fumbled for the phone. A very unenergetic "yep," was all he could muster.

"Hey Groom, rise and shine. It's the big day. I thought sure you would be up."

"Hi Todd, I stayed up late drinking beer and watching soft porn on cable. I figured it would be my last chance for a while."

"You should have called. I would have brought some good porn over and we would have gotten drunk together. I know it'll be a while before we'll have a chance to do that again."

"I should have, sorry. It was after ten when I got home from dinner with the family and I didn't even think about it."

"No problem. That's why I called. The wedding's at seven, right?" Todd did not give Russell a chance to answer before he continued, "and you can't see the bride until she walks down the isle. So it's the best man's job to keep you occupied until it's time to go to the church."

"What do you have in mind?"

"I'm glad you asked. Mark and Robert are working but Eric and Gene are coming over here and then we will come and get you. Kathy will kill me if I get you to the church late or drunk, so my idea is that we go someplace where the beer is real expensive and we won't drink much."

"Let me guess."

"You got it, titty bars."

"And you think Kathy will approve?"

"I'm not going to tell her. You can if you want to."

"Maybe tomorrow."

"We should be there in about an hour."

Russell hung up the phone and thought about what he was about to do. He didn't want to start off marriage by lying to his wife, but it would be better than telling her that he spent his wedding day looking at naked women. He couldn't tell his friends he didn't want to go.

Julie Hanson paced around her apartment wearing only panties and a bra. She would sit on the couch, turn on the television and surf the channels only to turn it off and look at the clock to see that only a few minutes had passed since she last looked at the clock. She could not understand why she was so nervous. It was her best friend getting married, not her.

By 10:30 Julie was at the end of her rope. She could not wait any longer to call Kathy.

"Hello," Kathy Beck said into the telephone.

"Hi, it's Julie. I couldn't wait any longer to call you. How are you doing?"

"Good. We just finished breakfast and we've been sitting here talking."

"I made an appointment for you to get your hair done, a manicure and a pedicure. Can you be ready in half an hour. It's like a wedding gift from me."

"That's so sweet. It sounds wonderful. I'll be ready."

Julie hung up the phone and went into the closet. She picked out a flowered romper which was very light. It was only May, but Houston was already having high temperatures in the 90's. She took her bra off and slid the romper on. On her way out she stood and looked in the mirror. Satisfied she looked presentable, she left the apartment, locking the door behind her.

"They're not going to make the last day easy for us," Agent Christian said as he looked at the locations of each suspect. "They're all on the move somewhere."

"At least several of them are together." Agent McBride said, "Moore, Evans and Lewis are together, and they are our main three. Moore wrote the original newspaper article, which is the only way we found any of them. Evans was with Simmons in San Francisco, so you know he is involved. Lewis is marrying the woman who lured James in front of the truck. I would be willing to bet Lewis was the driver."

Christian looked at the location board again. "Those three are together, along with Gene Thompson. Annie Simmons is still in her apartment. Beck is with Hanson at a salon on Westheimer. That leaves Mark Flanagen who is at his office. We should be able to round them all up without much difficulty if it becomes necessary."

"Alex, this morning Todd Evans called Lewis and told him they wanted to take him out. He said Gene and Eric were coming, but that Mark and Robert had to work. The only Robert we know about is Robert Green. He was not one of the ones we were planning to arrest. I think we may want to bring him in too."

"It wouldn't hurt. What do we have on him?"

"Not a lot. They're rechecking phone calls now to see if anything was missed that might implicate him. We should know soon."

"Good, but let's plan on picking him up anyway. It will give us a chance to do an investigation of his home."

McBride nodded, "do you want to do it now?"

Christian looked at the locations of the subjects and which agents were attached to them. "We're pretty thin. By the time we got mobilized, their locations could change. We have a good plan for this evening, I think we should wait. I would like to bust them before Lewis and Beck get married. If you are right about Lewis being the driver, he will get a lot more years than she will. I would hate to see her waste away waiting for him to get out of prison."

"She is an attractive woman. But do you think she could ever be interested in the man who stopped her wedding and put her husband-to-be in prison for life?"

The comment shocked Agent Christian. He stood speechless.

"You think I couldn't tell? Every time you look up there at her picture you look as if you just lost your best friend. You should have seen your face the other night when you were listening to the tapes of her and her boyfriend talking about their life together. I thought you were going to have an aneurysm. How in the hell could you fall in love with a woman you've never met? Actually, I know how. I've seen the pictures and listened to the tapes, but you know what I mean."

"I wouldn't say I'm in love with her."

"Bullshit Alex. I've known you a long time, not well, but long, and I can tell. If she were to walk in this room and ask you to take Lewis's place tonight, you would do it in a heartbeat."

Agent Christian wanted to argue with his colleague, but he knew he was right. At least partially right anyway. Every time he looked at Kathy Beck's photograph, or listened to one of her conversations, his heart would start pounding in his chest. It was an involuntary reflex and he could do nothing about it. He still didn't, couldn't, believe he was falling in love with her.

He looked around the room to be sure no one was listening. "John, I am not going to lie to you. I can't get her off my mind, but I don't believe I love her. Whenever we're after a particular suspect, I can't get them out of my mind. I'll admit this is a lot different. I wish I would have met her before she met Lewis and before she was involved in murder. I would have given her my best shot."

"Could you shoot her?"

"What?"

"You heard me. Suppose they are all more dangerous then we expect. Let's say she has a gun under her wedding dress. She pulls it out and is about to shoot me. Would you, could you shoot her? Could you kill her?"

Christian thought about the question. It was a very good question.

"You're taking too long. I'm already dead. Alex, this is your case, but if you think you may be putting another agent's life in danger by being there, I respectfully request you stay here."

"Luckily, I would put the chances of me having to shoot her near nil, but of course I would. I may never be able to shoot another person again and I'd have to transfer to a desk, but I would shoot her. Then again, if she pulls a gun, the SWAT team will probably take her out before I could react."

"That satisfies me, you know I had to ask."

"Of course. I would have asked too."

"So you want to storm the church just before they take their vows? That way they won't be married and you can play 'good cop' and protect her from us 'bad cops'. She is going to be quite vulnerable, she might even fall in love with you."

"And I could share her with the guards and inmates at Marianna."

"This day and age, with a good lawyer she may not be convicted."

"Then we could get married and live happily ever after. That would sure look good."

"At least we could assume she wouldn't be killing anyone else. Unless of course you pissed her off, then BAM, you're pinned between two cars. I don't know." Agent McBride laughed. He knew he had probably just crossed the line and he wanted to lighten the mood.

Christian was used to FBI ribbing and was surprised it took McBride so long to get to it.

"I was waiting for that. I am going to arrest her, AFTER she gets married tonight. I don't believe there is a chance in hell she would ever give me the time of day. I'll get over it."

Looking at his watch to check the time, Christian continued, "we need to start getting ready, the briefing begins in an hour."

Eric, Todd and Gene watched with envy as the young blond woman rubbed her leg against Russell's crotch and stuck her nipple next to his mouth. Russell would try to lick the dancer's breast, but she would move before his alcohol impaired reflexes could work. She would slide her silicon enlarged breasts down his chest and over his legs burying her face in his lap. She put her mouth over the bulging area between his legs, looked up and smiled, before turning around and sitting on his erection. Grinding her hips into him, she pumped Russell until he was very close to ejaculating. He held the woman by the hips and pulled her tight against him, rocking her back and forth as though they were having sex.

The music stopped and the blond twisted herself free of Russell's grasp. She turned, kissed him on the lips and said, "does that go on the tab." She smiled as she looked at Russell panting. She knew he was ready to come. He would be another easy twenty-five dollars. She looked around the bar to be sure the bouncers were not watching and put her hand between Russell's legs. "Want to go again?" She asked, already starting to dance for him.

The dancer immediately turned around and began rubbing his crotch. In just seconds she felt his hips shake and lurch as she brought him to climax. Russell dropped his hands from the woman's hips as he sat back and watched her perform the rest of her dance. When the music stopped the second time, she again kissed him on the lips. Todd handed the dancer fifty dollars. She kissed him as she put her short tight white dress on.

She leaned over to Russell and said, "thank you. Tonight when you're with your new bride, imagine you're fucking me."

Russell looked at the woman closely. She was extremely good looking but he would never think of her over Kathy. He smiled a big smile. "I will. You were great," he said.

The dancer smiled and walked off. The four men laughed and made a toast. It was all a game and it meant nothing to any of them. It had been fun, but now Russell had a problem. He excused himself and walked to the men's room, holding his hands in front of his crotch. His friends laughed at his predicament as he walked away, quietly wishing they had the same problem, but unwilling to spend fifty dollars to get it.

"After he dries out we should probably leave and go get something to eat. He's going to have to sober up some before the wedding," Todd said.

Julie went home with Kathy after their indulgement. Although the wedding was still several hours away, they needed time to pick out the right outfit that Kathy would wear as she and Russell left for their honeymoon. She also needed to pick out every outfit she would wear over the next week while they were traveling.

Like most women she would probably end up wearing the same outfit, or a variation of the same outfit every day. Most of the items she stuffed into her suitcase would never be unpacked. But she would have them, "just in case."

Julie's bridesmaid dress hung beside Kathy's wedding dress. Their hair and nails were done, their legs were shaved. Everything was ready. They just had to wait until time to get dressed and drive to the church.

Kathy's mom stuck her head inside the door and said, "how is everything?"

"Great. We're ready. I just wish it was time." Kathy replied.

"This may help." Mrs. Beck entered the room carrying two goblets of wine. "Relax, sip and enjoy."

"Why don't you join us?" Julie asked.

"Thank you, no. You two savor this time. Honey, you may not think so, but things do change." She turned and left the room.

Kathy and Julie sat on the edge of the bed and looked at each other, both on the verge of crying.

"Don't, you'll ruin your makeup," Julie said. The two friends laughed and hugged each other.

"Times have changed since mom got married, I don't think anything will be any different at all after tonight."

* * * * * *

Agent Christian addressed the assembled agents. "The church is on the corner of Auden and Nottingham streets. It's small compared to most modern churches. It was built when West University was truly a suburb of Houston. The front doors face the street, a small concrete path leads to the parking lot. The parking lot is to the north. There is only one other exit and that is in the back through the offices. There are no windows in the church itself and only one window in the office, next to the back door.

"The SWAT team will cover the back door along with two agents, Weiss and Holland. They will also cover the front door from three different angles. We will position ourselves around the front door. As they come out, we will pull the suspects to the right, our right as we face the door, and move the guests who are not to be arrested to the left toward the parking lot.

"I don't expect any of them to be carrying weapons, after all it is a wedding, so I don't expect trouble. As soon as we have our eight on the ground, I want them cuffed and searched. I said I didn't expect trouble, but we will not deviate from procedure. Lori, I want you close to pat down the women.

"Remember, keep the suspects quiet. I don't want them giving each other ideas. As soon as they are cuffed and searched. Load them in the cars. One person per car. We will bring them back here where they will be locked up in solitary.

"We have warrants to search all of their homes. Sam, I want you and Lori to escort the Becks home and search their house. A mobile lab truck will be standing by to meet you there. Everyone else lived alone, we will get to their homes tomorrow."

Agent Christian paused and looked around the room trying to think of anything he may have forgotten. The agents sat quietly reviewing the written information they had received from the logistics officer. The packets included everything their boss had just told them, as well as various personal assignments and radio frequencies which would be used.

"I hope I have not over simplified this," Christian continued, "we are dealing with a group of individuals who are responsible for the deaths of five members of the United States Congress, our bosses. These people are not to be taken lightly."

"What about the press?" Asked Lori Anderson.

"They monitor all HPD radio frequencies. As soon as the SWAT team begins to set up position, they will pick it up and be on us like flies. Houston Police is going to block off all roads leading into the area. They have instructions not to let the press in. Hopefully the wedding will be over quickly and we can take them down before any camera crews sneak in though the residential area."

"Once we have them arrested and are on the way back, the press will follow for sure. We will have to deal with them then. As soon as we get back to the command center, I will schedule a press conference and tell them what we have."

Agent Berg raised his hand as he spoke. "Sir, I will be here monitoring the situation, but I am curious, why don't you go in during the ceremony while everyone is sitting, except for the wedding party, and bring out the suspects? It seams to me that, with everybody coming through the door, it could get a bit confusing."

Agent Christian took a drink of water, sat the glass down, and said, "that's a good point. We thought about it. Four of our suspects are in the wedding and will be standing in the front of the church. If they see us come through the door, they may have time to grab hostages before we could get to them. They have to come out the front door two at a time, giving us the superior numbers. Not to mention as soon as they walk out a SWAT marksman will have them in their sights.

"The first two out the door should be Lewis and Beck, followed by Evans and Hanson. That's three of our four top suspects. Simmons is the only one that I think will have a chance to catch on that something is up, and she may not realize what all the commotion is about until she is outside. Let's hope not anyway."

Christian looked around the room to see if there were any other questions or comments. There were none. He looked toward the rear of the room. "Harry, what's going on?"

"The bride, Beck, and Hanson just arrived at the church a few minutes ago. Last report had Lewis and Evans still at Lewis's apartment, which is about fifteen to twenty minutes from the church." Berg checked his watch, "it's 1800 now, they have one hour."

Christian added, "we cannot show in front of the church until they are inside and the front doors are closed. As soon as the last of our suspects get into the church, we will move into the area on either side of the church. When we get the green light, we move in, quietly, don't come to a screeching stop in front of the church, and take up our positions. The SWAT team will be right behind us, then the police barricades will go up. We have no idea how long the ceremony will last, so we will have to get into position quickly."

"That's all I have. You all have been issued rifles and vests, and you should have your FBI jackets, be sure to wear them, the SWAT team will think a person with a gun is a bad guy unless they see 'FBI' on them somewhere."

Christian took another drink of water and again waited to see if anyone had any other questions. It was imperative that everyone know exactly what their assignments were. Satisfied that every-thing was in order, he said, "we've worked long and hard for this moment, let's do it."

39

Todd Evans scanned the church parking lot for late comers. Seeing no one, he closed the heavy wooden front doors of the church. He extended his right arm to Mrs. Lewis, and with Mr. Lewis walking behind, escorted them to their seats on the front pew. He returned and escorted Mrs. Beck to her seat. He then took his position in the front of the church next to Russell Lewis.

The music from the solid brass pipe organ filled the small church as Julie Hanson walked slowly down the isle. She was wearing a floor length pink gown and carrying a bouquet of pink flowers. She took her position in the front of the church as the organist began the wedding march. The congregation rose.

Kathy Beck, escorted by her father appeared from the foyer. She was stunning. Her hair was done on the top of her head allowing all the beauty of her face to show. The white gown with its long train accented her body perfectly. She was truly a vision of loveliness. Every eye was on her, not because she was the bride, but because she was the most beautiful bride any of them had ever seen.

As Kathy and her father walked slowly down the isle, a tear appeared in nearly every eye. Russell had to wipe his eyes as he watched his bride walk toward him. He almost asked Todd to pinch him to be sure he was not dreaming. Even the preacher, a kind man in his sixties caught himself with his mouth hanging open. Kathy's smile radiated as the photographer snapped her picture.

Earlier in the day, two agents had slipped into the small church and placed listening devises in strategic locations. An agent in the communications van had been monitoring the activity within the church. As soon as he heard the Wedding March begin, he signaled Agent Christian.

"They're moving down the isle. Go. Go. Go." Christian said into the voice activated microphone mounted on his head set.

Within seconds the first agents arrived at the church. With

great haste, but careful not to make noise by slamming car doors or running on concrete, the agents took their positions. All radios were monitored through an ear piece, the main speaker had been turned off.

Three minutes later, every agent was in place and the SWAT team had taken their positions behind them. Houston Police quickly secured the area, then joined the agents who were assigned to keep the local residents inside their homes.

Harry Berg and two other agents were busy at the Blind Luck Command Center monitoring all radio conversations. When every code word, a one word message meaning a specific agent is in position, was received, Berg relayed the information to Agent Christian. Everyone was in position.

Alexander Christian stood to the right of the front doors of the church. He wore a navy wind breaker, with the letters "FBI" in yellow, across the front and back. His revolver was still in his holster underneath the jacket. He said into the voice activated microphone, "all agents are in position. Remember we are dealing with murderers, do not take them lightly."

From outside the church, Christian and the other agents could here the music start. That meant that the happy couple had completed their vows. They would be starting their walk up the isle and through the front door.

"They're close, be ready," Christian said, his voice activating the transmitter which relayed the message to the other agents.

The heavy wooden door of the church swung open and Russell and Kathy walked out. They squinted as the setting sun, a bright contrast from the subdued light inside, temporarily blinded them. As the door swung shut behind them, Kathy, her eyes still nearly closed to block out the sun, reached up to kiss her husband.

As her lips touched his, she felt a hand on her arm. Before she could comprehend whose hand it was, or where it had come from, the grasp tightened and pulled her from her husband's arms.

"FBI. Please come with us and do not make a sound."

Kathy wanted to scream, but she was too stunned. Her mouth would not work. As the agent pulled her from the church steps, Russell took a step toward her, only to be grabbed by two more FBI agents.

As Kathy and Russell were hurriedly being pulled from the front of the church, other agents quickly moved into position. They would escort the next person through the door right, if they were a suspect, left toward the parking lot, if they were not.

The train of Kathy's wedding gown became tangled in her feet as she tried to keep up with the agent pulling her by the arm. She tripped and fell forward pushing the agent. He instinctively forced her to the ground, jamming his knee into her back. After driving her to the ground, the agent stepped back, drew his service revolver and began yelling, "put your arms out."

Unable to break her fall, Kathy landed hard on her chest snapping her head into the ground, causing a cut above her eye. The wind had been knocked out of her and the blow to the head left her slightly dazed and even more confused.

"Put your arms out!" The agent yelled at her. He was standing over her pointing his gun at her head. Kathy heard the agent's command, but it didn't register. Still trying to understand what was happening. Kathy tried to sit up.

To Russell it looked as though the agent had thrown Kathy to the ground and jammed his knee into her back. He twisted violently breaking the hold of the two agents who were also watching the scene in front of them.

Russell covered only about half the distance between himself and the agent who was yelling at Kathy before he was tackled by agents. He landed face down and was dragged to the point where the agents had intended him to be.

As his arms were twisted behind his back and handcuffs slapped around his wrists. Russell looked at Kathy lying just a few yards away. He looked at the agent standing above her, his .357 pointed at her head. The agent continued to yell at Kathy. He was telling her to stay on the ground and put her arms out. Slowly, Kathy continued to move to an upright position. Her face was expression-less. She looked at her torn wedding gown and began to reach under the train.

The look in the eye of the agent pointing the gun at Kathy's head scared Russell. He knew Kathy was in shock. "Don't hurt her. Please. Don't hurt her." Russell tried to move but couldn't under the restrain of the agents. He watched in vain as the agent began to squeeze the trigger of his service revolver.

As the door of the church closed behind Russell and Kathy, Todd Evans held his arm out for Julie Hanson. He walked her slowly up the aisle to the foyer, let her go, then turned to go back for the parents. Todd was half way down the isle when he thought he heard yelling. He turned to look just as the door was closing behind Julie.

He continued down the aisle trying to determine what he had just seen. As he got to the front row of pews, Todd realized it was letters. Three large yellow letters. FBI. He turned quickly, looking at the closed doors, wondering what was going on outside them. He tried to think of what else it could have been that he had seen. There was nothing else. It was the letters "FBI." The FBI was outside the church waiting on him.

Instead of putting his arm out for Kathy's mother, he gestured to Mr. Beck and to Mr. Lewis to escort their wives out of the church. As soon as the parents started up the aisle, Todd motioned for the remaining guests to follow.

Todd looked desperately for Annie Simmons. He wanted to tell her not to go out of the building. Wanting to be one of the first to congratulate the happy couple, Annie had slipped out while Todd was motioning for the parents to leave.

As Kathy Beck continued to reach under her wedding gown, the FBI agent standing over her began squeezing the trigger of his revolver. As the hammer of the weapon moved slowly backward, Agent Christian stepped between the agent and Kathy. The agent immediately released the pressure on the trigger and pointed his weapon skyward.

Christian pulled Kathy's arms behind her back and gently lowered her back to the ground. Kathy laid her head on the ground and looked Agent Christian in the eyes. Her forehead wrinkled as her expression asked, "what are you doing?" Her somber expression caused Christian to look away. Although she was a murderer, he felt horrible for what he had done to her on her wedding day.

Holding her hands behind her back, Agent Christian looked at the agent who had been very close to shooting her and said, "cuff her." The agent holstered his weapon and snapped his handcuffs around Kathy's wrists.

As Julie Hanson walked through the doors she was immediately grabbed and roughly escorted to the right. Annie Simmons walked out right behind Julie and was given an identical greeting. Both women were helped to the ground and handcuffed.

Kathy's fall and Russell's attempt to help her had caused the adrenaline in the agents to rise. Any restraint the agents may have been planning to show was now only a memory. These eight were now being treated as dangerous fugitives.

Mr. Beck held the door open for his wife who froze in her tracks. An agent took her by the arm. "FBI, please come this way," he said as he led her toward the parking lot. Mr. Beck and the Lewis's followed close behind as the FBI led them away. Kathy's father spotted his daughter lying face down in the dirt, her hands handcuffed behind her back, and froze in his tracks.

"What the hell is going on here?" he demanded.

"These people are under arrest sir. Please do not attempt to interfere."

"Under arrest! What for? What the hell is this?"

Agent Christian hurried to the confrontation between the agent and Kathy's father. He could easily understand a father's concern. He was glad her father had not see the agent pointing a gun at her head.

"I am Alexander Christian, Mr. Beck, Special Agent in Charge, Federal Bureau of Investigation," he said as he walked toward the church parking lot escorting the Becks and Lewis's.

"Your daughter and her friends are being arrested in connection with the murders of Representative Jack James and Representative Margaret Oliver. They may be charged with the murder of James and Oliver as well as three other United States Senators."

The family members slowly stopped and looked at their children, then back at Agent Christian. All of them stood silently agape. Mrs. Beck, too stunned to fully comprehend what was going on, simply said, "are you sure you have the right wedding?"

Gene Thompson, Robert Green and Eric Moore walked out of the church together. They were promptly hustled to the right. Each was placed on the ground and handcuffed as the last of the guests exited the church.

"Please stand here while we finish. I will talk to you once we have secured the building," Agent Christian said to both sets of parents as he left to rejoin the other agents. As he walked back to where seven suspects laid handcuffed on the ground, he heard an agent say, "we have one suspect remaining in the building. We don't know if anyone else is in there or not."

Todd got himself into a position to look out the door as people exited. Through the bright sun, he could see agents waving their guns in the air as they motioned for the guests to move quickly to the parking lot. He had yelled at Eric as he noticed him approaching the door, but it was too late. Eric was too close to the door. He could not hear his name being called.

Looking around the room for another way out, Todd noticed a single door in the back. He ran to it and slowly opened it. The preacher and his wife were sitting on an old tattered sofa in the corner.

"Is there a back door to the church?" Todd asked the couple trying not to look desperate.

"Yes, that door right there," the preacher said, pointing at the narrow wooden door. "Why?"

Without answering the question, Todd bolted for the door. Just outside the door Agent Weiss was standing, gun in hand. From where he was he could see the guests who had been moved to the parking lot. Weiss was watching the parking lot, wishing he could see what was happening in front of the church. Without warning, the door flew open, hitting him square in the shoulder and knocking him to the ground. His gun flew out of his hand and landed directly in front of Todd.

Todd saw the .357 hit the ground and took a step toward it. As he bent down he felt a burning sensation as the bullet pierced his chest. The concussion buckled his knees and pushed him backward. He sat on his heels as his arms fell limp to his side. Todd Evans brain shut down the instant the bullet from the SWAT team member's rifle ripped though his heart. His eyes were open. His head scanned the horizon, as if looking for his killer, but nothing the eyes saw made it back to the brain.

Todd's brain knew it was the end and turned out the lights before he even heard the sound of the shot being fired. Other than the slight burning sensation, Todd felt nothing as the .223 caliber bullet ripped a hole in his back as it exited his body. Todd Evans was dead before his knees hit the ground.

Everyone in the front of the church heard the thunderous crack of the M16. Kathy, still unsure of exactly what was happening looked toward the sky to see if it was beginning to rain. Everyone else looked around to see who was not on the ground.

"Todd." Annie screamed as she buried her face in to the ground.

"Fuck." yelled Eric Moore as he realized what had just happened.

Kathy Beck, her face bleeding from the small laceration above her eye, raised her head slowly in an attempt to look around. It was beginning to dawn on her what was happening.

"Report!" Christian said into his microphone. "What was that shot?"

"This is Weiss. Evans has been shot by the SWAT team."

"Shit!" Christian shouted before he realized every agent would hear him.

"The building's secure sir. We have all suspects accounted for."

"Thanks." Agent Christian said, not paying attention to which agent he was talking to. "Let's get these people up, searched and put into vehicles. Spread them apart, I don't want them talking to each other."

Christian watched as Lori Anderson patted down each woman for weapons. She paused briefly as she got to Kathy, contemplating the easiest way to check the wedding dress for concealed weapons. Lori brushed off some leaves and twigs that were stuck to the front of the wedding dress as she rubbed the material around Kathy's breasts. She then patted the entire outside of the dress before lifting the back and running her hands up her legs. Kathy flinched twice as Lori rubbed her hands up her legs, presumably as Lori reached the top. As Lori reached the top of Kathy's second leg, she slid her hands back down grabbing the ceremonial garter and sliding it off Kathy's leg.

Kathy did not know why the agent was removing her garter, but she obediently lifted her foot so she could slide it off. Agent Anderson folded the garter in half and slid it over Kathy's hand onto her wrist. "She's clean," Lori said as she walked away, never looking at Kathy.

The Becks and Lewis's were standing exactly where Agent Christian had left them when he returned. "This is Agent Anderson and Agent Zimmerman. They are going to escort you home. A lab van will meet you all there and search your home."

"I don't think so!" Interrupted Mr. Beck.

"Mr. Beck, I am going to try to make this as easy as possible on you. I am sure I cannot imagine what you and you wife are going through, but I am also going to do my job. We have a search warrant and we are going to search your home. You may return with these agents and cooperate, or I can retain you until they are finished."

Kathy's father was mad and wanted to yell at someone, he just wasn't sure who he should yell at. "We'll cooperate. But, are you sure you have the right people? You said murder, Kathy wouldn't kill anyone." Mr. Beck said.

"I don't know if she killed anyone, but I am very sure she was involved. I'm sorry, but I cannot tell you any more than that at this time. Do you have a lawyer?"

"She will have the best."

"I'm glad. She is going to need the best."

40

Kathy Beck sat at the table in the brightly lit square room. The handcuffs had been removed and the cut above her eye bandaged. The front of her wedding dress, which had been badly soiled when she was driven into the ground, was now soaked from her tears and stained with blood from her brow.

As she sat in the back of the car being transported to FBI headquarters, the emotions of the day, her wedding, her arrest, her friend being shot, she did not yet know Todd was dead, had become too much for her to bear. Kathy was unable to control her crying. With her hands cuffed behind her back, her tears streamed down her cheeks and onto the white silk of her wedding gown.

Kathy held a tissue in one hand as she twisted the garter around her wrist with the other. She did not know why Agent Anderson had slipped the garter on her wrist, but it had become a security blanket. Pulling and twisting on the garter, Kathy replayed in her mind, everything that happened. She jerked back in her chair as she remembered hearing an agent say, "Evans is dead."

She closed her eyes and tried to remember. *Was that really what she heard? Did he say he was "dead", or did he just say that he had been shot?* Kathy was sure that he said Evans was dead. Kathy held the tissue up ready to dab the onslaught of tears, but none came. She felt angry. Why did they kill him? There was no reason to kill him. He didn't even own a gun.

The lone door to the room opened and Agent Christian walked in. Kathy glanced at him then did a double take. She knew someone would be coming, but she expected an old, short, fat and balding man. This man was somewhat handsome. Before she could help herself, even with all her pain, heartache and anger, she found herself half smiling at him.

"Miss Beck, my name is Agent Alexander Christian."

Kathy stopped smiling and nodded at his introduction. They looked into each other's eyes and saw the corners of each other's mouths turn upward slightly.

"Kathy, may I call you Kathy?"

She nodded yes.

"Kathy, I need to read you your rights. You are being held for questioning in connection with the murder of Jack James, a former member of the United States House of Representatives. You have the right to remain silent. Anything you say can and will be used against you in a court of law. You have the right to talk to an attorney and have him present with you while you are being questioned. If you cannot afford to hire a lawyer one will be appointed to represent you before any questioning, if you wish one. Do you understand these rights?"

"Yes."

"I have talked to your father and he is hiring you an attorney. I would like to ask you a few questions, would you rather wait until your lawyer gets here?"

"Is Todd Evans dead? I heard someone say he was."

"Yes, I'm sorry, he is."

Kathy closed her eyes and put her head in her trembling hands, "I'd better wait for a lawyer."

Christian nodded and walked to the door. He knocked on it and waited for it to open. Before he walked out, he turned to Kathy and said, "if you need anything, or if you change your mind, tell the guard and he will get me."

Again, Kathy only nodded.

"They will take you, clean you up and change your clothes. Good night Miss Beck." Christian made a point of calling her "Miss Beck." He was glad that she did not correct him. She was now Mrs. Lewis.

Two agents came and took Kathy Beck Lewis to the women's detention center. She was stripped, washed, and dressed in bright orange coveralls.

She was taken to a small concrete cell which contained a stainless steel sink, toilet, and a mattress which lay on a concrete slab. Two sheets and a blanket were folded on the mattress. Kathy unfolded the sheets and made her bed. She looked for a light switch but could not find one. She lay on the hard mattress, pulled the blanket over her head to block the light and tried to go to sleep.

Kathy stuck her head out from under the blanket and looked around the cell. *Not exactly a honeymoon suite*, she thought to herself.

A similar scene was played with each of the seven remaining suspects. Each were read their Miranda rights and each said they wanted a lawyer present. The final suspect to be interviewed, Robert Green, had just been placed in a cell for the night.

Christian was exhausted. He still had a press conference and a debriefing to contend with. He would have liked to have had the debriefing and dismissed the agents. They all could finally go home, or to their hotel rooms, and have a good, long night's sleep. Unfortunately, it was after ten and he had scheduled the news conference for 10:30 P.M. He decided to keep it short and sweet.

Agent Christian straightened his tie and put on his sport coat. He stopped at the bathroom and the water fountain before walking to the lobby of the Federal Building. Word of the arrests had spread quickly. Every local and network television as well as hundreds of newspaper reporters had gathered. The lobby was the only area large enough to hold the throng of reporters. Luckily, less than three hours had elapsed between the first arrest and the first news conference. The news conferences which were to follow might require the Astrodome by the time all the journalists made their way to Houston.

"My name is Alexander Christian. I am Special Agent in Charge for the Federal Bureau Investigation. Tonight we detained eight people we believe are responsible for the deaths of Senators Carson, Abernathy, and Williams, and Representatives James and Oliver.

"I cannot release the names of the suspects tonight. However, we will give you a complete list as soon as possible. I hope you understand that our investigation in still ongoing and I cannot give you any more information at this time."

A television reporter from the crowd yelled, "is it true you shot one of the suspects? And if so, is he dead?"

"One suspect was shot and killed by a member of the Houston SWAT team, that's correct."

"Can you release that person's name?" Asked another reporter.

"No."

"Have you arrested everyone connected with the killings?"

"Our investigation is still ongoing. There may be more arrests."

"How long have you known about the people you just arrested?"

"As that is part of our investigation, I cannot answer that question."

"Did you know about them before Representative Oliver was killed?"

"I'm sorry, I have told you all I can tell you at this time. The fact is, we now have in custody, the people whom we believe are the principals in this case."

"Do you think the Congressmen and women are now safe?"

"They are safe from the nine individuals we believe are responsible for the killing of five of them. I cannot say for sure that they are perfectly safe. I realize I have not given you much information, but please understand my position. I will keep you informed as best I can. Thank you for coming."

Agent Christian ignored the questions being shouted at him as he turned from the makeshift stage and left. "I really hate these things," he said to Agent McBride as they walked to the elevators. "It wouldn't be so bad if I could get up there and tell them everything we know, but to tell them we arrested eight suspects and killed one, then walk off is terrible. Even worse, now they will start digging and speculating and the rumors will start flying."

The two senior agents walked straight to the briefing room where the other agents had gathered. As they walked into the room, the crowd burst into applause. They had watched the press conference on a television monitor set up in the large conference room.

"That's enough," Christian said smiling, "you all need to give yourselves a round of applause. You've done a hell of a job over the past weeks." Christian paused to allow the agents to settle down before he continued.

"I cannot say the arrests went according to plan. We still don't know how involved Evans was, and we may never know why he tried to run. Weiss, I would like a full report on the shooting incident as soon as possible. Also, make Evans' apartment first on the list to go over in the morning. That may explain a few things. Houston police have secured all of the suspects apartments, is that correct?"

An affirmative came from the back of the room.

"The only other thing that bothered me was the first two arrests. I think some of us let our adrenaline take over. We need to remember to stay in control and keep a level head under all circumstances. "That's it. Most of you can take a well-deserved night off, get out of here."

A young agent from Houston, who had been assigned to Blind

Luck specifically for the arrests, walked up to Agent Christian. "Excuse me, Mr. Christian?"

"Yes?" Christian recognized the young man as the agent who held the gun on Kathy Beck.

"My name is Peter Donahue. I've only been with the Bureau a little over a year. I'm in the International Bank fraud division. I was an accountant before I joined. Anyway, this was my first major arrest, and I almost screwed up, I wanted to apologize."

"There is no need. You were going exactly by the book. The book says get the suspect on the ground. Keep your weapon on them until they spread their arms, then cuff them. I jumped in between you and the suspect and, had she had a weapon, I would be dead."

"I thought she was going for a weapon, the way she was reaching under her dress. I think I was about to shoot her. Jesus, I was about to kill her. I should have been able to tell she was in shock."

"I thought you were going to shoot her too. Had this been a different circumstance, say we were busting Colombian drug dealers, who are as ruthless as they come, you damn well had better shoot him, because he would have shot you. Even though we were arresting her for killing five people, I didn't consider her ruthless, or armed."

Christian patted the young agent on the back and said, "don't worry about it, you did the right thing."

The agent left as Christian cornered Harry Berg. "Harry, public relations will be sending a press release down soon. After I add my changes to it, I want you to be sure Gary Stephens at the Phoenix Tribune gets a copy. Fax it to him signed, 'from a friend'. No, wait, on second thought, I want you to put together a memo with the names of persons we just arrested, including Todd Evans. Mention that Evans was killed during the arrest, and send the memo to Stephens as soon as you can. I want him to have it in time for the morning paper."

"Will he use it if it's just signed 'a friend'?"

"Put Eric Moore's name on the top of the list. He'll use it."

* * * * * *

The arrest of the eight people suspected in murdering five U.S. Congressmen, and possibly coercing Congress to pass legislation it may have never considered otherwise, was by far the most important arrest in Agent Alexander Christian's career. He went to his hotel fully expecting a fulfilling, restful night's sleep.

As it turned out, it was anything but restful. It was late, well after one in the morning, by the time he got in bed. He lay in bed rerunning the events of the day over and over in his head. Todd Evans was shot and killed. Why? He didn't have a weapon. Weiss is an experienced agent, what could have happened? Kathy Beck was within seconds of being shot. She was in shock and an inexperienced agent was scared. Had he pulled the trigger, a .357 at point blank range would have blown her head apart. Her husband of five minutes was ten feet away. Her parents less than fifty feet away, with twenty five or so of her closest friends. Thank God he didn't pull the trigger.

Christian knew he must have slept, although he would swear that he didn't. It was just past five when he got up, showered and walked the short distance to the Federal Building. He nodded to the lone security guard as he entered the front doors. The sky just beginning to show light in the east behind him.

As he made his way to the Blind Luck Command Center, Christian realized that nothing seemed different. He wasn't sure what he had expected, but he thought for sure things would be different. It finally dawned on him that most of the agents who were involved with blind luck were in the field most of the time. Throughout the night, it took just as many people to man the FBI headquarters whether he was running an operation from the office or not.

The command center looked exactly as it had for several weeks, both in Houston and Phoenix. Christian had tried to give most of his staff a well-deserved night off, but most, the agents from Phoenix in particular, had nothing better to do anyway. They loved their jobs and would much rather be working than sitting in a hotel room, even sleeping in a hotel room.

They all realized that apprehending the suspects was just the beginning. Now they had to deliver a case to the U.S. Attorney so charges could be filed. Without a case, and without charges, the suspects would have to be released.

Fingerprint samples already proved Annie Simmons was in Representative Oliver's room. Tissue samples and DNA analysis would prove she killed Oliver. Small scabs, not yet totally healed on Annie's legs that matched the exact size and shape of Margaret Oliver's fingernails would merely be icing on the cake.

They had five victims and one known murderer. They still had to determine who poisoned Carson and Williams, who shot Abernathy and who was driving the truck that rammed James.

It was important that each individual in custody was charged with the correct crime, either murder, accessory or conspiracy. Each charge, from murder down, would carry a lesser charge. It was important the individual who was actually responsible for the death be charged with the severest crime, capital murder.

It was just as important that the prosecutor be able to convict that individual of the charge. If the suspect was found innocent of capital murder, they would not be able to retry him on a lesser charge. It was up to the FBI to give the prosecutor enough evidence to convict.

Agent Christian was pleasantly surprised to see the activity in the command center at such an early hour. "Good morning all," he said as he entered the room. Everyone in the room glanced up, said "good morning," and returned to what they were doing.

Lori Anderson approached her boss. "Kathy Beck's house was clean as a whistle. Evidently she does not keep a diary, which would have been handy if she had written everything that she had done, and with whom, over the past few weeks. There were no weapons of any kind. We checked for poisons. None. Not even a box of rat poison. She owns several white rompers, the lab has all of them checking for blood stains. I don't expect they will find any."

"Without the video, we would have nothing. Is that what you're saying?"

"In a nutshell, yes."

"Let's hope we have better luck at the other apartments."

"We couldn't do much worse. If someone ever asks me to describe what I think Miss America's bedroom might look like, I will just describe Kathy Beck's room."

"How were her parents handling the situation?"

"Not bad, I guess. Mr. Beck was on the phone most of the time, I think he was calling his lawyer. Mrs. Beck just sat quietly in the living room. I don't think it has sunk in yet."

"Thanks Lori. Have you gotten any rest?"

"I'm fine."

Christian had seen Agent Anderson remove the garter from Kathy Beck's leg and slip it around her wrist. He wanted to ask her why she did it, but did not feel this was a good time. When he saw her do it, he thought it was certainly an odd thing to do, but he could not think of any rule the agent may have violated, so he ignored it. He did want to find out why, in due time.

The agents spent the early morning catching up on their busy work. Writing reports, reading reports, filing reports. All in triplicate. In a few hours there would be more attorneys than you could shake a stick at in the Federal Building.

All would come in saying they represented one of the suspects, and one or two actually would. One or two of the others would probably end up representing a suspect. Luckily, that was not something Agent Christian had to concern himself with. The suspects would be informed that an attorney was interested in representing them. It would be up to the suspect to choose which attorney they wanted. Christian prepared himself for a chaotic day.

41

The uniformed Houston Police Officer sitting on the porch in front of the yellow police tape stood up as Agents Zimmerman and Holland approached with members of the crime scene investigators. Holland showed the officer his identification and waited for the officer to step aside.

"Any problems?" Zimmerman asked as the officer removed the yellow tape from the doorway.

"Not at all. A few early morning joggers stopped and looked, but nobody's tried to enter. There hasn't been any reporters snooping around yet."

"Good, we'll be done this morning and we'll notify the next of kin. They are free to enter and remove items."

The officer nodded as the group entered Todd Evans' apartment. Nothing was touched until the area was photographed. The agents then began scouring the apartment for evidence. They read every piece of paper, looked under the bed and the mattress, checked every square inch of the closet, including the pockets of every item in the closet, went through every drawer with a fine-toothed comb.

"Look at this," Zimmerman said to one of the lab technicians as he pulled a medium sized cardboard box from the closet.

"That's a high quality respirator. One that would be used when dealing with highly toxic chemicals," a member of the lab team said as he looked into the box. He pulled the respirator out of the box and set it on the bed. He emptied the contents of the box on the floor. "These little tubes look like perfume sample's bottles. They would be the perfect size for filling with a lethal amount of a deadly chemical such as cyanide. We've got a tiny funnel, tube holders, rubber gloves, this guy was all set. Let's photograph it and put it back in the box for transport back to the lab."

The agents continued their meticulous search of Todd Evans' apartment. The small kitchen was last on the agenda. Holland was looking through the cabinets when he heard the agent from the lab say, "Bingo! You guys might want to back out and let me get this stuff out of here before you finish."

Holland looked at the agent who was on his knees looking at the inside of the refrigerator door. Holland did not have to be told twice. He went into the living room and waited with Zimmerman who had heard the warning.

The agent came into the living room and picked up an Igloo Playmate ice chest. He carried the empty ice chest into the kitchen and carefully placed the two small dark brown bottles in it. "This guy sure had balls, that's all I can say. I guess he didn't expect to ever get caught. We have two bottles. One is labeled Cyanide, and the other is labeled Anszoid. That's the chemicals used to kill Carson and Williams. He should have just hung a sign on the front door that said, 'I did it'. We will check it out, of course, but I imagine the contents of the bottles will be as advertised."

Zimmerman looked into the kitchen and said, "he had the poisons, but that doesn't mean he did the poisoning. He could have given it to any of the others."

"But he was the only one that ran. He's dead, so we may never know, but I would bet he did the poisoning," Agent Holland said.

"He may have been the only one to run because he was the only one who had a chance to run. Somehow he knew we were out there. I don't think any of the others did."

"Like you said, now he's dead. Unless we find something at the other homes, or we get one of them to talk, we may never know."

The crime scene expert, ignoring most of the conversation between Holland and Zimmerman, finished examining the refrigerator. "Everything else in the refrigerator is fine, a few beers, jar of mustard, leftover pizza. I am looking forward to the day I investigate a bachelor's apartment and don't find leftover pizza."

The team spent another hour going over the apartment. They double checked every item just to be sure nothing had been missed. Satisfied they had done a thorough job, they packed up their equipment and left. Zimmerman stood at the door and looked at the apartment thinking how fast things can change. Only yesterday someone had lived there, now he was dead. It seemed the apartment knew, it looked gloomy and lifeless. Zimmerman closed the door and caught up with his partner.

"That was very productive," Zimmerman said as he caught up with Agent Holland.

"The guys from the lab sure think so. They are taking the

bottles back before meeting us at the Lewis apartment."

"I hope we do as well there. I still think we need something more concrete to convict all of them."

"We'll find it. These people sure as hell didn't seem to be hiding anything."

As the lone female agent from Arizona assigned to operation Blind Luck, it was Lori Anderson's responsibility to lead the search of Annie Simmons' and Julie Hanson's apartments. It was a policy of the Bureau to have a female lead the search of a female suspect's residence whenever possible.

Not only was there a chance a female agent might detect something a male agent might miss, but if someone happened to witness a male agent lingering too long while searching the under-wear drawer, he would be labeled a pervert and charged with violating her civil rights. However inconvenient, it was much safer to have the female agent do the investigation.

The agents followed the same procedure as they had at Todd Evans' apartment. After two hours of thorough searching, the investigators had recovered a used airline pass to San Francisco, a tube of lipstick which matched traces of lipstick found in Margaret Oliver's flat and three small vials of a white substance wrapped in a man's sock.

Annie Simmons did not keep a diary. She thought about making notes so she could tell the world what she had done, but never got around to it.

The agents finished their investigation finding nothing to tie anyone other than Todd Evans, who had accompanied her to California, to the murder of Representative Oliver.

Eric Moore's apartment was next on the list for Zimmerman and Holland. He was the key to the whole investigation. Without the newspaper article, the FBI would still be spinning their wheels in Phoenix. Zimmerman began taking pictures as soon as they entered Eric's apartment.

"He's got a computer in the bedroom," Zimmerman said to Holland, "why don't we get Berg down here to check it out?"

"Sure, I'll call it in."

Zimmerman continued his search as Agent Holland used his cellular phone to call in the request for help from Berg. "He'll be here in a few minutes, Sam. He said not to touch the computer as it's possible he has it set up to destroy all data if tampered with. He said it's not likely, but it's better to be safe. . ."

The agents in the mobile crime lab arrived at the apartment the same time Berg did. They immediately began their task of checking for dangerous chemicals or other minute pieces of evidence that might tie Eric Moore to the murders.

Berg pressed the power switch and waited for the computer to boot up. He watched closely as the config.sys and autoexec.bat files executed their routines. The screen flashed and the computer beeped as Windows loaded. Carefully using the mouse to move the arrow over the WordPerfect icon, Berg clicked twice and waited for the program to load.

"So far, so good. If he had a program to destroy data, it probably would have been in the BIOS or autoexec.bat file. It would have asked for a password as the computer booted up. From here on in I think we are safe. He may have certain files password protected, but we can get around that easy enough."

As Berg was looking though a list of files on the computer, one of the lab agents asked if he could send something to the printer for them. Berg typed Eric's name and address, the date and each letter of the alphabet as well as the numbers one through zero. He clicked the small picture of a printer and waited for the paper to eject. "Thanks." The agent said as he picked the paper off the printer and dropped it into a plastic bag.

Berg continued his search through the documents stored on Eric's computer. "Here we are," he said as he viewed the document. "I sorted these by date and started looking at the most recent first. Here is the last letter received by the newspaper." He continued viewing documents. "Here are the other letters, they are all here. Of course it doesn't mean he wrote or mailed them, just means he has them in here. He could have copied them out of the newspaper."

Agent Berg checked the remaining documents but found nothing related to the case. He put a floppy disk into the disk drive and copied the letters to the disk. He exited the word processing program and went into DOS. Removing the disk with the copied documents, he replaced it with a disk of his own. He typed A:\undelete and waited as the computer executed the program. Berg entered the directory where he had found the letters.

"God Damn it!" He said loud enough to get the attention of all the agents in the apartment. "Here is a file he's erased called 'killers.doc'. It's been secure erased, meaning I can't retrieve it. I bet that file would have told us everything we want to know. Was there anything in the garbage?"

"Nothing, no printed documents at all."

"I'll play with this more when we get it to the lab, maybe we can get more out of it." Berg said as he turned the computer off and began dismantling it. "There may still be a way to retrieve those files."

The agents loaded everything up and returned to the Blind Luck operations center. All the teams assigned to search the suspects' residences had returned. Other than the evidence collected at Todd Evans' and Annie Simmons' apartments, no other evidence had been found to link the other suspects to the murders. Nevertheless, the mood at the Op Center was upbeat.

If the bottles turned out to be the poisons as the labels suggested, and there was no reason why they shouldn't, it would suggest heavily that Evans killed Senators Carson and Williams. Evans did, to some extent, fit the description of the Carson suspect. They had the letters on Eric Moore's computer and the fingerprint of the Hewlett-Packard printer would probably match those received by the newspaper. That should convict Moore, but only of conspiracy. And they had the video of Kathy Beck, which would prove she was the last person to be seen with James while he was alive, and her fingerprints inside the truck that killed him. It might be enough to convict her of accessory, if not murder.

* * * * * *

The phone rang in the command center and Christian picked it up on the first ring.

"Christian."

"Mr. Christian, Mr. Beck is here with his attorney to see you."

"Thank you. I'll be right out."

Agent Christian put on his sport coat and walked to the waiting area where all guests were required to register. He was not sure what to expect from Kathy Beck's father. Christian took a deep breath and walked through the door to meet Mr. Beck.

"Hello Mr. Beck, I'm Special Agent in Charge Alex Christian."

"Yes, I remember. This is our attorney, Mr. Barron."

"Bob Barron," the attorney said as he extended his hand to the agent.

"Please come with me, we can talk in my office."

The three men walked in silence to Christian's temporary office. He gestured toward the two empty chairs as he sat behind his desk.

"Mr. Barron, you are going to be representing Ms. Beck?"

"That's correct. I have been hired by the family to represent her."

Christian opened Kathy Beck's file and gave her attorney the proper forms to fill out so he could consult with her.

Mr. Beck was noticeably anxious. He fiddled in his chair as Barron and Christian discussed legal matters. "Can I see my daughter?" He finally said, tired of being ignored.

"Certainly. I will have to be in the room with you and I must advise you that you are not to talk to her about the crime."

"I must object. I believe my client is entitled to talk to her in private."

"Not until we have questioned her. She has refused to speak to us without an attorney."

"Jesus Christ," said Mr. Beck, "what has she done?"

"Barry," The attorney interrupted.

"That's OK, Mr. Barron. I am neither judge nor jury. My job is to supply the prosecutor with evidence, not determine her guilt or innocence. Mr. Beck, as I'm sure you have heard, your daughter is, in my opinion, involved in the murders of five Congressmen. We are still in the process of determining how involved. At the very least, I am sure we have accessory. We have a videotape that shows, through digital enhancement, your daughter at the rodeo arena the day Representative James was killed."

"That proves nothing!" Attorney Barron interrupted.

"As I said, that is not my job Mr. Barron, I only supply the evidence. Her fingerprints were also found on beer cans inside the truck that was used to kill James." Christian paused to look at Barron, waiting for another objection. There wasn't one. "I am certain we can prove that Annie Simmons killed Representative Oliver. We have an overwhelming amount of evidence against her. We have taped phone conversations proving that each of these suspects knew about the murders. It is my intention to see that the killers are charged with murder and the others with conspiracy or accessory. It is not my intention to see someone pay for a crime they did not commit. I believe it is much worse to actually kill someone than to talk about it. However, if they helped plan, or execute the crime, that's a different matter. To me, they are just as guilty as the person who pulled the trigger, or in this case, drove the truck."

Mr. Beck nodded, meaning he either understood or agreed, Christian didn't know which, and said, "I would like to see my daughter."

Christian picked up the phone and made arrangements for Kathy to be taken to an interrogation room. He hung up the phone and said, "come with me, it will just take a few minutes."

The three men walked to the elevators and rode up to the floor where the prisoners were being held. Neither man said a word. Agent Christian checked his weapon with the guard before entering the secured area. They walked to the only door which had an agent standing guard in front of it. The agent stepped aside as Christian approached. The three men walked inside.

Kathy was sitting at the table in the center of the room. She was wearing bright orange coveralls and white tennis shoes. Her face lit up like a Christmas tree when she realized her father had entered the room. She jumped from the table and hugged him, bursting into tears. Mr. Beck could not control himself as he held his only daughter. He began to cry.

After several minutes, Mr. Beck pushed his daughter back and looked at her. Agent Christian pulled a tissue from the box on the table and handed it to her. She wiped her eyes and blew her nose.

"Are you all right, can I get you anything?" Mr. Beck said. He really had no idea what to say. He had been told not to speak about the crime. He was not going to risk being told to leave for saying or asking the wrong thing. It was very awkward for both of the Becks. Mr. Beck didn't know what to say and Kathy was afraid to say anything with the FBI agent in the room.

"Mr. Beck, if you would excuse us for a little while, we could conduct our interrogation and then you could visit your daughter in private. I think you would be much more comfortable." Agent Christian said after several long moments of silence.

"That's fine with me. Bob? Oh, Kathy, this is Bob Barron. He is going to represent you," Mr. Beck said, choking back tears.

Kathy looked up at the attorney and began to tremble. The whole affair had seemed like a dream, but each new experience, the handcuffs, the orange coveralls, the hard mattress in the cold cell, and now her attorney, made her realize she was not dreaming. This was real life.

The attorney stepped toward Kathy and extended his hand. She took his hand and let him shake it, but said nothing.

Christian opened the door to allow Mr. Beck out and spoke to the guard. In a few moments, Agents McBride and Anderson entered the room. Lori set a tape recorder on the table and turned it on.

After stating the date and time and identifying the persons in the room, Christian said, "would you please identify yourself?"

"Kathy Beck, uh, Kathy Lewis. . . Kathy Beck Lewis."

Christian felt the urge to laugh at Kathy's concern over her name. It was the least of her problems. Christian asked Kathy, for the record, her birth-date, age, address and social security number.

"Mrs. Lewis," Agent McBride said.

Kathy did not look at the agent right away as, even though she had just identified herself as Kathy Beck Lewis, she had never been called, "Mrs. Lewis" before, and the title did not register.

When she finally looked up at McBride, he continued. "We have had you, your husband and many of your friends under surveillance for sometime. We know that you and Julie Hanson went to "The Cut-up," a hair salon that has wandering comedians to entertain you as you are getting your hair and nails done, the day of your wedding. We know your husband went to a topless bar and, for fifty bucks, a dancer gave him an orgasm. We could have picked him and the dancer up for public lewdness had we the desire."

Kathy's bottom lip quivered and her eyes filled with tears again as she heard of the exploits of her husband on their wedding day.

"And what was the point of that comment? That was outrageous! I must protest." Attorney Bob Barron was beside himself. He knew the only reason Kathy was told the story was to turn her against her new husband. From the expression on her face, he was afraid it may have worked.

"Mr. Barron, I only told Mrs. Lewis that information so that she would realize that we know every move she has made for quite some time," McBride said.

Barron did not say anything, he only stared at the agent, letting him know that he knew the real reason he told the story.

Agent Christian decided the blow had been dealt. "Kathy, we are investigating the murder of Representative Jack James. Do you know anything about his death?"

Kathy had been staring Agent Christian straight in the eyes as he asked her questions. She glanced up at her attorney.

"My client invokes the fifth."

"Uh?" Kathy said, surprised at the attorneys remarks.

"You are exercising your right under the fifth amendment to not answer on the question on the grounds you may incriminate yourself. After this initial interrogation, we can talk and decide if there is anything you should tell them."

"On the afternoon of April 20th, were you at a rodeo arena in Winnie, Texas and did you leave the building with Representative James?" Christian asked.

"No comment." Barron said before Kathy attempted to answer.

"Did you kill Representative James?"

"No!" Kathy said before her attorney could answer for her. She was looking Christian in the eye as tears filled her eyes.

"Do you know who did?"

Kathy sat silently as her attorney said, "no comment." Christian was now sure she did in fact know who was driving the Dodge truck that killed the Representative. He was also now sure, and somewhat relieved, that she was not the driver.

"Kathy, we know your friend Annie Simmons killed Representative Oliver. The evidence is overwhelming. I cannot predict how a jury will act, but with what we have on her, I cannot imagine her not being convicted. It would not surprise me to see her get the death penalty."

Kathy's stomach knotted and tears began to stream down her cheeks, but she did not take her eyes off Agent Christian. He kept eye contact with her as he said, "if you do not cooperate with us and tell us everything you know, we will assume you were the driver, you killed Representative James and you will get the death penalty!"

"Mr. Christian!" Barron shouted, "what kind of bullshit is that. I thought you would be above trying such scare tactics. Ms. Beck, do not say anything."

"Mr. Barron, I assure you, I am not employing scare tactics. If your client does not cooperate, you will be defending her in a capital murder case."

Bob Barron was about to offer his retort when Kathy interrupted. "What if I cooperate, I mean, tell you everything I know. What will happen to me? I don't want to go to jail."

"If you plead guilty to accessory, I will explain to the judge you cooperated and he might go easy on you. I cannot make any promises."

"If you will give me immunity, I will tell you every thing I know."

"You will have to give me something to take to the prosecutor.

How do we know you know anything?"

Kathy blinked, causing more tears to run down her cheek, but she did not take her eyes off Christian. She could have used her looks and personality to get just about whatever she wanted, for as long as she could remember, but she seldom did. Sitting across from a man who held her life in his hands, Kathy decided it was time she started. She bit her lower lip letting just a little of her teeth show as she looked at Christian with sad eyes. She could see him melting in front of her.

"I will tell you everything you want, but not until you promise I won't go to jail." She looked at her attorney, who was a bit stunned by her frankness. "Would you excuse us a second?"

"I don't think that's a good idea."

"Please, it's O.K., and them too." Kathy looked toward Agents McBride and Anderson.

Christian signaled for the other two agents to leave. They escorted Mr. Barron out of the room. Kathy waited until she heard the lock on the door click as it closed. "What is your first name?" she asked.

"Alex," Christian replied, very surprised at the question.

"Alex," Kathy said as she put her hand on top of his, moving very slowly as not to alarm the agent, "can we go off the record for a moment?"

"Sure," Christian said, knowing why he agreed but not wanting to accept it. He reached to the tape recorder and pressed the stop button.

The tears began to flow as she spoke. "I lured James out of the arena. I was told he had a reputation and he would try to seduce me, and if I ended up alone with him, like in his car or something, and I didn't give in, that he would try to rape me. I was going to go with him and then when he tried something, I was going to resist. I was to be rescued and they were going to kill James. But as soon as we left the building, he started groping me. When he pulled me up against him and squeezed my butt, I decided I didn't want to go through with it. I was going back to the truck and he followed me. I started running and he kept chasing me. I ran past the truck to get in the passenger's side, and the person driving floored it just as James got there. I was right next to him when he got crushed."

Kathy held her head in her hands as her shoulders shook. Her crying became uncontrollable. Christian jumped around the table to hold her. She stood and put her arms around him and held him tight as she cried. The crying was not an act. Whenever she thought of James, she would lose control. As she regained her composure, she eased her grip on Christian.

"Thank you," she said as she backed off slightly letting her head rest on his chest. Christian held her as he stroked the back of her head. Kathy allowed herself to grin slightly as she felt his touch. She had the hook in his mouth, now all she had to do was reel him in.

When Christian realized he had been hugging a suspect, he almost knocked her down pushing her back to her chair. Kathy slid her hands along Alex's arms as he backed away, clutching his hands in hers as they met. She held his hands for a brief instant before letting go.

"Thank you again. Whenever I think about it, I get like this."

"Who was driving the truck?"

"Off the record?"

Christian had forgotten they were off the record. "Of course," he said.

Agent Christian had moved back to his chair and was sitting directly across the table from Kathy. She slid her hand across the table and put it on top of his. "I want to trust you, I really do, and I'll tell you anything you want to know, but I don't, I can't go to jail."

Ordinarily, Alexander Christian would have told his suspect that she should have thought about that before she got involved. But here was an extraordinarily beautiful woman, holding his hand, tears streaming down her face.

"I'll see what I can do," he said as compassionately as he could. In a few more minutes he would have been crying with her. "I'll send your father back in."

42

Agent Christian reviewed his report for the Assistant United States Attorney. The preliminary hearing was to determine if there was enough evidence to hold the suspects while the grand jury determined if there was enough evidence to try them, and to set bail if it was decided they would they would be tried. The hearing was set for Tuesday morning.

Annie Simmons had killed Oliver. The poisons used to kill Williams and Carson were found in Todd Evans' apartment. Kathy Beck was at the scene when James was killed, it was unsure who else was at the scene. Eric Moore wrote the letters to the Phoenix newspaper informing them of the reason behind the deaths.

There was no evidence to suggest any of the suspects were in Florida at the time of Senator Abernathy's death. The local lab had determined the hair found in Abernathy's bedroom did not belong to any of the suspects. Not only was the hair found at the scene a different shade and texture of any of the suspects, it contained evidence of drug use. All the suspects in custody tested drug free.

After listening to thousands of hours of taped conversations, the FBI had proof that each suspect, with the exception of Robert Green, was involved in the conspiracy to kill a United States Congressmen. At some point or another each suspect had mentioned "the plan," or "our plan," when referring to the recent murders.

Agent Christian and other members of the FBI knew it was purely "blind luck" again that, in the two weeks they were under surveillance, not one of the suspects said anything about who actually killed who. Had the FBI waited, eventually someone would have talked. Unfortunately, sooner or later, one of the gang would have spotted the agent tailing them, it had almost happened.

The Prosecutor for the United States, Lane Jacob, walked into Agent Christian's office and introduced himself. The two shook hands and Christian motioned toward a chair.

"I hate to say this Mr. Jacob, but we have taken the people responsible off the street and stopped the threat of any more Congressmen dying from their actions, but I don't know if you will be able to convict any of them, other than Ms. Simmons.

"We found samples of the two different kinds of poisons and a respirator in Todd Evans apartment. As you know, he is dead. We don't know if he, himself, poisoned Carson and Williams, or if he had help, or if someone else did it and he was just supplying the poison. He did fit, in general terms, the descriptions we got at the country club after Senator Carson's death.

"A laser printer is just like an old typewriter when it comes to fingerprinting a document. Even the smallest piece of dust on the print drum will leave a minute mark on every document printed, until the print drum is changed. The letters received by Gary Stephens at the Phoenix Tribune were printed by Eric Moore's laser printer. That has been confirmed.

"We have a video that places Kathy Beck at the scene where Representative James was killed. The video never shows them together, only her sitting by herself and then walking away. Actually, the video never shows her face, but we have digitally matched up parts of her face, lower jaw and chin, and it matches perfectly. But like I said, the tape never shows her with James. We had witnesses that saw James and a woman leave together. We brought the witnesses in and put Ms. Beck in a lineup with five other fairly attractive women. All with great legs, all dressed similarly, and the witnesses could not identify Beck as the woman at the arena. Seems they only looked at her ass, excuse me, her legs.

"I think Moore had kept notes on his computer but he erased them before we arrested him. Actually, it looked like he had erased them before we were even on to him. We attempted to undelete the files to no avail. We even contacted the maker of the software which performed the secure delete and they told us there was no way to undelete the files. That was the point of their software. I imagine they will try to capitalize on this.

"To sum it all up, the only one alive you can convict of murder, in my opinion, is Simmons. You might get conspiracy convictions on the rest and an accessory conviction on Beck. But if you lose the accessory, you cannot try her for conspiracy, is that correct?"

"Yes, if a person is found not guilty on a charge, you cannot retry them on a lesser charge in the same crime. If we win, they can appeal till the moon turns blue, but if we lose, that's it. No matter what."

"Kathy Beck has offered to tell us everything she knows in exchange for immunity. I told her we could prosecute her for capital murder in the James case if she doesn't tell us who actually drove the truck into him. I don't think we have a case against her, but she doesn't know that."

"Actually, she was there. She is a known member of the group responsible for the other murders, we might get a conviction."

"Realistically?"

"She's got a top lawyer in Bob Barron. Realistically, from what you have told me about the evidence, I'd be lucky to get a conviction on accessory. If I really wanted a conviction, conspiracy is the best I could hope for."

"Should I offer her immunity?"

Lane Jacob stood up and stretched. He tried to pace in the small office but there wasn't room. There was no window and no pictures on the wall. He sat down. "None of the others are talking?" He asked.

"No."

"Beck's got a good attorney. He's not going let her make a deal until he sees the evidence we have on her. After he sees it, he won't let her make a deal. He'll know we don't have anything. Why was she in such a hurry to make a deal?"

"She's pretty upset. She seems to be very afraid of going to jail. Barron was in the room when I threatened the capital murder charge. He just blew me off, but I think it scared her. She asked if we could talk alone. That's when she told me she would talk if I could keep her out of jail. I said I would see what I could do."

"Even with her testimony, I don't know if it would do any good. The defense would argue she made a deal and lied to save her own skin. You said it yourself. She would do anything to stay out of prison."

"How 'bout I offer her a deal where she tells us everything, and pleads guilty to conspiracy. I'll tell the judge how cooperative she was, and she probably would spend less than a year in a minimum security federal prison. We have nothing to lose, she may finger Moore, or maybe her husband. At least it would give us something to work on them with, maybe get a confession. You don't sound like you want to try her for anything more than conspiracy anyway."

"Tell her she doesn't even have to plead guilty, but if she does she will probably get a lighter sentence, but depending on what she tells us, the worst charge will be conspiracy. We won't charge her with accessory. You are sure she did not kill James? If she admits to killing James or we find out she killed him, I will nail her ass to the wall. Capital murder, and I will fight for the death penalty if she's convicted."

"That sounds fair enough. I'll talk to her."

"Call me as soon as you have her answer. I'll be in my office all afternoon." Lane Jacob handed Agent Christian a card and left. Christian waited a few moments then called to have Kathy Beck taken to an interrogation room. He called the command center to tell them where he would be. He asked if the lab had come up with anything new. They had nothing.

Lori Anderson unlocked the steel door to Kathy's cell and opened it. Kathy was sitting on the bunk, her back against the wall.

"Kathy, will you come with me? Mr. Christian would like to speak to you," Lori said, holding the door open.

Kathy walked out of her cell and waited for the agent to close the door.

"Do you know what he wants?" Kathy asked as they began walking down the hall.

"No, I don't. I couldn't tell you if I did."

"I guess I should have known, I'm sorry." Kathy walked a while in silence before she said, "you were the one who put the garter on my arm, weren't you?"

"Yes. I knew what you were in for, and I thought you might need something personal to hang on to."

"Every time I think I am about to go crazy, I look at the garter, and rub it, it makes me feel better. Thank you for doing it, I'm very grateful, but why did you do it?"

Lori grabbed Kathy by the arm and stopped her. She looked up and down the hallway and said, "many years ago, I was still in high school and my brother had just graduated from college. It was 1969. He was very antiwar. Like a lot of young people, he demonstrated against the Vietnam war. But, unlike most, he decided to do something about it. He ran for the House of Representatives in Florida. He ran against a conservative named Abernathy. My brother had a significant lead in the polls. Everyone was getting tired of the war. A couple of weeks before the election, they found him in his car, dead. He had a needle in his arm. The police said it was a drug overdose and closed the case. No matter what we did, they would not reopen it. My brother didn't even smoke marijuana.

I know somebody killed him. I figured Chuck Abernathy had him killed.

"One of the reasons I joined the FBI was to look into the case. I waited until I had been with the Bureau six years before I started asking questions. It took less than a week for word came down to me to cease. I was married at the time, so nobody connected that I was related to the deceased. I hadn't made more than a few calls when word came down that I was to stop asking questions. I was told it was not a Bureau matter.

"Now I was really curious. Only a few people in Florida knew I was looking into the case. Somehow, they got someone at the FBI to tell me to stop investigating it. This was an old case, the FBI should not have cared, as long as I was doing my job. So I, very discretely, asked around and found out that word had come from Senator Abernathy's office that I should keep my nose out of that case.

"That proved to me that Abernathy had something to do with my brother's death. If he didn't kill him, he knew who did. So, when you all killed him, I wasn't too upset." Lori paused as she took Kathy by the hand, "I can't do much for you, but I hoped the garter would give you comfort. I know they take everything personal away from you in here." Lori squeezed Kathy's hand, "don't misunderstand, what you all did was wrong," again Lori scanned the hallway to be sure no one was listening, "but, I'm very happy you killed Abernathy."

Kathy was not positive the story she had just heard was the truth or an effort to trick her in to saying something she shouldn't. As the two women started walking again, Kathy said, "we didn't kill Abernathy."

"Sure you didn't," Lori said as she winked at Kathy. They walked in silence to the interrogation room. Agent Anderson unlocked the door and motioned for Kathy to go in. When Kathy was seated at the table, Lori closed and locked the door. Lori leaned on the door and thought about her brother. She thought about Abernathy and she thought about Oliver. It was ironic to her how she could feel so good about one death and so bad about another.

Kathy smiled as Agent Christian entered the interrogation room. As the door closed behind him, she stood up and slowly walked toward him. Like a beat dog returning to its master, Kathy slowly, and cautiously, put her arms around Christian and hugged him lightly. As the Agent returned the hug, Kathy squeezed harder. She put her cheek against his and whispered, "thank you for letting me see my father. He was very upset."

Christian could have hugged the woman forever. He loved the way she felt, her warm breath gently blowing on his neck. He was tempted to try and kiss her, but knew it would be the worst possible thing he could do. He tried to push Kathy away but she only leaned back, keeping her body against his. She placed her lips on his lower lip and very slowly kissed him.

Agent Alexander Christian's heart pounded as he pushed Kathy away. Kathy instantly sat down. "I'm so sorry. I . . ."

"Please, there was nothing meant by it."

She looked up at him as though he had hurt her deeply. Tears appeared in her eyes. She didn't say anything as she pulled a tissue from the box on the table and blotted her eyes.

Christian turned on the tape recorder and leaned forward toward Kathy, his elbows resting on the table. "Kathy, I am only the investigator. But I have talked to the Assistant U.S. Attorney and, as long as you did not kill James yourself, if you cooperate, conspiracy to commit murder will be the maximum charge he will bring against you. I will explain to the judge that you cooperated and you will probably get no more that a year in a minimum security prison. You might only serve two or three months. That's a hell of a deal, considering you all killed five United States Congressmen."

Kathy leaned forward on the table so she was only a foot from Christian. "Only you and I are in the room. How do I know I can trust you?"

Christian leaned forward closing the gap between them by half. "You can trust me. I give you my word."

Without moving her head, Kathy slowly raised her hand and turned off the tape recorder. She began closing the distance between her and the agent. Christian sat frozen, looking deep into her dark blue eyes as she came closer, until her lips touched his. Alexander closed his eyes as he and Kathy kissed deeply. Kathy kissed him with passion, then, slowly she backed back into her chair. Her eyes filled with tears as she said, "Alex, I'm a married woman. I can't do this. Not right now."

She turned the tape recorder back on.

43

The line to get into the court room began forming before midnight. Although it was only an arraignment, the nature of the crime had generated enormous interest. Judge Malcolm Winters did not allow cameras in his court. He believed prosecutors and defense attorneys began "performing" whenever a camera was present. They inevitably lost sight of what was in the best interest of their client and attempted to do and say whatever would make them look good on television.

Family members were the first to be allowed into the courtroom. Reporters with proper credentials followed nearly filling the courtroom to capacity. Reporters without credentials vied with individuals who just wanted to be in the courtroom for the remaining seats. Guards allowed two people at a time to enter, being sure there was room for them to sit, and that the count stayed below the room capacity, as mandated by the fire code.

When the occupancy level became precariously close to fire code capacity, the guards closed the doors and notified the Bailiff the court was full. The seven suspects were led in by members of the FBI and Federal Marshals.

Each individual was brought to the courthouse in a separate vehicle. They were kept in separate rooms within the courthouse until they were led into the courtroom. The suspects were led into the court and pointed toward a row of chairs set up behind a long wooden table. A second row of chairs had been placed behind the first row for the accumulation of defense attorneys.

Being an arraignment, charges would be filed and the defendant, or his attorney, would enter a plea. It's usually a given that the plea would be "not guilty." It was usually very routine and boring, except in this case no one knew exactly what charges the prosecutor was going to file against each suspect. Once the charges were filed, and a plea entered, a preliminary hearing would be held where the judge would examine the evidence and determine if there was probable cause to believe a criminal act was committed. If the judge found there was probable cause, the case would be bound over for trial.

Kathy Beck was the first to be brought into the courtroom. She was wearing a conservative short-sleeved pink dress which hung to her knees. Bob Barron greeted her and showed her to the first chair in the long row. Kathy said very few words to her attorney before taking her seat. Barron sat in the chair directly behind his client. Kathy looked over her shoulder and glanced at Agent Christian who was sitting in the first row of the gallery, directly behind the prosecutors. Christian had been staring at Kathy since she first entered the room. He looked her in the eye the brief second she looked at him, but showed no sign of recognition.

Russell Lewis was the last to be brought into the courtroom. It was the first time he had seen his bride since she was placed in the back seat of a police car and driven away. His heart pounded as he saw her. A small bandage above her eye was the only visible sign remaining from her ordeal the previous Friday evening.

As Russell walked to his chair, the only chair remaining on the front row, he stared at Kathy. She did not look at him, but continued to stare directly ahead. Russell thought that she must not have known he had entered the court. He wanted to say something to her but refrained. He had been warned not to speak to any of the other suspects.

Each of the other friends sitting in the front row looked up and nodded at Russell as he sat down. He kept looking at Kathy only to see her stare straight ahead.

The head bailiff, in an overly dramatic fashion, announced the court was now in session, the Honorable Judge Malcolm Winter presiding, all rise. Everyone in the court rose as the Judge entered the court and sat in his large leather chair. Russell continued to look at his wife who looked directly at the Judge, never glancing in his direction.

Russell had no idea why Kathy would not look at him. He had thought about nothing but seeing her for three days, and now she seemed to be ignoring him. A knot developed in his stomach as he tried to imagine the reasons she would not look at him.

The Judge gave a speech explaining why everyone was in the court and what the court was attempting to accomplish this day. He thanked everyone for coming and explained the rules that pertained to general courtroom etiquette as well as a few rules specific to his court. When Judge Winter finished his talk, he asked the lead prosecutor, Lane Jacob to present the charges.

Jacob, carrying a legal notepad, walked up to the podium. "Thank you your honor," he said as he reached the podium. "On behalf of the United States of America, I would like to enter the charge of capital murder against Annie Simmons for the murder of Margaret Oliver, who, at the time of her death was a member of the United States House of Representatives."

There were some murmurs from the audience, but the charge was not a surprise. Annie Simmons held her head high as the charge was read. Her expression did not change.

"Ms. Simmons." Annie and her attorney stood as Judge Winter addressed her. "You have been charged with capital murder in the death of Representative Margaret Oliver, how do you plead?"

Annie stood straight and said, "Not guilty."

Judge Winter wrote something on a piece of paper in front of him and said, "thank you. You may be seated."

Annie and her attorney sat down. They were finished for the day.

"Mr. Prosecutor." The Judge said as he looked down from the bench.

"Your Honor, with my authorization, FBI Special Agent in Charge Alexander Christian offered Kathy Beck Lewis a lesser charge in exchange for information pertaining to the case."

Christian was watching Russell Lewis as the prosecutor announced the plea bargain agreement. Russell was watching and listening to Jacob as he told the Judge about the agreement. Russell's eyes glanced from the prosecutor to his wife and quickly back to the prosecutor. He could not believe she would betray him. Christian was hoping for more of a reaction from Russell Lewis. A reaction that might indicate whether or not Kathy Beck had lied. It was part of the reason Jacob had made the speech.

Kathy Beck continued to stare at Judge Winter as the court was being told of her deal. She too gave no indication if the information she offered, was in fact, the truth. Russell kept his eyes glued to the prosecutor, never again glancing at his wife.

Prosecutor Lane Jacob continued. "I have examined the information received from Mrs. Lewis as well as all of the other evidence supplied by the Federal Bureau of Investigation, and after discussing this case with the Attorney General, at the present time, The United States does not wish to bring charges against Mrs.

Lewis."

The crowded courtroom became deafening as everyone expressed surprise at the announcement. Russell Lewis stared at his wife of three days in disbelief. Kathy stared straight ahead. Realizing she was not going to look at him, Russell swallowed his desire to say something to her and looked down at his hands.

Judge Winter pounded his gavel to restore order in the court. When it was quiet, Jacob continued. "Also from the evidence supplied by the FBI and Mrs. Lewis's testimony, it appears that Senators Carson and Williams as well as Representative Jack James were killed by Todd Evans, now deceased as well. We have no evidence to suggest that any of these eight were involved with the death of Senator Abernathy. That case is still under investigation."

Russell Lewis could not move. He had been thinking about Kathy and what she had done, and not listening to the prosecutor. Now he was trying to understand what was just said. He thought he heard him say that Todd Evans killed James, but he wasn't absolutely sure. He didn't dare look up. He stared at his hands, now listening to Lane Jacob very closely.

Jacob continued. "As you are well aware, your Honor, in this country once a person is tried for a crime, they cannot be tried again, as long as a verdict is reached. The government's option in these cases, in light of the available evidence, would be to charge each of these persons with conspiracy to commit capital murder, a felony punishable by a maximum of 10 years in a Federal prison. I am confident we could convict each of these suspects on conspiracy. However, we are not certain all the information we have related to this case is correct. We also believe that any one of these people could be directly responsible for the deaths of Carson, Williams, James and possibly Abernathy. At this time the Government of the United States, declines to bring charges against, in addition to Kathy Beck Lewis, Robert Green, Julie Hanson, Eric Moore, Mark Flanagen, Gene Thompson and Russell Lewis. The Government reserves the right to bring any of the aforementioned persons up under murder charges as further investigation warrants."

Again, the courtroom erupted. Judge Winter pounded his gavel to restore order.

"Mr. Prosecutor, I would like to commend you on your forthrightness. It is not often a prosecutor will admit they have a lack of evidence. However, you do understand that since you have arrested these individuals for conspiracy, unless you bring conspiracy charges against these individuals at this time, you will not be able to in the future."

"Yes, your Honor, the Government understands. The Federal Bureau of Investigation will continue its investigation into the deaths of Abernathy, Williams, Carson and James until they are certain Todd Evans was solely responsible, or new evidence is uncovered which would suggest someone else was responsible."

Judge Winter made notes on the pad in front of him before addressing the court. He took off his glasses and looked around the courtroom. "As I look at the prosecution team, the defense attorneys and the accused, I am reminded of a situation which occurred in 1865. A group of young men and women who lived at a boarding house in Washington, D.C. conspired to assassinate, among others, the President of the United States. As I am sure you all know, John Wilkes Booth shot and killed Abraham Lincoln. The owner of the boarding house, Mary Surratt was found guilty of conspiracy and hanged. If you study history, you will find there is little evidence to suggest that Ms. Surratt was even aware of the plot. Nevertheless, she was arrested, tried and convicted. Although I do not agree with the hanging of Ms. Surratt, she was given a trail by jury. Unfortunately her jury was not impartial. Today eight of you sit before me accused with the deaths of five United States Congressmen and the prosecution had declined to press charges, mainly because they know your sentences for conspiracy will be nothing more than a slap on the wrist."

The Judge looked at the accused and asked them to rise. "Had you all been tried and found guilty in this court, no matter how much I would have liked to, I would not have been able to offer death by hanging to the jury for consideration as punishment for your crimes. If you all are indeed guilty of conspiracy, and at this time I am not passing judgment, I would have been very happy to see you spend time in a Federal Penitentiary.

"These crimes fall under Title XII of the U.S. Code, Terrorism, specifically, chapter 351, crimes against Congressmen or cabinet members. The statute of limitations on these types of crimes is eight years. I am encouraging the FBI to investigate this case as long as it needs in order to satisfy themselves that the killers have been brought to justice. Each of you, I'm sure, will remain suspects in this case. Remember, you are not protected against further prosecution for alleged criminal activity arising from the incident for which the arrest was made. That means you will never know when, or if, you are being watched and/or listened to. One mistake and you will be back in this court facing capital murder charges. I do not know how deeply any of you were involved in these murders, but I suggest you find something else to occupy your time. Remember, YOU ARE STILL SUSPECTS. Bailiff, please escort Miss Simmons back to her cell, the rest of you are free to leave." Judge Winter pounded his gavel. "Court adjourned," he said.

The reporters without cellular telephones ran from the court-room as those with telephones attempted to dial their editors. The suspects stood slowly and the men shook hands as the women hugged. Kathy Beck Lewis stood slowly and walked to her husband. She put her arms around him and said nothing as she held him. Alexander Christian watched Kathy hold her husband for a moment before leaving the courtroom.

44

Russell Lewis dove off the swim platform into the crystal clear waters of the Caribbean. He swam underwater gently surfacing next to the yellow float his wife was lying on. He hung onto the float as he admired Kathy's naked body glistening in the bright sun. He ran his finger between her breasts, leaving a streak in the suntan oil, till he reached her navel. He poked his finger into her bellybutton causing her to flinch, lose her balance, and fall off the float.

Kathy put her arms around Russell's neck as he held onto the float to remain above the water. They kissed deeply and passionately. They drifted together in the blue water, kissing and talking. "You really kissed that agent?" Russell asked.

"Yes, I did. How many times do you want me to tell you the story?"

"Lots. I love to hear how my brilliant and beautiful wife screwed the FBI."

"I only kissed him, I didn't screw him." Kathy laughed.

"I hope not, I can handle you kissing him, but that's it. Even though it still pisses me off that he got to kiss the new Mrs. Lewis before I did."

"I really don't know if it did any good or not. The lawyer never told me what they had on me or what they might do, but I could tell by his eyes that Christian liked me. I figured if he thought I liked him, it could only help our situation."

"You know that we are never going to be able to talk about this again. If they find out I was driving the truck that killed James, they'll fry my ass."

"I know, that's going to be really hard. We will never be quite sure if anybody is listening to us or not. Even when we're in bed making love, somebody could be listening."

"That's probably part of the reason they let us go. Had they found us guilty of conspiracy and sent us to prison, we would have gone to a minimum security prison for, how long, maybe a year?

Probably only a few months the way the prisons are revolving doors these days. And that would have been the end of it. Now we are going to have to be careful what we say to each other for the rest of our lives. I'm not so sure we got the best deal."

Kathy stroked her arms to move the flotilla toward the white sloop. As she got to the teak swim platform, she pulled herself onto the edge. She leaned back on the platform, pulling Russell as she reclined. Russell came out of the water and laid gently on top of his wife.

They made love on the swim platform, shaded from the afternoon sun by the boat's bimini. A cool breeze blew in off the ocean. "I think we got the best deal," Kathy said as they finished.

Russell kissed Kathy on the lips and rolled into the ocean. Kathy rolled to her side and waited for her husband to reappear. Russell emerged from the water and put his arms on the teak platform, his chin resting on his arms.

"Do you think you could be happy living on a boat?" He asked.

"For how long? This is wonderful, but I don't know about living like this."

"Actually, we wouldn't be living like this. We couldn't afford a boat this big, but we could get one that was probably 34 to 36 feet, and capable of cruising oceans. We would sail where we wanted and when we wanted. We could make love when we wanted and not have to worry that the FBI is listening."

Kathy sat up and swung her legs into the water. She leaned back against the transom and looked at the island behind them. She looked down at Russell who was still resting on his arms, but now he was between her legs. She hadn't realized she had straddled him as she sat up. She was sitting on the back of a boat, naked, with her husband resting between her legs.

"I'm glad nobody can see us." She slid forward until she joined her husband in the water, wrapping her legs around his waist. "I hardly see my parents since they moved to Europe. We probably shouldn't associate with our friends anymore, at least for a while. I can't think of any reason we should stay in Houston. I'm all for buying a boat and living on it. Will it be safe?"

"Safer than driving a car on the freeway. In our case, safer than talking in our sleep."

They laughed and kissed until Russell said, "race you to shore." Kathy pushed him under the water and began swimming toward the white sand beach.

Epilogue

Lisa Thompson became the first woman vice-president of the United States in 2020. Upon the President's death in 2022, Ms. Thompson became the first woman to be President. At a fund-raising rally in Minneapolis in 2023, a lone assassin stepped from a crowd of supporters, pointed a small caliber handgun at the President and fired one round. The bullet entered through her left eye becoming lodged in her brain. She was pronounced dead-on-arrival at Minneapolis Memorial Hospital. She was 51.

Bubba sold his property to a large amusement corporation and bought a beach house in Marathon Key, Florida. He rents mopeds to tourists.

Annie Simmons was convicted of capital murder and sentenced to death by lethal injection. Twenty three years after her conviction, at the age of 48, while awaiting execution, Annie died of cancer. Her conviction and sentence was still being appealed at the time of her death.

Eric Moore, Julie Hanson, Gene Thompson, Mark Flanagen and Robert Green sold the rights to their stories for one million dollars each. They are all living in an American town in Mexico.

Agent Alexander Christian retired from the Federal Bureau of Investigation following the trial of Annie Simmons. He opened a private investigation firm in Phoenix where he worked some and played golf more.

Russell and Kathy Lewis sold the rights to their stories for one million dollars each and bought a forty-two foot sailboat. They became seasoned sailors as they cruised the Caribbean and South

Pacific for six years. A late season typhoon hit as they sailed from Tahiti to the Hawaiian Islands. Kathy and Russell were lost at sea. Their luck ran out.